And the Freak
Shall Inherit
the Earth . . .

The troupe. The freak show. People with green skin, white skin, furry skin, reptile hide, with no eyes, with extra eyes, extra digits, no digits, with wings, with visions, with no vision, with one face, with two faces, with every face. It was a gathering to give many a towner nightmares for life, but to Oz they were beautiful. They were his kin. Brother and sister were not forms of address he took lightly. They *were* kin. For they shared a common parent, a *third* parent that had left an indelible imprint on their genes.

The Otherness. Each had been touched by the Otherness. . . .

—FROM "Winter Quarters" BY F. PAUL WILSON

HORROR WRITERS OF AMERICA PRESENT

FREAK SHOW

Edited By F. Paul Wilson

POCKET BOOKS

New York   London   Toronto   Sydney   Tokyo   Singapore

An *Original* Publication of POCKET BOOKS

POCKET BOOKS, a division of Simon & Schuster Inc.
1230 Avenue of the Americas, New York, NY 10020

ISBN: 0-671-69574-6

First Pocket Books printing September 1992

10 9 8 7 6 5 4 3 2 1

POCKET and colophon are registered trademarks of
Simon & Schuster Inc.

Cover art by Jeff K. Potter

Printed in the U.S.A.

Copyright Notices

The Route Card

WINTER QUARTERS *(F. Paul Wilson)*   1

OKEFENOKEE SWAMP, GA
  (Brad Strickland)   13

ATHENS, GA *(Gregory Nicoll)*   34

SIKESTON, MO *(Rex Miller)*   53

LEESVILLE, LA *(Nancy Kilpatrick)*   69

BOIS D'ARC, TX *(Scott Cupp)*   79

PALOMITA, NM *(Kathryn Ptacek)*   94

VENICE, CA *(Douglas Borton)*   111

LA CAÑADA, CA *(Morgan Fields)*   131

SEATTLE, WA *(Richard Lee Byers)*   148

ELM HAVEN, IL *(Dan Simmons)*   162

CHICAGO, IL *(Yvonne Navarro)*   196

BATTLE CREEK, MI *(Steven Spruill)*   218

DROOD HOLLOW, WV *(Lee Moler)*   236

BIRD-IN-HAND, PA *(Chet Williamson)*   261

ROCHESTER, NY *(Craig Shaw Gardner)*   285

QUARRY, MA *(R. Patrick Gates)*   303

OYSTER BAY, NY *(Thomas F. Monteleone)*   330

THE PINE BARRENS, NJ *(F. Paul Wilson)*   353

THE AUTHORS   369

Dear Reader . . .

Freak Show is not another run-of-the-mill anthology. We're going to take you on a tour, starting in Florida, heading across the South, up the West Coast, then across the Midwest on our way back to the East Coast. Nearly all of the contributors now live or have lived in the locales of their stories. They'll not only give you a good tale, but you'll get the tastes, tangs, twangs, and textures of different parts of the country as well.

This particular anthology is different in another way: You shouldn't pick and choose your stories in random sequence. *Freak Show* has a beginning, a middle, and an end. Each story, though self-contained and written by a different author, is a separate stone on a path that leads to a final climax. Each story builds upon the others, borrows characters and incidents from stories that preceded it and from stories yet to come. The events within and between these stories *accumulate* until the Peabody-Ozymandias Traveling Circus and Oddity Emporium reaches the end of its around-the-country tour.

And then all hell breaks loose.

So do yourself a favor: Start at the beginning.

F. PAUL WILSON

July 1990–June 1991

FREAK SHOW

WINTER QUARTERS

Okeechobee County, Florida

"That's a difficult offer to refuse," Joseph Peabody said.

The crusted bowl of his briar was warm against his palm as he struck a wooden match to it and befogged his immediate vicinity. Ashes sprinkled the latest issue of *AB* lying open on his lap. He eyed his visitor through the blue-white smoke.

Jacob Prather's son—Ozymandias. Weird name, that. Almost as weird as the fellow standing in front of him now. Well, Jake Prather hadn't been too tightly stitched himself. Peabody had known him long ago when they were both with Taber & Sons mud show. Peabody had been assistant manager and Jake had had a gig in the sideshow—some sort of weird apparatus that didn't do anything, just sat there and looked strange. Jake was a nice enough fellow, but he got decidedly weird after his son was born. Finally quit the circuit just about the time Peabody got the wherewithal to buy Taber's failing show and rename it after himself.

Peabody's Traveling Circus—he'd match it up against any other two-tent mud show in the country for giving a family their money's worth when they bought a ticket.

Peabody never saw Jacob Prather again. And now, years later, here comes his son, back in the business.

The circus has a way of getting into your blood.

1

Ozymandias Prather looked nothing like his father. Jake had been a small, stoop-shouldered, bespectacled field mouse. His son was tall—six-five, maybe. He didn't stand, he *loomed*. Lank dark hair, parted on the side and plastered down; pale skin, lips so thin his mouth looked like a skin crease, and blue eyes as warm as a mausoleum. A funny-shaped body: his shoulders were narrow, his arms long and thin, yet he was barrel chested, with a broad but paunchless abdomen set upon wide hips. His head was normal-size but his torso made it look too small for his body. The overall effect distorted perspective. Looking straight at him made Peabody feel like he was standing in a hole looking up.

"Why should you want to refuse?" Ozymandias Prather said in a deep voice that seemed to come from everywhere in the room but his lips.

"A freak show . . . that sort of thing's never been my style. You should know that. As a matter of fact, it's *out* of style."

"Gawking at the deformed is never out of style."

Bitterness there—a *load* of bitterness.

"I don't know, Ozymandias . . ."

"Most people find it easier to call me Oz. You've seen my troupe, Mr. Peabody. If you don't think they can turn the tip, then you're not the showman I think you are."

"I've seen your troupe," Peabody said, repressing a shiver. In all his sixty-six years he'd never seen such a collection of oddballs. "Where on earth did you find them?"

The razor-thin lips curved upward at each end: a smile. Sort of.

"Diligence hath its rewards. But that is irrelevant. An offer is on the table: cash up-front for a forty-percent interest in Peabody's Traveling Circus. Your only concessions are adding my name to the logo and putting a few extra stops on the route card, but you retain control. A can't-lose proposition for you."

"I don't know about that. My people aren't going to like it." Peabody's general manager, Tom Shuman, and manager, Dan Nolan, were up in arms about sharing the stops with a bunch of freaks. "We run a clean show. We've got a reputation—"

"But you're losing money and you're almost broke. I've seen the balance sheets, Mr. Peabody. My troupe can bring in the extra crowds, the people who think high-wire acts and waltzing elephants and clowns and foot-juggling are passé. They'll come to see us, but they'll stay for your show, and they'll buy our flukum and popcorn and balloons and T-shirts."

"I want no grift," Peabody said emphatically, and he meant it. "No games, no monte, no prostitution."

He saw Oz stiffen. "I have never allowed that in my troupe. And I never will. We don't need grift to turn a profit."

Peabody believed him. Something in his gut warned him away from this man, urged him to throw Ozymandias Prather out on his ass, but he sensed a puritanical streak in this oddball and believed he'd run a clean show. And the hard truth was, the show was looking Chapter Eleven in the eye. Ozymandias Prather was offering him a way out. And at least he'd still be in control.

Reluctantly, he held out his hand. "You've got a deal, Oz." They shook. Oz's hand was cold but dry. "I'll have my lawyer draw up the contract. By the way, do we have a name for this new conglomerate?"

Oz rose and towered over him. His basso voice boomed.

"The Peabody-Ozymandias Traveling Circus and Oddity Emporium."

"That's quite a mouthful. By the way, how's your father?"

"Dad? He killed himself years ago."

Oz then stepped out the door, leaving Joseph Peabody alone in his chair, sucking on a dead pipe.

Outside the trailer, Oz stood under the stars and closed his eyes a moment. He wanted to celebrate, guzzle champagne, and shout his elation. But there was work to do.

As if on cue, a tall, lean figure separated itself from the shadows. An exquisitely handsome face with cold, cold eyes leaned into the light.

"He accepted?" said Petergello in his silky voice.

"Of course," Oz said. "He had no choice."

"A lot of money."

"What will money mean if we're successful?"

Petergello nodded. "And so it begins."

"And so it ends," Oz said. "For all of them. Drive me back and have the Beagles bring the players to the meeting tent."

"Everybody?"

"No. Just our kind."

George Swenson sat in his trailer trying out a new glue on his skin—he'd developed a rash from the old stuff—when the sudden pounding on his trailer door made him spill the glop all over his left arm.

"Damn! What is it?"

He heard a growl from the other side of the door and knew it was one of the Beagles. Daubing at the glue with a damp rag, he crossed to the door and wrapped his sticky arm around the doorknob. He hadn't had a chance to replace it with a lever and it was damn hard to turn these knobs when you didn't have fingers. Finally he twisted it far enough to slip the latch.

One of the five Beagle Boys was outside, pointing across the clearing toward the meeting tent. George tried to figure out which one this was. It was almost impossible to tell. The Beagles were identical quints; five muscle-bound hulks, virtually neckless, with tiny ears, close-cropped hair, deep-set eyes and toothy grins. All were mute but managed to get across what they wanted you to know, even if they had to get rough to do it.

"A meeting? All right. I'll be there in a few minutes."

The Beagle held up a meaty fist. The message was clear: Don't forget, or else.

"Yeah, sure," George said, undulating an arm at him. "I'll be there." Then he slammed the door.

George didn't know what to make of Oz's entourage. Some of them had been together for years, traveling the South and occasionally venturing up the East Coast. George was a newcomer, a "first-of-May" in the lingo. Oz had come to him a couple of months ago at the very nadir of his twenty-two-year life—out of college due to lack of funds, out of work because no one wanted to hire a guy with boneless forearms that looked like tentacles—and offered him a job. Not a great job. In fact, it was the worst job imaginable—a sideshow freak. He glued flesh-colored rubber suction cups to the underside of his tapered, hand-less forearms and—*presto!*—he was—

> *Octoman—The Human Octopus!*
> *Product of an Unholy Union*
> *Between Woman and Sea Monster!*

Yeah, right. His mother had never even seen an ocean and his father had been a car salesman. The closest George had ever been to a carnival before this was as a child when his mother would take him to the Taber & Sons show on its annual trip through Moberly, Missouri. She loved circuses and sideshows. She'd gone every year before he was born and saw no reason to stop after. He'd gawked at the bearded lady and pinheads and giants and dwarves, never dreaming that one day he would be a gawkee instead of a gawker.

Dwarves, giants, bearded ladies, pinheads . . . they were the Rotary Club next to this troupe. Yet for all the sinister shapes and bitter, suspicious attitudes, George had felt an instant kinship with these . . . *freaks*. God, he hated that word, but there was no other name for them. They were freaks of nature. Accidents who didn't belong, who had nowhere else to go, who were fit company for no one but each other.

Luckily George wasn't like them. He had a future. He was going to finish college, get his degree in computer science, and go on from there. He'd be so damn good at systems analysis no one would give a damn if he had no hands.

He finished wiping off the glue and headed for the meeting tent. Something had been in the air about joining up with a mud show for a long summer tour. Maybe Oz had struck the deal.

"It will be a long trip, brothers and sisters," Oz said as he walked among the members of his troupe. "Long in distance and in days."

Half an hour ago they'd straggled in and seated them-selves in a rough circle, and now they listened intently as he finished itemizing the mundane details of the coming tour and segued into the important part, the crucial part, the part they would have difficulty grasping and believing.

"And perhaps it is good that we make a full circuit of this country—better yet if we could make a circuit of the globe—for it will allow us a chance to see it so that we can remember it as it was—if we care to."

He let his gaze range over them as he allowed the words to sink in. All the important ones were here. The special ones, the ones like him. Carmella sat with Louella, Kysleen, and Emily, flashing sidelong glances at Lance who sat alone; as always, Virgie Bone sat alone too, not far from Haman who appeared to be staring at the closed tent flap; Herbert and Claude sat with Dub and Rattles, while Bowser occupied his usual place on Mr. Tane's lap; Senorita Gato and Quinta Romero had seated themselves up front next to George Swenson. And of course there was Malaleik, dear, precious Malaleik, the key to all of Oz's plans. Petergello hovered at the rear with the Beagle Boys, keeping them in line.

The troupe. The freak show. People with green skin, white skin, furry skin, reptile hide, with no eyes, with extra eyes, extra digits, no digits, with wings, with visions, with no vision, with one face, with two faces, with every face. It was a gathering to give many an ogler the creeps for life, but to Oz they were beautiful. They were his kin. Brother and sister were not forms of address he took lightly. They *were* kin. For they shared a common parent, a *third* parent that had left an indelible imprint on their genes.

The Otherness. Each had been touched by the Otherness.

George Swenson looked up at him from under a furrowed brow and posed the question Oz had known someone would ask.

"Remember it 'as it was'?" he said. "I don't get it."

"I shall explain," Oz said. "But first I must tell you that I did not arrange this tour merely to make more money. We will do that, but the money is unimportant." He watched the brothers and sisters nudge each other and mutter. He'd expected that. "What is important is the search. For while we are touring we will be searching for some important objects."

"Like a scavenger hunt?" said Dub's frontface.

"In a way, yes. But in this hunt there will be no single winner. If we are successful in this hunt, *all* of us will be winners."

"What will we win?" George said.

"Justice. Understanding. Acceptance. Compensation."

The expressions facing him—the readable ones—were frankly dubious.

"I don't get it," said young Lance Whiting.

"And you never have," Oz said. "Justice, that is. None of you have. You've been shunned at best, and at worst you've been reviled, abandoned, beaten, and tortured. But never . . . understood. With your cooperation, this tour will change all that."

"Will it give me hands?" said George Swenson.

"No," Oz said. "You won't need them."

"Will it give me eyes?" said Mr. Tane.

"No. You won't need them."

"Will it straighten my spine?" said Kysleen.

"No. You won't need a straight spine."

"Will it change this beak into a normal nose and mouth?" said Emily Gibbs Butterman, who toured as Mother Goose.

"No. You won't need them."

"Will it get me a keg of German beer?" said Dub's backface.

Everyone laughed.

"No," said Oz. "You won't need beer."

"I still don't get it," said Lance.

"A change," Oz said. "We have an opportunity to work a change upon the land. And the instrument of that change can be activated if we find all its components and reassemble them."

"A *machine?*" George said. "A machine is going to change the world?"

Oz nodded. He'd known this was going to be a tough sell. He barely believed it himself. But he had to have their cooperation. He could not succeed without it.

"Yes. When the machine called the Device is activated at the proper time in the proper place, it will, quite literally, change the world—change the way the world sees us, change the way the world sees *itself*."

He paused and let them mutter among themselves, then raised his voice.

"You need not believe me. I realize that might be too much to ask. But I do ask that you trust me. As we make a circuit of the country I will from time to time ask one of you to venture into one of the towns we are passing through and retrieve one of the missing Pieces of the Device. You do not have to believe that it will change our place in the world for the better, all you have to know is that it is important to me and to those of your brothers and sisters who do believe."

Oz turned in a slow circle, eying each one in turn.

"Have I ever lied to you?"

He noted with satisfaction that every head was wagging slowly back and forth.

"No. I do not lie." He pointed to the outer world beyond the tent wall. "*They* lie to you. I do not. And I say to you now that the Device is monumentally important to all our lives. Is there any one of you who will not help collect its component parts as we travel?"

Oz searched the members of his troupe for a raised hand. There were none.

"Excellent. And to give you some idea of the nature of the Pieces you'll be searching for, I've brought a few along to show you."

Oz withdrew the four objects that had been waiting in the pockets of his coat and handed them to the nearest members of the troupe.

"Here. Pass these around. Don't worry about damaging them—you can't. Just don't lose them."

George felt something very much like a cold shock when the first Piece was passed to him. The sensation ran through his boneless forearm up to the left side of his face; from there it seemed to penetrate his skull and shoot across his brain. Vertigo spun the tent and for that instant he thought he saw another place full of weird angles superimposed on the tent space—*coexisting* with the tent space—then it steadied again. He looked down at the thing in his hand, blinked, then looked again. Dull yellow metal, but strangely shaped. A couple of the sides met at an angle that didn't seem possible—shouldn't have been possible. He passed it on and reached for another. This one looked hard and glossy but felt soft and fuzzy, almost alive; he thought he sensed it breathing. He quickly dumped that one off and reached for the next—a flat ceramic oval. But there was something wrong with this one, too. He couldn't pinpoint it at first, then he noticed it didn't cast a shadow; it was solid, opaque, but no matter which way he turned it there was no shadow. The last object was a tennis-ball-size sphere and this one did cast a shadow—but one with sharp angles.

George cradled the last Piece in his coiled left arm and stared at Oz where he stood in the center of the tent. One strange dude. Aloof and yet paternalistic; even the freaks who'd been with him for years knew little about him, but they mentioned that no one had ever seen him eat. Full trays were delivered to his trailer and removed empty, but he always ate alone. His only close contact seemed to be with Petergello, another one who never ate—never even got trays. The freaks kidded about taking "a walk with Petergello." George didn't know what that meant but decided from the timbre of their voices that he'd rather not find out.

And now these Pieces. Strange little things to say the least. Almost . . . otherworldly.

One could only imagine the sort of Device their aggregate would produce. An instrument like that might be capable of almost anything.

Even Justice. Understanding. Acceptance. Compensation.

Oz stood with Petergello and watched the tent empty. As he pocketed the Pieces he had displayed, he glanced right and saw George Swenson standing beside him. George offered the end of his tentaclelike right arm. Oz shook it.

"Very moving," George said. "I want you to know you can count on my help if you need it."

"That's good to know, George."

"Of course, your Device will be more important to the others."

"Really?"

"Yes. I'm sure once I get enough money together to finish my education I'll be able to get by on my own. But I'd like to help the others. So just let me know what I can do."

"Thank you, George."

"Is our first-of-May also the eternal optimist?" Petergello whispered through a tight smile as George walked away.

"He still thinks he's one of them," Oz said, looking after him.

"You going to tell him the whole story?"

Oz shook his head. "George isn't ready for it."

"Want me to think of a way to make him ready for it?" Petergello said, his smile widening.

"Yes. Do that. Come up with a way to convince him that he will never be accepted by them, that we are his real family. And his only hope."

"Never thought I'd live to see the day," Tom Shuman said as he stood at the door of the office trailer and stared at the cluster of new trailers and campers parked across the field. "Joe Peabody touring with a freak show. Who'd believe it?"

Peabody looked up at his general manager. Tom had an angular body and a reedy voice. He handled the circus's performers and Peabody had known there'd be a ruckus when he found out about the freak show. He'd been dreading this moment.

"It's all a question of dollars and cents, Tom. We had all winter to raise the operating capital we needed for this year's tour. We couldn't get it. Not in this economy. So it's a choice: tour with them or disband the show. Which do you prefer?"

Shuman tossed his cigarette butt outside and turned toward the desk.

"You know the answer to that. But mark my words, there's gonna be trouble."

"There's already trouble," said Dan Nolan, a burly, muscular hulk in the chair near the inner corner of Peabody's desk. "A buncha my roustabouts blew the show this morning after seeing those freaks."

"Get some more," Peabody said. Nolan was his other manager, in charge of the workers.

"I combed every mission, homeless shelter, and Salvation Army office in the county to come up with these bums. Nobody wants to work."

"I have workers, Mr. Nolan."

Peabody started at the voice echoing through the office. Oz loomed in the doorway. Peabody introduced him to Tom and Dan. No one shook hands.

"I don't want your workers, mister," said Dan.

"How do you know that if you've never met them?" Oz said. "I'll call them."

He turned, raised a silver whistle to his lips, and blew. Peabody heard nothing, but a moment later, five burly figures were crowded around the door. They were identical, all stamped out from the same cookie cutter—neckless, deep-set eyes, pug noses.

"The Beagle Boys, Mr. Nolan. They follow instructions and don't talk back. And they're *very* strong. They're yours when you need them. Give them a tryout."

Grumbling that he didn't have much choice, Dan slipped past Oz and confronted his new roustabouts.

"Go with Mr. Nolan, boys," Oz said. "And do what he tells you." Then he stepped inside next to Tom Shuman and looked down at Peabody. "What's the route so far?"

Peabody reached into his desk and pulled out the route card.

"Let's see. So far we've got fifteen dates across the Deep South and Southwest in late May-June. A dozen stops on the Left Coast in July, ten across the Midwest and into the Northeast in August, then we'll make the home run down the East Coast in September. Hopefully, we'll pick up more as we go."

Oz handed him a sheet of paper. "Here are some extra stops I wish to add."

Peabody studied the list of locations. Some they were already booked into or near, but others were pretty far out of the way. But rather than get into it now, Peabody temporized.

"I'll see what we can work out."

"Excellent," Oz said. He reached into his jacket pocket and pulled out a foil sack. "And here's something for you."

Peabody took the proffered bag and unrolled the top. An exotic aroma wafted up from within. For an instant he felt almost giddy.

"Tobacco?"

"A gift. A special mix from India. I think you'll like it."

"Why . . . thanks." The unexpected gesture took Peabody completely by surprise. "Very kind of you."

"Enjoy." Oz waved and was gone.

"Trouble," Tom Shuman said, staring after him. "Nothing but trouble."

Joseph Peabody lit a bowlful of the new tobacco and drew a few tentative puffs. He felt light-headed again for a moment, then it passed. Strong, but smooth. An unusual flavor. He had a feeling he was going to like this blend.

"You worry too much, Tom," he told his general manager. "I've got a feeling we're going to have the tour of our lives." He drew another mouthful of rich, sweet smoke from his pipe. "My, this tobacco is good."

The show rolled.

Up through the northern Florida counties, breaking in the firsts-of-May, getting the kinks out of the acts in the tiny towns, playing big in Jacksonville, then sliding across the Georgia line into Charlton County. When the show stopped in Moniac on the edge of the great swamp, Oz called Claude Bledsoe into his trailer. Claude, known as Gator to the troupe and Alligator Boy to the public, did not speak so Oz asked Herbert Brooks along to sign for him. Herbert—"Mitts" to his friends—had seventeen fingers of varying length and extraordinary dexterity. He was one of the few members of the troupe with whom Claude communicated. Through the patterns woven by Herbert's spidery fingers, Oz told Claude where he wanted him to go, and what he wanted him to find.

F. PAUL WILSON

Okefenokee Swamp, Georgia

The Okefenokee is most alive in the afternoon.

Alligators cruise the black water. Long-legged birds stalk the shallows, spearing for fish. The water lilies splay white or yellow blossoms to the sky, and they hum with flies and bees. Frog songs become more strident, the zoom and *screek* of insects more insistent. Sunlight blazes off the water, and only in the depths of canallike alligator trails, arched over by towering cypress, is the air cool.

Here the fishing is good.

In his skiff Slim Surratt muttered to himself, an old habit. "Come on, you bastards, bite."

The catfish weren't going for chicken livers today. Or rather something was, but not catfish. Something clean stole the bait every damn time without the least tug of line or jiggle of cork to warn him.

Surratt lifted a quart jar, swirled the fragrant but colorless contents, and tilted it back, his Adam's apple bobbing. He wiped his lips. His left hand stole to the left front pocket of his khaki work pants and began to draw something out, but then he cocked his head and listened intently. "Damn."

An approaching motor farted along through the cypress stands, and Slim reeled in his line. He cut the leader, let the bait sink, and laid the rod next to his tackle box. Goddamn game wardens couldn't arrest a man for fishing without a license if they never saw him fishing. And if they tried—Slim nudged the tackle box with his foot, feeling the solid weight of the Colt service revolver inside—if they tried, a man could be prepared.

The boat growled into view, and Slim cursed the loss of his bait. It was just fat old Pig Carmody, who made good 'shine but who was good for little else besides scaring the fish. Pig waved and throttled back. "Hey, Slim. Busy tonight?"

"Why?"

Pig cackled in his phlegmy way. "Goddamn circus come to town. Helped 'em set up. Found some live ones for a little poker tonight. Ugly as all hell, but they got money."

Slim grinned. "Always ready to take a little money."

"Good," Pig said. "They 'specially wanted you to come."

Slim frowned. "What?"

"I'll pick you around sunset."

"What about them wanting me to come?"

"Same circus Big Billy Bledsoe run off with all that time ago. Guess these freaks and you is the only friends ole Big Billy ever had." Pig throttled up his outboard and passed on by, the wash rocking Slim's skiff.

"What the hell?" Slim asked himself. But he had no answer, and as soon as Pig was out of sight, he reached back into his britches pocket.

Late that evening Claude Bledsoe crouched in the moonlight outside the RV and listened to the poker game. Around him the thick south Georgia air thrummed: rioting insects, booming bullfrogs, and now and again the shriek of a night-winged bird. Claude had caught something good to eat, but it too made a noise, and Mitts apparently heard it. The RV door opened and Claude heard Mitts say, "Gentlemen, I must relieve myself."

He came and stood a few feet away from Claude. "Aw, Gator," he said with a sigh. "Man, you don't want to spoil your appetite before the show."

With a snap of his head Claude took in another foot of the diamondback snake he was eating, its twitching tail still burring. There was enough moonlight for Claude's stumpy fingers to spell out the sign language that he and Mitts had made up during the long winter layovers: *I was hungry.*

"You're always hungry." Claude heard the soft words clearly enough, but from habit the man's many long fingers moved, too, scattering syllables. "Did you spit the head out?"

Claude swallowed the last of the snake and pointed vaguely to his left. Mitts edged away, and dimly Claude recalled the time in Florida when a bitten-off rattlesnake head had snapped its fangs on a curious puppy's nose. The dog, he remembered, had died. Claude felt snake juice oozing from the corner of his mouth. He wiped it and then spelled out, *Ask the towner Slim about my father.*

"I will. But no more snakes, you hear me?" Mitts hesitated. "And I saw you peeking in. Listen, but don't look. Understand?"

Claude nodded.

Mitts sighed again and turned away. Claude edged back below the open window of the RV and heard the clump as Mitts entered. The window spilled smells into the swampy, humid air: sweat, the sour-corn tang of moonshine liquor, and the haze and pungent aroma of the cigars that Dub smoked.

"Took ya long enough," said a voice, Dub's nasty backface. "Piss that much, you're gonna raise the swamp a foot."

Pig cackled. "Don't that beat all? Din't I tell you these was the damndest fellers?"

"Deal," said another towner, the rail-skinny, silver-haired Slim. "And keep them goddamn hands where we can see 'em."

"The game is seven-card stud," replied the velvety voice of Mitts. Cards riffled as if he played them for music.

Claude sat with his arms circling his drawn-up knees and waited for mention of his family, his father, Big Billy Bledsoe. Claude was nineteen now, or so Mr. Ozymandias told him. He had to cast his memory back thirteen long years to dredge up a picture of his mother, MaMaw, thin faced, straw haired, a silent woman. With it came a vaguer image of his father, a tall black-haired man with big hands and eyes that squinted through you. . . .

With a start Claude sat up straighter, for he had heard his father's name.

". . . turned his boy over to the show a good while back," Mitts was saying. "Heard he lived around here."

Pig laughed. "He don't no more, does he, Slim?"

"Shut up."

"Don't wonder 'bout him givin' the boy away," said Pig. "Ugly dingy runt, all scabby-lookin', short stumpy arms and legs. And that head full a' teeth—folks said Big Billy'd raped a maw 'gator to get a boy that ugly."

Me, Claude thought.

"What happened to the Bledsoes?" asked Mitts.

"Nothin'," said Slim.

Pig cackled again. Everything was funny to Pig. "Don't ask Slim. Him and Billy went loafering around together—"

Dub's frontface murmured, "I'll see that, raise you one."

"Call," somebody said.

It took a couple more hands and a few more passes of the 'shine jar, but the story came out bit by bit: how years ago Big Billy Bledsoe had run off with the carnival, how after fifteen months he returned to his large family and the swamp. Then he'd lived on for years doing whatever came to hand, logging, paper milling, but mostly hunting and fishing in the swamp, as he had always done. And he had this keepsake . . .

"The Doohickey," Pig said. "Damndest thing you ever seen. 'Bout as long as the last two joints of my little finger, pointy at one end, flat on the other. Had a hole bored through the pointy end. Looked sorta like a slantways Ku Klux hood, but not round. The pointy end had lots a' flat sides to it. Only you couldn't count 'em."

"Shut up," Slim said.

"Sometimes you'd get six, sometimes thirteen. Looked like glass but felt funny, fuzzy, tinglylike. And it glowed, too, 'specially when it was in some dark place, shinin' all different flashy colors, red and green and blue and orange and some I don't know the names of. Well, sir, folks useta ask Billy to let 'em look in the flat end a' that thing, and they'd screech like a singed owl and beller and roll on the ground, and they'd never tell you what it was they saw in that Doohickey—"

Your father took a Piece of the Device, Mr. Ozymandias had told Claude before the show hit the road this season. He'd said it slowly, the way everyone did when talking to Claude. *We have to find your father.*

Pig was rattling on, but Slim's flat voice cut in on him: "Big Billy's dead. His woman still lives in the shack on Strange Island."

Crouched outside the RV, his knees aching, Claude felt his heart tighten.

"Don't know he's dead." Pig had grown more querulous as he lost money. "Hell, Big Billy useta go off into the swamp all by hisself and catch the damndest fish. Bass twelve, fifteen pound. All the time. Fisherman's luck, they called it, but nobody knowed how he could do it."

"He went fishing one day," Slim said with finality, "and he never come back. That's been eight, ten years. He's dead."

Pig's cackle had turned sour. "Slim got jealous a' Big Billy. Big Billy was the beatenest fisherman ever was, and now I reckon the title's done gone to Slim Surratt here."

"Ante up," someone said.

Mitts kept a calm tone: "And the—what did Pig call it—the Doohickey? What happened to that?"

"Hell if I know," Pig said. "I fold." Cards slapped the table. "Big Billy got so secretlike that he wouldn't never show it. But that was years before he took off."

"Died," Slim said. "He died in the goddamn swamp. It happens. Give me one."

Claude stood up, easing his stiff knees. So his father had taken off or died. He searched for some feeling and found only a remote hollow ache: His last memory of his father was of the big hands pushing him forward, the deep voice saying, "Go on. You'll be happier with your own kind." And the freaks waiting to welcome him. Claude did not much miss his father. But his mother—he'd like to see MaMaw again.

With sleep heavy in his head, Claude wandered across the grounds and stopped before the tent with a poster of him on it. Moonlight fell on the weird form of a human boy with an alligator's head, his limbs half concealed by scrolls bearing red and yellow lettering.

The colors were wrong. Claude's lumpy skin was a mottled tan, not the vivid arsenic green of the poster. And the anatomy was incorrect, because Claude's head wasn't really as flat as an alligator's, though he did have a long snout filled with pointed razorlike teeth, just like in the picture. Claude could not read the gaudy words on the scroll, but he knew them by heart, for Mitts had spoken them aloud to him.

> Alive! The Alligator Boy!!
> Born of the Swamp!!!
> $500.00 Cash If You Can Prove
> It's Not Real!!!!

Me, Claude thought.

With a last look at the yellow-lighted window of the RV, Claude Bledsoe heaved a sigh, licked his tongue around his sharp teeth to find any stray particles of rattlesnake, and trudged off to bed.

The next morning Dub drove Mitts and Claude to a settlement in the swamp: four concrete-block stores (Hop 'n Go Gas and Video, Peck's Package, Cribbs' General, and one abandoned) and a scatter of houses. Dub shelled out money to rent a squared-off green aluminum skiff and to hire a local to pilot it, tilted his foreign-legion hat at a jaunty angle, and sauntered into the package store to see what he could pick up.

When the redneck spotted what was waiting in the skiff, Mitts had to pay him an extra twenty. Even so he muttered, "You set between me and that or I ain't goin'." Obligingly occupying the center thwart, Mitts crossed his many-fingered hands, resting them in his lap like thick bristles of brown twigs. Dub came out of the package store, and as the boat pulled away from the dock Claude waved good-bye to him.

The black water lay mirror-smooth, each gray cypress standing on its own perfect reflection. A persistent clicking, like two marbles jostling together, filled the air. The first time Claude heard it he looked around expecting to see Rattles, his dwarf friend from the freak show whose head made just that noise. But then he remembered from his childhood that the sound came from little tree frogs. Sweet-tasting tree frogs.

Olive green alligators basked in the morning sun, soaking up the May warmth, or glided close in for a look at the boat before they dived. Crook-necked white egrets flew over, and a gray wading anhinga reared its snaky neck and dagger beak to give them a suspicious glare.

The trip to the island where Claude's mother lived took an hour, but at last they tied up at a splintered dock. Their pilot pointed inland. "Bledsoe house is over yonder."

Claude tugged nervously at his shirttail. He wore his best jeans, sneakers, and the bright red Alligator World T-shirt that a rube had given him to eat but which he had taken as his favorite item of apparel. Mitts and Claude made their way beneath scraggly pines and tangled beards of gray-green Spanish moss.

In a few seconds they came upon the house.

Claude had not seen his home in years, but it all rushed back: the unpainted wood shack on pilings three feet off the spongy earth, the rail fence enclosing the garden, the galvanized washtubs hanging on the wall beside the steps . . .

And his mother, MaMaw, appearing in the doorway, a thin straight-backed woman with hair the color of wet straw pulled into a tight bun. *She's old,* Claude thought. *She looks so sorrowful.* She stared, her bony right hand plucking at the flesh on her chest just below her neck, where the faded blue dress she wore made a vee. "Claude?" she whispered. "My God. Claude?"

He ran toward her, and she did not flinch. Her arms clasped him, his long chin rested on her shoulder, and he felt his throat tighten the way it did when he swallowed broken glass. She trembled in his embrace.

Mitts coughed delicately. When Claude pulled away from MaMaw, Mitts introduced himself. Claude moved his fingers while his mother looked on in wonder.

"He's glad to see you, Miz Bledsoe," Mitts told her.

"He can talk like that?" she asked, her voice rusty as if from lack of use. "Deaf and dumb talk?"

"Yes, ma'am. I can tell you what he says."

She bit her lip. "I reckon you better come in the house." She paused, giving Mitts a wary look.

Mitts held up his hands and said softly, "I was born with these. Just like Claude was born the way he is."

MaMaw blinked. "It ain't that. I just ain't never had a colored person come inside before."

Claude's fingers moved.

"He says to tell you I'm his friend."

"Then I reckon it's all right."

They sat at the table in the dark kitchen, which smelled of kerosene lamps and the wood the black cast-iron stove burned, and MaMaw talked to them for a long time, telling them how she had never learned where Big Billy had sent the boy, how she was glad he had friends.

Sad, Claude thought. *What made her so sad?*

Mitts gently urged her to talk about her husband. Big Billy, MaMaw said, was a good man, not church-good, but he kept food on the table. Lord, she missed that man. Life was hard without him, even though her youngest girl, older than Claude by ten years, came over from Moniac every other day to help her out.

MaMaw had a habit of plucking the skin at the base of her throat. Claude saw that it was scarred in dozens of places, as if years ago something had bitten her there. Mitts nudged him out of his reverie, and Claude spelled out, *What do you want?*

"Miz Bledsoe, Claude wants to know about something his daddy once told him he could have. It was a kind of unusual thing. You'd know it if you saw it. It looked funny, felt funny . . ."

Yes, she remembered the Doohickey. Scary it was, somehow not like anything she could put a name to. "I seen strange things in the swamp," she said. "Seen an alligator turtle big as that there tabletop bite my brother's foot clean off. But nothing ever made me shiver like that thing, like the Doohickey.

"Big Billy come back from his carnival tour with that thing and showed it around for a while, but then he got right jealous about it, especially after he hit on the idea of using it to fish with."

To fish with?

"Yes, he took and warped on a wire leader, running it through that hole in the pointed end, and he tied on a treble hook, and he trolled that plug through the swamp and brought in the biggest fish. He got secret about it after he found out how good a lure that Doohickey made. When he wasn't fishing with it, he took to wearing it around his neck on a thong to keep it safe. He never removed the hooks.

"He always wore it," MaMaw said, and her bony fingers plucked the scars at the base of her throat. "Day and night."

Claude knew about making babies, though he'd never had a chance to try it with a live girl. He imagined his pa on top of MaMaw in bed, them straining together, the treble hooks in the flesh of his chest and in the flesh of hers, binding them, their blood blending, streaking over sweaty skin, spreading in crimson blotches on the sheets . . .

Me, Claude thought. *Their blood ran together, and together his blood and her blood made me.*

MaMaw had birthed Claude after she'd been through the change of life and thought she wouldn't have no more younguns. Billy had taken Claude off when the boy was six. And two years after that . . .

"Him and Slim Surratt used to be fishing buddies," she said in a colorless voice.

Mitts nodded. "Somebody told us how close Billy was to Mr. Surratt. We met Mr. Surratt last night."

MaMaw looked away. "One day Big Billy went into the swamp. A little later that morning Slim come by and I told him Billy was off fishing, and he went to see if he could find him, but he never could. Nobody ever could."

And the Doohickey?

"He had it with him." MaMaw bit her lip, looked down in her lap, and then her faded blue gaze hit Claude hard. "Son, I hope you don't want to come back home. Billy never told me what he done with you, but he said you was better off with your own kind. I reckon you are. There ain't nothing in the swamp for you."

Claude could not break that stare. He slowly signed something, and he dimly heard Mitts saying, "He wants to know if you're sad because your husband is dead."

"If I knowed what got him, I'd kill it," MaMaw said. "It would be a pure pleasure."

Her blood, Claude thought. *Her blood and his blood. Me.*

They didn't stay much longer. There was a pile of rubbish in a corner of the yard, and in saying farewell Claude did a little of his act for his mother, eating a tin can and crunching up a broken quart mason jar.

"I hope he eats better than that," MaMaw said to Mitts.

"Yes, ma'am. Mr. Vitale—he's our cook—sees he gets regular meals. And he serves Claude up twenty pounds of fresh meat every two weeks." He smiled. "We have to watch his appetite, because if Claude eats too much, he doesn't want to do a thing in the world but sleep."

Claude spelled out a thought.

"Yes, Claude," Mitts said. "That's a good idea." With two of his long fingers he took a salmon-colored card from his vest pocket. "Here, ma'am. Claude says he'd like to give you something. This is a complimentary ticket for the show."

"I'll have to get my girl to bring me."

Mitts flourished a second ticket. "Our last show's tomorrow afternoon at one."

"I thank you kindly."

The sun was hotter. Their pilot started the outboard. Over its noise Mitts yelled, "Slim Surratt live around here?"

"Edge of the swamp."

"He a good fisherman?"

The man leaned over the edge of the boat, scooped up a handful of swamp water, sucked it into his mouth, and swallowed. "Godamighty, is he. Catches the biggest damn bass you ever see, lotsa other things, too. Caught this goddamn two-headed catfish one time. No shit, two heads. And one of 'em cried just like a little baby."

"Show us where he lives," Mitts said.

Surratt's house stunk of fish. They stood on the ramshackle porch—Surratt had heard the boat and had stepped out to meet them—but the reek of fish rolled through the open doorway.

"Be goddamn," Surratt said. Claude's nostrils twitched. Even the sweat staining Surratt's blue chambray shirt smelled fishy. The man was so short that he had to look up to Claude. "This his boy?"

"Yes," Mitts said. "This is Claude. We call him Gator."

"Gator, huh? Don't favor his old man much."

"We hear you and Gator's father were fishing buddies."

"Told you that last night." Surratt spat over the edge of the porch. "First time a damn freak nigger ever won money off me in a game of poker." Claude felt Mitts clench a little at the word *nigger*.

"Miz Bledsoe says you came looking for her husband the last time she saw him alive."

Surratt's brown eyes narrowed. "Reckon I did. Never found him, though. He went off into the swamp all by hisself and died. It happens."

"They never found his body?"

Surratt shrugged his skinny shoulders. "Hell, airplanes have crashed in there and never been found. And one man's body? Swamp's full a' gator holes." He flashed a yellow grin.

Claude felt his own lips pulling back, baring his teeth. To get his mind off Slim he concentrated on a sapphire blue dragonfly playing around the end of his snout. He held utterly still as it hovered. Mitts asked, "Did Billy Bledsoe say anything about his fishing . . . secrets before he died?"

Surratt snorted, his left hand rubbing the top of his left thigh. "Ain't no such a thing. Just luck, good or bad. He had good luck once, I got it now. No secret about it."

Claude snapped his jaws, and the others started.

"Godamighty," Surratt said, his gaze on the transparent wings between Claude's tough lips. "He's eatin' a goddamn *bug*."

Claude signed to Mitts.

"He says," translated Mitts, "that he's hungry."

* * *

Slim's luck in the swamp that afternoon was no better than it had been the day before. He tried a spoon, but nothing hit. "Fishing secrets," he muttered to himself. "Bledsoe bitch told him. Sure she did." The silver lure came back empty again. Some days it was like this. Some days nothing worked, except—

A cottonmouth, either out early or out way too late, wound through the water eight yards away from the skiff, spreading lazy ripples over the mirrored swamp. "What stirred you up?" Surratt asked it. The snake dived and did not come up again.

Well, some days nothing worked except—

Surratt hauled his line in and cut the leader. He dropped the spoon into his tackle box beside the revolver and then pulled a rattling snuff box from his pocket. Billy Bledsoe had wore the Doohickey around his neck, where a body could see it when his shirt blew open, but not Slim Surratt. No sir, Slim carried it safe in his left front pocket, close to his balls.

The wire and hooks gleamed in the muted sunlight as Surratt tied the leader to the hundred-pound-test braided line. He'd never caught a hundred-pound fish, but with this plug you never knew. He cast it out and began to troll it back, slow and lazy.

You could imagine how it looked under the water, twisting, shimmering, flaring its uncanny colors; how the fish saw it cloudy through the swamp water, which was the color of strong tea if you were under it looking up. How they saw it and wanted it, just like—well, just like anything would want it. Or any*body*, for that matter.

"You should a' sold it to me, Billy," Surratt said aloud. "I offered you cash money."

The lure came back, and Surratt cast it again. Sometimes it took a few tries, but the Doohickey never failed. "Shouldn't a' laughed at me, Billy," Surratt crooned. "Shouldn't a' been so biggity about how you could catch 'em when yore ole buddy Slim couldn't. Man can't take but so much."

The line went taut, and Surratt twitched the rod, setting the hook. He grinned. "What we got, Billy? Big old bass, reckon?" He cranked the reel a few clicking turns.

The catch ran, bowing the strong rod. It was *heavy*,

whatever it was. Surratt grunted and gave out a little line. The first few times he used it he had been afraid of losing the Doohickey, but somehow it never snagged. The lure made a live catch every time. That was good because if it ever did get tangled, he wouldn't ever be able to find the Doohickey in the swamp.

"Nobody'd find it 'cept maybe you, huh, Billy?" Surratt mused. He felt sweaty-cold all at once, for a picture flashed across his mind: him hauling the lure up to the surface and finding it caught in a rotting corpse, only the corpse *moved*—

"Nothin' left of Big Billy Bledsoe," Surratt reassured himself. "Nothin' but gator shit."

Damn, but the fish was a big bastard. Surratt played it, taking in line whenever he could, letting it out when he had to. It took twenty minutes, but finally his catch broke water before dipping under again.

"Shit," Surratt said. "Hooked a gator."

It looked like a middle-size one. With both hands holding the rod, Surratt pulled his tackle box over with his foot. The revolver lay within easy reach.

Surratt took up line, the reel whirring now as slack wound in. The fish, gator, whatever it was, seemed to be going beneath the boat.

No. It stopped when the line was straight up and down. Surratt cautiously cranked the reel, trying to peer down through the black water. A flat dingy head broke the surface.

Something red behind it: blood? Hell, alligators don't wear *shirts*—

A stump-fingered hand rose from the water and clamped onto the edge of the boat.

The Doohickey gleamed between sharp, clenched, grinning teeth.

Surratt screamed, dropped the rod, and snatched the Colt.

His first wild shot blew a hole in the side of the skiff, raised a fountain of water, and sent a screaming explosion of birds bursting from the cypress thicket. The hand slipped away, the head submerged.

Surratt stepped on the rod, felt its slackness, and realized that the damned freak had bit through the wire—

Two thuds, underneath the skiff. The swamp here wasn't but four feet deep, but God, the water was black—

Surratt grabbed the engine cord and yanked. The outboard barked, blatted, and then jittered the boat in an uncontrollable, bucking circle.

What the hell has that thing done to the propeller?

Surratt killed the motor before the lurching craft threw him into the water. The boat pitched, bumping over something—

Two hands appeared on the other side of the skiff.

This time Surratt aimed carefully, and his finger twitched on the trigger the second the evil pebbled snout showed.

But the thing was damn quick, and the slug tore through empty air, hitting only swamp. Cursing, Surratt lunged to the side, making the boat slew dangerously, and fired straight down into the concealing black water. Then the freak was under him again, rocking the boat, trying to toss him out.

"God damn you!" The pistol roared twice more, punching slugs through the skiff's bottom. Twin tea-colored geysers spewed from the .45 caliber holes.

Surratt glared at the trees a dozen yards away. Tepid swamp water already gushed into his brogans. Four foot deep. A man could wade to the cypress stands, might even live if the gators didn't get him in the water, if the snakes didn't . . .

The stub-fingered hands grasped the near side of the skiff again. The grinning snout leered at him, the Doohickey flashing a color that Surratt had never seen. The boat tilted.

The thing turned the Doohickey in its teeth, so the flat side faced Surratt, and even from across the boat where he had crabbed backward he could see in it an image of Big Billy's face, dead but alive too, grinning like the creature that flopped into the sinking boat. Surratt was screaming, sobbing, gibbering, raising the heavy Colt . . .

He used the last bullet on himself.

Although attendance was light at the final show, Claude's mother and sister came. His sister left the tent just after Claude's act began, but MaMaw watched as he listlessly ate a live chicken, a liquor bottle, the junk the customers threw him. One rube bawled out, "Bet ya he won't eat my pocketknife," only to lose the bet. And then the show was over, the towners were gone, and the carnival began to fold. Claude's sister went and sat in the car, but MaMaw came to stand beside her boy while the roustabouts broke down the show.

The two snuff-colored tents came down like magic, the huffing and tromping of the elephants drowning out the endless drone of insects. In the sunset glow, MaMaw stood watching it all, her son beside her.

When the circus folk had cleared the meadow, leaving nothing but scraps of paper, trampled black earth, and heaps of elephant shit, the black man with too many long fingers came over, nattily dressed and smiling. "Miz Bledsoe, it's time for Claude and me to go."

MaMaw nodded, her lined, thin face solemn. "I'll wash Claude's shirt and britches and mail them to the address you give me. Lord God, he got them muddy." She stroked her boy's head with her large-knuckled hand. "Claude, you be good now." She hesitated. "Your pa was right. You're better off with these folks. Swamp's a bad place. Dangerous . . ."

Torpid, Claude didn't respond. Mitts said gently, "Come on, now. Tell your mother good-bye."

"Dangerous," MaMaw repeated. "This morning somebody found Slim Surratt's skiff a-floating empty."

Mitts sounded politely interested: "Is that a fact?"

"Bad things happen in a swamp. Menfolks disappear. My Billy did years ago. And now his old friend Slim has." MaMaw's voice was a dreamy murmur. "You all must take right good care of my boy, mister. He looks plumb stout." Her pale blue gaze met Mitts's for the first time that day.

Mitts looked at Claude in some surprise. "He does, at that. Let's go, Gat—uh, Claude."

The man helped Claude climb into an RV, then turned and gave MaMaw a graceful bow. She nodded back. Engines coughed and rattled to life, headlights blazed, and the Peabody-Ozymandias Traveling Circus and Oddity Emporium began to move.

MaMaw stood there in the dusk until the last vehicle

had rumbled out onto the highway and turned north. Absently MaMaw's fingers touched the scarred flesh above her sternum. Somewhere behind her, Claude's sister leaned on the car horn. "Claude looks right well fed," MaMaw murmured to herself.

For the first time in years and years she smiled.

BRAD STRICKLAND

The show rolled on . . .

ALONG THE MIDWAY (1)

Glascock County, Georgia

"Another pair of workers blew the show last night," Nolan said.

Joseph Peabody puffed his pipe and watched his manager prowl the office, sporting the red bandana he affected when they were on the road. Workers blew the show every season. They were mostly winos, drifters, petty criminals, or all three in one. They slept on bunks stacked four high in smelly converted semitrailers, spent their off-time guzzling Mad Dog, and usually did their work with blistering hangovers. But there were always more where they come from. Why was Nolan so worked up?

"It's those freaks," he said, as if sensing Peabody's question.

"Got enough men to get the top up when we get to Athens?"

"I've got enough *bodies* to do it. Those Beagle Boys . . ." Nolan shook his head. "Jesus, they're strong. Work as hard as the bulls."

"Then what's the problem?"

"They make my skin crawl, Joe—that's the problem. And the animals ain't too fond of them, neither."

"As long as we get the canvas up and the lumber moved in, go with it, Dan. The crowds have been good so far. Oz's folks are bringing them in. If these first two

29

weeks are any indication of how the season's going to go, we'll be looking at the biggest end-of-tour bonus we've seen in ten years."

"No kidding?" Nolan's dour expression mellowed a bit. "All right. I'll make do with what we've got left."

"I'm counting on you, Dan," Peabody said.

When Nolan was gone, he sighed and repacked his bowl. He'd hired Dan to oversee the workers and Tom Shuman to nursemaid the performers, but he in turn had to nursemaid Nolan and Shuman. He lit his pipe. He'd grown quite fond of this new blend from Oz. Each bowlful offered him a quiet pool of tranquility amid the hustle and turmoil of the tour.

A tap on the door. He looked up and smiled. It was Ginger.

"You wanted to see me?" she said.

"Come in, come in. I always want to see my favorite niece."

How true. His sister Rosemary's daughter was damn nice to look at. Sweet face, sweet figure, sweet heart. Blue eyes and red-gold hair that Peabody swore his sister must have seen before she named her. A little headstrong, a tendency to pout, but cute as a bug. Peabody hadn't wanted Ginger in the circus, but Rosie had been an aerialist in her youth and had infected her daughter with the spirit of the circus. He had made a spot for Ginger in the deal when Peabody had to hire the Fugazi family a few years ago. She'd worked out fine.

Ginger wrinkled her nose as she sat down.

"Something wrong?" Peabody asked.

"Is that your pipe tobacco? Smells strange, like . . ." She seemed to run out of words.

"I know what you mean," he said. "I can't identify it either. But it tastes wonderful. Anyway, I called you here to tell you what a good job you're doing. I watched you in the Spanish web last night and you were perfect. And your trapeze act with . . . what's his name? The Fugazi boy?"

"Carlo."

"You two work very smoothly together, like you've been doing it all your lives."

"He's a good teacher."

"I'm glad to hear it. Just wanted to let you know I'm proud of you, and keep up the good work."

Her smile was sunlight as she waved at the door. "Thanks, Uncle Joe."

Ginger was feeling pretty good about herself as she walked through the backyard. Her mom had tried to discourage her, her uncle Joe hadn't wanted to hire her, but she'd hounded the hell out of them and here she was, aerialist with the Fugazis. Skill and hard work had a lot to do with it, but so did luck. The younger generation of Fugazis was almost entirely male and they needed a certain number of women for their act.

The roustabouts had the tents down but some of the older performers were still hanging around the backyard, sitting on lawn chairs and jackpotting. Ginger loved to listen to their tales of the old days on the kerosene circuits along the back roads of the South, but she had no time for that today. She had to get her trailer hitched up and ready to roll.

She was passing near one of the animal trucks parked in the shade when she noticed a young man sitting on a picnic bench with Neely, the circus's new baboon. Neely seemed to think she was human. There were no other baboons around, so rather than be lonely pining for one, she'd decided she was human and hung out with humans at every opportunity. She liked everybody and everybody liked her. She would groom anyone who sat near her and loved to be groomed in return.

Ginger hadn't seen the young man before. He seemed about her own age. He sat hunched forward, elbows on his thighs, hands between his legs as he let Neely groom his hair. He was kind of cute. She noticed his muscular shoulders and back—not iron-pumping bulk, but lean, sleek, hard-work muscles. Neely was working her long fingers through the dark blond hair that curled over his ears and down the nape of his neck to the collar of his Jane's Addiction T-shirt. She considered that neck. It was clean. You didn't see many clean necks in the circus, what with bathing limited to bucket baths. Though worn, his shirt was clean, too. She liked him already. And when he turned and smiled at her over his shoulder, when she saw his pale blue eyes and bright, warm smile, something tugged within her chest and she caught her breath. He was gorgeous.

"Hi," he said. His voice was like his face—light, open, friendly. "I hope Neely's not finding anything."

"Doesn't seem to be," Ginger said, stepping closer. His hair was clean, glossy. Obviously he took good care of himself. "She doesn't have to to be happy. I think it's some kind of ritual with her."

"I only wish I could return the favor."

She leaned forward and stroked Neely's fur.

"That's easy. All you've got to do is—"

At first she thought he was exposing himself, or playing with himself, or something equally sick. Then she noticed that the smooth fleshy tube wasn't coming out of his fly, but was attached to his arm. In fact it *was* his arm. Both of his arms tapered gracefully to long, curving, prehensile . . . things . . . ropes . . . *tentacles.*

The sight of those twisting, coiling arms was an icy slap in the face. All the rising warmth Ginger had been feeling toward him plummeted through the hole that ripped open in the bottom of her stomach.

She'd been about to ask if he'd just joined the show but the question was unnecessary now. She'd avoided the freak tent and had stayed away from the freaks' section of the backyard. The whole idea of deformed people putting themselves on display repulsed her. And here was one now, right in front of her, making a fool out of her.

She spun and hurried away.

George felt an aching void form in his chest as he watched the girl's retreating back. He'd seen her before, watched her bikinied form in rapt wonder night after night from the back door of the big top as she did her spins and poses on the vertical rope of the Spanish web, and her graceful, vaulting glides from trapeze to trapeze. He even knew her name: Ginger Cunningham. And just a moment ago she'd been standing not two feet from him, speaking to him, smiling that beautiful baby-faced smile—

Until she'd seen his arms.

Long ago George had stopped being self-conscious about his arms. After four years as a high school gymnast, a foreshortened year as a college gymnast performing in front of crowds of all sizes, and a couple of weeks now of displaying himself as Octoman, he'd doubted he could ever feel self-conscious again.

But he realized now he'd been wrong. The way her eyes had widened, the way her smile had withered into a tight line of revulsion . . . he'd felt naked. He glanced around. No one seemed to be watching. No one except Petergello who met his eyes for a second, then turned and sauntered away.

George stood and pulled away from Neely. He gave her a quick stroke along her back, then headed for his trailer. Despite the heat he felt a sudden need for a long-sleeve shirt.

Athens, Georgia

"Hey, Rattles, wake up—we're almost at Stonehenge," said the face on the back of the driver's head.

The dwarf lying across the backseat blinked at the unexpected intensity of the afternoon sunlight beaming through the van windows. The air inside their slow-moving 1982 Volkswagen campmobile was heavy with the lingering cologne of diesel fuel and thick with the ghost-like haze of pungent Maduro cigar smoke. Beneath him the van's rear-mounted engine rumbled powerfully, oscillating the vehicle. A soothing sound. A soothing feeling.

Rattles's python-long left arm reached to unfasten his safety belt. With his stubby, muscular right arm he pushed himself up. His head rose with a series of sharp clicks, like marbles snapping together repeatedly.

He rubbed his eyelids, sighing. His mouth was dry as cotton, and he felt a burning need to piss. "Tell me, Dub," he asked, his German accent rich as Black Forest cake, "how long vas I asleep?"

"*Too* long," Doubleface's backface snorted. He removed the smoldering cigar butt from his frontlips, stubbing it out in the dashboard ashtray. "Hours," answered his front, its voice calm.

"What is zee time?" asked the dwarf.

"Time for you to buy a watch," muttered the backface. Front glanced down at the dashboard clock. "Almost four P.M."

"Zo long," the dwarf marveled. He shook his head, its tiny loose bones rattling in their cage of skull and cartilage. "Zo long mitout any mechanical problems . . ."

"There was some talk on the CB about that," said Dub, speaking through his front. "The fat man's motorcoach has acceleration trouble, but you can fix it when we make camp."

"Zat is all?" asked Rattles.

The back answered. "That hundred-year-old Mercedes of Oz's had a flat tire outside Atlanta, but the Beagles changed it. We decided not to wake you up, Rip Van Rattle."

The dwarf sneered, tugging his little yellow baseball cap with its embroidered *Diesel Power* patch onto his lopsided head. He slid off the seat and opened the cabinet near the van's sink. Stabilizing himself against the vehicle's roll and pitch with his short arm, he used his long arm to unsnap his lederhosen and ease his trouser snake into a plastic bottle. Something began to writhe in a glass case nearby, its yard-long segmented body flexing its muscles. The thing hissed.

Rattles chuckled. "Calm yourzelf, Slither. It is only me." He wagged his dripping penis at the thing in the case and smiled as it twisted excitedly. "I vill fetch you later, my pet."

The two-headed monster called Slither hissed again and went limp, settling slowly back into its bed of curling excelsior.

Refastening his pants and closing the cabinet, Rattles took the seat beside Doubleface, his skull bones clicking. "What did you say about zis Stonehenge?"

Dub's front smiled. "Just a replica. The truckers radioed that it's at the end of this highway, right outside Athens." He switched on the turn signal. "Should be just ahead—*There!*"

The replica of the ancient circle of stones stood majestically on the roadside, though the modern commercial property nearby compromised the effect. An odd dozen of the troupe's vehicles including Ozymandias's massive trailer and Mother Goose's bus were parked helter-skelter beyond it. The peculiar arches of white rock were already crowded with the equally peculiar shapes of Oz's followers.

The auburn-haired psychic Carmella Cerami stood off in the distance, and looked as though she were in the spell of another of her disturbing visions. Mitts squatted in the center of the ring with his eyes closed, his rows of surplus misshapen fingers curling and flexing around the neck of a rosewood guitar. He seemed to draw inspiration from the site, like Robert Johnson at the Crossroads. Near Mitts's feet Gator slumped idly, unusually motionless for this time of day. Louella Snard and Octoman were posing for a picture being taken by Lance Whiting. As they leaned together in the shot, Octo's longest rubbery arm strained to wrap around Louella's girth.

At the periphery stood the five Beagles; hulking sentries poised at the points of an invisible pentagram. One of them cocked his head curiously at some spray-painted graffiti on one of the stones: This Is Bulldog Terror-tory— How 'Bout Them Dawgs!

"Looks like it's all *our* people here," Dub's front commented as he piloted the camper slowly past. "And none of Peabody's roustabout scum," his backface sneered.

The door of Oz's trailer swung open and for a moment their great, mysterious leader appeared. He stood in the doorway, raised his silver whistle to his dry, thin lips, and blew. Though there was no sound whatsoever from the whistle, all five Beagle Boys immediately turned to face him. Oz beckoned, and the Beagles obediently lumbered back toward the vehicles. Without protest the other freaks gathered themselves and followed, their little intermission clearly at its end.

"Cretins," Dub's backface commented as he regarded his fellow oddities. "They've forgotten that we're here to find a helluva lot more important kinda rock for Mr. Oz."

The dwarf sighed. "Und a much, much *smaller* one."

"Clogged fuel injectors again?" Doubleface's backmouth asked, its voice slightly muffled by the cloth drape now concealing it.

Rattles slid out from under the huge motorcoach which belonged to Gore Edmund, the World's Fattest Man. Streaks of grease crossed the dwarf's face like zebra stripes. He waved a dirty wrench. "Vat passes for motor fuel here—*Ach!*—it is a crime!" He sighed. "At least two hours' work."

There was a hiss from beneath the motorcoach and Slither dangled nearly his entire three-foot length from the undercarriage. His two tiny doll-size human heads leered on his segmented gray body, now discolored by grease. Speckled with short bristles of hair, the heads were fused as though partially melted together. Their eyes were small beads, their noses tiny pairs of dots. The wide mouths opened up, flashing crooked teeth.

Rattles smiled. "It would be *four* hours mitout zuch expert assistance as Slither provides." He waved at the thing. "Back to work, my pet. Zee entire injector assembly must be removed. Zertainly a more pleasant duty than turning zis big fat man's feeding intake valve—or his *drainage* valve!"

Slither hissed agreement, then coiled back up into the gargantuan vehicle's undercarriage.

Dub took a deep breath. The cool breeze stirring the distant tent wings was already heavy with the smell of boiling macaroni from the cooking area and the popcorn–cotton-candy perfume of the vending concession. The hammering and thumping of tent and sideshow construction was punctuated by the periodic bellow of an elephant casually tormented by a Beagle Boy.

"Doesn't take a seer like Carmella to tell dinner's gonna be macaroni again," Dub observed, both noses sniffing. "Don't know how the fat man puts away that macaroni *paste* of his, which is about fifty times worse. Even Gator won't eat *that* crap."

Rattles shrugged. "Gator has no appetite lately."

Vittles Vitale marched sullenly toward them, a steaming bucket hanging from each calloused fist. A tiny stub of smoldering cigar balanced impossibly on his meaty lips. Dub's four trained nostrils at once recognized the tobacco as a Tampa Nugget Blunt—a cheap, papery, workingman's smoke.

The cook glowered at the two of them but said nothing

as he placed both buckets on the cinder block step of the
motorcoach. Casually he flicked his cigar ash into one of
the buckets, where it speckled the whipped-macaroni
paste like a black pepper garnish. He knocked once on
the motorcoach door. *"Dinner!"*

Almost immediately the massive coach tilted to the
side, its springs groaning and creaking at the redistribu-
tion of weight as the fat man leaned within. With a frantic
hiss, Slither dropped from the undercarriage and writhed
wildly on the ground.

Rattles knocked his fist against the vehicle. *"Achtung!
No moving while zee wagon is under repair, Schwein!"*
He banged on the coach again, skinning a layer of flesh off
his knuckles this time.

The cook leaped backward as a huge steel hook
pushed open the coach door and snagged the bucket
handles, hoisting them inside. Vittles tossed his cigar and
marched back to his work.

The dwarf looked up at Dub. "By zee fine French
foreign legion hat you wear, I zuspect you are going into
town, yes?"

Dub nodded. "Gonna ride in on Morrison's sound
truck. I'll try to score some tobacco, maybe some beer,
and find out what I can about this town. Anything for
you?"

Rattles nodded emphatically, his loose bones knocking. "Yes—a *dinner!"*

The huge, grotesque canine wore a hat emblazoned
with the letter *G.* The beast snarled down from the poster
in the window which proclaimed: This Is Bulldog Terror-
tory.

Doubleface studied the image with disgust. Everywhere he turned in this little city he saw the same monstrous, muscular bulldog. This bizarre totem grimaced
from signs, decals, T-shirts, bumper stickers. How 'Bout
Them Dawgs? Wuf Wuf Wuf! The streets were alive with
its image, staring from the panels of cars and trucks,
leering from the cotton clothing of the healthy, laughing,
well-groomed young people crowding the sidewalks.
Many of those who didn't display the animal on their

garments wore instead one of two monograms—*UGA* or *R.E.M.*

Dub pushed open the badly painted brown door of Barnett's News and Tobacco. Wood creaked and a tarnished brass bell jingled weakly as the door swung. The shop was spacious and cool, softly lit, its air heavy with the smells of pulp paper, newsprint, and the tempting aromas of fine tobaccos. Spanish Maduro commingled teasingly with Virginia Claro and African Cameroon. Wire racks of books and magazines crisscrossed the interior in ersatz alleyways like the great labyrinth of Crete.

Dub reached up to a swivel display rack of postcards and lifted out one depicting the bulldog. He turned to the store's only visible employee, a pale, baby-faced man with curly brown hair and huge horn-rimmed glasses. "Sir, what's the significance of this animal to your city?"

"Why, that there's Uga," Horn Rims answered, "the team mascot of the university. You know—the *University of Georgia*." When Dub stared blankly back at him, the clerk pointed out the window toward a distant black iron arch with a cluster of white-columned buildings behind it. "That school's the main reason this little town's on the map, 'cept maybe for R.E.M."

"Uga?" Dub's backmouth snapped, its voice muffled by the cloth of the legionnaire's hat concealing it.

"Why, sure," explained the clerk, oblivious to the source of Dub's voice. "Uga—*U-G-A*. You know, University of Georgia."

"Then what is *R-E-M?*" asked Dub, speaking through his frontmouth this time.

Horn Rims shrugged. "They're a local rock band that made it big. Cover of the *Rolling Stone* and all. I kinda enjoy one song they do—a version of the old Everly Brothers' hit 'Dream.'"

Dub smiled, front and back. "I've sung that one myself," front said. "Good for harmonizing," added the back. "Nice duet."

The clerk blinked, then smiled. "You in show biz, mister?"

Dub nodded. As he replaced the bulldog postcard in the rack he noticed another, a picture of an oak with the title *The Tree That Owns Itself.* "What's this?"

The clerk's smile became a grin. "Oh, 'bout a century ago one of our citizens died and willed that tree to itself so nobody'd cut it down. Damn thing's in the middle of a street!"

Dub's front smiled politely. His backface sneered.

"Yeah, if you like that, look at this one." Horn Rims plucked out another card, this one showing a double-barreled cannon. "That's right up the hill in front of city hall. Long as you're in town, you oughta check it out. Real piece of local history. Our side maybe coulda won the Civil War with it."

Dub turned as if to examine the card in better light and the clerk turned with him. But Dub's backeyes were looking through the panels of his hat at the prizes within easy reach: handmade Cuesta-Rey Dominican No. 2 Maduros. By the time Horn Rims finished his lecture about the cannon, nine of the fine cigars rested in Dub's coat pocket.

The walk up the hill toward Athens City Hall was pleasant. The cool late-afternoon air was fragrant with honeysuckle and thick with the sizzling beef smell from the Grill, a crowded eatery on the corner. It reminded Dub of his promise to pick up dinner for Rattles, but that could wait.

A color poster for the Peabody-Ozymandias Traveling Circus and Oddity Emporium gleamed on a corkboard near the crosswalk. As Dub walked past, his backface noticed a smaller handbill tacked beside the circus poster. He stopped and went back.

The Rosetta Stones, it proclaimed, Live in Concert Tonite at the 40 Watt Club! Reproduced in the center of the ad art was what looked like the Rock of Gibraltar on fire.

Something tugged at the back of Dub's mind. The picture disturbed him in some unique, inexplicable way. *I wonder what Rattles would make of this*, he mused. Keeping a lookout with his backface, he pocketed the poster.

The crowd thinned as the sidewalk sloped up. College students' decal-covered cars puttered past, interspersed with farm vehicles and rumbling Du Pont trucks. Dub watched the students dressed in bright clothing, Italian shoes, and designer jeans. They reeked of deodorant soaps and trendy colognes.

He passed retrowave kids with Potter's House wardrobes, clown-colored hair, berets, sandals, and tie-dyed R.E.M. T-shirts. They studied his desert-gear hat with envious stares.

Cresting the hill, its sides lined with dogwood trees, Dub walked by aging merchants and farmers who had obviously lived here all their lives. Their hands were rough, their checkered shirts and dirty overalls moist with sweat. These weary men with bourbon-bloom noses probably spent hours every Saturday retelling their great-grandads' stories about fighting for the Stars and Bars under Beauregard or Stonewall Jackson.

Dominating the park bench in front of the double-barreled cannon were two big guys conducting a boisterous conversation. The larger was a hairy, dark-bearded fellow with a pompous, mad-professor air. In contrast, his graying companion wore a black T-shirt over jeans held up by bright red suspenders, and was mild and deferential.

Dub took up a spot between them and the antique cannon. While examining the double-barreled field piece through his front, he carefully observed the two men with his backeyes. He reached into his coat pocket and took out one of the prize smokes he'd so easily lifted from Barnett's, snipped off the end with his cigar cutter, and carefully lit it.

"Bulldog Ale?" bellowed the hairy man on the bench. "The import fee from England makes that stuff way overpriced for this market, Klon. But Wild Boar Amber is local, a *Georgia* beer."

Klon countered quietly, "But, Ort, a boar is the Razorbacks' mascot. No self-respectin' Georgia fan's gonna buy that."

Half listening to the Great Ale Debate, Dub examined the freakish cannon and read the historical marker explaining its origins. Developed as a Confederate secret weapon, Athens' startling contribution to the Civil War was designed to fire twin cannon balls linked by a chain. Ultimately it failed because the two barrels wouldn't ignite simultaneously.

"Klon," said Ort, "you know my pal Kurt, the new drummer for the Rosetta Stones? He said *their* favorite beer—"

Dub turned, his front facing the two men. "Excuse me," he blurted. "Did you say you know someone in the Rosetta Stones?"

Ort nodded his huge, shaggy head. "Yes, indeed."

Dub unfolded the Rosetta Stones' concert poster from his pocket. "What can you tell me about the rock in this picture?"

Ort shrugged. "That's the gimmick they use in their stage lighting. It's a lot *smaller* than it looks there, though. . . ."

When Dub flung open the campmobile's sliding door, he found Rattles reclining across the rear seat with Slither coiled around his wrist. The monster's two tiny heads lapped hungrily at the dwarf's skinned knuckles.

"Hey, midget!" shouted Dub's backface. "What's eatin' you?"

Rattles sat up, his head knocking. He grimaced. "It vas time to feed my pet. *Blood,* Dub, zat's Slither's diet." He uncoiled the monster gently and set it aside.

Dub placed a small red and black cardboard box on the van floor. It was from a burger joint called the Varsity and smelled of onions, a dark grease stain already spreading on one side. "Here's your dinner."

As Rattles opened the red box, Dub unfolded the concert poster. "Take a look at this. I think I've found one of Oz's Pieces. We gotta show him right away—maybe he'll give us the night off to crash this rock show."

The dwarf swallowed a mouthful of onion rings. "It is already arranged. Carmella vas here—she had a vision zat Doubleface, the Man With Two Faces, would find what Oz wants."

Rattles grinned as he chewed his greasy meal. He held up Oz's silver dog whistle.

Night had fallen when the long black 1969 Mercedes limousine pulled up to the curb outside the 40 Watt club, its diesel engine knocking.

A door swung open and two figures emerged—a tall

man wearing a foreign legionnaire's hat and a dwarf with mismatched arms. On a chain around the tall man's neck hung a silver whistle. Encircling the dwarf's waist twice was a segmented reptilian belt. The Mercedes pulled away slowly, five other hulking figures dimly visible through its tinted windows.

Inside the dark nightclub the air was heavy with smoke. The hall was crowded with young people, crushed elbow to elbow, shouting to sustain conversation above the roar of "Pinhead" by the Ramones, which boomed from the PA system.

In the control booth above stood a heavy, severe-looking woman with a bouffant hairdo. She studied the crowd carefully through narrowed, suspicious eyes.

Debra Rose Lacoste took a deep breath. The turnout for her band's show was better than she'd hoped. That was good, but she'd developed another of those infernal jack-hammer headaches, and now her period had started two days early. Tonight's show was important, and she knew that without her precise diddling of the special effects, a performance by the Rosetta Stones wasn't worth sour owl shit. The light show was everything. And the light show was the Rock. No way was Debra Rose Lacoste ever going back to the third shift at Du Pont. This was her express ticket to The Big Time.

She worried again about the Rock. Was it safe back-stage? The kids in the band—did they really have any idea how much it was worth to her? Why the hell wouldn't they *get real* and carry those pricey razor-edged Buck knives she'd bought them?

And as if she didn't have enough to worry about already, now there were two weirdos down there crowding the edge of the stage. They looked like trouble, par-ticularly the little shit with the *Diesel Power* cap. She'd mention them to the club's security.

She sighed. Her head throbbed. Menstrual cramps twisted her insides. She felt profoundly awful.

The Ramones tape ended and the club manager was onstage now, reading aloud an exhibition game score somebody'd phoned in. The Bulldogs had won, luckily—and the crowd reaction was the pathetically predictable explosion of jubilant cheers and idiotic shouts of, *How 'bout them dawgs?! Wuf wuf wuf!!!* She hated it.

If only her little musical ensemble could one day command such loyalty, they'd give even R.E.M. a run for the money.

In the downstage darkness, her musicians were taking their positions. Kurt carried out the Rock, then jogged back behind his drum kit. Ignoring her physical discomfort, Debra Lacoste began adjusting the equipment settings, ready for the assault.

Showtime.

The distorted voice cutting through the smokey darkness of the club was a woman's, though its Rod Serling mimicry was inspired. "In the beginning there was the sound. And the sound was The Rock. And from The Rock, the power flowed. Ladies and gentlemen—*the Rosetta Stones!*"

Psychedelic guitar music mixed with snapping drumbeats, swirling keyboard melodies, and a pulsing bass line. The tune was a lurching cover of the Rolling Stones' "Citadel."

Dub winced at the volume, grateful that he was born with four eyes and two ears instead of the opposite. His front watched the stage while his back kept vigil on the control booth. Not much to see onstage yet—shapes in the dark—though he noticed the Lacoste woman working the spotlights up in the booth. Dub remembered what he'd overheard about the light show. . . .

And then it happened.

Pink-hued footlights brightened at the rear of the stage, revealing silhouettes of the long-haired musicians thrashing at their instruments. But at center stage was a raised platform on which turned a six-inch chunk of gemstone resembling a miniature Rock of Gibraltar. A thin beam of carbon arc light burned at it, colors spreading out as if through a prism. But something was moving in the colors. Something *alive*.

Dub felt the earth sway beneath his feet, pitching and rolling like the floor of a moving bus. His backface saw the crowd dancing, but they danced as if floating in molasses, almost weightless, a rose-tinted movie in slow motion; time itself seemed to become fluid. The sound of the band faded low, like a stereo turned down. When he spoke, he heard his own voice, hollow and haunting, as though it were the only sound in the universe. "Rattles, d-do you f-feel it?"

The dwarf answered with a gasp. His bones knocked like hammers. The music seemed to be miles away. There were only Dub's and Rattles's voices.

Without stopping, the band eased into the second song of their set—"2000 Light-Years From Home." From the control booth, Debra Lacoste trained a laser beam on the Piece.

And then the show turned into a nightmare.

The amorphous scenes, which danced and flickered in, around, over, and *through* them, resembled Stoneman's cavalry raid through Georgia as if reenacted in Tallulah Gorge by ninety-foot maggots. Gargantuan two-headed pterodactyls carried the monsters, their beaks vomiting beads of dark liquid which expanded into quivering, explosive balloons of flesh. These wiggling wet earth-sperm wobbled among the crowd, warring and mating. The mounted maggots waved distorted tusklike swords from dozens of vestigial arms on their sides.

The colors were outrageous, the smells worse.

Kurt, the drummer, leaned against the cold cinder block wall of the club's tiny dressing room and tightened his grip on a sweating bottle of Bulldog Ale, his fifth brewski since the end of the band's opening set. He was comfortably numb.

Kurt's ears still rang from the percussive finale of "In Another Land," and his skull felt like the business end of Godzilla's own pogo stick. *Weird how I never feel bad when we rehearse,* he mused, *but I always feel dead as Keith Moon after our stage shows. . . .*

He grimaced. *It's gotta be this damn Rock of Debra's.* He prodded the little wooden platform on which it rested. The Rock shook on its mounting, as if nodding at him.

Kurt glanced around the sweaty-smelling room, its gray walls defaced with rainbow spirals of graffiti, everything from crude erotica to loopy Howard Finster art. *It's just not fair, Vince and Mike partyin' with that little purple-haired groupie and her bottle of JD while I gotta stay here and guard—What the hell?*

Slithering across the dressing room floor was the weirdest snake Kurt had ever seen. It looked like a yard of Wrigley's Spearmint sticks and it had the funniest looking head.

It whipped under Vince's gator-hide guitar case.

Kurt set down his beer bottle and knelt on the cold concrete floor for a closer look. Then something hit him across the back of the head with the force of a sledgehammer.

As he blacked out, the last thing Kurt heard—dimly through his numbed ears—was a peculiar, faraway rattle.

"Vee got it," whispered Rattles as he joined Dub in the narrow, brick-lined alley out back. He patted a prominent bulge in the front of the blouse he wore under his lederhosen.

Dub smiled front and back as together they enjoyed a quiet moment of triumph. Casually he tossed away his smoldering cigar.

Rattles stroked Slither, once again concealed as a belt. "Zee three of us vill now be among Oz's most favored." He stroked the bulge proudly. "Already I feel zee Piece's power."

Dub raised the dog whistle toward his frontlips.

At that moment the club's rear door banged open and Debra Lacoste stood framed in its arch, her face sick with panic. "Hey, you guys," she choked, "did anybody come outa here with—"

She froze. Though only a single bare bulb lit the dim alley, Dub saw her eyes widen and her brows lift. "Wait a minute! You're the ones I saw down by the stage! And *you,*" she said, pointing an accusatory finger at Rattles, "weren't you—"

The freaks stared calmly back at her.

Her gaze locked on the lump in Rattles's embroidered shirt. *"You* took it!" Her voice began to quiver. "Y-you've got it right there! *Give it b-back to me, now!"*

They shook their heads slowly. Rattles's loose bones knocked.

"You've *got to*," she choked, her eyes fogging with tears. "I need it . . . it's my future . . . m-my only chance . . . I . . . I-I'll show you . . ." Slowly she removed the tall wig from her head, revealing a gruesome burn across her entire scalp. She had no hair above her ear line, the top of her skull blistered and shriveled as fried bacon. Swollen fleshy knobs rose like horns.

Even Dub was horror-struck.

She replaced the wig and looked back up at them. "The Rock you took is th-the only thing that's letting this band m-make money. I n-need it," she pleaded, a tear drooling down her pale cheek. "It's my only chance— *please*. Oh, dear God, I'll do anything—*anything you want*—j-just *please* give it back!"

Dub was astounded at what happened next.

Rattles gracefully removed his *Diesel Power* cap. "I am zo zorry, zo zorry for you, *Frau* Lacoste," he said quietly, with what seemed to be genuine compassion. "All my life, I too have been *different*. But zis Piece—zis Rock, as you call it—it belongs to my people. Vee have come far to retrieve it, and vee have a long journey ahead to find others like it. I am zo zorry, but it is *ours*."

Dub, startled by Rattles's unusual display of sympathy, could only nod. When he saw the blade it was already too late.

"*Aeeegrrrhhh!*" Rattles screamed as the woman's gleaming silver Buck knife punched into his rib cage. He tumbled back, his longer arm whipping behind to break his fall.

Dub smashed his fist into Lacoste's face. She stumbled backward, her arms windmilling crazily until her head cracked hard against the alley wall. Her body went rigid and she slid down the wall, her eyes fluttering weakly. The knife fell from her grasp, clinking as it hit the pavement.

The dwarf gasped hard, his breath coming in ragged spurts.

Dub turned to his fallen comrade and knelt on the pavement beside him. "How bad is it?" asked his front and back together.

Rattles drew another ragged breath, choking. He coughed up a small fleck of blood. "Bad . . ." He tapped his segmented belt, and Slither uncoiled from his waist. His next breath came a little easier. "Vee must go now . . . get back to zee camp. . . ."

Dub's frontface contorted with rage. Turning again to Lacoste he picked up the Buck knife and raised its gleaming edge to her face. She blinked groggily as the blade reflected the glare of the lone bulb over the door. "I'll slice out your eyes," said Dub's front. His backface added, "And then your heart!"

"Nein!" Rattles coughed. "No, Dub! Leave her alone—vee vant no trouble from zee police!"

The tall man held the knife to her throat, where its edge raised a tiny red bead of blood. Then he dropped the knife, his backface cursing fiercely. He raised the dog whistle to blow but was distracted as he saw Slither zigzagging past him. Before he could move to stop it, the creature's two tiny heads lunged at Lacoste's neck.

Lacoste jolted upright with a ripping wet scream. She lurched to her feet as blood spread down her front. Slither wormed its way hungrily inside her throat, the tip of its tail whipping like a strand of slurped spaghetti as it vanished inside her.

Dub blew hard on the dog whistle, then bent down to scoop up Rattles's tiny body. He placed the *Diesel Power* hat on the dwarf's chest. Rattles's longer arm drooped like a dinosaur's tail.

The air smelled suddenly of diesel smoke, and massive feet scuffed at the alley's end. The Beagle Boys had arrived.

As Dub carried Rattles toward the waiting Mercedes, he pointed the Beagles toward the club's back door. "Don't let *anybody* outa there till we're gone," his backface commanded.

Lacoste sprawled dying on the alley floor as Slither slowly wiggled out of her. With a satisfied hiss it snaked off after Dub, leaving a curling red trail on the pavement behind.

The Beagles slammed themselves against the club's door just as excited cries and frantic pounding erupted from inside. They sealed the exit by locking their arms together, a wall of canine muscle that no mortal could pass.

As the black sleep claimed her forever, the last sound Debra Lacoste heard was Dub's backface shouting: *"How 'bout them dawgs!!!"*

GREGORY NICOLL

The show rolled on . . .

ALONG THE MIDWAY (II)

Crockett County, Tennessee

"It's not fair," Ginger said, biting her trembling lower lip. "I won't do it."

She was in her uncle Joe's trailer but they weren't alone. Someone else was there—that big ugly man with the lank hair who ran the freak show. The one they called Oz.

"I thought you were a trouper," her uncle Joe said, puffing furiously on his pipe. "You wanted to be in my circus, I got you in, and now the first time something goes wrong, you want to blow the show. What kind of gratitude is that?"

What was wrong with him? This wasn't the Joe Peabody she'd known all her life. Didn't he realize that this wasn't just some tiny mishap? Carlo—her partner, her aerial soul mate—had a broken shoulder. She was devastated and her uncle was treating it like she'd stubbed her toe or something.

The Fugazi family did another series of acts in the show under the name of the Amazing Armanis. Carlo's bit as an Armani was to ride a motorcycle on the high wire. He'd started when he was twelve and could do it with his eyes closed, but last night the front wheel had come loose in midwire and he'd fallen, cycle and all. A freak accident . . .

Freak . . . that seemed to be the word of the day. That

sinister character from the freak show, the one called Petergello, had been hanging around the Fugazi corner of the lot lately, and now her uncle Joe wanted her to do her act with one of the freaks, that one with the tentacles—Octoman.

"It has nothing to do with gratitude, Uncle Joe," she said. "I just don't want to cheapen my act by adding a freak."

"If it's okay with the Fugazis, why shouldn't it be okay with you?"

Ginger was stunned. "Papa Fugazi said okay?"

"Of course—right after I told him what I'm telling you: You do as I say or you'll never work any circus, anywhere, ever. And I can back that up. I get it around that you blew my show on the first leg, and no one'll want to risk taking you on."

"Wh-why are you doing this?"

"Because it'll make a great show. You up there flying through the air toward that guy with no hands—you'll have the crowd on its feet every time."

"But . . . but . . ." She was at a loss for words, desperate for some way out. "He's not qualified."

"George Swenson is an excellent athlete," said Ozymandias Prather in his basso voice. "He had a full scholarship to Florida State as a gymnast before the other schools in the conference changed the rules to exclude him."

Ginger felt as if the walls were closing in on her. She looked to her uncle one last time, hoping he'd respond to the plea in her eyes.

"Uncle Joe . . ."

"I've said all I'm going to say on this, Ginger. Now you get over to the Fugazi trailers right away. Oz's man is already there. Papa Fugazi will begin coaching the two of you this afternoon. We've got no time to waste."

Fighting the tears, Ginger turned, slammed out the door, and almost tripped going down the steps. Petergello, who seemed to be Oz's shadow, was waiting outside. He grabbed her elbow and steadied her as she stumbled. His touch was cold, like death. He smiled. A beatific smile in a handsome face, yet without the slightest trace of warmth. She yanked her arm free and continued on her way.

She stopped a moment later. On her way where?

To her trailer and then home to Momma like a spoiled child? Like a loser? Or grit her teeth and go over to Fugazi country and get on with it?

The show must go on—and all the rest of that bullshit.

What had Oz said his name was? George Swenson?

She shuddered at the thought of touching those boneless, fingerless arms. Like touching snakes. But she'd show Uncle Joe and the rest of them. Ginger Cunningham didn't choke.

She smiled to herself. She might throw up, but she didn't choke.

She headed for Fugaziville.

"You think I was too rough on her?" Joseph Peabody said as Ginger left.

"Not at all," Oz told him, glancing at Petergello as he entered the office trailer. "It's for the good of the show. We all have to make sacrifices for the show. Look at poor Carlo Junior. He broke his shoulder for the show." Oz caught Petergello's fleeting smile. "The least your niece can do is cooperate with the replacement we've chosen for him."

"Yes," Joseph said, nodding and puffing. "The least she can do."

Oz turned to Petergello and lowered his voice. "You're sure George will fall for her?"

"Quite sure. You should see his face when he watches her perform. He's already infatuated. And she loathes him."

"Excellent." A shame, Oz thought, to have to bring pain to one of his brothers, but George had to learn who was his true family. And speaking of family . . . "How's Rattles?"

"Recovering well. He's tough. We're all tough."

"And you, my friend. I understand you've added some new items to your collection."

Petergello smiled. "A few interesting pieces, yes. And in Sikeston I may find a Piece for *your* collection."

"I'm counting on it," Oz said.

Sikeston, Missouri

The exquisitely good-looking man with the odd last name, Petergello, was not alone in his private quarters. A drunken Hercules appeared to be watching him, while holding his absurdly outsized penis in a small, but well-formed right hand, urinating. It is well-known that a drunken man will urinate almost anywhere, and the classical strongman of antiquity was performing this biological function in the presence of both Ptah Sekar and—unforgivably—the lovely Isis.

The mighty Hercules, dick in hand, stood pissing into the face of eternity. Five-and-a-half centimeters in burnished bronze. A freak from before the birth of Christ—perhaps circa 1000 B.C. He was flanked by Ptah Sekar, the bandy-legged dwarf, standing with his hands on his hips, a monstrous thing sprouting from his groin. On his right, Isis, goddess of motherhood and fecundity, suckled Horus as she took the massive engine of a bull. The figurine retained its original turquoise blue glaze, and on the mighty cleaver one could see a witty representation of Uraeus, the sacred asp! Delightful.

Petergello found it most amusing. Definitely a worthwhile addition to his collection of antique erotica, and one which he would now share with the few who could appreciate such an acquisition on at least a superficial level.

Petergello peered out the window in the direction of Gore Edmund's mobile home, and he could see roustabouts preparing to drop the outer wall, readying Edmund for display. Petergello smiled, thinking of the way the passersby would flinch, gasp, and jabber at the sight of the monstrously obese human inside the rectangular box.

Petergello tapped Edmund's familiar number through the keypad of his Nipponese cellular phone, listening for the unmistakable voice.

"Yeah?"

"Is this Mr. Wolfe's residence?"

"Of course," the high, squeaky voice assured him.

"Is Mr. Goodwin in?"

"Mr. Goodwin is no longer in my employ. Mr. Goodwin has been *terminated*."

"With prejudice?" They chuckled.

"Extreme."

"Then this must be . . . Mr. Wolfe himself?"

"No. This is *not,* sir." A pause. Petergello could hear the whoosh of air-conditioning fighting to maintain a reasonable temperature in the sweltering southeast Missouri heat. "I am Stout," he said, playing on both the name of a world-famous mystery author and Edmund's own obesity.

"I can see that," Petergello said dutifully, smiling as he heard the voice on the other end of the connection wheeze with good humor. "You *are* stout indeed, which no man can deny. While I, on the other hand, am Hercule. Hercule Poirot at your service." Petergello gave the last words his best Gallic flourish.

"Where the bloody hell are we?" The high voice squeaked, Gore Edmund having tired of their word game.

"You, sir, are in Mr. Wolfe's brownstone on West Thirty-fifth, while I—"

"No, I mean where *are* we?" Edmund demanded.

"Sikeston, Missouri," reported Petergello.

"I should have guessed as much. I was sure that I sniffed something making its way past the filters. Where are we specifically, in some fucking stockyards?"

"We're in the lovely home of"—Petergello made a noise of effort as he craned his neck to read the billboard that was visible through his office window—"the Sikeston Bootheel Livestock Show."

"And you found something *here?*" asked Gore, who had a passion for collecting things himself.

"We'll soon know. I have an appointment after we close this evening. But I'm optimistic. The person I've been talking with promises an eclectic selection," Petergello said.

"In any event," he continued, "the reason I phoned—I got the Hercules statuette. And it is quite charming. I know it isn't your thing but I'll bring it by and show it off on my way across town. Also, what did the guy in Michigan have—anything?"

"Our man in Lansing. Yeah." The high voice wheezed, rummaging through notes which Petergello knew were probably scattered about the top of the mattresses where Gore Edmund lived out his existence—such as it was. "Uh—he has three pieces: *guilloche*-like Luristanian cast Ibex erect. What the hell is that?"

"It's just a type of ornamentation. It's a wild goat with a hard-on," answered Petergello.

Edmund wheezed with laughter. "Closed pyriform vessel with top like phallus. What's pyriform?" he asked.

"Means shaped like a pear. Like someone we know," Petergello teased gently.

"Creature of unknown origin—like someone *I* know," Edmund parried, "with twin lance tongues fit into the female apertures of a recumbent gnu of steatite. What's steatite?"

"It's like soapstone," Petergello said.

"What's a gnu?"

"Not too much, really." This evoked another bout of wheezing from Edmund. "I can see you'll be in rare form for the slugs," Petergello said.

"The Sikeston slugs. Yes. I foresee slugs, hemoflagellates, and assorted eupeptic imbeciles. I wouldn't mind contracting for a little souvenir here," said Edmund.

"Umm," Petergello grunted noncommittally.

"Did you want any of that stuff?" Edmund asked.

"No. It's all junk. The third is probably a repro anyway. But please tell the Lansing chap thank you for me," answered Petergello.

"All right," said Edmund, ready to rest from this burst of activity.

Petergello heard background noise like feedback, which meant Edmund was probably monitoring the exterior speaker. "I am now visible. I think I'll try to find something decent on the telly and have a bite."

"See you later, then. Bon appetite."

"Um-hmm. Well, you know what they say. Paste makes waste." Petergello simulated a chuckle and they each disconnected.

Petergello was lucky and he never failed to count his blessings. He was one of the few affected by the Otherness whose abnormality did not lend itself to display. Perhaps it was the reason why he felt such a great affinity for the huge freak. Because his was not an apparent physical oddity, he had been assigned a far more important function than entertaining rubes. He was the circus's bounty hunter. And he had proved to be very, very good at his work.

It took half a dozen roustabouts to lower the hinged wall of Gore Edmund's mobile home.

The basic unit of Gore Edmund's mobile home was a modified Ultracoach, custom-built to specs by the Worldwide Mobile Homes Company, Inc., of Elkhart, Indiana. The exterior measurements, fifteen-by-fifty-five, exceeded the national highway code provisions by a foot, and so the company had to preplan its road schedule accordingly, obtaining special permission to move Edmund's oversize trailer.

Since they worked at the job routinely, lowering the hinged wall for display was no more arduous for the carnies than setting up the juice joints and flat joints along the midway—roughly the equivalent of a small ride—but once a week the job became a nightmare.

Every seven days the team had to don gas masks and empty out Edmund's waste tank, which was considered the most odious job. Ozymandias Prather, the wizard of odds, planned to terminate Edmund's display at the first opportunity, but he was troubled by mitigating factors.

Petergello had formed an uncharacteristic alliance of sorts with Gore Edmund, which was unique in the history of the circus. While the phrase "regular freak" may be an oxymoron, technically, it nevertheless described Edmund's role. He was a human oddity left over from the sideshow days; neither circus performer nor one of those whom the Otherness had touched.

Petergello, a loner among loners, responded perhaps to some inexplicable vibes of kinship. He was the only one of *them* who didn't look down his nose at what they perceived as a gross, hated outsider, and a disgusting one at that.

It was a bizarre bonding. When properly attired, Petergello could blend into the most fashionable high society dinner party or gala, while Gore Edmund was unable to move outside his mobile home—more specifically from the pile of mattresses that served him as an easy chair and bed. (His only movement was to shift his poundage from time to time and apply petroleum jelly to the reddened areas of flesh that bore the brunt of his punishing weight—a condition of constant bedsores.)

Some of the carnies called them, when out of earshot, Peter Jello and Jelly Belly. An odd couple, to be sure. But while neither would classify the other as a friend, there was an area born of mutual need, trust, and—however unlikely—fellowship.

Both men were collectors, and the quirky collecting fraternity often makes for strange bedfellows. Whatever factors were responsible for the relationship, Oz was loathe to tamper with it. He was not about to risk the ire of one of his most dangerous freaks unnecessarily. Especially one with such a genius for finding Pieces. Petergello had a genuine gift for finding the things, having turned up three. And here he was on the track of another.

At the moment Petergello was far down the midway, but he could hear the screams and shouts of onlookers from the Oddity Emporium. Some of the loudest noises came from outside the Gore Edmund display.

It was indeed shocking to witness the thing inside the glass. Behind thick, soundproof, shatter-resistant one-way glass, installed inside-out so that the occupant would not have to watch or hear the crowds as they screamed and jeered at him, sat Gore Edmund, a one-of-a-kind sight. One saw a *human* freak, of inhuman proportions.

Initially one saw the belly: an impossible eight-foot-wide obscenely white roundness of skin stretched beyond all proportions, topped by a pair of pendulous pillows of breast fat, and resting at the sides of this weather balloon of bloated humanity, immense, doughy arms that looked as if they might be made of rubber. Each arm suggested a Michelin Tire man. This thing, this human thing of indescribable fatness, this travesty of gravity, had hands, feet (fat aprons covered most of the legs), and then . . . one saw the head.

The head was the most frightening thing about the sight because it was so tiny. There was something extremely alarming about the look of that perfectly featured face and head, like a shrunken head on an elephant, sitting atop the pile of naked mounds of flesh.

The head, no larger than a big grapefruit, had perfectly normal eyes, nose, mouth, and ears, and was the final touch to this caricature.

Once the spectator got his breath back, there was time for a more reasoned viewing of the thing—the man—and you realized that it *was* human, a living being, and you saw the visible feeding hookups. Two transparent tubes were apparent. One ran to the mouth, another to the center of the lowest fat apron, where it disappeared. (A third tube, which carried solid waste, was mercifully not visible.)

To those observing him, the mountain of blubber appeared to be looking vaguely straight ahead, or perhaps slightly to the side, but never making eye contact with those watching. They did not know he was watching a bank of monitors, which were placed along hanging shelves that ran the length of the room, flush against the ceiling. The back of the monitor bank was constructed to resemble the exterior of the trailer itself, so that onlookers had no idea that there were multiple viewing screens across the top of the room they were observing.

In each hand Gore Edmund clutched a remote control unit, the small buttons worn smooth by the hot, pudgy fingers that caressed them every waking hour of every day.

The controls ran to hookups labeled PASTE and WASTE (the life-support system that fed and cleaned this eating machine), and TEMPERATURE, and in his other hand the controls for TV, VCR, EXT FRONT and EXT TELE—the video-audio units for monitoring the people outside, and for talking on the telephone.

Gore Edmund was, in that sense, the ultimate couch potato. Which, in a roundabout way, is the second reason why the heartbreakingly beautiful Petergello, and the man upon whose display glass was the painted legend—Mr. Gore Edmund. Age: 29. Height: 5′ 11″. Weight: 1,869 pounds. The heaviest man in the world!—had formed a bond.

There was the terrible *rage*. Inside Edmund a fire of hatred boiled that only a freak like the dangerous Petergello could understand. Each of them had such an unrelenting and passionate hatred for the human race. Edmund hated, superficially, because of his morbid obesity, Petergello because he had been denied normality—yet given the cruel gift of superficial beauty. In fact, each of them hated because they could not love. The degree to which they detested everyone, regardless of color or origin, transcended psychopathy. Gore Edmund was *sustained* by his rage, Petergello was *nourished* by his.

Later that night, Petergello awoke from his nap, smiling as he anticipated the pleasures of the evening ahead. He phoned the Sikeston antiquarian dealer to reconfirm their appointment, and sat quietly, gathering his powers, focusing, enjoying his latest hobby find.

With a sigh Petergello forced himself to his feet, gathering up some of his items for trade, which he carefully placed in a foam-rubber-lined carrying case, and the other hardware he would need for the evening.

Lastly, after removing Piss Hercules from the case and tucking it into a traveling box, he dialed Gore Edmund's trailer again.

"Yeah?" growled Edmund.

"I'm coming," Petergello intoned musically.

"Another first."

Petergello laughed loudly and hung up, locking his private quarters and heading down the midway.

The crowd had thinned out. Hicks. Redneck townies on the cruise. Marks aplenty.

He approached the trailer from the rear, rapping

sharply on a metal fitting behind the huge man inside.

He walked around and stood in a gathering of townies, the most dangerous shill ever, working his way to a position in direct line with the hidden video camera.

He could see Gore Edmund's lips moving slightly, not looking anywhere near the place where Petergello stood, in between a family of four and a young couple, all of whom seemed to be giggling. The tiny head was in animation atop the mounds of pulsating, quivering lard, which always seemed to be moving slightly.

Petergello knew that Edmund would be watching him on the monitor, having been alerted by the call. Doubtless he'd also have the audio on. "Paste makes waste," Petergello said in the direction of the glass, showing the treasure.

"Oh, God, yuck!" a young girl gasped behind him.

Petergello said, loudly enough for anyone near to overhear, "Wouldn't it be funny if all the freaks were on this side of the glass?" He carefully covered the prized figurine, waved, and left.

The same teenage girl who had gasped at the sight of Edmund turned to her friend as Petergello walked past, saying the Lord's name again, but in a different tone. "Oh, God," she of the limited vocabulary said. "What a hunk."

The normal teenage girl, yearning innocently for the handsome man vanishing into the night, had no idea what he was. Hunk he was indeed, but a hunk who was unable to consummate the act of physical love, much less procreate. Freaks like Petergello had evolved *not* to reproduce. The Otherness had seen to that. They were *sui generis*, these unique, freaky one-shots.

The other freaks were always after Oz to urge that an accident might befall Gore Edmund. They could never understand why Petergello catered to this repulsive remnant from the Peabody's Traveling Circus days of painted-tarp sideshows. There had been times when Petergello had wanted to share the secret with Oz, but he didn't dare. For all his ruthlessness Oz could be absurdly puritanical at times. Oz could never be told about the rows of jars and bottles and glass frames that lined the secret shelf of the trailer where no one other than Gore Edmund ever ventured. Crammed between monitors and other gear, on display solely for Edmund's pleasure, his private collection rested.

The dark and nasty things that Gore Edmund collected, the hideous horrors bought and bartered from others as mad as he was—from the venal, from those with secret weaknesses of their own, from those whose professions brought them in contact with the criminally insane—could only be shared with a brother who prowled the same shadows. As Edmund liked to sometimes say, "You can't fake a taste for paste."

The display, Gore's hidden treasures, included leathery skin flaps, oiled vaginas in apothecary jars, the infantile penis of one of the most famous film actors of all time. There was the thing that a notorious bandleader had once forced his wife, a beautiful singer, to wear whenever she performed: a combination chastity belt, pessary, and double anal/vaginal dildo. (Petergello assured him there was a primitive antecedent.) The nipples of a legendary sex symbol, preserved and mounted, stared like dead eyes from the breasts of her nude photo. There was, shadowboxed with his bronzed baby shoes, the awesome schlong of a show business figure whose name had once been a household word. How on earth had he obtained these pieces of the famous and the adored?

By networking. He had obtained them from grave robbers and physicians, mortuary assistants and medical examiners, lawyers and honest johns. There was in fact a bustling, teeming, secret cottage industry that was sustained by a clandestine network of such collectors. Each had his or her own perverted peculiarity. The trick was to find what X wanted—via fax or phone, tape or typewriter, and make a deal to get it—because X had what *you* desired.

Gore Edmund's network was Petergello's sub rosa path to the Pieces. It was why he was so proficient a hunter. The network was perfect for turning up those special, weird "eclectics," that never seemed to surface in the ordinary collectibles marketplaces.

In less than a quarter hour Petergello had found his

way across the small town to the address of the antiquities dealer. He carried his display case to the door and rang the bell. A pleasantly plump gentleman of advanced age answered.

"Yes?"

"I'm Petergello. The one who called."

"Of course. Please come in."

The dusty shop was crammed floor to ceiling, wall to wall, with curiosa, ephemera, and small collectibles of every description. Galle and miniature guillotines, Daum Nancy, French cameo art glass, and Civil War daguerrotypes. It was a jumble of junk, junque, and—here and there—genuine rarities. Just the kind of shop where the Pieces sometimes ended up.

"You're the gentleman into Ancient Greek and Roman erotica, correct?"

"No, not just that," Petergello said, shaking his handsome head. "Everything. Byzantine. Islamic. Mayan. You name it. Erotica and eclectics."

"I've got some beautiful pieces," the dealer said, unaware of his inadvertent tease.

"I see that," Petergello said, trying to simulate normalcy, but feeling the focused rage hot in his throat, the closest he came to salivating.

"Here's a beauty," the man told him, reverentially, placing a small item on a velvet pad.

"Umm."

"Schist," he told Petergello, as if he thought he'd never seen the metamorphic crystalline rock before. It was a common phallic piece.

"Charming. Fourth century B.C.?"

"Very good," the dealer said, nodding. "Here's a nice pair. See how they fit?" He placed two tiny figures together. "Sobek has an interesting patina—eh?" He placed the figure on the female with open legs and Sobek the crocodile god performed the act for which he'd been created.

"Oh, yes. I like that. Quite amusing. I'm not turned off by the green patina. You know"—he looked up with his beautiful eyes—"I'm really hot for the offbeat stuff. Abstracts. Eclectic pieces . . ."

"As I told you on the phone, Mr. Petergello, I do have an exceptional piece. But it's not presently for sale."

"I understand, but I'd still enjoy seeing it. Perhaps down the line, if you should ever decide to run an auction on it . . . ?"

"Certainly." The plump dealer turned and took something from a locked case behind him, handling it with exaggerated care as he placed it on the velvet pad. "Please don't handle it."

"No. I wouldn't think of it. *Ah!* Yes. Oh, say—that is special."

"One of a kind, I'm sure," the dealer whispered. "Beyond price."

"Beyond price," Petergello repeated, as light danced from iridescent biconical mosaics. At first it appeared to be a prism of cornerless cubes, but it was much more.

Imagine a talisman or statuette that on closer inspection revealed the details of a tiny piece of incredible automata: a miniature model of a futuristic cityscape, sculpted to scale. Mysterious, like a smoked rock crystal by Gustave Miklos, and lit on the inside by some microscopic fire.

Serpentine highlettes snaked and pirouetted on filigree balls of brecciated black chlorite. Conjoined surfaces glowed with inexplicable core energy, as if it were alive. As the fiery internal light sparkled, Petergello saw yellow-gray chalcedony and the suggestion of minuscule oil slicks. "I've seen a few like this before," he said. "Believe it or not."

"I'm guessing Iranian—but who can say?"

"Not for sale under any conditions?"

"Sorry." The dealer started to reach for it.

"Before you put it away"—Petergello reached for something in his case—"compare it with this." He squirted something in the face of the antiquarian dealer, who coughed and fell back against a showcase.

Several pieces of art glass toppled to the floor and broke, and a Greco-Persian piece—obviously a fake—shattered into fragments.

"Certainly no loss here," Petergello said quietly, stepping behind the counter, lifting the other man easily, the focus of rage surging through him like hot blood as he tenderly snapped the neck, holding him and swallowing as he nurtured on the life taking, feasting sumptuously, and not bothering with appearances.

Petergello fed on killing. It was his pig-out. A massive coronary was his lobster, a nice pulmonary embolism his pizza. He was a *gourmand* of mayhem. It filled him like a seven-course meal.

He placed the Piece in his case, then took Sobek and the female slave for himself. He was very full. Oz would be ecstatic. They would be out of town, in all probability, before the antiquarian dealer would be missed. With the new Piece, they were that much closer to the Otherness.

Petergello smiled his handsome smile, and decided he'd look around for something sharp so he could take a souvenir for Gore, before he cleaned up the mess he'd made.

REX MILLER

The show rolled on . . .

ALONG THE MIDWAY (III)

Yell County, Arkansas

She was almost used to his touch now.

Ginger remembered how she'd gagged the first time they practiced the catching grips. Not that the freak's skin was slimy or anything. In fact, it was warm and soft and smooth and dry, just like anybody else's. Maybe even better. But the way the ends of his arms coiled and locked about her wrists filled her with a trapped, claustrophobic feeling that nearly sent her on a screaming dead run from the Fugazi corner of the backyard.

But almost being used to something didn't mean she looked forward to it. No way. Her gorge didn't rise at his touch anymore but still she hated to get out of bed in the morning knowing she'd have to practice with Octoman.

The other performers were giving her a hard time as well. Ginger had crossed one of the lines of the circus world's caste system. There were performers, there were musicians, there were bosses, there were workers, and there were sideshow freaks. Each had its own caste. No one—except for musicians—mixed between those castes. And even the musicians—the sober ones, at least—steered clear of the freaks.

Not fair. This wasn't her idea. She hadn't wanted to bring a freak into her aerial act. It was all her uncle Joe's doing. But nobody seemed to appreciate that.

65

And because of Uncle Joe she was here on this platform now, forty feet above the soggy ground, waiting to
swing out, do a release, and let the freak catch her. God
Almighty, how had she got herself into this?

"Please, Ginger," said Papa Fugazi from below. "We
haven't got all day."

Okay, okay!

She wanted to scream at them to leave her alone. Just
let her be. What did they know about how she felt about
this? She wasn't just practicing grips now. This wasn't a
practice trapeze a few feet above the safety net. This was
full height. Sure, the net was still there, but this time she
was going to have to hold on to those freaky arms for
real—really *hold* on to them. And there were few em-
braces more intimate than those between people suspended forty feet in the air.

She looked across the void in the freak's direction.
Without making eye contact, she nodded.

"Go."

She watched him swing out, build up his arcs, then flip
so he was hanging from the bar by his knees. He was
good—limber, graceful, excellent timing and balance. If
only he had real hands.

Okay, Ginger, she told herself. Now or never.

When his backswing reached its high point, she
dropped off the platform and swung toward him. Papa
Fugazi had set the trapeze ropes long so that she and the
freak practically bumped when they swung together over
the middle of the safety net. Ginger matched her arc to
his, then reversed herself into the knee-hang position.
Nothing fancy here—no flying, no free-fall, no flips or
spins or somersaults like she'd been doing with Carlo
before the accident. A simple catch and transfer, nothing
more. She'd grab his arms, he'd grab hers, then she'd
unhook her knees from her bar, and they'd swing in
tandem from the freak's trapeze.

Kid's stuff.

"Okay," Papa Fugazi said from below. "On the next
swing."

Ginger swallowed, arched her back, and headed into
her final swing. The freak was heading toward her, his arc
perfectly timed. She straightened her knees to release

them from the bar, reached out her arms as he extended his—

—she saw those tapered, fleshy, snakelike things stretching toward her, the tips coiling and uncoiling in anticipation of grasping her—

No!

At the last second her hands pulled back, seemingly of their own accord, and she was falling.

Ginger knew what to do. She'd fallen countless times before. She turned, tucked, and landed on her back in the springy mesh safety net. When she rolled out of the net, Papa Fugazi was there to meet her.

"Ay, what happens?"

"I can't do it," Ginger told him. "I just can't."

She heard a weight hit the net behind her, then saw the freak rolling out and landing on his feet. She turned to him.

"Sorry."

"Yeah. You're sorry." His eyes were hurt, his voice was bitter as he turned and walked away. "What a jerk I was to think this might work."

Ginger suddenly hated herself. She took two steps after him.

"Look, I said I'm sorry."

He whirled on her and now he was all anger.

"That doesn't cut it. *You're* sorry? You've got two normal arms and *you're* sorry?" He held up his tentacles. "How'd you like to grow up with these?"

And suddenly Ginger saw it all. Toys, doorknobs, utensils, appliances, even pencils—nothing recognized his particular deformity. And school—what kind of hell had recess in the schoolyard been for a kid with tentacles instead of hands?

She realized he had a lot more guts than she did, and that she was letting this get the best of her. Ginger never had backed down from anything before and she wasn't going to start now.

She forced her own hand to reach out and grab his arm as he turned away again.

"We'll try again."

"Don't do me any favors. I don't need this kind of humiliation."

Now it was her turn to get mad. "Hey, give me a break, okay? I haven't known you that long and you take some getting used to, in case you haven't noticed. I mean, how long did it take for your folks to get used to you?"

He looked at her and in that instant she saw the answer in the bleakness of his stare.

Oh, God. They never did, did they.

"So maybe it'll take me a little longer," she said quickly. "One more try. If I screw up again, we call it quits for good."

He hesitated. "Okay. One more try."

Ginger headed back toward her pole and steeled her gut as she climbed. This wasn't going to be easy but dammit she was going to do it.

Leesville, Louisiana

Ronee Sue stands at the gray tent flap, half-in, half-out, trembling. Malaleik, The Dream Catcher, is a blinding light lurking behind the low white screen. A townie, female, always a female, sits in the chair. She lets The Dream Catcher hold her hand. Cold sweat slides down from Ronee Sue's armpits and from under her breasts. Her heart hollers in her chest and her legs feel planted in the earth. She wets her lips, ready to warn the girl, but hesitates. Her job is clearing lots, setting up tents, selling tickets, cleaning stalls, whatever's useful. If Nolan, or Mr. Peabody or, God forbid, Ozymandias Prather catches her interfering with business . . . She calls out anyway— "Don't give away your dreams!" but her words are ignored. Each night the girls are different but the same. Young, vulnerable, full of hopes for the future, hopes that will erode just from living. They shell out to have their narrow lives expanded with false promises.

The Dream Catcher listens patiently, a freak therapist feeding the girl what she longs to hear. Suddenly Malaleik rises. The Dream Catcher has grown large. In the belly. The girl too stands up, but slowly. Her husband catches her hand. The two turn. They walk toward Ronee Sue. The young thing smiles, but her eyes are icicles. The warmth that should be there has been sucked out. She looks like hard winter. . . .

Ronee Sue burst through her trailer door. She staggered down the metal steps into a blazing midday sun, grateful for the searing light. It burned away the nightmare images and snapped her back to the reality of the campgrounds.

Shit, another scorcher, Ronee Sue thought. Way too hot for May. The oppressive heat began prickling her skin. She raked her fingers through her short dark hair and looked around. The last two times Ronee Sue Baines crossed the country—by thumb—she'd been unlucky enough to get stuck right here, in this swamp some demented visionary had named after General Lee. She favored warm weather, but 100-plus degrees was pushing it. Yesterday, while clearing the lot for the freak tent, she'd accidentally stepped on a dead coral snake, except it wasn't dead, just too heat-exhausted to slither away. At least the show would be out of this pit day after tomorrow.

"Hot one, Mr. Peabody."

The easygoing man nodded in passing. He looked tired and older but she wrote it off to the humidity.

"Makes for business," he said. "Folks swelter all day, come nightfall they crave excitement. That's us."

Ronee Sue took a deep breath. The air was heavy and thick; it was like trying to inhale hot water. A childhood terror of suffocation seized her. She thought about returning to the cooler comfort of the trailer, but that was where the nightmare lurked. Instead she dragged herself across the parched dirt to the cook tent. By the time she got there her pale blue *Lifestyles of the Broke and Obscure* T-shirt was splotched with sweat.

Malaleik, The Dream Catcher, sat at the only table with a vacant seat and Ronee Sue hesitated. If that empty chair was next to a performer, or even one of the other creepy freaks, she wouldn't have thought twice. But Malaleik rattled her. White hair and bleached skin, born without finger- or toenails, in Ronee Sue's opinion there was something, well, lacking. And those unearthly eyes. Colorless. When they locked on, it was like being stared at by a husky, only worse—they made Ronee Sue feel like she was buried in snow, trapped under packed ice, freezing to death. Suddenly the heat felt just fine.

She grabbed a cup of coffee and a slice of soggy toast from the steam table then squeezed onto the edge of the picnic table bench directly across from Malaleik, who had been watching her. Ronee Sue smiled quickly, careful to turn away.

"Another dream?" The freak's voice was permafrost.

"How'd you know?"

"I'm The Dream Catcher. It's my job." Malaleik sipped iced lemonade. In the month since Ronee Sue joined the show in Florida, she had yet to see Malaleik eat food. She did not even know if The Dream Catcher was a man or a woman. Most people said "he," but Ronee Sue wasn't so sure. Especially lately, since she'd noticed the swells beneath that blousy shirt and fuller hips stretching the white pleated pants. Of course, Malaleik had gained weight. A lot. Most of it in the belly. Once skeletal, The Dream Catcher must have loaded on thirty pounds in half as many days. Ever since . . . well, ever since Ronee Sue's nightmares began.

"Give me your dream and the terror will evaporate. Money-back guarantee."

Ronee Sue shook her head. "Can't remember." She swallowed coffee and munched toast. No way would she reveal the repetitive nightmare, especially because it was Malaleik who made the dream scary.

"You'll come to trust me." Glacial fingers touched Ronee Sue's bare forearm. Frozen metal sticking to human flesh. The chill penetrated. Skin. Muscle. It struck bone. Ronee Sue jerked her arm free. Their eyes met. She felt like she was falling. Empty whiteness caused her head to hurt. She wanted to sleep.

"Hey, first-of-May!" She didn't have to look up to know who was putting her down by calling her a new-comer. Still, she grabbed the opportunity. "Help Okie hose the bulls. And clean the turds."

Nolan always assigned her the worst jobs. She liked the elephants, and cooling them down was okay. But burying their mounds of stinking shit was bad news, especially in this heat. She was hired as an all-around helper, a job men usually do. Being new to circus life didn't help.

"Sure," she said, standing. Her appetite had faded and

this seemed like a good chance to escape. From both of them.

She'd nearly made it out of the mess when Nolan yelled, "Tonight you're on sideshow, front door."

"Why me again?" she grumbled.

"Peabody's orders. Seems Malaleik, here, likes your company."

Malaleik, The Dream Catcher, stood. Ronee Sue watched that bloated stomach sway toward her and stop. A cold voice whispered in her ear, "Would you like to join me in my trailer?"

The chortles and macho wit from nearby tables chased Ronee Sue out the door.

By five-thirty Ronee Sue was beat. She had half an hour to duck in the trailer she shared with Clara the Clown and Mitzi, a contortionist who'd joined up last week, both of whom resented bunking with a nonperformer. She took a quick bucket bath and changed her clothes. Zipping up her jeans, Ronee Sue wondered what sorry sense of adventure had compelled her to sign on with this mud show. There were easier ways to travel.

But she had signed on and she was a sticker. The show would take her out west and eventually up north where she'd spend part of the summer with her dad in Chicago before heading back to Orlando for the winter to see her mom.

Her mom. She could still hear the warnings. Everything from "Don't go gettin' yourself knocked up," to "Flittin' around the country all the time. You ain't livin' in the real world." Hell, if reality meant ending up like her mom—seven babies in as many years, and alone to boot—Ronee Sue would pass. Twenty-five still left plenty of years to settle down and have kids. If she was living in a dreamworld, she wasn't about to part with it yet.

Her cot looked comfy. A nap would do the trick. But she had to be at the sideshow. Now. And then there was the nightmare. Lying in wait. Hungry. Burning away at her soul like dry ice chewing through skin. Every damn time she shut her eyes.

She took a breath of close air and headed out.

* * *

All Ronee Sue had to do was stand inside the flap at the entrance and collect tickets. It wasn't hard work. But everybody in their right mind hated this job. Nobody could stomach being close to the freaks for long.

Inside the tent the air was wicked with stink and moisture. She tied the canvas flap back; oily grit. There was something eerie about this night. As the sun sank, the heat rose. She opened another button on her plaid shirt.

It was early and there were few townies for the barker to catch. But two kids peeked in. Both still teenagers, blond and painfully wide-eyed. The girl was very pregnant—her gold wedding band sinking into a puffy finger. The reedy husband grinned—he had a tooth missing, bottom front—and nodded, then handed over the tickets.

They looked around the dimly lit tent, confused, sweating, a bit scared. "Just wander through," Ronee Sue mother-henned them.

Carmella sat closest to the flap. Her third eye put a lot of people off. When the psychic winked, the future momma's face paled. Ronee Sue watched a look pass between the couple. They changed direction pronto and headed for Gore, whose mounds of flab seemed ready to burst the plate glass wall he sat behind. They looked revolted. And it got worse.

Mr. Tane. Mother Goose. Haman. Lance. The whole weird tour. And Ronee Sue knew just how those two kids felt. Here it was, weeks later, and she still wanted to puke or run screaming from these freaks. It wasn't so much the physical deformities that bothered her. They gave off a kind of diseased energy that sucked in everybody who came near.

Finally young Mr. and Mrs. Leesville got to Malaleik. "Listen, hon." The girl—it was always the females who noticed—read the sign tacked to the low white screen: Give Me Your Dreams.

Hubby, sweat dripping off his nose, wanted out but the Mrs. plunked herself onto the chair. Malaleik, hidden by the screen from the collarbone down, cool and rigid as an iceberg, smiled that Arctic smile and took the girl's hand. And Ronee Sue shivered.

Suddenly she remembered. The nightmare. Every night. A mirror of freak show reality. The other players changed, but not she nor Malaleik. The terrifying dream, she now knew, was trying to tell her something. To warn her.

The way The Dream Catcher listened to the dream reminded her of a swamp sucker feeding on blood. And when it was over, that girl looked empty. Stone cold. Just like all the others before her.

As Ronee Sue watched the couple leave the tent, she realized something was different. She turned. The Dream Catcher stood. Their eyes locked for a moment then Ronee Sue looked down and gasped. Malaleik was skinny again. Bone thin. No belly. A skeleton, grinning, frozen in time.

It tore at her all through the shift. How could somebody shrink like that in just a few hours. She covered the possibilities but only one made any sense. The Dream Catcher was pregnant. And had a miscarriage. Or an abortion. There was no other answer.

As business picked up, the intense heat weighed on Ronee Sue's head. She couldn't breathe and things looked hazy around the edges. Her thoughts darkened. By ten o'clock, when Joey took over for her, Ronee Sue had herself convinced that Malaleik had done something nasty.

It was too hot to eat and a cool drink didn't help. The air felt like solid fire when she took it in. She moved fast through the backyard behind the big top. Nobody saw her slip into The Dream Catcher's trailer.

She turned on the light and looked around. The place was stark, colorless, odorless. A bunk was made up with white sheets. There were empty white cupboards. The small space looked unlived in.

The real oddity was the full-size freezer, running off propane. Next to it, stacked neat as could be, were a dozen black boxes. Ronee Sue picked one up—it was stone, maybe eight inches square—and lifted the lid. Empty.

Ronee Sue didn't know what devil had caused her to sneak in here. There was no dead baby on the bed, no fetus floating in a pail of blood. Maybe the heat was frying

her brain. She'd better hightail it before she got caught.
Just a peek in that freezer, then I'm on my way, she
thought.

"Oh, God." She sighed. Cold white puffs wafted out.
She leaned into the relief. As the cloud evaporated she
saw another onyx box. She reached in and lifted it out.
Icy cold zipped through the nerves of her fingertips and
up her hand.

The lid was stuck and she tapped it open. Nothing but
frozen water. A big gray ice cube.

She was closing the box when she thought she saw
movement. Ice is solid, she reminded herself. But there it
was. Squiggling. A flat dark form? A thin white shadow?
A tadpole maybe, half a foot long. She squinted and
looked closer. Nothing. I'm losing it, she thought, but
then had a brainstorm.

Ronee Sue went to the Coleman and moved the cof-
feepot so she could put the box on the grill. In seconds a
blue-yellow flame rushed up to meet the bottom. She kept
the lid off the box to watch the contents melt.

The form seemed to twitch. As ice liquified, whatever
was in there jerked like an animal caught in a trap trying
to free itself.

Black and white blurred. A frosty rainbow buckled
and swirled in the center and rippled away. Shards of light
stabbed her eyes and penetrated her brain. Ronee Sue
screamed. Everything went black. Then gold beetles with
silvered backs, millions of them, scurried toward her,
biting through her eyelids. She panicked and tripped. As
she fell, she smacked the side of her head on the floor,
hard enough to burst an eardrum. Pain streaked through
her head and the insects faded into sparkling, glittering,
crystalline stars. They pulsed against a colorless background until the sky fragmented, so fast it made her
hyperventilate. By the time she got her breath right, she
wished she hadn't. The reek of sickeningly sweet cedar
and honey; a stink like tar and putrid skunk filled the
room. Overpowering stenches of life and death washed
her cells. Air—light—sound—smell—form throbbed and
raged. Objects flew every which way. And people long
dead, plus ones she prayed had never lived, paraded past.

Monstrous creatures chewed her flesh, slurped her blood.
Punishing voices. And beneath it all a rumble, like the
fury of an earthquake, or too many bad dreams.

The room went subzero and Ronee Sue shook until
her muscles locked in understanding: These were all the
dreams that Malaleik had stolen. No human being was
meant to experience this.

Blind, half-deaf, she struggled to her feet. Primordial
energy, oozing with violence, erupted. Frigid tentacles
seized her. Frostbite strangled her cries. She felt snow-
bound, buried under impacting ice.

And then she heard The Dream Catcher. An ava-
lanche. She plummeted through glacial space, grateful to
be losing feeling, getting sleepy, melding with a great
inhuman nothingness.

"Give me your dream!" Malaleik demanded.

And Ronee Sue did.

NANCY KILPATRICK

The show rolled on . . .

ALONG THE MIDWAY (IV)

Nacogdoches County, Texas

Oz chipped a small piece off the corner of the latest fruit of Malaleik's special talent and dropped it into a small copper cup. He placed the onyx box in his freezer with the others like it, then carried the cup to the tiny room at the rear of his trailer. There were two pieces of furniture in the room: a small table and a single chair, crowded in with an antiquated X-ray machine and a sagging bookshelf. Oz seated himself before a square, black wooden platform—two inches high, two feet on a side—that occupied most of the tabletop. His collection of Pieces rested in the platform's copper-lined depression.

He was satisfied with the progress of the tour so far. He had seven Pieces now—two of which actually fitted together—and that put him approximately a third of the way home. He hoped. For he was not sure exactly how many Pieces had made up the Device when it belonged to his father. He had old photos and even X-rays taken by his father when the thing had been intact, but the very nature of the Device and its link to the Otherness made photographs unreliable. Even in real life, face-to-face, you could not be completely sure what you saw when you looked at the Device. Oz remembered many times as a boy when he'd sit and stare at the thing for hours. When he'd cocked his head this way and that it had seemed to change shape; and as it turned on its stand, parts of it seemed to fade in and out of view—perhaps out of existence. Sometimes it had glowed and flashed unearthly colors.

When his father discovered the truth about the Device—what it could do, what it had already done—he'd tried to destroy it but learned he couldn't. The Device was indestructible. It couldn't be smashed, it couldn't be melted. But it could be disassembled. And so Jacob Prather took it apart and made one final tour of the country, scattering its components as he went.

And then he killed himself.

But he left a journal to his son, explaining everything, including how he had disposed of the Pieces. Oz had read it countless times and had gradually come to the realization that his father viewed the Device from a perspective wholly different from his own. To Jacob Prather the Device was the problem.

To Ozymandias it was the answer.

He noticed that the chip from one of Malaleik's boxes had melted. He dribbled it over the Pieces. It fumed a little but nothing more.

Nothing. Maybe this search was nothing more than a wild hope, a mad fantasy, an exercise in futility.

No. It's too early yet, Oz told himself. I need more Pieces. Many more.

Bois D'Arc, Texas

Señorita Gato paced throughout her trailer while the roustabouts began setting up the show. The fur on her arms rose in hackles of rage. She hated being confined in her trailer, but Ozymandias had said she must stay put. Too many people watched the setup wanting to see the freaks for free.

"Let them stare," she muttered. "I want to be outside, to run free in the Texas air. To smell the bluebonnets and Indian paintbrushes growing wild in the spring sunshine. To be home again—even if I am alone."

She pulled back the curtains to watch the work. To the east, just across the highway, she could see the permanent structure of the Bois D'Arc Rodeo Arena. The Great and Powerful Oz had managed to book the show for the weekend in the immediate vicinity of the arena, allowing him to draw from the rodeo crowd as well as generating his own. To the west, she could see the high-rise office buildings that were downtown Dallas. She tried in vain to make out the figure of the red neon Pegasus atop the Magnolia Building. Her mother had spoken often of it. Of how on a clear night in the old days, before Big Business really found its way to Dallas, you could see that majestic horse flying through the night from as far as twenty-five miles away. And if you wished hard enough, the bold steed might carry you and your dreams on to Olympus or

Valhalla or wherever your shining knight might be waiting.

Now her mother and the dreams were gone, driven away in a car wreck that deprived her of both family and hope. The Magnolia Building was now dwarfed and surrounded by gleaming towers of chrome, steel, and glass. Still the red horse flew every night. But few people ever saw it anymore and fewer still wished their dreams upon its wings.

Bored with the routine of the circus setup and her confinement in the trailer, she found one of her tattered historical romance novels, curled up on the floor in the sunshine, and began to read. She placed herself in the role of a Saxon maid falling for the charms of the conquering Norman warrior. She felt his strong arms around her waist. She felt his hot breath blowing down her neck, raising goose bumps all over her body. She heard him whispering her name. "Juanita," he would say. "Be mine and I will deny all my birthright and the honors that I have gained. I will be content just to be a peasant with you." He placed her atop his brave stallion, a red horse with huge white wings. He joined her there and placed his arms around her as he took the reins. She felt the wind rush through her whiskers and fur as they rode among the clouds without a worry. They had their love and their dreams.

She sighed. All she really wanted was someone who would willingly give up that which he loved the most, just for her. Just for love.

She'd never really experienced love. Her mother had kept her isolated from the beginning. Good folk didn't have demon children. Their children didn't have whiskers and fur and pointed ears. She had only begun to feel part of the world during the last two years as she traveled with the show. Her mother's death had taken away her support, and Oz had offered her a position. But all of that was reality and she had seen too much of that. She turned back to her novel.

She purred softly to herself, content to be back in her home state. Lost in the romance and chivalry of a world long gone, she never even noticed that she was crying.

* * *

John Bob loved the smell of the rodeo. Loved it to death. The smell of the livestock, the smell of the earth as it was thrown from hooves, the smell of the leather tack combined with animal and human sweat. He'd inhale these odors and let their flavors linger in his lungs. And the Bois D'Arc Rodeo was one of his greatest joys. Since it ran in the spring, he got its flavor combined with that of the abundant wildflowers and the rebirth of nature bursting forth all around him. Texas in the spring was heaven.

The cattle loved the rodeo, too. They loved the work, the bounding, the racing, trying to throw the rider from his horse or from their back. They loved John Bob, too. They told him so.

John Bob talked to the cattle every day. Being a top wrangler with the rodeo, he was expected to ensure that the bucking bulls were in the proper chutes ready for their riders when the announcer made the call. He'd found out years ago that he could talk to the bulls, that they would do whatever he asked of them, and that they, in turn, could talk to him and ask things of him.

This made the daily work at the rodeo a breeze. John Bob had only to explain what he wanted to any small group of cows and it happened perfectly. The other wranglers didn't understand exactly what was going on. They knew that John Bob had a way with cows and it was better to leave him be than to try and cross him. The rodeo riders knew it, too. Only the newer ones ever treated John Bob with anything less than respect. Talk crossly to him or curse at anyone when he was listening and that sweet Brahman bull that anyone could ride might just try to do a double somersault while you was trying to hold on for eight seconds.

But John Bob hated the rodeo, too. "It ain't fair!" he'd say to whoever was near. "Look it them yahoos struttin' around like they had peacock feathers growin' out their butts. Are they any better than I ever was? Hell, no! They're gettin' the money and the girls, though. And, me! I ain't gettin' dick! All I got's a job, a bum leg, and a big toe that says it's gonna rain come next Thursday."

Harry Longabaugh, the big Brahma bull in stall three, said, "Christ, here he goes again! Look, JB, you was good. You just weren't great. So, your leg got tore up. It happens. You're alive. Enjoy it. Besides, how many of those easy riders out there got a silver buckle, all-around cowboy belt like you do? They ain't shit and you know it. Quit searching for sympathy and get me some food."

John Bob hung his head a little. Harry was right. His fingers brushed over the buckle, feeling the bright red stone, vaguely in the shape of Texas. He'd won it right in this very arena, not eight years ago on a night when everything had gone just perfectly. He was twenty-one and full of coyote piss. He'd ridden the horses like he was tied to the saddle with barbed wire. He tackled bulls and calves with a lasso that couldn't miss. That night he was, by God, King of the Goddamned Cowboys.

The belt was a symbol of all that—what he had been and what he could have been. He polished it every week, buffing the silvery surface until his arm ached. It was all of his dreams made real. It shone with the fire of the sun.

But the bulls were right. He'd been good, but good just didn't cut it anymore. Anyone could be good. Hell, there were girls over at Bois D'Arc Junior High that was good at ropin' and ridin'. It took something else beyond good. He might have had it, certainly he had pieces of it. But the horse that took his leg and made spaghetti out of it killed all those hopes.

One of the calves called to him. "JB, you gonna think shit all night till we die or you gonna feed us?" Others added their voices to the question. They were right. When you're thirty, it don't do to dream 'bout bein' twenty.

The rodeo was set to start in about four hours. He needed to get the bulls fed and settled before it came their time. They were restless. Cyclone Red and Useless Lou didn't like the circus and freak show setting up across the road. They claimed the smell of the people wasn't right. The other bulls sided in with them. John Bob tried to reassure them that the freaks would stay on their side of the road. Deep down he wondered what it was they were really afraid of.

Señorita Gato rose from her nap and stretched her body to its full length. As she extended her hands, tiny claws appeared at her fingertips then slowly retracted.

She picked up her novel and placed it on the table. It was nearly time for the first show. She hoped she wouldn't be put into the cage tonight. Oxymandias sometimes had one of the more normal freaks appear next to the barker in a small cage to entice the customers into the show. Recently he'd taken to using her there, making her wear a tiny bikini to emphasize the suppleness of her body and show off her fur.

She draped her cloak over her shoulders, raised the hood to cover her ears, and crossed the backyard to the sideshow tent. Hundreds of customers were wandering around the midway trying their hands at impossible games of "skill," eating hot dogs and cotton candy, spending money, and gawking at the sights. The gate will be big tonight if this keeps up, she thought.

As she entered the freak area, she heard Petergello talking.

"There's a Piece nearby and it may be attracted to the Device. So be on the lookout for it."

Two of the Beagle Boys were hanging around inside. She could see Gore's trailer house with the glass sides and waved limply to him. She liked him. She didn't like the Beagle Boys and had clawed one or more of them in the past for getting fresh with her.

Petergello turned to her. "Señorita, we have a long three-day stay here to capitalize on all the weekend crowds frequenting the rodeo. We want to make the most of our opportunities for money and . . . other things. Oz wants you in the cage again tonight. He wants you to drag all the male population in the county here. He wants you to display your charms, smile your smile, and make them *all* come to us."

John Bob watched the rodeo crowds closely. Something was in the air. Most of the bulls were restless and wanted to do some damage, if not to a rider, then at least to a horse or the arena itself. It took a great deal of cajoling to keep them docile. They were upset by a feeling that things were not . . . right. Maybe the problem wasn't at the arena. Maybe it *was* the circus across the street, as the cows kept saying that it was. John Bob had finally promised Cyclone Red, the big Brahma, that he'd check out the freak show as soon as possible after the rodeo closed and report back to the bulls. He assured them that there'd be no more problems.

As he crossed the parking lot separating the shows, John Bob wondered out loud why he was going. "Buncha dang fool stupid cows. Get a bee up their butt when someone moves in next to them. There's something funny going on. Ain't nothin' but a damned circus. Next thing ya know, the mailman'll have a cleaver and a meat grinder and be talkin' about openin' a McDonald's around the corner. It ain't nothin' but the weather. The boys are just feelin' a big spring storm comin' on. I oughta just turn right on around and go back. Anyone says anything, I'll just say I'm thinkin' of bringin' out my old Bar-B-Q pit and did any of them want to come help me with the first party? That's what I oughta do."

His feet wouldn't turn around. They just kept right on going, straight as a Baptist preacher's spinster daughter. Something was pullin' him to the circus and it wasn't Dumbo.

Strolling through the midway, John Bob thought it looked like most any small traveling circus he'd ever been to. There was the smell of various animals, including the elephants, the sounds of the concession barkers hawking their wares, and the constant din of the crowds of laughing children and adults.

He was seriously considering a corny dog and Dr Pepper when he heard the freak show barker begin his spiel.

"Look here, ladies and gents. Watch her as she dances. This is Señorita Gato! No fakes here. Take a look! She's got the ears, nose, and whiskers of a beautiful pedigreed cat. But, she was born a woman in this very state, down in the Rio Grande Valley. Her skin is covered with a fine fur. Her hands and feet have retractable claws."

Señorita Gato splayed open a hand, showing the claws, and made a scratching motion at an imaginary foe. Someone called out from the crowd, "Here, kitty, kitty." She hissed at him. She hated to be called Kitty. She was Señorita Gato and proud of it!

"No fakes here, ladies and gents. Take a close look.

Watch her ears move with every sound. See those whiskers twitch. And, ladies and gents, she is just *one* of the many attractions at the show. There's more on the inside. Now listen close here! The show is only two bucks a head. That's it! Two bucks. See the sights that have astounded men for ages. See the freaks and thank God that you're normal. Step right on up and pay the man. Show starts in ten minutes. Come on in and see them. . . ."

John Bob couldn't take his eyes off the cage. He was having trouble breathing and his heart was beating so rapidly he checked his pulse to make sure it was really his heart. The crotch of his jeans was suddenly hot and tight. The cat-woman was beautiful in a way that he couldn't describe.

Most women didn't do much for him. They'd smile and flirt and he'd smile and fumble for a word, but something told him that the rodeo groupies were desperate women looking for something he didn't want to provide. This woman showed confidence and assurance, yet had a vulnerability that he found fascinating. He wanted to talk to her. Hell, he just plain *wanted* her. He wondered how he would make her know that. He wondered if she minded cattle.

Señorita Gato absently watched the crowd as Matt made the bark. They were the usual assortment of geeks and goops wandering around, looking for something, anything, that might make them forget their own problems. She danced and writhed to the musical rhythms that accompanied the bark. She could smell the desire of several of the crowd members. They wanted her badly. Tough. Then, she saw . . . him. Something in his appearance caught her eye and she couldn't let go. He was tall and so very different from the rest. He was wearing denim pants and a chambray shirt—clothes that he had obviously worked in. He smelled of cows. But that wasn't it. There was more to him than that. She wanted to know who he was, where he was from, what he was like. She stopped dancing and stared at him. He stared right back at her.

She smiled. Slowly a picture formed in her mind of the

two of them in bed. She liked the picture. She'd never had a man before. Her mother had seen to that.

Suddenly, it hit her. A feeling unlike any she had ever had. Her body *ached* for him. She wanted that man inside her. She wanted him *now!* She began to howl inside the cage, her claws began extending on their own volition. She clawed at the air. Her body burned from the inside.

Matt quit barking the show. Instead, he began to stalk the outside of the cage. He began calling, "Here, kitty, kitty. Come here, little Gato. Daddy's got something for you." She wanted a man, but Matt wasn't the one. She swiped at him with an open claw.

Another man pulled Matt away from the cage, cold-cocked him, and tried to get in. "You shore looking fine, Miss Gato. You and me, we gonna have some fun now." He began to rock the cage back and forth.

Juanita looked out at the crowd. Every male in the immediate vicinity seemed to be stalking her. They were all determined that they were going to be the one to get her.

John Bob was close to the stage when the pheromones hit him. He had thought the girl attractive, but now she was totally irresistible. He wanted to take her with him, to rip the thin fabric off her body, to take her, to make her his. She *had* to be his.

He began to fight the crowd to get to the stage and the cage. Other men had the same idea. He was hit, he was scratched, he was kicked in his bad leg as he approached. Someone pulled a knife and began to brandish it at anyone who came near. Another knife appeared and the two men squared off. Someone else pulled a gun and shot both the knife wielders.

The crowd got even uglier. The women took off, abandoning mates and boyfriends for safer confines. John Bob saw no way of getting to the girl without help. He reached out mentally and found Cyclone Red alert. The bull had sensed trouble coming and was ready.

"Can you boys get out of the pens?" John Bob asked. The ache in his crotch was becoming unbearable. He needed a release and soon.

"Hell, yes! The only reason we stay put is 'cause some

big hunter's liable to shoot us for being deer. I'll bring Harry and the boys. Meanwhile, you go get the girl."

Two men were attacking the cage. Señorita Gato seemed to be enticing them into it. She was strutting back and forth inside the cage, howling for a man. They were fighting each other to be the one who would get in. Other men were trying to storm the stage. Circus workers could be seen trying to fight through the crowds. They ranged from regular roustabouts to characters who might have been freaks. People were fighting all around the stage.

John Bob made it to the stage about the time that Cyclone Red and twelve other bulls charged onto the grounds. John Bob looked at them and gave them instructions.

"Get yore butts over here. We got us a girl to save. Use your horns to poke guys out of the way. Try not to hurt anyone too much. Clear me some space."

The bulls began making their way toward the stage, muscling men out of the way. The girl inside the cage was howling and dancing, clawing at the men trying to get in. John Bob threw one off the stage. The other man came swinging at him, all out of control. John Bob dodged the first punch and threw one of his own, pivoting on his right foot, sliding his full weight behind it. The man's head rocked back and he slowly fell off the stage.

John Bob found himself alone with the girl. Only the bars of the cage stood between them. He felt the blood pounding in his ears. He kicked the door open and entered the cage. He wanted her here, now, on the floor of the cage. But there were too many people around. Somebody might take her away. He had to get her somewhere away from all this.

The girl came at him, claws extended, arms flailing. Her hormone aura was almost overpowering. She threw herself at him, wrapping arms and legs about his body, scratching at him. Controlling himself, John Bob grabbed her arms and pinned them to the sides of her body. He turned her around so she was looking the same direction he was. Cyclone Red and the bulls had conquered the stage area and formed a small circle for him to enter. All around the bulls he could see the sea of men boiling with fights and blind-crazy attempts to break the circle of beef.

He saw carnies as well as straights trying to get to him and the girl. He saw the Beagle Boys punching Useless Lou. Lou wanted very badly to stomp on them for a while, but John Bob would not let him.

"Let's get the hell outta Dodge," he told them.

With John Bob holding the girl and the cattle encircling him, keeping others away, they made it to the edge of the circus. John Bob had a few bulls stay behind to keep others from following, then got the girl into his truck and locked himself in with her. He still wanted to jump her bones right there on the seat; instead he drove out Interstate 20 out past Lake Ray Hubbard. It was a short trip, thank God, since he had to use one arm to fend off her attacks. The claws ripped into his arms repeatedly, shredding a good shirt. Her yowling echoed through the cab of the truck.

He pulled off the highway and worked his way to a dirt road on his property. His balls felt ready to explode with every bump.

He grabbed the woman and pulled her out of the truck. He pinned her arms to her sides again and examined the damage to his arm. He decided he'd live. He took her into the house and threw her on the bed.

"All right, Miss Kitty, you been wanting this from most anybody, so I guess it's gonna be me as has to deliver it. That's just the way it's gonna be."

"No one calls me Kitty and lives," she hissed. She began ripping his clothes off with her claws. "I am Señorita Gato and never, ever forget that!"

He kissed her hard to shut her up. He squeezed her breasts and began to bite the back of her neck with a feverish passion.

The next morning he rolled her over to face him. "So, Kitty, you do this every time you want to meet a guy? I don't know as how I might be jealous if that was the case."

"No, no. John Bob, last night was the first time. I don't even really know what happened other than you and I got together out here wherever we are."

"What's happened is that when you saw me, your mind and heart said 'Goddamn, ain't he just the one that I been wishin' for and cravin'.' So your body says 'Let's see what he's really made of.' You, bein' yourself, just naturally went into heat. Strongest and craftiest one gets you. So of course, I won."

"I'm so glad. What happens now?"

"Well, as I see it, you go ahead and quit the show, come stay here with me, and we live happily ever after, or something like that."

Señorita Gato shook her head. "No, that won't work. Ozymandias won't let me out of my contract. I'm sure of that. What if you were to come with me? You have a way with animals, maybe you could get on with the show." She expected him to object because of the macho attitude that she had seen so often growing up: The man is the head and should make the most money, not live off his wife's earnings. But, then nobody had yet mentioned the M-word.

"Well, if that's our choices, I reckon I'd rather go with you. But, let's talk to this Ozywhatsis second." He got out of bed and began to put on his clothes.

"But what's first?" she asked.

"Why, we get married, of course. Unless you got a problem with that?"

Señorita Gato began to tingle all over. "Do you ride a red neon Pegasus, too?" she asked.

"Not unless I need to."

As he began to fasten his belt, she looked at the buckle.

"What type of stone is that?"

"Well, no one don't rightly seem to know. I won the buckle in the rodeo and the fellow that made it just liked the look and texture of the stone. Though it's not really a stone."

She leaped out of bed. "John Bob, you may have just found a way to break my contract."

"Oh, no! Not with my buckle, you don't!"

He started to say more but she kissed him hard and drug him back to the bed.

John Bob looked around the tent. This Oz fella was big. John Bob didn't like the looks of him one bit. He liked the looks of the others that filled the tent even less. He wished that he had Cyclone Red or Harry Longabaugh with him to even some of the odds.

"Well, Señorita Gato," Oz said in his booming voice, "that was quite a scene you caused last night. I hope you don't intend to make a habit of it."

John Bob stepped toward the man. "She don't. Ain't nothin' gonna be a habit here for her, 'cause she ain't stayin' with you. She's comin' to live with me."

"Really?" Oz said, and John Bob felt a menacing shift in his voice. "What makes you think so?"

"We done got hitched about an hour ago. She don't need to work for you."

"The señorita—or, should I say, señora—has certain contractual obligations to this show."

"Well, Ozzy, you can stuff the contract. We're walkin'!"

He turned to lead his new wife away and saw that they were surrounded by some of the ugliest people in the world. He thought about calling for the bulls. Oz must have read his mind.

"Don't count on any assistance unless you're ready to see your bovine friends hurt."

"Don't worry none about me and mine. I ain't the kind to drag my friends in where they're gonna get hurt. No, friend, this is just between you and me. Forget them yahoos back there. It's just us, *mano-a-mano*."

Oz said, "It occurs to me from your little stunt that you might be one of us. Would you care to join?"

"No way, no where, no how. We're gone. Kitty don't want to be here and neither do I. So, what's it gonna take to buy out that contract. Whose head am I gonna have to bust?"

"It'll cost the thing you cherish the most."

"No way. That's her!"

He felt her fingers tighten on his arm. There was love and gratitude in her feline eyes. He smiled at her and kissed her nose.

"How about the thing you next most cherish? Say . . . that belt buckle. That's your choice. You walk away alone with the belt buckle in place, or you can leave it here and take your bride wherever you please."

"My buckle," he said. He stared at the shiny surface

and its cool red ornament. It was everything that he had
been and thought that he could be. He ran a gnarled finger
over it.

He looked at the girl next to him. He loved the feel of
her next to him, the smell of her. With her, he could be
more than he had ever thought. She made him something
beyond anything he ever could have imagined.

He undid the snaps and slipped the buckle off the belt.
He took one last look at the trophy.

"Hope my damn pants don't fall down now."

He threw the buckle to Oz. Immediately the freak sea
parted behind him, leaving a clear passage home. As soon
as they were outside the tent, John Bob hugged her
closely to him.

"Let's celebrate! Where do you want to go? What do
you want to do?"

She pointed to the downtown Dallas area. "I want to
go there, to the Magnolia Building. I want to see the
Pegasus and to thank it for making my dreams come
true."

SCOTT A. CUPP

The show rolled on . . .

ALONG THE MIDWAY (V)

Bernalillo County, New Mexico

They were a hit.

George looked down at the crowd of sweltering New Mexicans as they fanned themselves with hats and programs and anything else they could use to make a breeze. But the fanning was automatic. Their minds weren't on the heat for the moment. George and Ginger had seen to that.

No denying his tentaclelike arms had something to do with it, as did Ginger's teeny bikini. But the plain truth was that he and Ginger were *good*. Especially Ginger. Once she'd got some confidence in his strength and his timing, once she knew she could rely on him always being there to catch her, she'd cut loose. She'd begun launching herself into great gliding, soaring leaps, dizzying spins, triple and quadruple flips, all with no apparent effort. Even Papa Fugazi was amazed.

And the crowds . . . George knew the crowds were mesmerized. They had never seen, never *imagined* anything like this. In a matter of weeks George and Ginger had become a star attraction. A beautiful girl, all shapely curves and damn near naked, flying through the air and being caught by a guy with no hands. Even though they still did their act with a safety net, people must have thought it was pretty neat, because the second-night crowds were always bigger than the first—a sure sign of good word of mouth.

The top was packed now. George tried to cap the excitement bubbling in his chest as he stood on the trapeze platform and waited for Ginger to start. To his amazement, he'd found he liked being the focus of the crowd's attention—from a distance. As Octoman in the freak tent, the scrutiny had been too close, the noxious comments too audible. Where he had been passive before, an *object*, here he was an active participant. His deformity merely heightened the attraction—what he was *doing* was more important.

And what he was doing was catching Ginger, allowing her to look and be the best that she could and then being there on the spot, in the precise locus in time and in space to catch her when she came out of her move. She was so beautiful to watch, George was afraid that sometime in the future when they did away with the net he'd become so engrossed in the wonder of her that he'd forget to catch her. And then she'd fall and be hurt or maimed or worse and George would have no alternative but to let go of his own bar and plummet into the earth beside her and join her in death.

He was hopelessly in love and he knew it. And he was being a sap about it. He knew that, too. He also knew he had to hide his feelings deeper than he'd ever hidden anything before. Because Ginger wanted no part of him.

He could live with that. You don't grow up with a name like Octoman without getting used to the idea that there are some things you'll never do, some things you'll never have.

She gave him the nod and they dropped off the platforms and went into their swings. Soon she'd be tumbling through the air toward him. Soon he'd get a chance to touch her, to wrap the ends of his arms around her wrists. Soon he'd feel truly alive for the first time all day.

Palomita, New Mexico

I eased up on the accelerator and tapped my fingernails against the steering wheel.

Just ahead men and women in their Sunday-best clothing mingled with gaudily clad tourists, cameras in hand, "outlandness" stamped across their midwestern features. The crowd shouted and laughed merrily as the people surged back and forth across the street, weaving intricate patterns in front of the battered car. There were torches and the clanking of liquor bottles, the popping of flashbulbs, the smell of spilled wine and roasting chiles, and the brassy too-loud sound of *mariachis*. No one in the throng spared me a second glance. I rolled up my window to shut out some of the noise. The tapping increased tempo.

I cursed myself for coming back today . . . tonight, rather. But I really didn't have much choice, now, did I? The circus would be leaving Albuquerque, some two hours' drive to the south, the following afternoon. I'd had to act now. Hadn't Oz made that abundantly clear before we arrived in New Mexico? He'd made other things clear, too. He had hinted—more than that, I recalled—that if I brought him this certain object that he wanted he had the knowl-edge—through the object—to . . . cure me, as it were.

I had almost laughed aloud when the great Oz had said that; there was no cure for me. *None.* And yet . . . what could it hurt?

At a crawl—and fearing I would stall the car any minute—I followed the celebrants down the narrow main street of Palomita, old cottonwoods like living columns alongside the two-lane road, then turned right several blocks before the plaza, leaving the light and laughter behind.

This street was barely that, almost a burro alley. It was unpaved, and dust rose because there'd been no rain recently. Narrow windows, with their blue wooden trim, overlooked the street. I was so close that I could probably roll down a window and rap on one of the panes. I smiled at the thought and wondered what the people inside would think.

I'd had little to smile about, though, on this trip home. I had been gone a long time.

Sixteen years since I'd left. I'd fled southward to Santa Fe one autumn night while I was in high school. I'd gone to see the fiesta and the burning of Zozobra—Old Man Gloom—and knowing what waited for me, I had never returned.

I'd never wanted to until now.

My mother had died shortly after my birth, a suicide. No one ever told me as much, but I knew it from what the villagers didn't say. I'd been raised by my uncle, the village priest.

My uncle. And my father. He had raped, seduced— what did the word matter?—his own sister, just fifteen at the time. The girl had not spoken much after that until she had been delivered of a healthy baby girl.

Yes, healthy; but with one alarming quality.

I checked the rearview mirror; nothing but blackness.

I didn't know if Padre *Tío,* as I liked to call him, stayed on at the church. He was already drinking far too much by the time I cut out, but that didn't mean the Church had relieved him of his duties. There were many drunken priests in churches in many towns. Many priests who made passes at their nieces . . . their daughters.

The anger . . .

I hunched my shoulders and gripped the steering wheel, feeling it cut into my skin. No, I told myself. No, not yet.

I forced myself to relax, little by little. Forced the anger away. Forced myself to think of other things.

I felt grimy after the drive. It had been hot and dusty, and the air-conditioning in this clunker hadn't been working; I hadn't had time for amenities before leaving the circus tonight, either. I'd rent a room, wash up and then . . .

I smiled. Grimly, but nonetheless it was a smile.

I located a small motel not far from the plaza where the culmination of tonight's fiesta would be held. I registered, took my one shoulder bag to the room. I washed and changed clothing, putting on a full white skirt and a white peasant blouse. Even inside the room I could hear the sounds coming from the plaza. It was a good thing I didn't plan on sleeping here tonight.

I had no sooner left the room, locking the door and dropping the key into my pocket, when someone bumped into me. I whirled around.

" 'Scuse me," the man muttered.

I moved back. He reeked of liquor. No doubt one of the fiesta attendees; God knows there were enough of them crawling around town. In the light from the motel's sign I saw that he was Anglo; there would be many Anglos here tonight; it was the town's biggest attraction, this Feast of San Ignacio held every May 13. Ignacio was a local *santo,* a man some in town whispered might have been Joseph the Carpenter. Or perhaps not. The village had suffered much until this man passed through; afterward the crops had grown, children had been born healthy, and the blind had been cured.

Or so the legend went. It was enough, though, for the start of an annual thanksgiving.

I said nothing.

He studied me, and I knew what he saw: a woman above average in height, almost unnaturally thin, yet with very firm and large breasts. It was always what they saw first, I thought; color of eyes? Oh, you have eyes. . . .

They never saw the paleness of my eyes, nor the solid blackness of my hair, a blackness that held no highlights, no glints, a blackness that was almost as complete as a starless sky . . . a void. . . .

" 'Scuse me," he repeated and shoved closer to me.

"You're in my way," I said, not even pretending politeness. This kind didn't understand tact. I started to move away.

He put one arm out to block my way. I pressed my lips together.

"How about you and me head over to the cantina to get a little drink?"

I had him pegged now; his speech condemned him as a Texan. I should have known with the enormous silver belt buckle shaped like a longhorn's head and the obnoxious behavior. "You've had a 'little drink' too many already," I said. "I don't think you need any more."

"The night's young."

"Go away."

"No." He pushed closer. I could feel the nearness of him, the heart radiating from his body.

Exasperation and something else whorled within me; I felt it stirring deep inside.

"Get away," I warned. At my sides my fingers curled and uncurled.

"Honey, I'd like to get to know you better. I like you Mexican girls."

Mexican. The fool didn't know the difference. Not one of my ancestors had been Mexican. Mine—and all the ancestors of those who lived in this town in northern New Mexico—had hailed from Spain. They were the descendants of the conquistadors who had come to this mountainous country over three hundred years before searching for cities of gold. They had discovered nothing but Indians and villages of mud and straw.

Mexican. Up here that was an insult.

But to this Anglo, this *Texan,* there was no difference.

Bitterness added to the brew inside me, and when he reached to touch me, I could feel the tingling in my palms. Warmth coursed upward in my arms. Without warning, I grabbed hold of his forearms, felt the hot dampness, heard the sizzling.

The Texan screamed in animal pain; I released him, and he whirled away from me, stumbled back into the darkness. And then he was gone. Good riddance.

I smiled.

I waited to see if anyone had noticed and would come rushing out, but everyone at the motel seemed to be elsewhere tonight. Celebrating.

I had to go back inside, though, and check. I entered my room and went into the bathroom, flipping the light switch on with the tips of my fingers. I stared into the mirror above the sink, saw the blood seeping from the line of cuts on my forehead. I gazed down at the palms of my hands, at the blood in the great gashes there. Even as I watched though, the blood receded, trickled away until there was nothing. I pulled up my shirt and examined my side; even the gouge there was gone. I did not look down at my sandals; I knew what I would see.

Once more I smiled.

Tonight would not be so bad after all, I thought.

Whistling, I left the room and headed for the church, not far away.

It took only a few minutes to reach it, and I paused on the sidewalk outside.

St. Anne's. An Anglo name. But Anglo money had built the mission and educated the kids and fed the old people during the bad times. The Anglos were good for something, I figured.

And yet the church, built of adobe, was not very well constructed for all the money and labor that had gone into it—the walls were always in need of patching, it was drafty in the winter and stifling in the summer. Something was always broken, too.

Inside the church was cool against the warm night air. Ahead I saw the flickering flames of the votives. I could just make out the rows of rough-hewn pews in the gloom; there was a smell of piñon, too, and old candle wax. The smells brought back many memories, and I shivered, suddenly cold.

One small light burned behind the altar, outlining the plaster statue of the crucified Christ. Occasionally as a child I had gazed at that figure and after a while I could see the signs of stigmata, could see the trickle of blood on His body. Of course, when I blinked there was nothing but the plaster.

I listened. The sound of something soft, and then: "May I help you?"

Trying not to tremble, I turned around. The priest stared at me.

"You." The one word was almost a curse.

I nodded, not trusting my voice at that moment.

"What brings you back here?" he asked harshly.

"You don't want to welcome home your niece, Padre?" I asked, advancing and holding my arms out, as if to embrace him.

Quickly his eyes shifted to my palms—guilty of nothing—and backed away.

"Stay away from me."

"Father, father," I said, shaking my head slightly. "That is not precisely a Christian sentiment."

"You're a devil," he said.

I looked him directly in the eye. "You made me what I am, father."

"Not me, the devil."

"I don't think the devil slept with my mother."

He took a step forward, as if he were about to slap me, then stopped. He knew what that would bring. He had seen it once before, once when I had been in bed sleeping and he had tried to press himself on me.

They say the burned hand teaches best.

"Why are you here?" he demanded again.

"To celebrate the feast, father."

"The truth. Although you've never told it before, *puta.*"

I bit back my answer. I had been a good child, truthful and obedient, and loving him to the end. How could he say this? Because he knew in his heart he was wrong. Because he had all those sins weighing upon him. He might have confessed; he might have even been forgiven by his priest; but he had never forgiven himself.

Nor had I.

Memories were burned into my soul, just as my grip could sometimes burn a man.

"The truth, father?" I shrugged. "I came back for something I left here a long time ago, something I think is mine."

He looked puzzled. I walked down the aisle toward the chancel rail.

"Where are you going?"

I said nothing. I opened the gate and went into the chancel. Once I had felt a power there, a presence; God, I had thought. Now I wasn't so sure. I felt a tingling once more in my palms, as if my body knew where the object was. I studied the altar, the embroidered cloth on it. There was a silver chalice in the middle and on either end of the altar vases of fresh-cut flowers that the local ladies brought in each day.

Father *Tio* had doggedly followed me.

"Where is it?" I asked.

He looked puzzled. I didn't believe his innocence.

I approached the statue.

"Get away from Him!" the priest warned.

"Or what?" I sneered. "Who will you call? The Spanish Inquisition?"

"He doesn't have to," said a new voice.

Behind the priest stood a handful of young men, all much bigger, much more muscled than I. They were all attired in dark monk's robes and sandals. I knew there was nothing frail about them. In the village there were whispers of these Brothers and an offshoot of the Penitentes sect, the sect that reenacted Christ's crucifixion each spring. The Penitentes playacted; as for these Brothers . . . what I had heard made me believe they took their reenactment much more seriously. And, too, I had seen the stripings left by a whip on the priest's back from time to time. They were not self-imposed marks.

"Ah, the good Brothers to the rescue," I said. "You were always *friendly* with them, Father *Tio*."

The youngest of the Brothers—and the most serious faced—now stood alongside the priest. His skin was pocked, yet he was vaguely handsome in a strange way.

What a waste, I thought.

"You should leave now, señorita, before you desecrate this holy place," the young man said.

I watched Father *Tio*. He was trembling, moisture glistening on his upper lip, but whether these symptoms were because of me or the monks I didn't know. Perhaps it was simply time for another pull on his alcohol teat.

"Go," the priest said. "Go now."

"I want it. I want the Piece."

The monk looked at the priest, then at me; obviously he was puzzled.

The priest shook his head. He wiped a hand across his forehead, then down the side of his black pants.

"It's not here. It hasn't been here for a long, long time."

"Then you know what I'm talking about. Good. But I think it's here . . . in this building . . . somewhere. And I'll find it." My eyes met those of the monk's.

I walked forward, and the priest jumped backward. "My, how skittish you are. Perhaps you should have a doctor prescribe a tranquilizer."

The monk headed toward me, but the priest waved him away. "No! She's the one I told you about."

The one I told you about. Not, *she is my niece* or *she is my daughter. The one.* There were connotations of an itness there, of being less than human.

But to him, I guess, I wasn't human. But the devil hadn't formed me; it had been the priest and my poor mother, just two simple humans who had made me into what I was.

I raised my hand to the priest, and he whimpered. I dropped my arm, walked away from the altar, down the nave, knowing that the men watched me.

When I was outside, I took a deep breath and didn't look back as I headed for the street.

I wasn't defeated, just stumped for the moment. I would find the Piece. Tonight. And neither the priest nor the Brothers could stop me.

I headed back to the plaza and found an open-air bar where I ordered a drink. I sat at a small table and watched as villagers I had known long ago made fools of themselves. All for a *santo* that was nothing but plaster of paris and bits of cloth.

The *mariachis* were closer now, the trumpets blatting. Maybe they would go away, I told myself, but I didn't think I would be that lucky. A little girl, hand-in-hand with her older brother, strolled by; she glanced at me, then away.

Never a Beauty, but always the Beast, I thought. There was nothing outwardly wrong with my appearance—not enough to make someone gasp with fear—but I had always had that effect on people, no matter how well they knew me. I guess that made me a freak who couldn't fail. Job security, right?

I watched a couple, not much older than I, sit at the next table. They were holding hands and their heads were bowed, close together. She said something, and he laughed. I looked away.

The crowds were becoming organized as people actually began lining the street. Soon the procession would begin. San Ignacio would be brought out on his special platform; he would be brought from the church down a maze of streets to the plaza and then . . .

I sat up, my hand twitching, and knocked my glass over. Wine dripped off the table, splashing my sandals. I didn't notice.

The procession. The *santo*.

I leaped to my feet, paid my bill, and ran back to St. Anne's.

The door opened with a resounding slam and I peered in. It was empty. I trotted into the sacristy; empty. Then the rectory. The statue of the saint was nowhere to be found.

San Ignacio.

The statue.

That was the answer. It had to be. Not even the priest would be so blasphemous as to put the Piece close to the Christ statue, but a statue of a local saint was something altogether different.

So obvious, I thought as I raced along the streets, and yet so cleverly hidden.

I could hear the sound of cameras clicking and people praying. I knew what I would see . . . the old and faithful on their knees, crossing themselves reverently, some weeping, all gazing at the statue as if it were something . . . someone . . . alive, as if it were someone who could make a difference in their lives. The fools, I thought.

I rounded a corner, saw the procession had gone farther than I thought, and I ducked down an alley. I would cut them off.

I was slightly out of breath, and could feel the heat from my exertion. The wind blew my hair, and I knew I must look crazed. I didn't care.

I was close by the plaza now and screeched to a halt. There was the *santo* upon its platform, borne by four monks. The platform, made of simple wood, was anything but simple now, decorated as it was with fresh flowers and bright ribbons and the shiny tin holy medals that the good and simple folk thought would be blessed by being next to a *santo*.

The priest, leading the procession, was chanting in Latin—old ways die hard this far north—with his hands raised. The monks were the first to see me, and they stopped. Suddenly the priest realized something was amiss; he looked to them first, then turned around and saw me. He went pale.

I approached carefully, deliberately. As I drew closer, I could see the *santo* was decked out in his finest: a white robe delicately embroidered by local women; in one raised hand he held a jeweled something or other; I never had figured out what the article was. At Ignacio's feet were the various objects that had been significant in his life: a handsaw, a hammer, and there, so close I could see its odd glint, was the object. It had been there all along, all those years when I had gone into the sacristy and looked at the *santo*. So close . . . and perhaps the cause of my deformity, or so Oz had suggested.

And the priest had known. He had kept that to himself, too, all those years. Another sin for him to eat.

My face flushed.

The priest retreated, closer to the monks now. Gently they set the saint's platform down. The young monk stepped forward. The people clustered along the street had no idea what was going on. Some must have thought it was all part of the program. They would soon learn otherwise.

I advanced. "Give me the saint."

"No," said the young monk. "He is ours."

Ours. Always ours. And you're not part of it—the unspoken words. Always on the outside; never accepted. I looked at the priest, my *father*, and he was trembling; he would not look my way.

My anger and disgust mingled. My hands were growing warm, and the monk gasped when he saw the droplets of blood appear on my forehead.

I reached for the man, and my hands locked on to his arms, and he screamed and writhed as the skin sizzled and scorched with a terrible odor. I saw the glint of white. Bone.

He dropped to his knees, whimpering.

The crowd was murmuring now. They didn't remember anything like this happening in last year's celebration. Was this a new script?

Oh yes, my friends, a very new script.

I moved toward the saint, and another monk stepped in front of me.

"You just won't learn, will you?" I said with a slight shake of my head. I could feel the blood inching across my right cheek now, down toward the low neck of my blouse. On my left a crimson stain had appeared on the cotton material of the blouse.

I placed my hand fully on the chest of the monk, and listened in satisfaction as my blood ate away his robe and then his skin. He flung himself away, clawing at his corroded chest.

Now the crowd knew something was definitely wrong, and when I glared at these stupid Anglos and villagers, they panicked. Someone—a man or woman or child—screamed, and as one they began to stampede away from the plaza. Some stumbled and fell in their haste to leave, and I watched as an old woman was trampled by her friends. No one would call the police; in town there was only the one fat officer, and he had no doubt run away just as fast as the others.

"Get the *bruja!*" the priest quavered over the shouting and screaming, and the cries of pain from the two injured men. "Stop her—she's unholy!"

First, whore. Now witch. Could he think of nothing more original for me? I grinned in my mask of red.

The two remaining monks glanced at each other uneasily. They weren't fools. They fled without looking back. It seemed they weren't so penitent after all.

I picked my way around the young monk, still thrashing about on the street. That element which was in my blood would eat away at any alien substance—that which wasn't me, in other words—until there was nothing left. Soon his arm bones would be in two parts. As for the other man . . .

I reached for the statue. Suddenly the priest was in front of me.

"Father," I said, "I am amazed. Courage at last? Or is it false courage? Did your own private communion renew you?"

"You are a blasphemer," he said. His face was ashen, and the sweat dripped down from his hairline. I could see that his hands were trembling, and he had gripped them in an effort to still the tremors. It didn't work.

"A blasphemer. A devil. A whore. A witch. You're quick to call me names. Why not add 'daughter' to the list?"

If possible, he paled even more. "It's not true."

"Ah, but it is. You have only to look at me to see the resemblance." I had his high-arched nose, the same thin lips. There could be no doubt. There had never been any in my mind, nor I suspect in the minds of his parishioners. But it was, after all, hard to get priests to leave cushy jobs in cushy parishes and come to backward places like Palomita. It was far easier to look the other way and ignore his . . . indiscretions.

Indiscretion. Another word to add to the list.

"It's not true," he whispered.

"It is. Admit it. To me. At last."

He shook his head.

I looked at him and wondered what had gone through my mother's head when her brother had seized her bodily and mentally. How fearful she must have been, how shameful. How she must have hated him, herself, life . . . me.

Inside the hatred twisted. It grew, and I could feel the heat radiating once more through my body. Could feel the blood as it formed upon my forehead, my hands, my side, my feet. A trickle, and I wiped it away from my eye with my fingers, then brushed them off on my skirt. The fabric smoked and shredded into a hellish design.

"Say it," I said.

He shook his head.

I thrust him away with the back of my hand. He shrieked before he realized he wasn't hurt. Then I grabbed the object. It was at once hot and cold in my wet palm, and I watched as the blood beaded on its curious surface. In its shiny surface I could almost see myself, could see faintly the red reflection of my face. I tasted blood on my lips.

I turned around. The priest was on his knees now, doing the only thing he knew how to do: pray. He was good at that.

His eyes were squeezed shut and he did not see me come to stand in front of him. A faint wind was blowing now, and my skirt whispered about my legs. A tendril of my hair, loose, clung damply to my cheek. I could smell the stench of destroyed flesh. The whining of the monks had quieted. Perhaps they were dead, or simply unconscious from their pain. It didn't matter.

I caressed the object, touched my tongue to its surface, and a shiver, almost sexual, coursed through me.

I slipped the object into my pocket and patted it. For now it would be safe. Who here would dare to take it away from me?

But what of the priest, my father?

"Say it," I urged once more. "Admit who I am, that I'm your daughter. Say it so that the words can be taken away on the wind, into the night."

"No, it's not true, it's not true. Never. I never touched her. Never, never, never, in a thousand lifetimes. She was just a child, I was her brother . . . how could . . . there was no way—"

"Liar," I said softly.

His eyes were open now, and silently he pleaded for me to leave him alone, with the truth, with his memories, his sins.

I had left him alone for too long. Fresh blood flowed downward, to my lips.

Smiling, I bent to kiss my father upon his forehead.

KATHRYN PTACEK

The show rolled on . . .

ALONG THE MIDWAY (VI)

Maricopa County, Arizona

At the top of the trapeze tower Ginger felt as if she were
suffocating. All the heat and sweat from the crowd that
had flocked in from Tempe seemed to have settled up here
in a moist, ripe cloud.

She rubbed extra resin into her palms. She was per-
spiring heavily, and from more than just the heat. Tonight,
for the first time, she and George were doing their act
without a net.

It shouldn't matter, she told herself. And so you
shouldn't think about it. Because if you think about it you
may hesitate, you may throw your timing off a fraction of
a second, and that fraction could mean the difference
between a catch and a miss.

Don't think about it.

After all, what was there to think about? They'd already done it so many times without a hitch, in practice
and in public, that the presence or absence of the net
should mean nothing . . . nothing but the difference between life and death.

Ginger readied herself inside and out. As she adjusted
the straps on her bikini top she looked across the void at
George, waiting for her signal. Everything was going to be
fine. She was used to the feel of George's handless arms

108

now, and she'd come to have complete trust in his flawless timing. She nodded to him, he nodded back. Ready.

She swung out, matched her arcs to George's, then began her series of flips. It went smoothly, just as it had all those other nights with the net. She started out simple and built the complexity, from spins to single flips, to double flips, to the big finish—the quadruple flip. She needed a strong swing for the finale—extra height, extra speed. She increased her arc, once, twice—

Some of her sweat had somehow made the bar slippery. She felt her left hand slip an instant before she released into her quadruple and she knew she was dead. Panic squeezed her throat and she made a futile backward grab for the bar which threw off her timing even further. Completely out of control, she tumbled upward toward the top canvas. She bit back a scream as gravity reasserted its control and began tugging her toward the floor. If she was going to go, she'd go quietly, not like a howling jackass. The crowd had no such compunctions. She heard it screaming in horror as she plummeted earthward. Ginger spread her arms to slow her fall on the one chance in a million that—

Suddenly a rope coiled around her wrist and nearly yanked her arm out of its socket, and then she was swinging instead of falling and it wasn't a rope; it was one of George's hands coiled around her wrist in a death grip, no, a *life* grip, and she looked up and saw his red face and bulging eyes as he strained to maintain his grip on her. He was hanging by his ankles and must have stretched his body to the breaking point to reach her. But reach her he had and now he was hauling her in. She climbed up his body until she reached the bar, then helped him back to an upright position.

Below, the crowd was cheering, utterly berserk with relief and amazement. Yet Ginger found herself completely calm. Her hands were shaking and her knees were weak, but that was the adrenaline. Mentally, emotionally, she was calm. She'd slipped, fallen, almost died. But *almost* was the key word here. She was okay. Her partner had saved her. They were a true team now, and something deep within her told her she'd never fall again. She straightened to a standing position on the bar and tugged George along to join her.

"Stand up, George," she said over the joyous tumult rising from the crowd.

"I can't. I'm going to be sick."

"Don't be sick. You're a star. They probably think it was part of the act, the greatest gag they've ever seen. Don't let them down. Wave. Smile. Bow. This is show biz, guy."

George did as he was told, but he looked pale and shaky. Not a trouper, but a good guy. He'd damn near killed himself catching her.

"I almost lost you," he said.

Lost you? What did he mean by that? Did he blame himself? He shouldn't do that. She gripped one of his tentacles and held it aloft for the crowd. The cheers redoubled.

"These things really came in handy today," she told him. "If you'd had hands I don't think you'd have caught me."

"Yeah," he said, finally smiling. "I guess they have their uses."

Venice, California

On Saturday morning, as the tents were springing up like toadstools and the troupe was preparing for another show, Mr. Tane went out for a stroll.

With a grunt of pleasure he scooped up Bowser, grateful for his friend's familiar weight in his arms, and left the trailer they shared, emerging into a warm haze of sun. He walked briskly through the side streets and alleys of Venice, passing many large murals splashed on brick walls, mostly landscapes and mythological vignettes, the colors vivid as a drug dream. Bowser was fascinated by the paintings. Mr. Tane, as always, remained indifferent to matters of art and beauty.

Ooh, look, Bowser exclaimed in his soundless voice. There's a pretty one, Tane.

It looks like all the others, Mr. Tane answered in his thoughts as he walked on.

But the reds and blues—

Quit turning your head to see, will you! I nearly tripped on the curb just then. Watch where we're going.

Bowser sighed. And just where *are* we going, exactly?

Supposed to be a beach around here someplace.

And girls? California girls?

I imagine so.

Like the girls in the movies? Bowser asked, and in time with his awed question he sent Mr. Tane a rapid-fire series of images from the many films they had watched together, a blur of beautiful actresses with hair like sunlit smoke.

Yes, yes, Mr. Tane replied. Just like in the movies.

Do you think Julia Roberts will be there?

Despite himself, Mr. Tane smiled. His small friend was touchingly naive about some things.

As a matter of fact, fuzzy, I believe she will.

Bowser lost all interest in murals then. He concentrated on guiding Mr. Tane to the beach, where he fully expected to find Julia Roberts waiting for them in a state of extreme undress.

Bowser was skilled at providing such guidance. He had been doing it for three years, ever since Mr. Tane joined up with Ozymandias Oddities on a stopover in Illinois. Mr. Tane had been blind then. In truth, he was blind still, but he no longer thought of himself as such, because he had Bowser's eyes to see with.

Neither he nor Bowser understood the telepathic link they shared. Nobody else in the show—nobody else on earth, as far as they knew—could tap into either Mr. Tane's or Bowser's thoughts. But each of them could read the other's mind perfectly. They conversed in voiceless dialogues, traded musings, memories, fantasies. And of course Bowser transmitted to Mr. Tane an endless stream of live images, the sights perceived by his own eyes, which had become Mr. Tane's eyes by extension.

In exchange for giving Mr. Tane sight, Bowser got what he had always been denied: mobility and voice. His wobbly, stunted legs could not carry him more than a few steps; but Mr. Tane's long strides could take Bowser anywhere by day, and at night his unfolded wings, magnificent in moonlight, could conquer the sky. And more important still, Bowser was able to communicate with Mr. Tane, share thoughts, express opinions and desires. No longer was his mind imprisoned by the malformed mouth that mashed his speech to barks and grunts.

They needed each other. Mr. Tane had been blind, Bowser helpless. Together they made one being, clear-eyed and able-bodied. Oz called it a perfect symbiotic relationship.

Mr. Tane and Bowser called it friendship.

They found the beach within a few minutes. There were girls everywhere, many gliding on roller skates down the wide paved promenade that served as a boardwalk; but Julia Roberts disappointed Bowser by her absence.

Maybe she'll show up later, Mr. Tane said.

Fat chance, Bowser answered. Then he added more brightly: But the ones who *are* here certainly are beautiful.

Enjoy them now, furface—Mr. Tane's telepathic voice was harsh—because before long, they'll all be extinct.

Mr. Tane walked along the promenade, carrying Bowser without strain. Anyone observing the pair would have seen a tall, handsome, gaunt man with white hair swept back in a tight skull cap, his upper body clothed in a jacket too bulky for summer—and, in his arms, a medium-size and very ugly dog, its jowly face, fish-belly pale, poking out of a thicket of frizzy reddish orange fur, its stubby nailless paws disturbingly reminiscent of an infant's grasping hands.

Bowser was not a dog, of course, despite the cruel canine name inflicted on him at the orphanage where he'd been raised. But he was not quite a man either. He was something in between, something even the other mutants found strange and mildly repulsive. The Beagle Boys, in particular, had teased and baited him mercilessly . . . until Mr. Tane became his protector. Once they saw what Mr. Tane's silver fingernails could do, they had left Bowser alone.

The promenade was lined with trashy shops housed in converted garage stalls, stocked with T-shirts and posters, power crystals and astrology charts, miracle vitamins and wheat germ capsules. Mr. Tane paused before a carousel display of Ray-Bans, but purchased none. His own sunglasses, a pair of opaque wraparounds, were perfectly adequate. Besides, it would have been awkward to try on a new pair in public, thus exposing, even if only for a moment, the smooth white flesh that had sealed his hollow eye sockets since birth.

He did buy a present for Bowser, however. A silly little gewgaw, one of those glass paperweights filled with water and plastic snowflakes. Holding it gently, careful not to scratch the glass with his nails, he shook the bubble and let Bowser watch the sudden flurry of snow.

For me, Tane? Really?

Take it easy, furball. It's no big deal.

They found a bench and sat watching the California girls in their swimsuits and short skirts, then broadened the range of their interest to include the other specimens of humanity passing by. Muscled surfers, ragged bums wheeling supermarket carts, street musicians and jugglers, hippies caught in a '60s time warp. A jogger thudded past, trailed by a dachshund on a skateboard, tail wagging. Nobody noticed.

Look, Tane! Bowser exclaimed suddenly, though the words were hardly necessary; Mr. Tane had no choice but to look wherever Bowser did.

Carmella, Haman, and Herbert Brooks were moving through the crowd. A tie-dyed headband, recently purchased, concealed Carmella's third eye; a hooded, baggy sweatshirt emblazoned with a pink palm tree and the HOLLYWOOD sign covered most of Haman's green skin. Herbert, swaying to the music of a Walkman, was snapping his fingers freely; his spidery hands drew no more attention than the skateboarding dachshund had. All three wore mirrored shades, price tags dangling from the stems.

Carmella pointed at Mr. Tane and Bowser, and the group quickly approached the bench.

"I'm surprised to see you out and about," Mr. Tane said without rising. He had little stomach for socializing.

"No reason we shouldn't join this crowd," Haman said. "We fit right in."

Carmella giggled. "I think the man who sold me this headband saw my eye." She tapped her forehead lightly. "He didn't seem to care."

"Can you imagine?" Haman waved his arms loosely. "In this place, we're not freaks!"

"In this place," Carmella said, *"everyone* is a freak."

Mr. Tane nodded. Similar thoughts had occurred to him.

Herbert's voice rang out, singing along with the cassette tape in the personal stereo. The song was "I Love L.A."

Then Haman's long-nosed face became serious as he leaned close to Mr. Tane and Bowser. "Oz sent us to track you down," he said, his voice dropping to a theatrical whisper. "He wants to see you. Says it's urgent."

Neither Mr. Tane nor Bowser liked the sound of that.

They returned to the vacant lot east of Main Street where the Beagle Boys and the elephants were raising the tents in a maelstrom of dust. Oz was in his trailer. A breakfast tray, the plates empty, lay on a table near the chair where he sat with folded hands.

"It's your turn, Tane," he said in his rumbling voice. "The next Piece is yours to find."

Mr. Tane drew a sharp breath. Bowser stiffened, his paws gripping Mr. Tane's arm.

"This particular Piece is a lovely thing. Shaped like a starfish. Chilly to the touch. Put it to your ear and you'll hear wind chimes."

He paused as if awaiting an obvious question.

Ask him where it is, dummy, Bowser ordered.

"Where do we find it?" Mr. Tane asked.

Oz did not smile, but there was humor in his voice when he answered. "You two will appreciate this aspect of the assignment, I think. Unless I've misjudged you. The Piece is in the possession of an actress named Kimberly St. Clair. Heard of her, Tane?"

"Certainly. She was in *Singapore Rain*. And *Fallout*."

Don't forget *Cutaway*, Bowser said. I think that was her best role.

"Miss St. Clair lives a few miles up the coast," Oz said, "in a rather exclusive community called the Malibu Colony. I want you to fly there tonight. Break in and steal the Piece for me."

"Yes, sir."

Will we get to meet her, Tane? Bowser was asking excitedly. Get her autograph, maybe?

Oz was speaking again, but Mr. Tane had trouble hearing him with Bowser's voice in his head.

Be quiet, he told his friend as he strained to hear Oz's

instructions. But Bowser was too far gone to listen.

Kimberly St. Clair, oh boy, oh boy. That's even better than Julia Roberts. Promise we'll get her autograph, and a picture too, one of those big glossies we can tack up in the trailer. Will you promise me, Tane? *Please?*

Shut up! Mr. Tane roared.

Bowser shut up.

Then they both listened to the rest of what Oz had to say, but neither of them remembered much of it later, except for his very last words:

"I shall be occupied in a small town near Pasadena, so I want no trouble with the law, Tane. Understand? There's to be *no killing.*"

Night tented the earth with its starry canopy, and in the big top the show was well underway, the elephants waltzing and the crowd enchanted, when Mr. Tane prepared for his flight.

Concealed behind the water truck, he stripped off his clothes, leaving only his sunglasses in place, and stood naked in the feeble light of a quarter moon. Majestically his wings unfolded, spreading wide. Bowser sat watching a few yards away, and through his eyes Mr. Tane saw himself from a distance, a bat-winged gargoyle, all lean muscle and alabaster skin and shining silver fingernails. The sight pleased him, as it always did.

He picked up Bowser and cradled him against his chest.

Ready? Mr. Tane asked.

When you are, boss, Bowser replied.

The great leathery wings flapped once, hesitantly, testing their stiff muscles. Then again, with new vigor. And then a furious thunder of wings—a swirl of beaten air—the ground dropping, horizon tilting—a sudden ascent into a fog of cloud—the cloud shredding to gauzy wisps, falling away—a clear sky now—unlimited distances to travel.

Mr. Tane looked down with Bowser's sight and saw a net of lights extending to the dark humps of mountains, and beyond the mountains still more lights blending with distance to form a ground cover of luminous mist.

He flew out over the sea, heading north. A few ships

passed below, bright jewels set in the black-velvet smoothness of the water. Airplanes crossed the sky, circling to land at faraway fields.

Oz had provided detailed directions to the Malibu Colony. With Bowser's help, Mr. Tane found the place easily. He glided over the row of beachfront homes, searching for a house that matched the photo Oz had shown them, an aerial shot clipped from *People* magazine.

It's that one there, Bowser said. And, ooh, it's all lit up. And noisy.

I don't like the look of this, Mr. Tane said grimly.

Cautiously he descended, perching in a tree. They watched the house. Music blared from the open windows. The oceanfront deck was thick with swaying figures.

Mr. Tane frowned. She's having a party, he told Bowser.

Are we invited? asked Bowser expectantly.

I think we should invite ourselves, Mr. Tane answered.

He waited, a vulture on a limb. After a few minutes a red Ferrari Testarossa slunk down the street and parked near the house. A man got out.

All right, hairball, here's the plan. We dispatch this late arrival, steal his clothes. Properly attired, I can get inside.

Dispatch him how, Tane?

A little love tap, nothing more.

Remember what Oz said. No killing.

I lack eyes, not ears; I heard him. Now hold on to my neck good and tight. . . . Ready. Set. *Go.*

Out of the tree like a dislodged kite. Swooping down, wings taut and silent, air rushing past. Mr. Tane knew how an arrow feels, or a bullet, or a bird of prey. The driver of the Ferrari never even knew what happened. One moment he was standing there, fumbling with his car keys, and a moment later Mr. Tane's shoeless feet, the toes bunched like fisted fingers, slammed into his back and knocked him sprawling on the pavement. He grunted once, then lay still.

He'll be out for hours, Mr. Tane said with satisfaction.

You think he's anyone famous? Bowser asked excitedly.

Oh, pipe down.

Mr. Tane dragged the man into the bushes near the car, stripped him, changed into his clothes. The fit was acceptable. Using Bowser as a mirror, Mr. Tane admired himself, then turned to be sure his collapsed wings did not print too badly against the suit jacket. No, they were fine.

With Bowser snug in his arms again, he walked briskly up to the house. He had never crashed a party before, any sort of party, least of all a Hollywood bash. He expected to be met at the entrance by some dour fellow demanding to see an invitation. But the door was opened and unguarded. The security officers at the Colony's gate must have already cleared the man in the sports car.

Elegant bodies in elegant clothes filled the cavernous living room, blotting out the moonlit ocean framed in the glass wall at the rear of the house, choking the spiral staircase that twisted upward to a second-story gallery lined with still more guests. Pounding chords from an electric band clashed with a frenzy of half-shouted conversations.

It's all so glamorous and thrilling, Bowser thought happily. What do we do now, Tane?

We mingle, Mr. Tane thought back. And keep an eye out for the Piece.

The trouble was, he did not have much experience at mingling. He stood there uncertainly, trying to imagine how one might begin a dialogue with a stranger.

"Rutger!" a female voice shrilled at his back. "Rutger, how *are* you?"

Startled, Mr. Tane pivoted and came face-to-face with Kimberly St. Clair. In his mind he heard Bowser squeal with delight.

"Oh, I'm sorry," the hostess said, a practiced smile fixed on her beautiful face. "I thought—well, from behind, you look just *exactly* like Rutger Hauer. Do you know Rutger? For that matter, do I know you?"

"The name is Tane," he said, extending one hand while holding tight to Bowser with the other.

She ignored the offered hand and instead kissed him lightly on the cheek.

Va-va-voom, Bowser thought.

"Oh, and *who* do we have here?" Kimberly cooed.

She petted Bowser. "Love your dog. Simply adorable. The ugly breeds are *so* chic right now."

Bowser bristled.

Easy, pal, Mr. Tane warned. "I always keep him with me," he said mildly. "He's much more than a pet to me. I hope you don't mind."

"Mind? Hardly. I'm an animal lover myself, oh, yes, dogs and cats, *wonderful* companionship, I give to all the charities. Honestly I am so *very* glad you could come, Mr., uh, what was it again?"

"Tane."

"Yes. So glad. I'm sure you know everybody here." Her busy hands fluttered around her face like butterflies. "They're all in the industry, of course, and in the industry everybody knows everybody, except for those who don't, but then they're not really *in* the industry, are they? If you see what I mean."

This broad's an airhead, Bowser thought with obvious disappointment.

"Anyway, let me introduce you around, even though I'm sure no introductions are necessary in *your* case, Mr. Tang."

"Tane."

She was already wafting away into the crowd. Mr. Tane followed obediently. Over the next hour he and Bowser made many interesting acquaintances.

An agent at Creative Artists: "I like that look of yours, Tane. Very slick, very different. You're a performer, am I right? Of course I'm right. Happy with your representation? Of course you're not, nobody ever is. Tell you what, here's my card, call me, we'll do lunch."

A producer with a three-picture deal at Paramount: "Points? Everybody wants points. And what do points mean? Howyadoin', Tane, pleased tameetcha. I'll tell you what they mean. They mean diddly-shit."

A director who had just wrapped his latest film, a teen comedy with a high-concept premise: "So the P.A. says to the A.D., he says, 'I can't find the shoes,' and the A.D.—Tane? Am I pronouncing that right? Great to know you, Tane—the A.D., he says, 'Then give him *your* shoes.' I mean, Jesus, can you see it? Eighty people standing around drawing union scale or better, and the fucking celluloid can't roll because of a pair of goddamned Hush Puppies, for Chrissakes."

Mr. Tane smiled and nodded and made what he hoped were the appropriate responses at the appropriate times. Kimberly St. Clair stayed close to him throughout the evening, her hand straying more and more often to his arm, her gaze meeting what she imagined were his eyes.

"How rude of me," she said suddenly. "I haven't even offered you a drink."

"That's quite all right. I don't drink anyway."

"Well, then"—she favored him with the sultry smile that had put her face on a thousand movie screens— "perhaps I can offer you something else."

Her hand crept inside his shirt and massaged his hairless chest.

Go for it, Tane, Bowser said. She's got a world-class bod, albeit the IQ of a lawn mower.

"Madam," Mr. Tane said, removing her hand from his shirt and kissing the delicate fingers, "that's by far the best offer I've had in a very long time."

"You're a gentleman," Kimberly said, flushed with pleasure. "Boy, do I ever love that in a man. Chivalry, courtesy, the old-fashioned virtues." She took his arm. "Come on, let's fuck."

She steered him through the crowd, up the winding staircase, into an unlit rear bedroom. A triangular window carved a wedge of white beach and creaming surf out of the shadowed wall. The floor vibrated with the band's throbbing noise.

She shut the door and reached for a light switch. Mr. Tane stopped her.

"No lights," he said gently. "More romantic in the dark."

"My God, you *are* a gentleman." Already her eager fingers were unbuttoning her silk blouse. "Put that dog down and come to bed, gorgeous."

Mr. Tane placed Bowser on the floor. Kimberly was bouncing on the king-size bed.

"Special things always happen to me in this room," she said happily as Mr. Tane removed most of his clothes, leaving only the shirt to cover his wings. "I've got a little pyramid under the bed to focus my energies, you know?

And the bed is oriented toward the east, because that's the direction of the sunrise. And I use incense—smell it?—and oh, yeah, there's this thing. I picked it up at an art gallery."

Her gaze had drifted upward. Bowser raised his head and saw a faint sparkle above the bed, a small metallic object in the shape of a starfish, suspended from the ceiling like a mobile.

The Piece.

"I don't know what it is, but it catches the light in funny ways, and I swear, since I got it, I've been having the most *creative* dreams. Call me crazy, but I think it's something mystical."

"I would never call you crazy," Mr. Tane said as his hands, guided by Bowser's excellent night vision, found the supple softness of her breasts. He squeezed gently, rubbing the nipples till they were hard, then kissed, nibbled, sucked.

Go get her, tiger, Bowser said.

"Beautiful," Mr. Tane whispered. "So beautiful."

"Oh, mister, that feels good, really good."

"I want to kiss you . . . everywhere."

"Muscles like iron, ummm, you shouldn't have left your shirt on, baby."

"Skin so soft, so smooth . . ."

"Love to feel your shoulders, your back, your . . . hey!"

Uh-oh, Bowser thought.

"Hey, what . . . what *is* this?" Sudden panic jumping in her voice. "Jesus Christ, what the *hell* . . . ?"

Her hands were under his shirt, moving blindly over the leathery husks of his folded wings, as a scream struggled to be born at the back of her throat.

"Kimberly—"

"You're a . . . some kind of a . . . you're a fucking *freak!*"

She jerked free of his arms. The first note of the scream escaped her parted lips. Mr. Tane clapped a hand over her mouth, and she flopped and squirmed under him, her fists beating his face and hands, her legs bicycling wildly. His free hand swept up, the metallic nails gleaming—

Don't do it, Tane! Bowser cried.

Reluctantly Mr. Tane decided to forgo the considerable pleasure of killing her. Instead he merely delivered a backhanded swat to her face. Her jaws clicked together and her eyeballs rolled up white in their sockets; she twitched briefly, then was motionless.

You didn't hurt her, did you? Bowser asked anxiously.

Just knocked her out, that's all—thanks to you and your stuffy moralism.

Mr. Tane balanced on the bed and yanked the Piece free of the wires that attached it to the ceiling. The five-pointed object was clammy in his hand. He felt it squirm like a living thing—no, impossible, some kind of illusion; had to be.

He snatched Bowser, gave him the Piece to hold, and ran to the window. It was closed, and he could find no handle on the damn thing. His nails raked the glass, scoring deep grooves with a chalk-on-blackboard screech; but before he could smash his way out, he heard shouts and knocking at the door.

"Kimberly? You okay in there? We heard a scream. Hey, Kimberly!"

What now, boss? Bowser asked.

We break up the party, Mr. Tane replied as his wings unfolded, shredding his shirt. Put your arms around my neck. And, whatever you do, hold on to that Piece.

The door burst open. Three men crowded the doorway. Their eyes went first to Kimberly, unconscious on the bed, then to Mr. Tane, standing by the window, naked, winged, his nails white as mercury in the moonlight.

"Holy shit," one of them said.

Mr. Tane came at them fast, jabbing with quick hard punches. The men went down in a tangle of limbs, groaning and cursing. He leaped over their prone bodies, into the hall.

Seconds later he reached the stairs, still clogged with people, the crowd making passage impenetrable. A woman, seeing him, started shrieking. He lashed out with one arm and swept her over the banister. She plunged onto a table of hors d'oeuvres directly below, starbursts of onion dip and guacamole spattering her dress.

Beating his wings, Mr. Tane launched himself from the

gallery, spiraling down into the living room where screaming guests scattered as if before a kamikaze plane. He
buzzed them, laughing, as they took cover behind sofas
and under tables. These people had thought themselves
powerful. Movers and shakers, yes. Well, they were shaking, all right.

Let me kill a few, Mr. Tane begged, blood lust ringing
in his ears. Just a few of them, Bowser. They'll bleed so
nicely.

No, Tane, please. They . . . they aren't worth it.

Oh, all right!

He allowed himself a final spin around the living room.
The CAA agent signaled him frantically from his hiding
place behind a potted plant. "Tane, baby, you and I have
got to get together! This bat-creature shtick—fantastic
gimmick—I'm talking *serious* money . . ."

The agent was still jabbering, saying something about
spin-offs and merchandising tie-ins, when, with a flurry of
wings, Mr. Tane flew out the front door into the street.

We did it! Bowser said happily. Home, Jeeves!

My plan precisely. Back to the mud show with our
prize. Oz will—

Mr. Tane had never heard a gunshot before, nor felt the
impact of one, and so what happened next took him
entirely by surprise. There was a sharp whip-crack of
sound, a thud in the center of his chest that drove the
breath out of him. He lurched in midair, dizzy, sick with a
wave of sudden intense pain.

It took him a moment to realize that the impressions
of agony and disorientation were not his own. They were
Bowser's thoughts and feelings, crowding his mind.

Bowser? Bowser, can you hear me?

Eyesight flickering, the world a blur.

Bowser?

It hurts, a frail voice answered.

With Bowser's eyes Mr. Tane scanned the street. Near
a slant-parked security-patrol car stood two uniformed
men, guns drawn, staring big-eyed at the apparition flap-
ping over their heads.

"Shoot it again, Joey!" one of them yelled.

More gunshots popped like firecrackers.

Wild rage seized Mr. Tane. These scum—these inferior

animals soon to be exterminated from the planet—had shot poor Bowser, hurt him, hurt him badly enough that he might . . . he might . . .

"No!" Mr. Tane howled, and then he was descending in a screaming dive, clawed hands extended, bullets streaking past him like tracer fire. There was a thud of impact as he plowed into the first guard and hooked two silver fingernails into the man's eyeballs. The guard wailed, a shrill womanish sound. Mr. Tane flung him onto the hood of the patrol car and heard the wet snap of his neck.

He whirled, still guided by Bowser's dim, fluttery vision, and fell on the other guard as the fool tried desperately to reload his weapon. A neat upward karate chop opened him up from groin to chin. Mr. Tane reached between the bloody skin flaps and unpacked the intestines, then flew in tight circles around the screaming man, draping him with his own innards like a Christmas tree garlanded with tinsel. The guard's hands were witlessly attempting to untangle himself when the news reached his brain that he was dead.

Mr. Tane watched him topple face-forward on the ground. He sprayed hot spit on the corpse. "Filth! Stinking *filth!*"

Then he was out over the sea, flying fast, thinking desperately that Oz would have some medicine or magic to save Bowser's life.

Hang on, fuzzy, he told the shivering shape in his arms.

He tried not to think of the many times he had said those words to Bowser during their night flights, afraid his friend might fall, and of what a long fall awaited him this time, that final graceless plunge into the dark.

Tears watered Bowser's eyes, smearing Mr. Tane's borrowed vision.

Hang on, he said again.

I will, boss, Bowser said. I won't let go.

Of course you won't.

I'm holding on good and tight to the Piece.

The Piece? Oh. Yes. That's good, Bowser. That's very good.

Mr. Tane hammered the air with his pounding wings.

You shouldn't have killed those two men, Tane. They didn't mean to hurt me. They were just scared.

Be still now. Save your strength.

A long silence followed. The night grew darker, Bowser's sight failing. The stars winked out like snuffed candles, and the black ocean became blacker still.

That was fun tonight, Bowser said suddenly, his telepathic signal nearly obscured by rising static. I mean . . . until the end. It was neat meeting real Hollywood celebrities.

I knew you would enjoy that.

You enjoyed it, too. We both did. . . . We've had some real good times together . . . haven't we, Tane?

Sure we have.

I liked . . . going to the movies with you. I liked . . . Bowser?

There was no answer, no presence in Mr. Tane's mind except buzzing heat. Moments later even that was gone.

He was in darkness, and alone.

Afterward, Mr. Tane could not say exactly how he found his way back to the circus. He must have used smells, he supposed, and air currents and faint sounds from the city streets. He flew for hours, circling and drifting, and finally he heard the circus music, the amplified voices of the barkers, the trumpeting of a restless elephant, and he knew he was home.

He had held tight to Bowser the whole time. He did not surrender his hold on the small limp thing that had been his friend even after he landed and told Haman to fetch Oz.

There was nothing Ozymandias could do for Bowser, of course. But he was happy to have the Piece, which Bowser had not relinquished even in death. That seemed to matter most to Oz.

Haman helped Mr. Tane find his way to the trailer he and Bowser had shared. Then, at Mr. Tane's urging, he left, shutting the door.

Mr. Tane laid the body in bed and ran his fingers over the soft familiar fur, stiff here and there with matted blood. He felt the bullet hole. Touching it jerked a sob out of him. He turned away, pacing the darkness of his world. His arms felt empty without Bowser in them.

Groping for a wall to lean against, he found the night-stand, and on it the paperweight he had bought this morning. He shook the small round object and imagined watching the drift of snow with Bowser's sight, his friend's thoughts mingling seamlessly with his own.

His fingers splayed. The paperweight fell to the floor. Glass shattered.

Mr. Tane knelt, naked and bloody, and covered himself with his unfolded wings. He hugged his knees and rocked slowly, slowly.

He wanted to cry. He wished desperately for tears.

But he had no eyes..

DOUGLAS BORTON

The show rolled on . . .

ALONG THE MIDWAY (VII)

Los Angeles County, California

After lying awake half the night planning it, George still needed most of the morning to get up the nerve to ask her. When they had finished checking the ropes and cables for tonight's show, he made sure no one was in earshot, then quickly turned to Ginger.

"Want to go see the town—you know, Beverly Hills and all that?" he blurted and steeled himself for the inevitable rejection. He just hoped she didn't laugh. "That is, I mean, if you don't already have plans."

"As a matter of fact, I do have plans," Ginger said.

"Oh. Okay." Mixed deep within the disappointment was a vague sense of relief. At least his life was holding true to form—no tricks, no curves, no surprises, just straight-ahead frustration. "Some other time then."

"Sure. But today I'm heading out on the highway and checking into one of those cut-rate executive motels and staying there till show time." Suddenly she turned to him and smiled. "Say. Why don't you come with me. We can split the rent."

George tried to speak but his mouth was like the desert they'd passed through on the way to L.A. Alone with Ginger . . . in a motel room. He swallowed.

"Uh, yeah. If you're sure you want to."

She gave him a puzzled look. "Why wouldn't I want to save a few bucks? Meet you in front of my trailer in ten minutes."

Ginger drove. George sat in the passenger seat and watched the scenery, trying not to let his fantasies run wild. But he needed some fantasies now, especially after what had happened to poor Bowser. He didn't understand what Ginger was up to, but he was quite willing to follow wherever she led.

He wasn't a virgin. That had ended during his freshman year in Gainesville, thanks to the expert tutelage of the redoubtable Toxic Terry—Theresa Marques on the student register. Terry had been a senior and the most outrageous woman on campus. Overweight, orange hair, black lipstick, lots of leather. She spotted George in mid-September and took him under her wing . . . or rather, under her breasts, under every part of her. She was voracious, insatiable. She taught George all about sex and devised ingenious uses for his tentacles when the rest of him ran out of steam. He had no illusions about their relationship. There was no feeling, only mad couplings. He knew that taking the freshman freak to her bed was just one more way for Terry to thumb her nose at the society she abhorred. George didn't care. He was a horny teenager that none of the girls in high school would even date, let alone allow to first base. College had proved *very* educational.

But soon Terry lost interest in him, and so did Florida State. He spent years scrounging around until Oz found him. And now he'd found Ginger.

And they were heading for a motel.

They found a Red Roof out near the airport.

"Didn't you bring a change of clothes?" Ginger said as he unlocked the door to their room. She was carrying a blue airline bag.

"Why, uh, no. Should I?"

"You're going to get all cleaned up and then get back into the same clothes? You surprise me."

Cleaned up? George followed her into the room. He closed the door behind him as she turned on the TV and began playing with the channels. He stood staring at her.

God, she was beautiful. That skin, that upturned nose, that fine red-gold hair pulled back in a banana clip, exposing the soft length of her neck. He stepped toward her.

"You can use the shower first," she said, still flipping the channels. "Take your time but don't take *too* long because as soon as you're through I'm going to take a bath, a good long soak." She turned and looked at him. "Well, come on, George. We haven't got all day."

The shower was great. Glorious, in fact. George shampooed his hair three times and let the endless supply of hot water run over his skin until he heard the impatient knocking on the door.

"Come on, George," Ginger called. "Save some for me."

He wanted to tell her to come in and *make* him get out but decided not to risk making things awkward. He was beginning to have an idea what this was all about.

"Doesn't it feel great to be *really* clean again?" Ginger said when he emerged from the bathroom. "I do this whenever I can afford it. I get so sick of bucket baths. No matter how hard you work at it, you never feel clean."

She squeezed past him into the bathroom.

"What do I do now?"

"Sit in the A-C and watch cable TV and enjoy just being alone. When was the last time you were really alone, George?"

He almost said, *I'm always alone,* but thought it might come off too self-pitying.

"See you in an hour," she said and closed the bathroom door behind her.

George flopped back on the bed. He understood the motel trip now. Nothing sexual. Just a chance for a shower, a bath, all the hot water you could use, the opportunity to sit on a real toilet—donniker, as the folks in the show called it—and to be alone. You were never alone in the circus. Always noisy, always somebody yakking a few feet away, always crowded, always something to be done. A motel room was an island of peace and a bastion of simple civilized comforts.

George closed his eyes and reveled in the quiet.

* * *

"Wake up, sleepy head."

Someone was poking him in the ribs. George opened his eyes. Some sort of weird-looking Hindu was standing over him. He blinked. It was Ginger, swathed in a terry-cloth robe, a towel wrapped around her hair. Her cheeks glowed red from all the hot water and scrubbing.

She smiled. "I thought you were dead."

"Sorry." He sat up and rubbed his eyes. How long had he been out? Thank God he didn't have an erection.

"Nothing to be sorry about." She dropped into the chair next to the bed, loosened the towel around her head, and began rubbing her hair dry. "I was thinking while I was in the tub: I don't know a thing about you. Where were you born?"

They talked then. Really talked. He told her about his boyhood in Missouri, his talent for gymnastics, his trophies, his disappointments. Ginger in turn told him about herself, her mother's circus ties, her own history in gymnastics, her determination to get into the circus.

And as she spoke, George realized how comfortable she was with him. Too comfortable. Almost as if he were another girl.

That was it. She didn't think of him as a male, didn't seem to ascribe any sort of gender to him. He was sexless as far as she was concerned. A buddy. A pal. Maybe even a pet?

He should have been hurt, but he wasn't. He was here with her, close to her, alone in a tiny room. He'd have to resign himself to the fact that this was as good as it was going to get. Was it enough?

Yes, he decided, blocking out the dull ache of desire in his pelvis. It was enough. What choice did he have? It had to be enough.

La Cañada, California

Since his mother died, it was worse.

Theron Rawley waited in the dark for his father to come home. No windows. Locked door. The dark was all right. He wasn't afraid of emptiness, or of being alone. It was what happened in the light that scared him—what happened when his father came home.

He twisted around on the floor, rolling his long body into the cloth of the scratchy wool blanket, dragging it closer to him and curling into a kind of human nest. Trying to stay warm. Trying not to be hungry, not to think about food. Trying not to remember his mother's eyes.

He could see her sometimes against the dark screen of this room, feel her presence like a touch still holding him, and see himself in the loving gaze of her eyes. She had said he was handsome, that he had the face of an angel. She'd cared about him—the only one who ever had—promised him things would be better soon, and stood up for him against his father . . . until that night. Until that bad night.

She'd saved him . . . but what would save him now?

We're not scared, he heard his brother's voice. It wasn't like real talking; he knew it came from inside his own head, but he heard it all the same. *Not scared.*

"I am. I'm scared, Thad."

Theron and Thaddeus—those were the names his mother had picked for them before they were born. Siamese twins, she'd told him, trying to explain what that meant: how their bodies had been made together inside her, thinking and moving like one child, joined at the legs and ankles. They had never completely divided. What would have been their leg bones had fused, with Thad growing in the other direction, becoming a long body like a tail with a knob on the end, a knob that should have been Thad's head, but Thad had never been born . . . never really been born.

The deadbolt clicked open, and the door pulled wide, flooding the narrow space with light. Overhead, a bare white bulb in the ceiling switched on, blinding him in its hard cage of electric glare.

Eight hours Theron had lain awake, waiting in the black cave of this room, eight hours while his father worked as a caretaker at Descanso Gardens, the park where they lived. Now, Jack Rawley blocked the doorway, his form high and wide, barring all escape.

"Tripper!" It was the name his father called him when he was drunk, when his feet stumbled over Theron's long body as it scooted across the floor. Deliberately stumbled. It was an ugly nickname from when he was a little boy. Only Tripper wasn't little anymore; he was a grown man, twenty now. Head to tail, he was over eleven feet long—he and Thad.

Without speaking, Tripper dragged his undulating torso across the width of the room, lifting his heavy head at the threshold where his father stood. Hesitating.

"Come outta there." Jack Rawley glared down at him, the words descending like sharp blades from that hawklike face: bloodshot blue eyes, razored nose, and snapping jaws of a mouth.

"You disgust me, like some kinda snake—Jesus!"

Tripper waited for the kick. Whenever the old man had been drinking, he found an excuse to sink the toe of his work-boot into Tripper's tail. Usually, just under the gut; that was his father's favorite. It happened more and more, now. Jack Rawley was less careful—about drinking too much, about work—since Tripper's mother had . . . His father was less careful of everything.

As expected, the kick had a force of hate behind it, tearing into the softer flesh of Tripper's belly, making him choke with the sharp stump of pain rising in his gorge, and nearly knocking him onto his back. He was heavy: a large head, neck and shoulders, no arms or legs, and a two-hundred-pound torso with two sets of tiny and useless flipperlike appendages instead of hands and feet.

"Go'wan!" Jack Rawley opened the door and stood out of the way. "Get out or I'm shutting the door."

He was excited to be allowed out. There was still daylight, and he could hear the squirrels running on the grass. But if he left, would his father let him back into the house again when he came home? Would he make him curl up on the porch all night, like he had those other times?

It was cold on the porch.

"You goin', or ain'tcha?"

The temptation of freedom was too great. Tripper arched his tubular frame over the splintered doorstep and moved across the front porch, down the four entry steps, and onto the black macadam pathway leading from the groundskeeper's cottage to the connecting roads and walkways of Descanso Gardens.

The park was 165 acres of camellia garden and oak woodland. The miles of shaded forest and meadows were home to a wide variety of ducks, geese, owls, squirrels, rabbits, and fish. At five o'clock, the main gates of the garden were closed to the public. That was when Tripper was set free.

It was late June, the days long enough to hold the light past eight o'clock. Tripper loved the extra hours of sunshine and warmth, before night poured across the earth and blackened the land like spreading ink.

Take us to the mound, Thad told him.

Thad was getting scary, a lot stronger since their mother died. When she was alive, she could hold Thad back. She would stay with Theron and tell him not to listen to those thoughts in his head, not to hear what Thad told him. She made him say Thad wasn't real . . . and he said it, for her. But he knew better.

Get the Protector, Thad insisted. *We need it.*

Thad had become more demanding, lately. He spoke

all the time, told Tripper what to say, what to do. Told him they were strong, together. And Tripper had to listen. Thad was right there, inside his head. He couldn't make him go away . . . not without his mother's voice to hide the sound. He wasn't strong enough, not by himself.

Thad always said *we*, never I, or you—always *we*. He knew what they were.

"I don't like the way it makes me feel," Tripper told him, trying to hold out, but knowing what would happen. "It makes me cold inside, makes me see things."

We need it!

Thad wouldn't have dared be so strong before . . . Now, he wasn't scared of anything. Their mother was gone, and Thad was free.

Tripper had to work hard to drag himself up the hill. His face was dripping with sweat, and his body left wet marks on the ground—from the terrible effort. The hill was where they'd buried it—the Protector—up at the top of the mound, with what was left of the animal carcasses.

He was dirty and thirsty when he got to the small knoll. More than anything, Tripper wanted a cold drink, but he had to dig. The earth was soft near the top of the mound—where over the years, he'd scraped away the surface soil to hide things: childhood treasures, toys his mother had given him that he never wanted his father to see, and other things . . . other things.

The Protector was easy to reach, lying just under the first thin layer of rabbit and squirrel bones, not disturbing the deeper grave. Tripper shoved the top crust of dirt aside with a muscled push of his torso, then dug carefully with his chin and flippers through the jagged, broken skeletons.

The Protector lay beneath these remains. He'd taken it from a drawer in his mother's room long ago. It was a pretty thing, small enough to carry in his mouth, clear as glass, but prismatic, with a thousand threads of color veining through the core of it.

Pick it up, urged Thad.

With only an instant of hesitation, Tripper slipped the smooth, multisided token into his mouth. The taste, where it rested against his tongue, excited him. It was that of ice, and the salt of rabbit blood, and something else . . .

something he thought must be the sweetness of human flesh.

They savored it, together, filling themselves with the intoxicating flavors, smells, and the myriad touch of the thing. When Tripper held it inside him, he could feel his brother's body—a prisoner within his own—and sense all his brother's thoughts. With the Protector, they became truly one flesh, one mind.

With a cunning that became easier and easier to understand, it told him things: how to shield himself—themselves—from everyone, how to use the Protector to survive, how to deal with their father. When they held the Protector, their body was not the slow-moving slug their flesh had become, but was transformed into a sinuous rope, with the quick movements and hunter instincts of a snake.

The world took on new shading, in the light of the Protector. Everything Tripper saw, smelled, and tasted was different. The sky was no longer a peaceful canvas of blue ceiling and white clouds, but blossomed before his all-seeing eyes into an open plain with chasms and tunnels, hills and mountainous reaches, reminding him of Earth.

He was different, too. His body rippled with sinuous muscle, coiled and pulsing with energy—with life. He knew he wasn't ugly, like his father said, but beautiful, his shape sleek and looped with powerful curves.

The rabbits on the hill were more than soft does with gentle eyes. Now . . . he could sense their beating hearts, feel their muscles stretch and move in graceful jumps, and taste their hunger-satisfying flesh . . . even as it moved on the thin crunch of their bones . . . even as they fled in terror from him . . . even as his mouth caught and held the final quiver in their throats.

It was late night when he stopped—when the shuddering took him, and the cold. His face was sticky, something like mud was caked dry in his hair, and the taste of salt was on his lips. A bit of furred gristle was caught between his teeth. His tongue worked it loose and he spat it out. Sickened.

In front of him was the carcass of a rabbit, the

brown doe eyes still gentle in the skull. Before him was a pile of slippery, damp fur. And a trace of bones. Of bones . . .

"Mama!" he cried, shuddering harder. Scared, so scared. Remembering her eyes. Remembering the way she'd looked at him. A handsome face, she'd said. "Mama, help me!"

Our belly is full, said Thad.

"Go away. Go away!" Tripper shouted. Feeling sick. Feeling too sad to breathe, too sad to live.

Our belly is full, and we're stronger. Thad wasn't going anywhere. Thad was there inside him, listening to all his thoughts.

Tripper dropped the Protector into the small basin of dirt at the top of the mound, covered it with a lumpy layer of fur and bones, then pushed the earth around it, shaping the soft hill with the curve of his back. He covered the rabbit eyes with dirt, and the steady fall of his tears damped the shallow grave.

"Why did you do it?" he asked Thad. "It was so beautiful. So soft and—"

We were hungry, brother. Thad was weaker now, with the bright call of the Protector beneath the ground. *We wanted it,* he whispered, and then was silent.

"I never . . ." Tripper cried, cold and angry. "I never wanted this."

Even without Thad's voice covering the thoughts of his mind, Tripper knew the truth. It came to him like the chill wind, like the cold rabbit blood on his cheeks.

We, the gust of heart-pulsing sound rustled in the night. *We . . . we . . . we . . .*

He held his face in the cleansing water of the pond, before he went home.

"I didn't know what he did," Tripper said to the staring ducks. "I didn't know."

The moon shone a white radiance on the face of the water—glossy, like the cool eyes of the ducks—listening, but the tumble of words had become harder and harder to believe.

Slowly, empty of heart, and full of belly, Tripper dragged himself home.

*   *   *

From the sheltering cell of his room, he heard the throaty rumble of the engine. It stopped, just outside the house. Not his father. Not the small car Jack Rawley drove. A heavy *thunk* sound followed, and the scrape of footsteps leading to the door.

From within the black heart of the room, he heard the pounding. Unrelenting. Steady beating of the door.

"Go away, go away, go away," he begged it. The dark was not deep enough to swallow him, the cave not secret enough to hide within.

A metal *crack*, and the front door burst open. He heard it slam against the wall, felt the impact, and coiled in fear. For this, he was alone. Something moving through the house, opening doors, shoving furniture aside. He heard the terror of his own blood like a weighty hammer at his temples—*throb, throb, throb*. Alone.

The deadbolt turned and clicked back. The door to his room opened, slivering the dark like the blade of a knife. A thin track of light arrowed its way into the black, finding him.

"Aaghh!" Tripper squealed. Fear flooded his veins, his throat, his eyes. Fear caged him, like the room.

Someone would see him. Someone would know how he looked, what he was. Someone would—

The light snapped on; sharp, revealing light.

A man stood in the doorway, the cold reach of sun edging his large frame and tunneling its way across the floor. He was tall, his body extremely wide at the chest, but his arms and legs thin as narrow pipes.

Tripper didn't move. His throat seized shut; he could barely breathe. A whimper rose from him, spiraling through the close, cold air. It squealed . . . like the sound of the rabbit . . . like the desperate cry of a silent beast. Caught in that same terror, he remembered the sound. In the silence which followed, his thoughts pleaded—*Thad? What'll we do?*

"I'm sorry, you're frightened. What's your name, little brother?" the man asked. His voice was deep, crushing the weight of space between them.

He wanted to say Theron, or even Thad, but that other identity came from him before he could hold it back. "Tripper."

"Wait in the car," the man at the door said to someone behind him.

Tripper heard growls and the sound of many footsteps leading away. He thought about trying to break free, to force his way between the man and the open doorway. If he could make it to the park, he might—

"It's all right, I won't hurt you. I won't let anyone ever hurt you again." He moved farther into the room. "We share something; can you see that? Look at me, Tripper."

His escape was completely open. He could try to scoot himself around the man and through the doorway . . . but the words held him like a leash keeps a tamed pet, held him with a tether of hope.

The stranger moved closer, and his hand—a thin-edged wedge at the end of his skinny arm—reached out . . . *Don't hurt me! Don't, please don't* . . . reached out, touching Tripper's head.

"My name is Ozymandias Prather."

Oz told Tripper to fetch the Piece—the name he called the Protector—and have it ready when he came back for him. It was what he'd broken into the house to find. Carefully, Oz explained about the Device, about Otherness, and the circus . . . where he would be accepted, among family.

He wrote a note for Jack Rawley, and read it to Tripper before he left. Although he claimed to have known about Tripper, this wasn't true. He'd known about the location of the Piece. The note said nothing of that. It read: *I will be back for Tripper tomorrow,* and warned, *If anything unfortunate happens to the boy, you will face serious criminal charges with the police for a long history of child abuse.* The best part was at the end. *Tripper will be joining others of his kind at the Peabody-Ozymandias Circus.*

Others of his kind! The excitement, the way he felt hearing those words, stayed with Tripper long after Ozymandias had gone, long after Tripper had dragged himself up to the mound in broad daylight—hiding in the brush when he heard anyone nearby—and even more urgently, after he tasted the Protector, alive against his tongue. *His own kind.*

They talked about what Ozymandias had told them, worried it through, he and Thad. Tripper was afraid to do what Oz had suggested, but Thad wanted it. He wanted it bad.

Fear made Tripper weak; it always had. When he was afraid, unable to move, Thad surfaced, ready to strike. When he was afraid, Tripper Rawley became lost in Thad. Disappeared.

You remember how it was . . . when Mother came for us, Thad pressed harder on his mind.

"No." The image was too sharp, too jagged with raw edges of pain.

Remember, brother? She thought we were evil . . . that she'd put an end to what she'd started. Remember the gun? She would have killed us.

"No! Mama loved me. Mama wouldn't—"

She shot us! Thad shouted. *Remember how that felt?*

Tripper felt himself slipping, slipping into a numbing black which covered him, hid him from what he saw . . . what he knew, and remembered.

She had brought him there, asked him to come with her to the top of the mound. "You can see the whole park from here," she'd said. "This is your place, isn't it?"

He remembered looking at the spot where the mound had been, where now there was a deep hole in the earth. The Protector was nearby; her digging hadn't found that. He felt the close presence of it surge through him, making him strong, making him see things as they were, as they really were.

"Come here," Mama told him. "I have something for you."

She was standing at the edge of the pit. Her eyes were shining with wet. He moved closer, but a trembling started in him. A trembling . . .

"I love you, Theron," she said, stretching out her arm.

He thought she was leaning forward to touch him, to stroke his hair, or . . . but her hand held a gun. There was no time to wonder at it, for in that instant, a slash of brilliant pain sheared across his back. The bullet continued, and hit the trunk of the tree behind him. He heard the sound, and knew she had meant his death.

A smothering of terror encased him. "Mama!"

Away! He pulled into himself, into the dark center of them, where he could hide. In his absolute fear . . . in the nearness of the Protector . . . he felt Thad rise within them like a water snake . . . hurtling to the surface in a striking track of white anger. He knew . . . even in the dark chamber of his cell, he felt the powerful rope of their body twist around her, squeezing the last breath from her lungs.

To all, he closed his mind. When he woke later, and she was lying in the deep pit—in the grave—he knew what they had done.

We had to kill her, Thad's voice spoke to him now. His strength grew as Tripper's diminished. *She hurt us. She hated us. Hated . . . hated . . . hated!*

It was quiet and warm inside the dark place of Thad's mind. Tripper would wait here until he felt stronger. He'd been here before, those other times, when Thad killed the squirrels . . . the rabbit . . . their mother. Afterward, he'd always been able to come back. This time, he closed everything out—all memory, recognition, sight, and sound. It was peaceful in the concealing dark. No one could find him here. And no one would ever hurt him again.

"My son's insane, has multiple personalities—calls himself Thad, sometimes," Jack Rawley told the circus owner. "He can be dangerous; that's why I keep him locked up."

"Dangerous?"

Mr. Prather had come to pick up Tripper, but the boy had gotten out of the house, and was somewhere in the park. While they waited for him to return, Jack tried to explain his actions.

"You think I treat him this way because of what he is, how he looks?"

Prather didn't answer.

"It isn't just that." Jack felt his nerves crinkle up inside his skin. The kid was out there doing God knew what. Where the hell was he?

Jack moved uneasily around the room, looking out the

windows, the door. He took a couple of deep breaths and went on. "My wife saw it clear, finally; Tripper had become too hard for her, too much of a risk. I told her—I'd told her for years—but she couldn't stand the idea of putting the boy away in an institution, not with a bunch of strangers laughing at him. Never could bear people starin'. Maybe that came from her own days in the circus. She made up her mind to finish it, to stop him before . . ." His throat choked, closing together as if his air were being squeezed off by some unforgiving hand.

Prather said nothing.

"I wanted to put him away right then, but she made me promise never to do that. Made me swear on my mother's grave I'd never let people lock him up." Jack slumped into his chair. "I should have done it, anyway. Before long, he started killing things. Little animals. Digging like a dog in the sand. And then, when she tried to . . ." Rawley felt his voice metal and warp like tin on the wind.

"I can't say for sure what happened. She went walking with him one morning, and didn't come back. That's all I know. Maybe she couldn't stand it anymore. Maybe she ran off and left me with him. Or . . . maybe he killed her. His own mother—Oh, Christ!"

"Why would he do that?" The expression on Prather's face hadn't changed.

"How the hell should I know what a creature like him thinks!" Jack Rawley's eyes hurt, feeling swollen and hard with anger. "He's not human; I know that."

"No." Prather stood and crossed to the door. At the threshold, he turned. "I'll be back in three hours for Tripper. Have him ready."

"If you take him," Rawley shouted, "you don't bring him back, hear? You don't never bring him back!"

Prather opened the door and got in beside the driver of an old Mercedes. Jack saw him, staring back at the house, his slack face and neck framed by the margins of the window—unreadable.

"When your son leaves here," Prather said in final words to Rawley, "there will be no reason for him to come back."

The car drove away, the sound of its tires scraping on the pebble and shale access road. Jack Rawley picked up a stone and threw it after the retreating back window. The rock fell short of its mark and Rawley's arm dropped to his side, the fuse of his anger falling well short of its mark, too.

Thad watched from behind the high brush, across the road. He had seen Ozymandias leave and wanted to go with him, but he wasn't ready . . . not quite yet. With the Protector firmly clamped between his teeth, he shot out across the rough macadam drive, gliding over the cool, sweet-scented grass, hurrying, wriggling like an eel, and slipped his way into the still open door of the house.

It was nearing dark when the Mercedes returned to the groundskeeper's cottage. The lights were off in the house. That didn't surprise Oz.

"Wait here," he told Petergello.

Oz got out, walked across the lawn, and climbed the four steps to the front porch. He didn't knock. The door was unlocked, slightly open. He knew it would be.

"I'm coming inside." His voice was calm and kind. "It's all right. Don't be afraid." He opened the door, and stepped into the dark.

The smell of savage death saturated the room. It had a copper odor, sharp, cloying. He breathed it in. "I'm turning on the light."

Against the far corner of the room, the snake-boy sat coiled and ready to strike, his head held high above smooth loops of his body, slowly moving, weaving side-to-side. His cheeks were a wet sheen, his body glazed red and slick with blood.

"Tripper, you can come with me now. It's all right. I know what you've done. I understand, little brother." Oz stepped carefully over the savaged carcass. There were black ruby holes where Jack Rawley's face and throat had been. The body was twisted and broken, as if it had been squeezed in a giant vise.

"Stay back!" the snake-boy hissed, moving closer to Oz.

"Tripper?" Prather backed up, unsure.

"He's gone. Too afraid. Thad's the one. Thad's the one."

Prather stood his ground and waited while Thad entwined himself around his legs, his body. He felt the snake-boy's muscles inch their way around his waist, twisting higher . . . higher . . . until they were face to bloody face.

"Wanted to say hello," said Thad, his glassy eyes glittering in the light.

"I had thought to take you to dinner, but perhaps you won't be needing a meal after all," Oz told him, glancing down at what was left of Jack. "Let me help you clean yourself up, Thad, and then I'll take you home. The others are waiting, anxious to meet you."

"Not in a cage . . ." said Thad, still holding Prather in an iron grip.

"No." Oz didn't flinch. He felt the vise grip tighten, a closing fist, but he didn't try to pull away. "Locked doors are for animals. I don't put members of my family in a cage."

The brown-black eyes blinked. Slowly, Thad released his hold. His body slid down the length of Oz's, like sloughing off an old layer of skin.

"I'll need the Piece," Ozymandias reminded Thad. They were at the front door of the Rawley house, ready to leave. "That was our bargain, remember?"

Thad held the Protector in his mouth, the taste of it singing through him in chords of light. He wasn't afraid. Nothing scared him, anymore.

"I'll take you home with me. You'll love it with the others," Oz promised, ". . . after you give me the Piece. You'll have to give it up for now, but when the Device is complete, the power will be there for all of us."

"Tell me again about the circus." Thad made no move to release the Protector. His tongue slipped around it, caressing the edges. Loving. He knew its strength, savored it.

"It's right here in town—in La Cañada—at a place called Oak Grove Park."

Thad had lived in this city for twenty years, but hadn't known the name. He'd never seen any other park. "And the others? What did you call them?"

"I told you about Claude; you'll like him. There's

Carmella, and lots of others. You'll be among friends, Tripper."

Thad allowed Oz to use that name. It was who he was now—who they were, he and Theron—Tripper Rawley, the Snake-Boy. Oz said he would have an act, that people would come to the circus to see him. He would be like the other freaks, Mother Goose, or Gore, or Mitts; those were the names he remembered.

He wanted to meet them, wanted to leave this place and see the city, and the circus . . . but hesitated. "Will there be squirrels at the other park?" he asked.

"Oh—yes, I think there will," Ozymandias told him, reaching a hand out to brush the long hair out of Tripper's eyes. "You don't have to worry, little brother. No one will ever starve you again. We're your real family, understand? You belong with us, Tripper, and we'll take care of you. You have my promise."

Thad's eyes were circles of brimming wet when he dropped the Protector at Prather's feet.

"That's fine." Oz reached for it, quickly scooping the Piece into his hand, and dropping it into the inside pocket of his coat. He opened the front door and led the way down the porch steps, and to the waiting car.

Thad followed.

Fool!

Thad's head turned sharply, looking behind him.

He's got the power, now. Can't you feel it?

"Theron?" Thad was scared. It was Theron's voice coming to him, talking inside his head.

Don't trust him too much, Thad. Don't trust anyone— but me. I'm coming with you.

"No!"

"What?" Ozymandias turned and stared questioningly at Thad. "Something wrong?"

Don't tell him. He's not part of us. You're getting weaker, Thad. You needed the Protector. I'll have to help you, brother.

Thad shook his head, but couldn't make Theron go away.

It's all right. Don't be afraid. I'm coming back.

"Are you coming?" Oz called to him. The door to the

car was open. A new world of freedom was open to him, too.

Thad moved slowly, dragging his sluglike body over the rough stone walkway. Inside him, the chords of song from the Protector were gone. Another sound had intruded.

With the whisper of his twin brother alive in his mind, Tripper Rawley, the Snake-Boy, left the house where he had spent the first twenty years of his life a prisoner, and at last . . . headed for home..

MORGAN FIELDS

The show rolled on . . .

ALONG THE MIDWAY (VIII)

Clackamas County, Oregon

Oz sighed with relief as Virginia Bone squeezed her doughy girth through the door and exited his trailer. She was gone but her sour effluvium remained, like the refrain from an old song. Small wonder why the other members of the troupe disliked her—she was as unpleasant on the inside as she was on the outside. But she had a right to be bitter, more bitter than the rest of them. After all, who else in the troupe was perpetually, parthenogenetically pregnant? Virgie gave birth several times a day. Her newborn children, always deformed, could run around like squirrels and obey her mental commands. But only for a few minutes. Then they died. Perhaps that was the source of her bitterness. She said she mourned the passing of her countless children, but Oz wondered—it didn't stop her from bottling their remains in alcohol and selling them to a concern in Del Rio, Texas, for twenty-five dollars apiece.

Whatever her true feelings, Oz had promised her that once the Device was operational, all her children would survive.

He almost hoped that wasn't true.

But Virgie was now responsible for acquiring the next Piece during their upcoming stop near the Boeing plant outside Seattle. She was vaguely acquainted with the man who currently possessed it and Oz had given her strict instructions to get the Piece *quietly*. Ask for it, *buy* it. At all costs avoid attracting any official attention.

He shook his head sadly. They'd had to keep Mr. Tane hidden away during all their stops since the Los Angeles debacle. Not that Tane cared. He was in a black depression since the loss of Bowser. Too bad. But strange how things work out: An old member of the troupe dies as a new one joins.

Petergello entered then. He fanned his hand before his face. "Virgie?"

Oz nodded. "The one and only."

"I keep leaving bars of soap on her doorstep but she doesn't get the hint."

"Did you drop off fresh tobacco for Peabody?"

Petergello grinned. "He sends his thanks. He's totally malleable now. If you suggested driving the circus off the edge of the Grand Canyon, he'd think it was a marvelous idea."

"And how's our friend George doing?" Oz said.

Petergello fluttered his hand over his heart. "Hopelessly in love. *Unrequited* love."

"Is there any other kind? How long before he confesses his feelings, do you think?"

"And takes the Big Fall?" Petergello scratched his head. "Before Chicago, I'd say."

"That soon? No, I think George is shy enough to wait until we get into the Northeast. I'll say Massachusetts. Bet?"

"You're on," Petergello said.

They shook hands.

Seattle, Washington

Mrs. Ortiz had a weak bladder, and it got the better of her about halfway through her counseling hour. Whining an apology, which Sullivan graciously waved away, she gripped her tripodal steel cane and levered herself to her feet. He waited for her to hobble out the office door, then scrambled around the desk, snatched her purse off her chair, and dumped the contents on his blotter.

He passed over the gold compact. It was expensive, but the old fossil had bought it for herself only a year ago, so it wouldn't have much sentimental value. He popped open her worn brown leather wallet, flipped past her identification and credit cards to the ancient black-and-white snapshots she'd shown him a hundred times, and found the baby picture of her oldest daughter. It was one of her favorites; she'd be horrified when she noticed it was "lost," and grateful to the tune of a few hundred bucks minimum when the spirits found it for her. He began to draw it from its plastic sleeve, and then a floorboard creaked in the hallway behind him.

Jesus Christ, she'd never made it to the shitter and back in under eight minutes before! But there was no reason to panic; as long as he kept his cool, she'd believe any ridiculous thing he told her. He turned, not convulsively, not guiltily, but *casually*, then blinked in surprise. It wasn't Mrs. Ortiz back after all, but the most pregnant woman he'd ever seen. Her distended belly virtually filled the doorway; her stumpy, doughy limbs and her round head with its wide, thin-lipped mouth and broad, flat nose seemed almost vestigial.

Sullivan felt himself relax a little. She surely wasn't a cop, not working in the field in what must be her ninth month, not with that dandruffy, uncombed hair, not dressed in a mustard- and pizza-stained muumuu and holey sneakers. He smiled, making no effort to hide the rifled bag. "Good afternoon, dear lady. May I help you?"

For a moment, she didn't answer, just leaned sideways to peer around him at the polished cherry desk, the gleaming leather chairs and couch, the framed celebrity photos with their forged inscriptions, and the oil paintings of Jesus, Mary, and various lamas, yogis, and Indian braves that adorned the office, as if she were looking for something in particular. Her gaze lingered on the file cabinet, where he stored his props, and for some reason he shivered, was suddenly glad he kept it locked. "Classy setup," she finally rasped. "Bet you like this better than being a stick, or doing your magic act, or any of the other things you done when you was on the road."

He frowned. "I'm Reverend John Sullivan, the pastor of this church. I think you have me confused with someone else."

She grinned, exposing irregular yellow teeth. "Save it, Jackie. I'm a carny, too. My name's Virgie Bone, and my family was with Geraghty Brothers the same time you was there. Course I've changed, so I don't blame you for not remembering me." Her stomach twitched, and she clutched at it. "Look, I got to sit down."

"Actually, I'm in the middle of counseling a parishioner . . ."

She waddled to Mrs. Ortiz's chair, dropped into it with a grunt, interlaced her hands protectively on top of her midsection. He winced at the stink of her, a smell compounded of cigarette smoke and BO. "This doesn't have to take long. I want the red egg."

He suppressed another shudder, then felt annoyed at his timidity. It was weird that she even knew about the thing, let alone wanted it, but there was still no reason to feel so spooked; after all, she couldn't just *take* it. He raised his eyebrows. "Red egg?"

Virgie grimaced. "Do we have to play games? I traced it to you. A zillion people have seen it here. You use it as a lamp in your séances."

"Oh, my *focus.* I couldn't possibly part with that. My astral guides—"

"Come on, Jackie, I'm not one of your spiritualist marks. And I don't expect you to *give* it away." She rooted in her pocket, produced a crumpled pack of Camels and then a wad of bills. "Seven hundred, all the money I got in the world."

The sight of the cash dispelled the last of his jitters; now it was time to go to work. Maybe she wasn't a mark when she operated her hanky-panky or flat store or whatever the hell she did, but she was on *his* lot now. He pretended to consider. "Well . . . all right, sure. But I don't keep it here in the church. Can you come back around six?"

She lipped a Camel out of the pack. "I don't guess you'd try to sell me a ringer, you being a *minister* and all. But maybe I ought to mention that I know what the thing's like. Glassy, smooth, and round, but it's got like invisible blades, and it can cut you if you grab it wrong. It looks like it ought to be cold and hard, but most of it feels warm and rubbery. It—"

He wondered if he could show her the real egg, put it in a box or a bag, and then switch packages. No, she'd never fall for it. He sighed. "Okay, I guess you really aren't a sucker. Sorry, but the thing just isn't for sale." Certainly not for a lousy seven bills, and she sure didn't look like she was good for any more. "Give my regards to carnival land."

She lit her cigarette with a plastic lighter, took a drag. Her belly quivered, and she patted it. "There, there, dumplin', it's only smoke, it can't hurt you. Look, Jackie, I *need* your fucking egg."

"Yeah? What for?"

She blinked, screwed up her face, and after a second he realized she was trying to cry. The effort made her even homelier. "All I want in the world is to be a mommy," she blubbered, "and my babies always die. But if I can get your dingus, maybe they won't."

"What, somebody's going to buy it, and give you enough money to have an operation?"

"No, it's nothing like that, I need it to keep."

He started putting Mrs. Ortiz's purse back together.

"Yeah, right, I suppose Jesus told you this in a vision. Level with me, why do you really want it?"

"I can't explain, but I swear, I'm telling the truth." She snuffled, then knuckled her nose and eyes.

He shrugged. "Fine, stick to your story, but it wouldn't help even if I believed you. Why would I care about your problems?"

Her mournful expression twisted into a snarl. "I don't guess you would. So get this: If you don't sell me the egg nice and easy, you're really gonna be sorry."

"Right," he sneered, "I hear you, and I'm shaking." But, absurd though it was, he realized he *was* uneasy again. Well, he supposed it was never fun to be threatened, even by some bimbo so bloated she could hardly stand, let alone do anything to hurt him. He picked up his phone. "Now are you going to get out of here, or should I call somebody to drag you out?"

"I'll go." Groaning, she struggled up out of her chair. "But this ain't over."

He followed her to the front door, locked it behind her, watched her through a window. She crossed Pike Street by the fish market, lumbered past the used-books store, and collapsed on the wrought-iron bench at the bus stop. By the time he escorted Mrs. Ortiz out, she was gone.

Gone, but he found he couldn't stop thinking about her, perhaps because her odor still hung in the air. Eventually he decided she must want the egg because she hoped to go into the medium racket herself. But how could she know what the thing actually did?

He'd stumbled on it, a rounded, fist-size object casting an anomalously jagged shadow, in one of the neighborhood's ratty little antique stores. It looked so odd he had bought it to use as stage dressing, then fortuitously discovered that if he touched it to a flame, it would emit a shimmering crimson light for several hours afterward.

That radiance not only looked impressively eerie, it baffled the eye. It seemed bright enough that no medium working inside its light could move a muscle without somebody noticing, but in reality it hardly provided any illumination at all. Sullivan sneaked around his séance room as easily as other spiritualists prowled around in total darkness.

The gimmick had made him one of the hottest spook wranglers in the Northwest, and he meant to hang on to it no matter what this Bone bitch tried to pull, not that he believed she'd really do anything more than threaten him. People like her were losers, scum, otherwise they'd find a ticket out of the crummy gillies like he had.

Later he ate supper, boliche, yellow rice, and black beans with onions, in the Spanish restaurant on the corner, prepared for the evening's séance, then parked himself in the vestibule to wait for the marks. Predictably, Mrs. Ortiz showed up first; she'd just live in the church if she could. Then squat, balding Frank Grimaldi, one of Puget Sound's richest real estate developers and the chairman of the church's board of directors. Sullivan had selected him for the latter eminence because he consistently donated more than any other sucker.

"Reverend!" he boomed, his breath smelling faintly of rum. "How you doing? How are the vibrations tonight?"

"I'll see," Sullivan said. He lifted one hand to his temple, knowing they'd track the motion, and simultaneously slipped the other hand into his pocket, took out a paper rosebud, and tossed it into the air. The marks gasped; to them, the flower seemed to tumble out of nowhere. He stooped and picked it up off the floor, presented it to Mrs. Ortiz. "Well, I guess that answers that question. The spirits are here already."

The door creaked open again. He turned to greet the rest of his pigeons, but the words caught in his throat.

Paul and Maxine Ryan *had* arrived, but they were clinging solicitously to Virgie Bone's flabby forearms, more or less holding her up. The carny had scoured the flakes out of her hair, scraped the stink and greasy sheen off her skin, and traded the grubby garments she'd worn that afternoon for a voluminous pink maternity gown with a lacy white collar and a pair of pink plastic flats. She simpered, then lowered her eyes demurely.

"The most wonderful thing has happened," prattled Maxine, her voice even shriller than usual. "This girl has seen a *vision!*"

"A vision of *Jesus*," Virgie cooed. At least it sounded like she was trying to coo, though actually it was more of a croak. "I was just walking down the midway—I'm in a circus—and I saw Him floating over the donniker. He told me to come to this address and ask to sit in a Reverend Sullivan's séance, so the spirits could bless my babies."

Sullivan opened his mouth to order her out, then reconsidered. He wouldn't look very compassionate, very *holy,* if he bounced an expectant mother who claimed she'd been sent by Christ, and if he tried, she'd probably retaliate by denouncing him as a phony. He didn't think the marks would believe her, but he'd rather not put it to a test.

On the other hand, she might be planning to spoil or expose his tricks to pressure him, or simply get revenge. But he knew how to guard against that. Worse, she might try to snatch the egg, but she was scarcely in any condition to fend him off if he had to wrest it back. If he waited till she created a disturbance, he could kick her out with impunity, because at that point the suckers would be too pissed to listen to a word she said.

He decided to let her stay. "Goodness," he said, "that *is* wonderful. Let's go to the séance room and begin."

The rubber-shod feet of Mrs. Ortiz's cane thumped along the floor. "What do you do in the circus?" she asked.

"A stunt," Virgie replied. "It's nothing other women can't do, but I do it different. On cue, a bunch of times every day."

Sullivan wondered what she was talking about. He'd figured her for a jointee, not a performer. Even cleaned up, she had all the charm of a mound of dog turds.

His regal fan chair stood on a dais, and the glowing egg sat on the oval table in front of it. Virgie stiffened when she saw it.

Eat your heart out, Sullivan thought. He moved a fifth

chair up to the table and seated her between Ryan and Grimaldi. "Let me explain how this works," he said. "You'll all join hands, to generate a current of energy the spirits can use to manifest themselves. It's important that no one break the circle, except when I say you can. Otherwise we might lose contact and not be able to get it back." *And good luck fucking me over with two strong men holding down your arms.*

To his surprise, she grinned at him. "Got you, Rev. No problem." She took the men's hands, slumped back in her chair, and spread her legs apart.

He felt another chill and angrily shrugged it off. So what if she was humongous, ugly, and creepy; he was damned if he'd let her psych him out. He strode to his own chair, sat down, and twisted the rheostat knob built into its arm.

The cut-glass chandelier dimmed and went dark; the egg seemed to shine brighter. As usual, Sullivan *felt* that he could see almost as well as before. He had to concentrate to perceive that Virgie and the marks had faded to shadows swimming in a dim red haze.

He led them in a prayer, and, secure in the knowledge that they could no longer make him out inside the fan chair, slipped on a hood and gloves as black as his suit and shirt. Next he did a little groaning; he'd found that suckers appreciated the manifestations more if they thought the medium had to strain to crap them out. Then he ducked out of his chair and off the dais.

Even though he couldn't quite shake his jitters, it was still a hoot to be invisible again. He jingled a bell over Mrs. Ortiz's head, stroked her pruny cheek. She jumped, then giggled. After that he took out his atomizer, spritzed some lilac scent into the air. And then he circled the table chattering greetings, constantly changing his voice, creating the illusion that a *slew* of ghosts had appeared in the room.

The parishioners clamored in response, each eager to talk to dead friends and relatives, their personal Master Teachers, and other pet phantasmal personalities. Sullivan decided to open with a bang, by trotting out the son the Ryans had lost in a boating accident a year ago, a spirit he'd supposedly never managed to "locate" before.

He turned his back and drew a chiffon mask and tapered, ankle-length bib out of his shirt, unfolded them and slipped them on. When he spun around, the gauzy silk would gleam in the crimson light, and the marks would think an ectoplasmic figure had popped out of nowhere.

Virgie grunted. Something squelched, then thudded twice. An instant later, Maxine squealed.

Sullivan sidled back toward the fan chair, so the medium's voice would come from the right direction. "What happened?"

"Something bumped my foot," Maxine quavered.

"Is the circle intact?"

"Yes," Grimaldi said.

"Then perhaps it was just a shy spirit's way of saying hello," Sullivan told them. "At any rate, I'm sure everything's all right." He didn't understand why or how Virgie had produced the squishing sound—maybe it was just her guts gurgling—or what she hoped to accomplish by kicking and stomping, but he was reasonably certain that that alone couldn't do any real damage. And if she kept it up, the marks would catch her.

He edged away from the dais again, his back still to the table, and jumped when something rustled. It sounded like it was right behind him, but of course that wasn't possible; it was probably somebody's shoe scuffing around under the table.

He pivoted, drew a breath to say, "Hi, Mom, hi, Dad," and something seized his ankle.

He staggered several steps, struggling desperately to keep his balance. The monkey, or whatever Virgie had sicced on him, he couldn't tell in the dimness, scrabbled at him, tearing his pant leg and sock and then his skin. "Oh, look!" Mrs. Ortiz cried. "That spirit's dancing!"

Sullivan finally booted the animal away and immediately lost sight of it in the darkness. He heard it mewl, then start to creep. He was rattled, but not enough to forget that he had to keep the marks believing he was a ghost. Since he no longer wanted the Ryans going nuts with joy, not right at the moment, he decided to be White Deer, his principal assistant on the other side. He tried to gutturalize, the way the fictitious Arapaho usually spoke, but it came out as more of a wheeze. "That'um right. White Deer do dance of welcome."

Then suddenly the animal was at his feet again. It grabbed the end of his bib, yanked him to one knee, and started climbing his body. Its lower half seemed to be all tail, a broad, flat, thrashing appendage that was slapping him in the stomach. Its hairless skin was slick with a rancid slime.

He fought to keep it out of his face, wished to God he could make out what it *was*. What kind of animal had arms but no legs?

Its tail nearly clipped him in the balls; he struck it a glancing backhand blow. It shocked him by screaming something very like a human shriek, squirmed even more frantically, then went limp in his grasp.

Panting, he dropped it and peered up at the table. The egg was still there, the circle of hands unbroken, but the suckers were craning and yammering questions. He wanted to collapse on the carpet and snivel, or better still, beat Virgie Bone over the head with the little beast's carcass. Although his bruises and scratches were twinging, sweat was stinging in his eyes, and his chiffon bib was tattered, he dragged himself to his feet to reassure the idiots who paid the bills instead.

He was sure they'd glimpsed the animal, but equally sure they hadn't seen it clearly; hell, he still hadn't seen it clearly himself. White Deer could tell them they'd been watching a friendly ectoplasmic wrestling match, two rambunctious spirits cavorting together, and the scream was just a joyous Indian war whoop. Then—

The chandelier lit up.

Sullivan cackled, suddenly convinced that he was dreaming or delirious, that none of this could actually be happening. No one could smuggle in *two* monkey-sized animals when she wasn't even carrying a purse, release them without using at least one hand, and direct one to find and turn a rheostat control in a dark and unfamiliar room without even speaking.

Ryan goggled at the dais, murmured, "Shit!" The pint-size, bat-eared cyclops in the fan chair waved its arms and chortled.

Grimaldi, Maxine, and Mrs. Ortiz didn't notice it; they

were busy gaping at Sullivan. The older woman said, "Reverend, it's *you!*"

Virgie was looking at him, too. She leered, then groaned and squinched her flushed, sweaty face. Her belly juddered, and her thighs spread even wider. And then it all came clear. When he realized what she was doing, how she'd done everything, it jolted the giddiness right out of him.

Grimaldi stood up. "You goddamn fake."

"I can explain everything," Sullivan babbled, ripping off his headgear, bib, and gloves. "It was all part of a trap to catch this woman. She's *possessed,* makes *monster babies,* cranks them out like an assembly line and then they do any awful, evil thing she wants. Just look over—"

It was about as close as he'd ever come to telling a mark the truth, and he was shocked when Grimaldi raised his fist. As he hastily stepped back, he heard another squelch, then felt the vibration when something else plopped onto the floor. The new baby, green, scaly, and ten-legged, shot out from under the table, hissed, and, perhaps because it had misunderstood its instructions, darted up the would-be assailant's body and sank its fangs into his cheek.

Grimaldi reeled, howling and trying to fling the creature off. The other marks shrieked, leaped up, and scrambled backward.

Virgie's arm shot out to seize the egg, but she couldn't quite reach it; her belly kept her from leaning forward. Sullivan shoved Maxine out of his way, lunged, and grabbed it.

Unfortunately, he'd forgotten about the invisible blades. His fingers spasmed and the thing tumbled out of his hand to roll clattering across the tabletop. Virgie crowed and scooped it up, heaved her bulk up out of her chair and joined the general stampede for the exit.

He started after her, tripped on something, banged his elbow on the edge of the table as he plummeted to the floor. Still chortling, the cyclops baby wrapped its arms around his legs.

He couldn't kick or pound it loose, but after half a minute its chuckle turned into a rattle. Its arms tightened convulsively, then relaxed.

He sprang to his feet, ran, stumbled over the corpse of the green baby and nearly fell again. At the end of the hall, Mrs. Ortiz was just gimping into the vestibule. The front door stood open.

He dashed past her, out onto the concrete steps. The other marks were scurrying for their cars, but he didn't see Virgie. He clenched his fists, spiking pain through his lacerated palm. How had she gotten away so fast?

Then he smiled. It was obvious: she hadn't. She couldn't move much faster than Mrs. Ortiz, and the old bag hadn't even made it outside yet. She must be hiding in the building, hoping he'd run off on a snipe hunt. He stepped back inside and jerked Mrs. Ortiz's cane out of her hand, spilling her against the stand supporting the poor box, then stalked into the sanctuary.

As he slunk toward the front of the vaulted chamber, he kept glancing downward, kept the steel stick cocked at his shoulder, but no lurking infant appeared. Perhaps the supply had finally run out.

Red light glinted on the pulpit. A moment later Virgie hauled herself up from behind the altar, the egg glowing in her right hand. "All right, Sherlock, you found me. So what're you gonna do now, knock my brains out?"

He paced toward her, still checking the floor: There was still nothing crawling, scuttling, or slithering around. "I'm thinking about it. You and your little freaks just wrecked the sweetest setup I ever had. But you know what? I can live with it, because you didn't *win*. When I pull out of here, I'm taking the egg with me."

She smirked and shook her head. "No way, so you might as well lighten up. I mean, fuck, we're both carnies, ain't we? Brother and sister. Two of a kind. Now that you see how things are, you ought to feel sorry for me."

He decided he actually was going to kill her. He swung the cane over his head, bellowed, and charged.

Overhead, something buzzed. He looked up, spied a baby with a normal head and a shiny black torso clinging to the ceiling. Just as he spotted it, it dropped.

It smashed into him, knocking him down, wrapped its six spindly limbs around his head and ground its acrid, chitinous thorax against his face. A white-hot needle jabbed into his shoulder.

His body went numb, and the cane slipped out of his fingers. When he tried to pull the infant off his head, he discovered he couldn't move.

Virgie picked the child up and cuddled it, crooned baby talk and kissed it. The thing buzzed and goo-gooed happily for a minute, then retched and convulsed. When it stopped thrashing, she tucked it under her arm, kicked Sullivan in the ribs, and lumbered out.

At first he was afraid he was paralyzed for life, but eventually his hands and feet started to tingle, and he found that if he strained he could make them twitch. He floundered around for a while, finally managed to sit up, and then two bunco cops and an animal control officer came in and arrested him..

RICHARD LEE BYERS

The show rolled on . . .

ALONG THE MIDWAY (IX)

Sweetwater County, Wyoming

Oz hovered over the tiny table in his back room. The Device was taking shape now. Still a long way to go, but he'd been able to interlock five of the Pieces. He compared the construct seated on the platform before him to one of his father's old photographs. Yes. Some of the larger supporting elements were missing, but it looked right.

Now . . . the test.

He rotated the copper cup, swirling the melted residue of another chip off the frozen contents of one of Malaleik's onyx boxes, then poured it over the assembled Pieces and the loose extras. As he had so many times before, Oz watched the thick liquid run over their surfaces, steaming as it began to evaporate. Once again he was ready for another in a long series of disappointments.

That was why he thought it was a trick of the light when a shimmer ran over the surface of the uppermost Piece. He leaned closer. It happened again. The shimmer spread, rippling down over the other Pieces, even the ones that were not interlocked with the central five, dancing over the bubbling surface of the liquid pooled on the top of the platform.

Suddenly light blazed from the Device. Oz squinted into the brightness—pale violet light suffused the tiny room, shadows moved around the Device—and then with a soft *pop* like air rushing to fill a vacuum, the light was gone.

Oz blinked at the Device, at the dried residue of the liquid, and squeezed his fists so tightly his arms trembled to the shoulders.

"Yes!" he said softly. *"Yes!"*

Elm Haven, Illinois

Night has always been, for me, the only gentle time. Night is the Forgiver and the Acceptor. Night is the time to stir abroad and to walk the empty streets of our small and dying town. I sometimes dream of Night being a sister to me in my suffering; I hear her consoling whispers in the summer shuffle of leaves above the shadowed walks and imagine her lullaby in the slide of snow on snow during the long winter dark.

But most often, Night seems a parent to me. She is the mother who takes the place of the one who abandoned me three days after my birth; he is the father who replaces the one who died or disappeared the week before that birth. Night is the coddling parent who rocks me with its breezes, breathes on me with its warm summer fragrances, and who conceals me from all the cruel and curious eyes.

I only go out at night. The people in our little town—this dying little town—know the scrape and shuffle of my dragging walk. They know the tap of my cane along the dark pitches of tilted sidewalks between the streetlights. They know the rasp of my breathing and the rustle of my beekeeper's veil. They know my stench.

They do not fear me. No one locks their doors at my approach. I am part of their town and a piece of their night. Sometimes there will appear a pale face at a window as I lurch by in the not-quite-shrouded dimness of a late summer twilight, but the face is always as familiar to me as my veiled countenance is to them, and more often than not I will receive a wave and a smile.

I wave back with my good hand, my uncloaked hand. But I do not smile beneath my veil.

And then, one mid-August night in this summer just past, everything changes. Everything.

Old Settlers Weekend is, I think, as old as our town of Elm Haven, Illinois. I have seen photographs that go back to just after the Civil War. Old Settlers has always fallen on this same weekend in August—in the heart of summer but close enough to its end that generations of Elm Haven's children have taken the weekend carnival as the last knell of freedom before the descent of school, hard weekends of work in the harvest-rich fields, and winter, and the end of everything that childhood is about.

So I was not surprised in the dark hours of a late-Thursday, early-Friday night to see the colored lights and to hear the shouts of roustabouts from just beyond our sheltering ring of city trees. The Old Settlers carnival was being set up—as it always was—in the fields north of town and east of First Avenue, out in the meadows beyond the city baseball diamond and overgrown football field, between the water tower and the town.

I dragged and scraped my dead leg and misshapen foot down Depot Street to the abandoned Somerset place, through the overgrown yard reeking of wisteria gone wild, and then over a sagging fence—tugging my cloak and veil away from brambles and wire—and finally out into the field where the carnival was being erected. The bright lights had been extinguished now, the generators were silent, and only starlight and the gleam from a waning moon illuminated the pale canvas of tents being raised and the paler sheen of skin on the bare backs of roustabouts laboring to raise them. The carny rides already had been set into place, the dark shapes of the Ferris wheel and Mad Mouse looking like metal gallows designed by madmen. The tents were rising quickly. I stood there in the predawn chill and listened to the hollow thud

of great mallets pounding stakes deep into the chest of
our Illinois earth.

This was not the Old Settlers I had known for almost
three decades. Usually, Old Settlers Weekend is cele-
brated with fish fries and fireworks and baseball tourna-
ments and water fights between our local volunteer fire-
men. The three huge tents always belonged to the
JayCees, the American Legion, and the WCTU. Two of
the big tents sold beer and food, the third only food and
soft drinks.

The carnival itself was a smaller, secondary thing,
usually consisting of a three-ride midway and half a dozen
smaller tents where our citizens could lose their money at
the ring toss or shooting galleries or Guess-Your-Weight
or other pleasant silliness.

But not this year.

This year the tents and rides and booths and sideshow
trucks filled the meadow and lopped over onto the dusty
football field. The main tent was larger than the three-pole
American Legion tent that had always dominated Old
Settlers. The rides were bigger, more dangerous looking.
The game booths filled a hundred yards of grassy avenue
like the midway of a real circus.

This *was* a real circus. I could hear large animals
breathing and smell their reek over my own stench. Somewhere in the huddle of dark trucks at the far end of the
field, an elephant trumpeted softly. A second later a lion
or tiger or some other big cat coughed.

I felt goose bumps rise along the skin on my normal
arm. I moved forward from shadow to shadow until I was
in among the long trucks. I ran my hand—my cloaked and
deformed hand—over the baroque letters of the painted
sign along the trailer's side: Peabody-Ozymandias Traveling Circus and Oddity Emporium.

The words seemed charged with electricity. I felt what
little hair I had rising along my deformed brow and the
fingers on my good hand twitched as if from palsy.

There was movement in the shadows. Gasping more
loudly than usual, almost unable to hold my head erect in
the dizziness that suddenly assailed me, I crouched low,
pulled my veil tighter inside the neck of my cloak, and
scrabbled for the darkness of the overhanging trees. But

other shapes moved faster, dodging between cab and trailer, between tent and sideshow booth. Men's deep voices set up a hue and cry.

Panting, wheezing, my lungs full of liquid and my bad leg dragging, I lurched around a dark corner of a truck and began scraping toward the dark row of trees thirty yards south.

Two men were on me in a second.

"Jesus," said the first. "What's that stink?"

"What the fuck . . ." said the second, and ripped away my beekeeper's hat and veil. I winced at the fresh air.

Both men stepped back. One raised a bare forearm to his mouth and nose. "Hey, Nolan!" shouted the first man.

A third man appeared. Even in the dim moonlight I could see the muscles on his thick upper body, the blood-red slash of bandana tied around his head.

"Look at this, willya?" said the first roustabout. "I never seen one of the freaks tryin' to sneak *into* the show before. You believe this shit?" He leaned lower and tugged loose my cloak. The second roustabout stepped farther back and made a gagging sound.

"He looks like a melted candle made outta lizard skin or something," said the first roustabout. "Makes ol' Tripper Rawley look like Tom Cruise, don't he?"

"Shut up," said the man named Nolan. He gestured toward the second roustabout. "Take him to Prather."

I closed my eyes and did not resist as they lifted and carried me back into the maze of canvas and steel.

Despite the late hour, the man they called Prather was awake and at the table in his trailer, looking toward the door as if expecting me. He waved the two roustabouts away and then gestured me toward a chair. I did not sit. Regular chairs are difficult for me.

"My name is Ozymandias Prather," said the big man in a voice that sounded as if it were being boosted by microphone and amplifier. The light was dim in the trailer, but even so I could see a certain slackness in the large man's face that did not seem to match the energy in his voice. The muscles of that face twitched into a smile. "My friends call me Oz," he said.

I blinked. The roustabouts had tossed my beekeeper's

hat onto the floor of the trailer and I longed to put it on, but bending and lifting it would be too awkward in front of Mr. Prather. I pulled my cloak as tight as I could and backed away from the lamplight.

"No," said Mr. Prather. It was a command. I stood still in the light. "What is your name?" he asked softly.

I did not answer. Few could understand my speech— Old Sook could, but she was dead; Father O'Rourke could, but he was not here.

"What is your name, brother?" Mr. Prather said. The "brother" startled me. The big man looked to be in his early or midforties; I was thirty-one. But the word had come easily enough to him and it still echoed in my consciousness. *Brother.*

"Benjamin Willis Ashley-Montague," I muttered, knowing that he would not catch a clear syllable of it.

"Well, Benjamin Willis Ashley-Montague," said Ozymandias Prather with a smile, "we'll have to come up with a shorter version of that or we'll both be worn-out just saying each other's names. What do you say I'll be Oz and you'll be Benjamin?"

I could only blink stupidly. *He had understood me.*

"Don't move, Benjamin," said Mr. Prather as he rose quickly, pulling me slightly toward him. "No, no, it's all right. I just want to see you in the light."

I winced as he came so close, and watched his eyes and nostrils, waiting for the usual narrowing and flaring as he saw my deformed flesh, smelled my fungous stench. His slack face showed no reaction. His hands were firm but impersonal as they moved over my bulbous skull, the terrible proboscis-shelf that was my cheek and upper lip, the wattles of tumorous reptile flesh beneath my neck and above my chest.

Finally, he stepped back. "Do you know the cause of your condition, Benjamin?"

I nodded, a ponderous dip of misshapen skull. "Elephant Man Disease," I whispered. I knew the words sounded like nothing more than a random rattling of stones in a broken cup.

"And what is Elephant Man Disease, Benjamin?" Mr. Prather's soft smile had not wavered.

I took a breath, trying not to expel it in his direction. I

knew that my breath stank of inner decay. "Multiple neurofibromatosis, von Recklinghausen's disease," I said, knowing that even Old Sook could not have understood me now. "A genetic disorder. It affects about one person out of every three thousand . . ." I paused, but Mr. Prather seemed to be waiting for more. I could not believe that he could make out what I was saying.

"In most cases," I continued, hearing the rasp and slide of my own tongue in the malformed cave that was my oral cavity, ". . . in most cases, it just results in discoloration . . . spots on the body . . . some small tumors . . . and a ten percent chance of retardation. In more advanced cases . . ."

Mr. Prather tilted his head, a tutor ready to prompt a faltering student.

I did not falter. "In more advanced cases . . . like mine . . . there are freely hanging pedunculated tumors distributed irregularly over the skin, other tumors made up of fibrous and connective tissue cells and malformed nerve fibers along the subcutaneous nerves. Also . . ." I took another breath. "Also, I have the Elephant Man syndrome of scoliosis . . . severe curvature of the spine . . . and a malformed skeletal structure." I waved the paddle of my bad arm at him, tugging up the cloak a second so that he could see the finlike *thing* that grew there where a hand should be. I did not offer to take off my slippers so that he could see the malformed feet, or lower my cloak so that he could see the thirty-pound, hanging, wrinkled masses where my buttocks and thighs should be.

Ozymandias Prather nodded, went around behind his desk, and sat down. "No," he said.

I blinked three times. "No?" Old Sook had taken me to the best specialist in Illinois when I was a baby. I had read volumes on the disease. *Multiple neurofibromatosis. Elephant Man Disease.* There was no doubt.

"No," repeated Prather. His voice was firm. "You have the same disease as Joseph Merrick, Benjamin . . ."

Joseph, I thought. *He knows.*

". . . but it isn't NF. The doctor who diagnosed you was wrong. Dr. Treves . . . Mr. Merrick's surgeon . . . was wrong."

I shook my head in confusion and had to brace myself against a chair to keep from falling. "But—"

"The disease you and Joseph Merrick share is called Proteus syndrome," he said. "It wasn't described until 1979. Drs. M. Michael Cohen, Jr., and Patricia Hayden were the first to isolate it. Proteus syndrome explains the grossly abnormal bone growth you and Merrick obviously share . . . the malformed, wrinkled bumps on your feet and elsewhere . . . the bony bumps on your head and cheek." He paused, perhaps seeing me writhe in what he might have thought was embarrassment but was nothing more complicated than self-disgust. "Proteus syndrome," he said again.

I tried to speak, but no words formed, only rattling, echoing noises in my slippery proboscis of a jaw: a malodorous wind in a damp cave.

Ozymandias Prather knew what I was so desperately trying to say. "No," he replied softly, sadness audible in that booming, oddly amplified voice, "there is no cure, Benjamin. Proteus syndrome is even less well understood than neurofibromatosis."

He did a strange thing then: Mr. Prather bent, retrieved my beekeeper's hat, set it on my misshapen skull, tucked in the little elastic strap Old Sook had attached so that my malformed chin held the hat in place, and arranged my veil so that my face must have been less than a shadow to him.

I turned to leave.

"No, wait just a moment, Benjamin. I have something to tell you."

I paused by the door while he spoke. The explanation took only a moment or two, but I felt as if I were riveted there for days, weeks, while new worlds opened at my feet.

Ozymandias Prather explained about his father's dismantling of a wonderful Device . . . I could hear the capital *D* in his voice . . . and about the Piece that he was sure was still around Elm Haven somewhere. He explained how the completed and activated Device would realize a wonderful change in the world, how it would somehow confer both justice and a new appreciation to those of us who had been unfairly treated as freaks. Mr.

Prather explained how he lived for that day of ultimate justice.

"You are how old, Benjamin?" he asked at the end of his story.

"Thirty-one," I said, my voice choked with emotion now as much as with phlegm. No one had ever asked me my age before.

"And your birthday?"

I felt my eyes water beneath their bony ridges. "August eighteenth, nineteen-sixty."

Ozymandias Prather nodded to himself. "That would be about right, Benjamin. One of the Pieces could well have been left in this area just about that time."

I did not understand. In my confusion, I turned to go. Beyond the open door, the sky was beginning to pale.

"Benjamin," he called as I made my way clumsily down the trailer steps, across the dew-dampened grass, "if you find the Piece I spoke of, I will grant you your wish."

"What wish?" I said. My garbled voice made one of the big cats growl beyond the wall of trailers.

"Your wish to join the freak show," said Mr. Prather as he closed the door.

I stood there for a long moment, not blinking, barely breathing. *How did he know?*

Finally it was daylight that drove me back into the darkness of the trees and then home.

Despite what you have heard, or read, or seen in the movies or on stage, the Elephant Man's name was *Joseph* Merrick, not John Merrick. The Elephant Man's friend and savior, Sir Frederick Treves, had inexplicably (and incorrectly) referred to Merrick as *John* in an essay written years later, and John he has remained.

Joseph. Joseph Merrick.

Socrates once said, "A name is an instrument of teaching and of distinguishing natures."

Dr. Treves, in the same essay where he repeatedly referred to Joseph as John, wrote of his disfigured friend's nature: "As a specimen of humanity, Merrick was ignoble and repulsive; but the spirit of Merrick, if it could be seen in the form of the living, would assume the figure of an upstanding and heroic man, smooth browed and clean of limb, and with eyes that flashed undaunted courage."

I have the quote hanging over my bed in the tunnels behind the mansion, the ink on heavy parchment still as legible as the day I copied it when I was seven. Old Sook was a good tutor. And I was a willing student.

Joseph Merrick.

My name is Benjamin Willis Ashley-Montague. A name is an instrument of teaching and of distinguishing natures.

All that long August Friday, I lay in the cool tunnels beneath the greenhouse behind the ruined mansion and thought of where the Piece might be hidden. In the early afternoon, four or five of the town kids visited me—the Cahill boy, the Catton girl, the Daysinger twins, and, I think, the retarded Sperling youngster who rarely spoke. The children were not afraid of me; their parents had grown up with me and the children themselves had seen me all of their lives. Still, it required somewhat of a dare for them to come down into the chilly tunnelway under the greenhouse to talk to me in my home.

Today their excitement could not be contained. They wanted to tell me about the wonderful circus and freak show that had come to town. Only Tommy Cahill realized that the prattle about freaks might embarrass me, and he elbowed little Judy Catton every time she babbled on about the "Oddity Emporium," but Judy and the others were so enthralled and oblivious that they would elbow Tommy back and continue with their breathless descriptions.

"You gotta see it, Bennie," Judy finished, her grin showing her missing front tooth. "It's the neatest thing that's ever happened to stupid old Elm Haven. Honest!"

Then the children were gone, rushing home for more fudgesicles and then back out to the fairgrounds to watch the JayCees finish putting up their tent in the stultifying heat.

I lay in the suddenly quiet dimness and thought about where the Piece might be. Mr. Prather had said that it might have been hidden in or around the town about the time I was born.

From what I could tell from Old Sook's senile prattle before she died, from old photographs and newspapers I had seen, and from my own earliest memories, our town was nothing like what it was in 1960, when I was born. Like me, Elm Haven had been dying and decaying almost since the day it had been conceived.

I had read in the *County Historical Gazette* that Elm Haven had had more than 4,000 people in 1875, the year a huge old county school had been built in town to hold the droves of children of the new residents the community had anticipated. The droves did not appear. The school was built, abandoned by sections, and had burned down the summer I was born. There were fewer than two thousand people still living in Elm Haven that year of 1960, but photos of the old town then still reflect a certain vitality and hopefulness.

It was the three decades between then and now that seemed to have delivered the *coup de grace*.

In the year I was born, the bastard child of a Peoria millionaire and a poor white-trash Elm Haven girl, Highway 151A still was the main thoroughfare between Galesburg and Peoria, and the traffic helped keep two restaurants, a tavern, the A&P, a dry goods store, and half a dozen other downtown establishments running. In the late sixties, Interstate 74 bypassed the town by six miles and traffic on 151A all but disappeared. Now the only people going *through* Elm Haven are probably driving *to* Elm Haven . . . and that is very few people indeed.

By this summer, the town's population has dropped below a thousand and most of them are old. The children of my generation have mostly fled to cities for work and for the ease of commute and for the civilized amenities of cable television, decent restaurants, and movie theaters, as well as for the anonymity which seems so necessary for sanity these days. Even when Elm Haven had restaurants and the occasional Free Show movie, it never offered anonymity. It never will.

By this summer of 1991, the great elm trees which had given our town its name more than a century earlier are dead—carried away by the Dutch elm blights of the sixties and seventies—and the previously leaf-shaded streets lie naked to the sun. The once-fine old homes along Broad

Street have been sold by the heirs of the families who had owned them since the Civil War, have been bought and "renovated" by Peoria or Chicago yuppies seeking a quieter life, and most have been sold again by those same yuppies fleeing back to the city. The "renovations" mostly consist of shag carpet, sybaritic open "master bathrooms," and rewiring projects that were never completed. Some of the big old homes still stand empty, their garish paint jobs and add-on redwood decks looking like cosmetic finery hastily applied to a corpse. Other homes have been sold to locals at bargain prices and are rotting away without maintenance or care. Only a few, like Doc Staffney's old home and the Grossaint place, still attempt to keep up standards.

By this summer, Elm Haven's Main Street, Old Highway 151A, looks like a smile that has lost most of its front teeth. The old A&P has long been closed—locals use the Stop'N'Shop QuickStore out at the I-74 exit eight miles away—and, after a short reincarnation as a secondhand thrift shop, the old market was bulldozed to leave room for future expansion along Main Street. The dry goods store also was leveled, along with Myers Hardware next door. But no future expansion has occurred. So now, at least along the north side of Main Street, there are a few remaining buildings with cheap facades—Farmers' Commercial Bank, the empty Catton Mercantile building, Mr. Denofrio's barbershop—separated by great gaps of gravel and weeds.

Nothing has been bulldozed along the south side of the two blocks of Main, but it might have been a mercy if they had done some razing. The old Texaco on the east edge of town has been closed since 1964 and only the most desperate tourist, low on gas, pulls into the ancient pumps there. I have watched, late at night, as tourists in the glare of their own headlights stand peering at the prices frozen beneath the glass of those dust-covered pumps—twenty-seven cents a gallon, read the tin numerals—and I have smiled beneath my veil as the tourists curse and bang at the pumps as if threats will bring back those days, those prices.

West of Ernie's Texaco, the Parkside Cafe has been

closed since '74—I remember going to the back door for free Cokes until I was well into puberty—and the John Deere dealership down the block closed in 1976. (Sarah Dean Sperling, the untalented daughter of the town's mayor that year, was paid two hundred dollars to do a huge Bicentennial mural along the side of Farmers' Commercial and that awkward excrescence has survived all of the entropy that has claimed so many of the good things about Elm Haven. It flakes there now on the east side of the bank, the stick-figure pioneers and coonskin-capped frontiersman looking faded but indelibly idiotic.) Bandstand Park next to the abandoned cafe is treeless now, the once-proud gazebo bandstand reduced to a slab of pea green concrete, the benches no longer painted or repaired. Only the pigeons, a few senile old pensioners and I patronize Bandstand Park. I sit there frequently on summer nights and try to imagine the days when my grandfather (and then my father) showed outdoor movies there—the Free Show—between the early days of World War II and the year I was born. It must have been a pleasant thing, lying there on blankets on the new-mown grass, in the shade of the elms, watching the Free Show while evening settled in and the stars came out between the leaves.

The park is empty now, the grass overgrown by weeds or worn away by erosion, but the War Memorial Monument near the sidewalk is still cared for and updated. Three names were added to the bronze plaque for service in Vietnam—Father O'Rourke's is one, I was amazed to note some years ago—and I hear that one will be added for the Persian Gulf War. Young Greggie Whittaker, an idiot during his high school days who almost killed himself in his daddy's Subaru, did manage to kill himself while driving an army truck over there in Saudi Arabia three weeks before the air war began. The older residents in town flew American flags all during that conflict, but only the Whittakers felt it was worth flying theirs at half-staff.

Carl's Tavern was the last place to die, closing down in the early eighties. Local patrons now drink out at the Black Tree near the Catholic cemetery, or drink at home. There's been a lot of drinking at home through the recessions of the seventies and eighties and, now, the nineties. The trickle-down theory never trickled all the way down to Elm Haven.

So where can Mr. Prather's Piece be? I ask myself as evening falls. I climb up to the greenhouse and set my knobbed brow against the grimy glass. Bats flit and dodge above the brambles and between branches over the ruins of the mansion. *Where could it be?*

Every town has its unsettling places. Some are outright evil. Others are just . . . unsettling. These places seem to gather power in Elm Haven in the late summer, when perspiration lies between your skin and clothes from morning until night, when the cornfields have grown until they block out the light like walls of green darkness, and when the sky seems haze-hidden and brooding.

Where?

As the older residents and few remaining children of Elm Haven move off toward the lights and circus noises of Old Settlers, I hobble out into the all-but-abandoned town, seeking out the Piece. Seeking my salvation.

Dr. Frederick Treves revealed in his essay that Joseph Merrick used to have two recurring fantasies. The first was that of being a lover—in the Victorian sense—a gentleman who charms the ladies. "He was amorous," wrote Treves. "He would like to have been a lover, to have walked with the beloved object in the languorous shades of some beautiful garden and to have poured into her ear all of the glowing utterances that he had rehearsed in his heart." Merrick himself fell in love with almost every lady he met after his admission to the safe haven of the London Hospital. It was for his actress-friend, Mrs. Madge Kendal, that Joseph Merrick constructed the elaborate model of St. Philip's Church as a gift. That model still stands in the hospital, framed near the glass case holding Merrick's twisted skeleton.

Joseph Merrick's other dream was to visit a land in which everyone was blind.

I understand both dreams. To be loved and admired. To be seen for oneself. And I understand that for him—as for me—it could only happen in the kingdom of the blind.

Even as I enter the warm embrace of Night, seeking

Mr. Prather's missing Piece as my admission to his family of freaks, I dream of loving and being loved. I dream of the happy time after the Device is finished.

That night I searched the bad places.

While the calliope tunes from the merry-go-round and the shouts from the last game of the evening's baseball tournament and the screams from the Mad Mouse drifted east and south across the town, I scrabbled through the charred ruins of my father's family's mansion.

The timbers and broad oak floorboards had charred and fallen into the basements and subbasements, and all of this wreck and rubble was overgrown by brambles. But Old Sook had shown me the secret way in from the greenhouse basement near where my own tunnels began. I squeezed and puffed and panted and tugged my cloak free as I wormed my way between old foundation stones.

I found nothing but spiders and rats there in the cellar of the house my great-grandfather had burned down in his fit of madness just after World War I. As a haunted house, the ruins of the Ashley-Montague Estate held only promise or disappointment, no reality.

Pulling on my hat and veil, I scraped my way down the sidewalk along Broad Street. The branches of the Chinese elms and young oaks that had grown up since the death of the great elms there came nowhere near spanning the wide arc of street, but they gave me deep shadow through which to move.

The Duggan house was empty, boarded-up, either truly haunted or merely run-down enough that not even our yuppie invasion of the early eighties had threatened it with purchase or renovation. I let myself in between planks of loose plywood on the side door.

The place smelled of mildew and rot and rat droppings. Small things scurried in the walls where I was and larger things scrabbled claws along the hallways of the second floor. I was not afraid. Night was my sister and mother.

Mrs. Duggan, the last occupant of the house, had been no local witch or monster, only a pedantic old sixth-grade teacher who had died of cancer months before I was born. But local legends among the kids then and now insisted that the old teacher had been seen in town after she died, that the old woman's rotting corpse had been spied shuffling through the corridors of the abandoned school in the months before the structure burned down.

It was nonsense, of course. Kid stuff to frighten future generations of kids. But it had done its job; even now, thirty years after the poor lady's demise, Elm Haven parents could finally call in their playing children from the last bit of play in summer's long twilight by shouting—"You'd better hurry, before Mrs. D's ghost comes out!" The kids would come galloping for the safety of electric lights.

There were no working electric lights in the ruins of Mrs. D's once-proud home. But I had brought a flashlight in my cloak.

Every town deserves a haunted house like this one; Mrs. Duggan's furniture had never been removed. Childless, without heirs willing to travel to the wilds of central Illinois, the teacher could not have foreseen that her house would remain much as she had left it when she left for her final hospital stay. In recent years, prowlers and vandals and thrill seekers had carried away souvenirs until only the heavier pieces of furniture remained, shrouded in dust and cobwebs and darkness.

I spent almost two hours in Mrs. D's haunted house. I searched the downstairs rooms where footprints in the dust showed me where the adventurous had gone before me; I searched the velvet-shrouded upstairs rooms where there were fewer footprints and cobwebs had reclaimed the doorways. Incredibly, the old woman's hairbrush and toilet set were still laid out on an age-yellowed and dust-grayed doily atop her bureau. A begrimed mirror made me lower the veil from my hat, even though I could barely see in the dark. The canopied bed had been soaked through from the leaking ceiling and had collapsed into a rotted mass on the floor. Small white things burrowed into the mattress as I shined the flashlight beam across it.

Nothing of interest upstairs. No Piece.

Mr. Prather had said that he did not know the shape or size of the Piece, but that it would be small—almost certainly smaller than six inches in length or circumference. He had said that it would probably be made of metal, but might also be made of ceramic or something like it. He said that it might be buried or hidden among junk or held as a prize possession in someone's safe, but that I would know it when I saw it.

How? I had asked.

You will know it, Benjamin, he had said.

There was nothing in Mrs. D's haunted house that struck me as anything but a relic of some sad teacher's moldering legacy of rot and local superstition. I even searched the basement, where legend had it that Mrs. Duggan's dentist father had left his chair and tools.

They were there. The dental picks and cumbersome drills were rusted so badly that they looked like some barnacle-encrusted instruments of torture brought up from a Spanish galleon. The dentist chair had rat holes chewed in the dusty fabric. Small things scraped and scurried behind dripping brick walls as I wheezed my way up the stairs.

There was no Piece.

North and west of town, out along the gravel roadbed where the Monon Railroad tracks had been torn up a quarter of a century earlier, there was an old tallow plant cum grain-elevator complex where even the most adventurous of high school students would not go on a dare.

I took my flashlight with its fading batteries and hobbled out there. A child could have run there from Broad Street in five minutes. It took me almost an hour to make the trip.

The door of the central building was sagging free of its massive hinges. There were no cobwebs here, no dust-covered portraits with eyes that followed the intruder— none of the Disneyland haunted-house ambience of Mrs. D's home. But the emptiness was somehow worse.

There were large iron hooks that hung down over a steel trough running across the center of the first-floor space. The hooks had been added after the grain elevator had gone out of business in the recession following World War I. It had been a tallow plant for only a few years, but the hooks were stained with something deeper than rust, and the steel trough had been scoured black. A chill wind blew in through broken panes.

It was the perfect place for Mr. Prather's father to hide

a Piece. The place would already have been abandoned thirty years ago—even forty or fifty—and, in the back room, there was a heap of scrap iron of every possible shape, size, and function. I spent hours there, my flashlight beam growing weaker and weaker until I was sorting shapes of iron in almost total darkness, until finally I gave up, laboriously rose from my good knee, and felt around for my cane.

The Piece was not there. I felt no recognition. The cold iron was only cold iron. The only resonance I received from that place was the disgust and loathing when I ventured too near the hooks and trough. Something had been butchered and bled there.

Something not meant to be butchered.

Sighing, my breath rattling in my proboscis of a mouth, I began scraping and pulling my way back into town. It was after two A.M., the lights of Old Settlers had been dimmed for almost an hour, but I would wait in the line of trees along the water tower ditch north of the playing fields until it was safe to see Mr. Prather.

Again, he seems to be waiting for me.

I begin to explain my failure, but he holds up one hand. "No explanations are necessary, Benjamin. I know that you will find it."

I have nothing to say to that. Embarrassed to stay, unwilling to leave, I touch my veil the way a man will stroke his beard when at a loss for words.

"Come here, please, Benjamin," he says and leads me to the dark end of his trailer.

There is a machine there: something Gothic and clumsy out of the twenties, all vacuum tubes and heavily shielded wires and glass plates the size of upended tables. I begin to back away.

"No, no," Mr. Prather says softly, taking me by the arm and moving me between the glass plates. "It is only my father's X-ray machine. Very old, but I've modified it to be very safe."

I make a series of sounds that no living person could have understood.

"Why take an X-ray?" he repeats. Even while he speaks, he is positioning the equipment, throwing a switch that brings a deep hum to the room, and sliding in heavy photographic plates. "My father used it . . . I still use it . . . to make sure that the . . . ah . . . performers in my Emporium are in good health." He smiles at me. "It is amazing how few doctors, even specialists, have any idea of the health needs of the physically exceptional."

He smiles again, steps far back into the dark, and says, "Take a deep breath, let it out, and do not move until I tell you to."

I inhale and then rattle an exhalation. The hum grows louder. The ancient apparatus clicks and groans.

"Fine, fine," says Mr. Prather. He removes plates, hands them to someone waiting just outside the door. "Why don't we have some tea while we wait for them to be processed, shall we, Benjamin?"

I do not actually drink the tea. The noises would be too embarrassing. But I do pretend—lifting the delicate china cup to my proboscis, the little finger of my good hand lifted as I do so. Time passes.

There is a knock and Mr. Prather excuses himself. He carries three large X-ray transparencies to a small light table between his closet and the rear of the trailer. I am standing only three feet behind him, but I cannot see the pictures. I feel it would not be polite to ask to do so. In truth, I do not want to see them; I have seen the photographs of Joseph Merrick's skeleton from the London Hospital.

Mr. Prather clicks off the light. His face seems more slack than ever as he turns. "I'm sorry, Benjamin. Actually, I had been hoping that the problem with your spine might be cured. Treatment of scoliosis has come a long way since Mr. Merrick's day. But I'm afraid it is too severe." He looks down a second and when his face bobs back up, the smile is attached again. "But the good news is that you seem very healthy. All of the internal organs that I can make out are well-formed. Do you feel well?"

"I have never had a sick day," I say in all honesty.

"Good, good," says Mr. Prather and he moves me to the door. His hand on my twisted shoulder feels firm, friendly. "You know that we will be leaving before sunrise on Sunday?"

I nod. My face does not allow the usual expression of

emotion—both smiles and frowns are impossible for me—but I feel the tears forming in both eyes. I tug down my veil to conceal them.

"I *know* you will bring me the Piece by then, Benjamin. Have no concern. I have none. You will come by after the last show tomorrow night, yes?"

I nod again. I almost stumble on the small step of his trailer, but he touches me again, steadies me. I realize that he is patting me on the back.

Moving away through the dark maze of tents and trailers, I no longer try to stop the tears.

Old Sook brought me to the specialist in Peoria when I was six years old. I remember the tests, the stares, the whispered comments as more and more specialists were brought in to look at me. I remember the equipment, how cold and large and intimidating it all was. I remember how I hated to be naked in the bright lights and how chill the air was.

When it came time to report to us, I remember the consternation on the doctor's face as he held his report in his hand and frowned at the old woman and the bizarre child across the desk from him. Finally he had set the report down, given me a candy to suck on, and taken Old Sook into an inner room to speak simply to her. I remember her cries and shouts from the other room before we left the hospital.

But most of all, I remember the taste of the peppermint candy as I turned the report around and began reading it. I was only six, but Old Sook had taught me to read almost two years earlier. I knew that I would not have time to read it all or to work out the hard words, so I lifted the carbons out of the file and slipped them in my shirt.

Now, almost twenty-five years later, the carbons are smudged, the paper yellowed, but I can still make out the words:

> The subject is a slight male Caucasian, six years two months old. Intelligence appears normal or above-normal (Wexler) and there is no sign of emotional disability other than an extreme shyness

which may be the result of physical abnormalities and a home environment in which the child is being raised by a seventy-two-year-old "Auntie." . . .

Radiology: The skull is the seat of extensive asymmetrical bony outgrowths affecting the frontal, left, parietal, left temporal, and left half of the occipital and sphenoidal bones. Osseous growth is not accurately bordered by the sagittal plane, but extends to the right frontal and occipital regions. Bony masses involve the entire frontal region except for a small area above and behind the right angular process. These masses are extremely irregular and may be divided roughly into three portions by two deep longitudinal sulci. The left sulcus is practically continuous with the supraorbital notch. . . .

The bones of the subject's face are deeply affected. The lower end of the left nasal bone is prolonged into a rough prominence which encroaches on the anterior nares. The left malar bone has a prominent boss just external to the infraorbital foramen. The alveolar process of the maxilla projects strongly outward at its lower extension while a second, rougher mass runs nearly horizontally inward.

Spine: The subject exhibits extreme scoliotic curvature to the right in the dorsal region, the vertebrae being also rotated. The transverse processes in the mid and upper dorsal regions are oversize and rough on the right side. The atlas has a large boss, nearly two-and-a-half centimeters in thickness, on the right side of the anterior arch. The left lamina of the fourth cervical vertebra is also thick and extruded.

Epidermis: The subject's skin is subject to papilloma ranging from a mere roughing of the integument to great masses of hanging papillomata. Such masses cover the back and gluteal region. Subcutaneous tissue is massed in regions where the integument is raised prominently above the surrounding epidermal layers. This tissue is loose and can be raised from the deeper parts in great folds.

In the left pectoral region, at the posterior aspect of the left axilla, on the inner sections of each thigh, and over the buttocks, the affected epidermal layer forms heavy, pendulous flaps which may be manipulated with only slight discomfort to the subject.

The subject's left ulna is large and rough. The greater sigmoid cavity is distorted. The malformation of the inner lip of the trochlea throws the forearm out from the arm at an angle of 150 degrees. The bones of the left carpus are large and friable. The metacarpals and phalanges of the index, left, and little fingers are distorted, cartilage-webbed, soft in texture, and incapable of articulation. The bone of the left thumb presents normal characters but is imbedded in a fibroid mass.

Supplementary observation: The diffuse lobulated tumors which cover the subject's back, chest, and buttocks, as well as the undifferentiated papillomas, reflect direct involvement with innumerable sebaceous and sweat glands, as well as with other secretions from internal vessels and cavities. The resulting bacterial decomposition of secretions within these papillomatous masses causes the subject to emit a powerful and unpleasant odor.

Diagnosis: Multiple Neurofibromatosis with scoliotic rotation and generalized Hyperstosis with Pachydermia.

Prognosis: Anecdotal evidence and examination suggests a rapid spread of the neurofibromatosis symptoms within the past year. While surgery can eliminate some of the more obvious papillomata and relieve some of the scoliotic effects, irreversible involvement of bony masses on the skull, left arm, pelvis, and spine, as well as the rapid spread of tumors throughout fibrous and nervous tissues, suggest continued spread of the disorder through puberty and beyond.

I lie in my nest of pillows in the tunnel and remember the first time I read those pages, and I remember the look on Old Sook's face as we rode home in her friend Gabriel's 1948 Buick, and I think about how Joseph Merrick chose to die.

He laid his head back on his pillow and went to sleep.

Like me, Joseph Merrick had to sleep sitting up in a nest of pillows, his ponderous head propped upon his knees. Otherwise, the weight of his own skull would break his neck.

He laid his head back on his pillow and went to sleep.

I have thought of this every night and morning of my life.

But this morning, as Elm Haven slowly comes to life after its long night at Old Settlers revelry, this morning I listen to the few traffic sounds and I am not tempted. Not this morning.

I will find the Piece.

On Saturday evening, just after dusk, I begin the long trip out to Calvary Cemetery.

I make the long walk up the alley between Broad Street and Fifth, cut through the fields north of Catton Road, come down around the water tower past the lights and sounds of Old Settlers, and strike out through the edge of the cornfields bordering Jubilee College Road. It is a little over a mile and a half to the cemetery. I figure it will take me four hours to make the walk.

The car pulls over before I can blend away into the tall corn and a voice says, "Ben? Is that you? Come on out, Ben."

It is a voice I can not ignore. I move out of the darkness of the field.

"What the hell are you doing out here, Ben?" asks Father O'Rourke. "Where are you headed?"

I tell him.

The priest stares at me a moment and then opens the passenger door of his Honda Civic. "Well, the pope-mobile's headed that same direction, kiddo. Hop in." I believe that Father O'Rourke only calls the parish car the popemobile when it is just the two of us talking. It is, I think, a private joke that I never understand and he never explains.

We roar the remaining mile and a quarter in less than

two minutes. There are twenty or more trucks and cars visible as we pass by the Black Tree Tavern, tucked in like piglets to a sow's teats, Father O'Rourke says, and then we zoom down the narrow paved road through the woods, and then up to the cemetery.

It is not quite full dark when Father O'Rourke opens the black iron gate and waits for me to enter. He sees my hesitation. "I'm just going to pray out here for a few minutes, Ben. You do what you have to. I'll wait for you in the car until you're finished."

Still hesitating, I look at the priest . . . my friend. He is in his early forties but even with a beard he would look younger if it were not for the thin spiderweb of scars that creep up the left side of his face. His hair is cut short and is thinning on top; he has a sunburn. When I finally drag myself through the gate, I notice his own limp as he follows.

Father O'Rourke is an Elm Haven native, one of the few of his generation who stayed. Returned, rather, for the priest had first left as a young man of nineteen to go to war. It was in Vietnam that Father O'Rourke had lost much of his left leg. I had not failed to notice the symmetries of our afflictions.

Rumor in town has it that the priest had been a tunnel rat—one of those unfortunate volunteers who crawled into Vietcong tunnel networks. Rumor in town says that he had been very good at his job of tunnel rat, right up to the time he tried to squeeze past a decomposing NVA trooper's body in a narrow passage only to find that the body had been booby-trapped. Rumor in town whispers that Father O'Rourke spent fourteen months in the veterans' hospital, that he joined the Franciscans as soon as he was released, and that he had been an outspoken defender of the rights of the poor in Central America right up to the time two years ago when the Church had forced him to leave because *they* were fearful for his life even if *he* wasn't. Rumor in town has it that Father O'Rourke could have taken a teaching position in any Catholic university in the nation, but that he chose to return to Elm Haven as a simple parish priest even though his parents had died and his sisters and friends had moved away.

One never immediately notices Father O'Rourke's slight limp or the plastic prosthesis of a leg. With Father O'Rourke, one notices the laughter and the enjoyment of life that seem to gleam behind his gray eyes. One notices his kind voice and strange sense of humor. One notices his courage.

I watch him limp away down the first row of headstones, and then I turn and limp away myself, toward the back of the cemetery.

The utility shed there is in little better shape than my great-grandfather's mansion, but there had been no basement, so whatever tore the north and east walls apart and collapsed the roof had left the bones of the old structure intact. The shed is not on consecrated ground. There is enough left that the groundskeepers still kept their shovels and lawn mowers stored there.

There is no padlock on the door but I do not open it. I set my good hand against the warped wood. The door seems to vibrate slightly.

Children hate this place. I have heard about "Van Syke's Shed" from children of my generation and the others that followed. Kids who would happily spend the night in an open grave in Calvary Cemetery will make wide arcs around the shed. No one knows why. There is no legend surrounding the place, no campfire tales of ghosts or ghoulies.

But children hate this place.

The vibration against the door seems to fade. I feel a vague nausea, a dizziness that moves from my feet to a place behind my eyes.

But it has nothing to do with the Piece. I know that now.

On the ride back to town, Father O'Rourke speaks softly. "You're looking for something, Ben." It is not really a question.

He glances at me. "Does it have something to do with the circus, the new mud show that the town council brought in?"

I do not know what a mud show is, but I know what he means. I look away, absurdly fearful that he can read my eyes through the darkness and the veil. The night wind through my open window is redolent with the smells of moist earth and growing corn.

"There's something wrong with that show, Ben," says Father O'Rourke, his eyes moving from the road to me. We are only going fifteen or twenty miles per hour and there is no other traffic along the county road. "Do you feel that?" he asks.

I do not answer.

Before we reach the area where the lights of Old Settlers fill the intersection of Jubilee College Road and First Avenue, Father O'Rourke stops the car. He reaches over and grips my good hand. "Ben, I know you're lonely, but whatever the hell's going on, don't let loneliness guide your actions."

I can hear the midway sounds coming down the dark road.

Father O'Rourke sighs. "Are we friends, Ben?"

I have to answer that. "Yes."

He squeezes my hand. "Then, as a friend, do you promise that you will come to me before you do anything . . . before you have any dealings with those people at the freak show?"

I hesitate only a second. "Yes," I say. At this moment, I do not think that I am lying.

Father O'Rourke keeps his gaze on me a second, then squeezes my hand a final time. "Okay. Good enough. Where do you want me to drop you?"

"The schoolyard," I say.

If the shed behind Calvary Cemetery was avoided by kids, the schoolyard in the center of town was shunned a hundred times more earnestly. No one knew why it was hated by children. There was no school there and had not been one there for three decades, but the land had never been used for anything else. Playground equipment stood rusty and unused. Town kids would walk blocks out of their way to play baseball at the city diamond out by the water tower rather than venture onto the old playing fields of the schoolyard.

I could have started my quest for the Piece here, but I also hated the schoolyard. There was no reason for my fear, but the fear was real enough. This was the only place

I had ever encountered where the Night was neither sister nor parent, but something dark and malevolent.

Father O'Rourke watched me for several minutes as I stood by the edge of the schoolyard. I stood staring back through my veil. Then the priest held up his hand in what I first thought would be a fist or beckoning gesture; instead, he made the sign of the cross, a benediction. I did not move until he drove away, the taillights of the popemobile disappearing down Depot Street.

The foundation of the old school lay in the center of this square of blackness in the heart of Elm Haven. The old stones and bricks were almost flush with the ground. The deep basement had long ago been filled in, the charred timbers carried away to the landfill out beyond the dump. There was nothing to mark the site of the old school except the foundation stones, looking like the low headstones I had just seen out in the cemetery.

Teenagers in Elm Haven dared each other to step across that line of stones. None did.

I did. Closing my eyes, cursing my own cowardice, I stepped across the foundation stones and dragged my dead leg out into the center of the great, dark square. Cinders scrunched under my good foot and left a wake behind my bad one.

I stopped in the center.

I hated this place. I hated the feeling that flowed over me here like black water in a cave. I hated the darkness deeper than darkness that seemed to rise from the foundation stones behind me and seal this place from the rest of Elm Haven . . . from the rest of the world. I hated the quiver that started in my good leg and worked its way through my malformed body until I was shaking like a palsied thing, vibrating like a victim of electroshock. The pendulous masses on my chest and back and buttocks quivered like pulpy cockscombs. If my jaw had been anything near normal, my teeth would have been chattering. As it was, saliva flew from the open proboscis of my bone-thrust of a mouth and I drooled on myself even while I wept.

I went to my good knee in the cinders and then forced my other leg down. It would be very difficult to rise again without anything to grip, anyone to help me up.

At that instant I did not think that I would rise again.

The cinders cut through the thin cloth of my cloak and cotton trousers into the flesh of my knees.

This would be where Ozymandias Prather's father would have brought the Piece. This is the heart of the heart of evil. Whatever was here would have welcomed him . . . accepted the Piece into its dark keeping.

I heard a rustling above and around me as if large wings were being opened. I looked up but there was only darkness, storm-cloud dark, raven-black. A great weight seemed to press me closer to the cinders.

I fell forward onto the rocks. I broke my fall with my good hand, but my bulbous forehead still scraped the cinders. Blood dripped onto the black stones.

He laid his head back on his pillow and went to sleep.

My breath rasped. My face was pushed downward as surely as if there were a taloned hand on my neck, forcing me into the sharp-edged cinders.

Something stirred under the stones.

The kids had told of basements and subbasements, catacombs where things moved deep out of the light. The corpse of Mrs. Duggan dragging its rotted remains up varnished stairs. Worse things moving behind it.

I heard stirring and shifting under the stones. There came a deep sliding and then an upward shift. The cinders moved under me like earth suddenly turned rubbery in an earthquake. I tried to grab the ground with both hands but the pulpy flipper that was my left hand slipped out of its cloak and flailed helplessly. The cinders slashed at the soft, gangrenous flesh there until blood splattered my cheek.

I allowed the weight of my horrible skull to pull me the rest of the way down, my brow pierced to the jutting bone by cinder edges now, my gasping mouth against the iron-flavored rock. The shifting continued until the entire center of the square was bowing upward like the water above a shark on its final run.

I felt the *something* directly under me then . . . knew that it would be mere seconds until the long white fingers thrust up through cinders to close on my throat . . . knew that the long teeth would be seconds behind that . . .

could all but hear the walnut-cracking snap and crack of bone and cartilage as the jaws just inches below me now surfaced and closed on my face and skull. . . . I could imagine the last glimpse from those multiple eyes, red beyond the knowledge of red, swallowing my soul in my last moment of knowing. . . .

I gasped and sat up.

The great square of cinders bowed five feet above the level of the foundation stones and collapsed like a trampoline suddenly losing tension.

I could see beyond the stones. Leaves on the oaks across the street stirred in a sudden chill breeze. There was no other noise.

After several moments . . . after I was sure that whatever had almost come for me had nothing to do with the Piece, or Mr. Prather's Device . . . I rose to my good knee, managed to leverage myself to my feet, wiped the streaming blood from my brow, and limped toward my greenhouse and tunnel and home.

One of my favorite bits of poetry comes from Shelley's strange homage to John Keats, the pastoral elegy *Adonais:*

> Life, like a dome of many-colored glass,
> Stains the white radiance of Eternity,
> Until Death tramples it to fragments.

As a child, after reading that, I used to lie awake in my bed in the tunnel, listening to Old Sook rattle and snore behind the curtain of burlap that separated our niches, and I would imagine that dome of many-colored glass . . . I would imagine coming up from the tunnel in daylight, not night, and emerging in the beautiful dome of many-colored glass, not the pale and shattered wreck of the greenhouse.

I can hear the trampling of my dome to fragments this final night before the circus lifts stakes and leaves, these final hours after the total midnight of my soul.

I think that I might kill Ozymandias Prather for the false promise he had made me. He had invited me not just to the Kingdom of the Blind, where my terrible ugliness might not be found, but beyond that . . . to the Ultimate Kingdom where my ugliness would simply cease to exist.

Where I would be normal.

Where the world would cease to be a robe of razor blades flaying me more surely than the cinders had, and become a warm blanket wrapped around a shivering child. Would become my mother's arms.

Goddamn Ozymandias Prather to hell.

But even as I see myself killing the tall man with the dead face, I know that I will not touch him. I have never knowingly hurt any person.

Except the twin you murdered, I correct myself.

I groan and turn my face to the cold stones. *This was not my fault,* I tell myself. *It was not really a twin. Not yet. Only cells.*

Old Sook told me, the night after we returned from the specialist in Peoria. She had been drinking the black cherry wine that she made up each autumn. "You not the only one in your mama's belly before you was born," she said, not looking at me, her wrinkled face flickering from three dimensions to two in the candlelight. "That professor doctor-man we called back when your mama went into the labor pains two months too early, he look through that little shiny scope of his and say that you have a baby brother, a twin baby like you. Only you swallow him up like a big fish swallow a little 'un. He say you gobble up this little 'unculus so's you can live your own self. What we wonder now, my little darling baby, is was it worth it? Was it worth it?"

And she had started crying and had not stopped until she had started snoring. I was sure the next day that she did not remember telling me. It was months before I found the word she had been trying for: *homunculus.*

Not the tiny human child I had imagined then, nor even the fully formed fetus I had nightmares about later, I know now, just a bundle of cells not much smaller than the bundle of cells that I was then.

But would we have been normal if we had both developed?

I scrape my bleeding forehead against the stone and try to think of other things. Once I had tried to speak to Father O'Rourke in the rectory garden about this thing, but I had begun weeping and slobbering instead. Father O'Rourke had hugged me to him, ignoring the stench and slobber.

Time to tell Prather that I failed.

For the last time, I push away my pillows, fling my blanket into a corner, and drag myself up stone stairs into the lighter darkness of night.

The WCTU women had their tent down by midnight, the American Legion half an hour later, and the JayCees by one A.M. By two-thirty the rides had been dismantled, the Freak Show canvas folded back in trailers, the midway disassembled, and the circus animals fed and sent to sleep in their traveling cages. Only the elephants continued to make noise, their trumpeting sounding like the cries of scalded women in the night.

By three-thirty A.M. the Peabody-Ozymandias Traveling Circus and Oddity Emporium was nothing more than a series of trucks and trailers on a filthy field. The roustabouts had quit shouting and grunting, even the elephants had quieted, and now the diesel engines began growling on the trucks. I scraped my way out of the line of trees and shuffled to Mr. Prather's trailer. He opened the door immediately.

"Come in, Benjamin."

I hesitated on the step. Most of my wounds had caked over, but some blood still found its way into my eyes. "I failed," I rasped.

Mr. Prather shook his head and pulled me into the darkness of his trailer. His touch was firm but gentle. "You haven't failed," he whispered. His voice seemed to be coming from his belly rather than his face.

"I failed," I said again. "I could not find the Piece. The Device will not work."

"Come here, Benjamin," whispered Ozymandias Prather and pulled me deeper into the dark. I could hear others breathing in the room. There were large shapes—not normal shapes—on the couch at the end of the room. I realized that some of his freaks were here. I did not want to see them.

"Look," he said and turned on the light table.

I glanced over my shoulder toward the couch, despite

my wish not to see. The light did not reach that far, but I could make out a young man who looked like a snake, another man—thin, with skin as green as very new cheese or very old meat—and there, in the corner beyond the ancient X-ray machine, something larger and much more terrible . . .

"No, here," said Mr. Prather and turned me back toward the light table.

My own X-ray photograph was there. I knew it was me . . . the twisted spine, the massive, misshapen upper arm, the fused ribs . . .

Mr. Prather's strong finger stabbed down just above the white glow of my sternum in the X-ray image. "See?"

I saw. It was not very large really, no more than a few centimeters across. It looked almost, but not quite, round. There were teeth there, rather like the ratchet teeth on a small gear, but far more irregular. A thin, rodlike extension of the thing ran deeper, between the fusion of metal and rib cage, like a filament through my heart and into the spine.

"What does it do?" I whispered. I could not have understood the rattle of my own words.

"We don't know what it does, what part it plays," whispered Ozymandias, "but it is as necessary as any other part of the Device."

I turned to look at him, aware of the stirrings on the couch, in the corner.

"We will need it, Benjamin," he whispered. His mouth was inches away but there was no breath from it.

I turned to run but they had me before I got halfway to the door. I was weeping, but not at the terrible reality of my situation, only at the absurdity of the thought that I could successfully run away from someone.

Outside, all the diesels roared to life at once. The noise made me clap my hand and flipper over my ears. My beekeeper's hat and veil rolled away under the X-ray machine.

"Take him to his cage," said Mr. Prather. He had never turned away from the light table, as if the only thing about me that was worth his attention was there.

I tried to scream then, but whatever noise I made was

lost in the roar of diesels as the first trucks began pulling out of the field onto First Avenue, one after the other.

As they hurried me out the door, Ozymandias Prather finally turned from the glowing board. "I promised you, didn't I," he said in that oddly booming, barely human voice, "that you could join the freak show?"

They found Joseph Merrick dead, in his bed, shortly after three P.M. on Friday, April 11, 1890. Although his body had continued to degenerate and become more terrible to behold in recent months, his spirit had been at peace for some time.

Joseph had realized his lifelong dream of visiting the theater. He had visited a country estate called Fawsley Park for six blissful weeks and had walked its fields, picked violets along its streams, and taken tea in its garden. Dr. Treves later wrote of receiving a gift of flowers from his friend in the country; they were the commonest of hedgerow plants, but Merrick had pressed, banded, and wrapped them as if they were the rarest and most lovely specimens ever gathered.

The wonder of the theater, and the country, and of his newfound friends never left Joseph Merrick. He was to say a few weeks before he died, "I am happy every hour of the day."

After Merrick's death, his friend Dr. Treves directed the taking of plaster casts of Joseph's head and limbs, performed the autopsy and dissection, and supervised the mounting of Merrick's bones onto a wire armature so that the skeleton could be displayed.

It is displayed until this day in a side hall of the Medical College of the London Hospital. Nearby, also on display, are the cap and burlap mask he wore, and a model church he had given a lady friend as a gift. Almost unnoticed in the rear of a secondary display case lies a small bunch of dried flowers wrapped in a ribbon from which all color has fled.

The Night seems gone because the lights of the midway gleam brightly whenever they open the fourth wall. Whenever I am exhibited.

I call for help, try to reason with those who have paid to see me, but the crowds shrink back from the stench and senseless noise. I think that they see my tears, but I cannot be sure.

I dream of the familiar streets of Elm Haven and the familiar faces at the windows of the houses there, faces watching me without fear, frequently smiling and waving as I pass. Sometimes I awaken to the sounds of the tires on pavement and the roar of the engines, and realize that I have lifted my good hand in a return wave.

The others do not speak freely when my cage is opened, but from the excitement behind their hushed voices, I sense that the journey is continuing. The Device is growing.

Perhaps they need only a few more Pieces.

Sometimes I convince myself that Father O'Rourke will track them down, find me, free me. If there is anyone in my life who I believe has confronted evil in all of its arrogance and terror, it is Father O'Rourke. Sometimes, when I have wept for hours and feel that the Night is nearing its end, I truly do believe that Father O'Rourke will find me and take me home.

At other times I know better.

There is a single high window on the far wall of my cage when the fourth wall is drawn shut, and by pinching my fingers in front of my eyes, I can make the midway lights through the glass gleam like a dome of many-colored glass. When I do that, I try to remember the penultimate stanza of *Adonais*.

> That light whose smile kindles the Universe,
> That Beauty in which all things work and move,
> That Benediction which the eclipsing Curse
> Of birth can quench not, that sustaining Love
> Which through the web of being blindly wove
> By man and beast and earth and air and sea,
> Burns bright or dim, as each are mirrors of
> The fire for which all thirst, now beams on me,
> Consuming the last clouds of cold mortality.

Father O'Rourke once told me that all choices are ours to make. All futures are ours to choose.

Joseph Merrick had simply removed all pillows except for one. And then he had laid back his head to sleep. He was twenty-nine years old.

It is cold here tonight, but the blanket they give me is warm. My head is so much heavier these days that when I doze off sitting in my nest of pillows, my forehead touches my knees and the pain brings me awake in an instant. The cuts and scars across my brow have never healed properly. The temptation to kick the pillows aside, to lay one soft pillow down upon the cot they gave me, to lay back my head and close my eyes . . . the temptation is very strong.

But not quite yet. There may be pantomimes yet to be enjoyed, flowers to be gathered by streams I have not yet visited. Though the season grows toward its end, the leaves brittle, and the Night as cold as a dead mother's breast, I think that there is time still to dream, and wait, and perhaps to hope.

All futures are ours to choose.

DAN SIMMONS

The show rolled on . . .

Chicago, Illinois

"Hello?"

Kysleen waited a moment before answering, studying the slender, dangerous-looking teenager slouched in the tent's entrance. The sticky heat of the city mixed with the exhaust fumes from Ashland Avenue and drained her strength; already today she'd taken three jobs. No more than usual, but it was enough to make her long for a rest in her trailer, a half hour with a glass of iced tea and her feet up while the clip-on fan bathed her in temporary coolness.

But a lean and finely muscled young man was here, and her hunger was ever present. She stretched and touched his thoughts briefly, seeing the tent and herself through him: a small, twisted toad of a woman, squatting across the table in the murky light, repulsive despite her glittering tawny eyes and the spill of ink black hair framing pearly skin and red, inviting lips. His name was Collis, and he had come to ridicule her.

Kysleen smiled. "Please," she said in a silky voice. "Sit down."

He came in and lowered himself to the chair with unconscious grace. "Yeah, okay. So now what? The sign says *Have Your Fantasies Come True*. What the hell does that mean?"

She leaned forward, hands splayed on the pitted table.

"Do you dream, Collis?" she whispered; he twitched when she used his name. "Of things you can't have, things you can't . . ." The word ended on a hissing note, like the soft kiss of a snake. ". . . *do?*"

Someone passed close outside the tent and a breeze opened the flap momentarily; dust motes spun on the sudden, thin blade of sunlight that split the hot darkness. Collis cleared his throat. "Yeah, so what?"

"I can give you those things," Kysleen said in a low voice. "In your mind." She paused, let her voice drop to a sensual whisper once more. "For a little while, I can give you *anything.*"

His gaze became sharp. "Anything I want, huh? No shit? And what if my . . . fantasy is, say, a little—"

"Out of the ordinary?" Kysleen asked smoothly. "It makes no difference to me. I can—and will—give you whatever you like. All you have to do is pay."

He lowered his gaze and she bit back a smirk; it was funny how the marks could tell her almost anything, yet couldn't look her in the eye while they did. She ran a pointed, lacquered fingernail across his arm; he didn't pull away.

"There's an old fucker who lives upstairs from my mom and me," he said at last. Bad memories made his voice hoarse with rage. "Makes my mom miserable all the time, always calling the cops when she brings a friend home—"

"Don't lie to me, Collis."

He swallowed. "Okay. When she tries to bring in a *john,* all right? Anyway, we've been living there since I was little, we can't afford to move someplace else. Bastard's always banging on the pipes, beatin' on the floor with his broom. Never lets up."

"But that's not all, is it? That's not what he's done to . . . *you?*"

"What is this?" he snarled and started to stand. "A fucking counseling session?"

"You'd like to *kill* him for that, wouldn't you, Collis?" she interrupted. The teen froze. "You never told your mother, never told anybody, but you'd like to kill him for what he did to you in the basement that night."

Collis sank back onto the chair, his eyes black pools of hate. His tongue flicked across his lips. "You can do that?"

"No," she answered serenely. "But I can make *you* think you did, make you enjoy it as though it actually happened. Would you like that?" She gave him a dark smile.

"How much?"

Kysleen touched his mind again, her eyes narrow. Yes, there were things in him she might want, but honor demanded that she give first. In reality, the money meant nothing. "Twenty dollars. In advance."

He pried a bill from a small wad in his pocket, then held back. "That's pretty steep," he said craftily. "What if I don't like it? Do I get my money back?"

She smiled again, full and wide, and he blinked, dropped the money to the table and leaned away. "Of course," she said soothingly. "But I *guarantee* this will be what you want. Now, just relax and close your eyes." She ran a finger lightly across his arm and he flinched, then forced his arm muscles to loosen. "That's right, don't worry." Her finger made a figure eight, then returned to his wrist; she slipped her hand around it and immediately found the strong pulse below the skin's surface, beating . . .

> beating . . .
>> beating . . .

The building, an old hotel converted to small apartments, squats on the corner of Bryn Mawr and Winthrop like a huge and stinking dinosaur, pale bricks mottled with stains and mold, windows gaping in the sweltering heat like crooked mouths gasping for breath, the ragged curtains tongues searching the air. Unafraid, Collis moves through the people clustered on the sidewalk, the pimps, the whores, the pushers with their endless, powdery treats and voracious greed. Someone approaches him, a young Latino with slicked-back hair and pants sporting a dozen pockets; he presses a small white packet into Collis's hand. "Gratis," the dealer says with a decayed smile and saunters away.

Collis tucks the packet in his jeans and continues

*along the sidewalk, pausing at the entrance to the build-
ing where he and his mother have lived for so many years.
He looks up and the old man is there, leaning from his
third-floor window, his eyes hooded and gleaming with a
knowing smirk that Collis can see even from sidewalk
level. He grins openly in return and the old man jerks in
surprise at this teenager who has ignored him for so long;
for the first time in years, the secret laughter of his glance
is replaced by a momentary shot of fear that quickly
dissolves into speculation. Collis's grin becomes more
menacing and the old man pulls his head inside.*

*The elevators haven't worked for a week and the mid-
dle stairwell is narrow and dark, full of trash and whispers from the air shaft it follows through the building. It
smells of urine and rat droppings, but Collis has numbed
himself to the scent long ago and his gaze slides unseeing
across a broken bag of rotting garbage and the rodent
that burrows industriously amid the scraps.*

*He pauses at his own door but does not go in. From
beyond the scarred wood he hears the grainy sound of
television laughter and music; an uncomplicated woman,
his mother has always been fond of the morning cartoons.
He is supposed to be at work, but the boss is out for the
morning—taking his wife to the doctor or some bullshit—
and his buddy Miguel will swear that Collis never left the
shop.*

*He steps lightly along the landing between the second
and third floors, the one that leads to the man's door,
which he knows will be locked. It doesn't matter; the man
is a nosy, mouthy old fuck and Collis knows there are
ways of bringing people like that into the hall. He waits
quietly at the entrance to the third floor, watching the
dusty, dim beams cut through the sludgy air currents and
listening to the building and its life sounds for long minutes before gliding forward. Ten feet from the man's door
he hardens his steps, his feet hammering against the
creaking floorboards. He paces in front of the door, back
and forth, back and forth; on the third pass he can hear
angry wheezing from the other side.*

"Get the hell away from my door!"

*Collis passes again, stomping now, his footfalls vibrat-
ing the door; his response is a mocking, girlish giggle as*

his fingers slip into a back pocket and fold around spring-loaded stainless steel.

The laughter is the ultimate insult. "What are you, some kinda wise guy?" the man bellows. Bolts turn and slide, the sound racheting through the gloom as the door is yanked in and Collis steps to the side with feline quickness. He expects a weapon to lead the old man's entrance into the hall and is not disappointed; he feels a stale breeze kiss his face as a splintered baseball bat swipes the hot air. Then the bastard steps from his apartment, cussing as he turns to inspect the hall.

Collis happily buries the knife in the old man's stomach.

The bat clatters to the floor as the fat, sweaty face re-forms into an elongated oval of shock. The moment draws out in exquisite slow motion: Collis feels the muscles in his arm bunch as he twists the blade, then pulls it upward as though he is lifting a particularly weighty shopping bag; metal parts skin and muscle, even bone, with obscene ease. There is a heavy, wet warmth spilling over Collis's hand as the man he has hated for most of his life does a death dance on the end of his stiletto.

Collis's pulse is a pounding, triumphant beat of revenge, tainted only by a quickly receding pain, a sort of mental bee sting on the memory places of his mind. . . .

Collis jerked and sat up, eyes bulging as he searched his hands for blood, but they were as clean as they could be considering he worked in a body shop.

"I—I killed him!" he said incredulously. "I *felt* myself do it." He stared at his hands again and rubbed a thumb and forefinger together experimentally. "Didn't I?"

"Only in your mind, Collis," Kysleen answered. "I think it's time for you to leave now, don't you? That is, unless you want your money back."

He shook his head as he pushed to his feet, then stumbled. At the tent flap, he hesitated and started to speak, changed his mind and clattered away.

Kysleen sat back and relaxed, let her eyelids lower as her mind turned inward. *There,* tucked in a small corner of her thoughts, was the teenager's true payment, a side-memory she'd chosen because of the drug packet in his fantasy. She went through it hungrily, feeling, *living* this piece of Collis's memory, experiencing the numbness along her gums and nostrils, feeling the rush as the drug blasted through her bloodstream. He had used cocaine so often she knew he would never miss the single recollection she had stolen—

No, Kysleen reminded herself as the fantasy-high tapered off, not stolen; taken in *payment*. For what good would this pathetic green paper do her—in what way could it enhance or change anything? All the twenty-dollar bills in the world couldn't lengthen or straighten her deformed body, fill the loneliness she had known all her life, or—most of all—hide that her parents had abandoned her as a young teenager and kept her twin sisters.

How she hated this city, this *state*. The fact that she had been born in Bartlett, Illinois, thirty miles west, only made it worse. A few more stops and the show would curve into Michigan; in the meantime she couldn't stop the bitterness that swelled at the old memory, couldn't help but condemn herself as a failure, the result of some poorly directed attention on the part of Mother Nature.

A freak.

Still, the tears dried as quickly as they had appeared. It wouldn't always be like that. She believed, she *had* to, in the promises that Ozymandias made of a newly formed world where Kysleen's role would be reversed and she would move freely and unashamed.

Her lips stretched into a grin amid the lines of moisture on her cheeks, and in the dull, musty light her teeth looked like a dark row of daggers.

Late afternoon: The midway was nearly suffocating, the air within her tent unbearable. Night would bring no relief; during a short respite in her tiny trailer, the radio had sputtered out the news that the temperature was expected to rise this evening and tomorrow might see a record-breaking 105 degrees. In spite of the difficulty she had standing, Kysleen struggled out of the tent to lean, gasping, at its entrance, ignoring the stares of the people roaming the show. From the other side of the lot she could hear the elephants bellowing their discomfort and knew they cried for a dousing; one such bray was cut off abruptly and she wondered if the Beagle Boys had whacked the animal with something to quiet it.

Her gaze wandered over the tents and booths, the occasional animal wagon with its miserable, heat-beaten prisoner. How did these people take it? Kysleen could understand the kids, little half-naked apes in shorts and tattered T-shirts, but the adults—some with ugly, doughy bodies squeezed into undersize Bermudas, others mercifully swathed in sweat-soaked polyester—how could they maintain this frantic pace among the shows and games, stuffing themselves with the worst from the junk food stands, then using the rickety, deteriorating rides to whip it all up?

Just thinking about it made her nauseous; too much time standing, even outside the oven-like interior of the tent, made her sway slightly and she clutched at her cane, wobbling like one of those stupid doll-faced punching bags with a weight in its bottom. Turning and groping at the tent flap, preferring its sweltering privacy to the greasy, flushed faces gawking in her direction, Kysleen almost ran into a thin, sad-eyed boy waiting silently behind her.

"What're you doing?" she asked harshly. Between this infernal heat and this stealthy kid, she thought she might as well lie down and have a heart attack right now.

The color along the boy's sunburned cheeks deepened. "I—uh, was, uh, waiting for you," he finally managed.

"Well, go on in," she snapped. "And hold that flap open, will you? I can't take any more of this damned sun!" He lifted the canvas obediently and she lurched through, feeling her way along the table when her eyes couldn't make the abrupt adjustment to the dimness. The muscles in her back and neck were spasming in pain and she found her chair and sank onto it with a groan. The boy stopped uncertainly just inside the tent, one hand still holding the flap as his gaze skittered around the gloomy interior. Kysleen sighed and waved at the chair across the table. "Come in and sit, kid. I won't bite. What is it you want?"

He surprised her by speaking clearly. "My name's David. My cousin Ryan was here this morning. He says he paid you ten dollars and you gave him a fantasy about—"

"A girl in his class named Rochelle," she finished for him.

"I can pay you twice that," the boy continued. "But I want a bigger fantasy. I want a *better* one."

Kysleen lifted an eyebrow. "Oh?"

"I want you to make me think my parents aren't dead."

"Close your eyes," Kysleen told him. "And give me your hand." David followed her instructions without hesitation. At thirteen, he was still more child than teenager and his hand was grimy and tipped by chewed nails bearing traces of crystallized cotton candy sugar; she could smell the soap scent of his skin despite his heat-soaked shirt. Touching him made the memory search quick and easy, and she saw a flash picture of his parents as they had been before, ironically, they'd been killed when the car of the Octopus ride they were on, part of a fly-by-night mud show, had pulled free of its corroded housing. Eight-year-old David had watched in horror as they plummeted to the ground, his thin arms clutching the family things that his father had entrusted to him: Mom's change purse and floppy straw hat, Dad's 35mm Nikon and windbreaker, a huge black-and-white stuffed dog that David himself had somehow won in the ring toss, and a star-shaped object of shimmering reddish gold that looked like a wayward puzzle—

Piece!

Shock nearly made Kysleen lose the contact, then she recovered, quickly working to build the boy's dream. Both his parents had been in their late thirties when they died; they would look older now, a little softer around the middle, more lines in their faces. Knowing David actually had a Piece of the Device somewhere within his reach had rattled her and Kysleen tried frantically to think. What memory would have been important enough to stand out in his life?

An idea struck, and she smiled. His eighth-grade graduation—perfect. His aunt and uncle had attended, and she could still feel the solidity of their love in his mind, but it was no substitute for his long-dead folks or for the empty place in his heart their death had caused. For a second a hot, nearly liquid jealousy filled her as she realized how very *loved* this boy had been, then she squeezed past it and pushed on with the fantasy—

He stands on the stage, straight and shy, his face red above a rigid, bright white shirt collar that smells of soap and starch. His teacher has placed him at the end of the first row, next to a girl he sort of likes and about whom he and his dad talked last night. He does not have a speech or anything special to do for the program like some of the kids, but that's just as well; the auditorium is so full of people that they seem to spread from the stage like a huge sea, and he doesn't need them all to see his face get any redder or hear him try to stammer through a page of meaningless words.

His mom and dad arrived early so they could sit close to the stage, and he can see them in the third row. His dad is accustomed to wearing a suit and looks cool and comfortable in his tan jacket and the jazzy floral tie bought last weekend just for the occasion; his mother is wearing a pink silk dress with a cream-colored lace collar. There is a sweet moment of sadness when he realizes that the sunlight slanting from the high, narrow windows on the south wall glimmers on silver strands that have worked their way along his father's temples and within the gentle curve of bangs on his mother's high forehead. He concentrates on their faces and gets the impression that they're smiling . . .

But only the impression.

—then yanked out of his reach.

"Hey!" David gasped. "Wait—"

She leaned back, carefully adjusting her aching spine against the hard chair. "That's it," she said. "Sorry."

"But that can't be *all!*" He squirmed, the stringy muscles along his arms and shoulders trembling. "Ryan said you could, you know, make me actually *believe* things. I couldn't even see their *faces.*"

She made herself wait, feeling David's need palpitate through her senses, fighting the urge to prod him along, afraid he might pick up on the sheer *oddness* of it. He said nothing, merely stared at her in desperation and bewilderment; she found his blind belief in his cousin's farfetched accounting of his own early morning visit unsettling.

"*Please.*"

A few heartbeats more, until she felt his disappointment slip toward despair, then she spoke, her words softened by regret. "I'm sorry, David. It's just that they've been gone a long time, and your memory—"

"I remember them just fine!"

"—is a bit blurred. You were very young when they were killed, and they would've changed by now. It's been so long since you had close contact with them that it's very difficult to pick up . . . *vibrations,* I guess you'd call them."

He slumped over the edge of the table, fighting tears. "Can't you try again?" he pleaded. "One more time?"

She shook her head. "No, it won't do any good. It's been too long." A tear snaked from the corner of one eye and he slapped at it angrily and started to stand. "Unless . . ."

He stopped. "Unless what?"

"Unless I could *touch* something that belonged to each of them," she said slyly.

The boy looked pained. "You mean like clothes? All that stuff's gone. The Salvation Army got it." His expression brightened. "I've got tons of photographs, though."

"No," she said, choosing her words carefully. "Photographs won't work. I need something they actually handled, the closer to the time they died the better."

David chewed absently on the edge of a fingernail. "I know what I can bring you," he said finally. "My mom had a little wallet she always carried, and my dad had this neat thing, sort of like a paperweight with points, that he'd just won from one of the game booths. Dad really liked it, said he was going to make it into a key chain. I was messing around with it right after Ryan told me about you. . . ." His voice trailed off and he looked at her hopefully.

She nodded. He'd put a folded pile of bills, mostly singles, on the table and she pressed the money back into his hand. "You bring those things tomorrow and we'll try again."

"Why not today?" he asked. "I don't live far."

"No," she answered. Instinct screamed at her, but she needed filler time. Once she had the Piece she'd never return it, and she would be safer if Ozymandias Oddities was on its way to another town in case a relative or friend connected its disappearance or any change in David with his visits to the show. "I'm through for today." She made her voice tired and apologetic. "I'm afraid I just can't take this heat. Besides, your fantasy will be better if I'm well rested." He started to disagree, but she held up a hand. "I'll see you tomorrow. Good-bye, David."

Kysleen had once believed that the most frightening thing in her life had been watching her family drive away, afraid they would never come back and knowing she'd hate them even if they did. She still remembered her father, a handsome magician with a traveling wagon that occasionally followed Oz's freak show for want of any better route. Her mother had been exquisite, a cream-faced child-woman with a halo of hair that always seemed charged with static electricity. Beautiful parents, yet fate chose Kysleen as its plaything within the womb.

But she had been wrong about that old fear. Waiting for this boy David to return was far, far worse, and the idea that he might do so based only on leftover love for his long-dead parents was something she found difficult to accept. Would her life have been as warm and full as his had her parents not left her behind like some broken, unwanted doll? It was impossible to imagine, out of the realm of even her abilities.

Anxiety made the hot and sticky night seem never-ending. Concentration was impossible, and she didn't even try to run her tent. She never pulled a crowd anyway, and the only thing that made the wait bearable was watching the towners from the window of her trailer while her cheap drugstore fan labored to bring relief from the heat. A few stops this summer had seen Kysleen's trailer set up next to overloaded circuits and stuck without electricity, but this time Sparky had done right by her and at least she had a breeze to keep her from fainting. She wished she could move like the others; how she longed to get out of this tin sweatbox, stroll east and away from that sweltering, setting ball of fire called the sun. Kysleen had heard the roustabouts talking about Lincoln Park and Lake Michigan, but the ten blocks that separated her from cool greenery and cold water might as well have been the width of a country. And what would she do if she got there anyway—sunbathe?

In the end, Kysleen simply waited.

"Hello, David," she said warmly. "I thought you'd changed your mind."

"No." He set a plastic grocery bag on the table, along with the same crumpled money she'd returned yesterday. "I brought the stuff like you wanted." He looked thin and fatigued; an old man's eyes peered from his boyish face.

Kysleen squeezed her hands together, stilling the urge to snatch the bag. "Your parents touched these things the day they died?"

"They were holding them before they got on the ride." His expression was questioning; yesterday's fantasy fragment had already faded and his faith in her was starting to disintegrate. For a moment they stared at each other, then he shrugged and reached inside the bag. The first thing he pulled out was a small, tan change purse, smooth from years of use, its leather smell long rubbed away.

Then he pulled out the Piece.

It was the most beautiful thing she'd ever seen, sitting in the center of the table like a small, fierce sunburst that gave off no heat. She touched it tentatively with one finger, then recoiled when its center flared to a nearly blinding gold and the object *drew* warmth from her, momentarily sending a rush of coolness over her hand. David watched impassively and she realized that the Piece's throbbing brilliance was for her eyes only. After a second she let one hand drop to the soft surface of the change purse and pointed to the chair with the other.

"I think I can give you what you need, David. Sit and close your eyes, relax. Rest your hands on the table. Don't think of anything—let *me* think for you." When he obeyed, Kysleen quickly slid the change purse to the floor, then swallowed and closed her fist around the Piece.

Golden light bled from between her fingers and it felt as though she clutched a pulsing chunk of ice; the coldness faded as she tucked it into the pocket of her dress. The Piece *belonged* here, with her and the others who were the heart of Ozymandias Oddities, not in a bottom drawer somewhere as part of a youngster's long-dead memories.

She rubbed her fingers, dispelling the last traces of cold, then covered David's hands with her own. Images from his past flooded her mind, the worst of his recollections like black, pounding waves. Again she saw his parents on the day they died, saw them hand the boy their things and climb into an ill-maintained ride, watched the car pull free of its housing and crash to the ground. Sweat beaded on her forehead and crept stinging into her eyes as she went back further, looking for happier times and dreams, searching for tools with which to build a false future. . . .

The singing and speeches finished at last, he follows his classmates down the steps from the stage, looking up when he hears his mother call his name amid the excited chatter of the graduating class. She enfolds him in an embrace that smells of Shalimar and kisses his cheek as his father claps him on the shoulder and grins, showing the chipped front tooth that makes him look so comical at times. . . .

Another stage, this one eleven years and three schools later. He sweats beneath his black robe, blinks as an insect buzzes around the silly tassel dangling along the side of his face. His parents, with their perpetual penchant for front-positioned seats, watch as he receives his diploma from John Marshall Law School. His father's hair is white and starting to thin in the back, his mother has used a rinse to soften the gray. He resembles them more with each passing year, though their faces are mapped with lines now, the road marks of love and laughter etching crevices alongside eyes and mouths. . . .

The church is cool and hushed, awash in a hundred colors from stained glass windows that stretch from shoulder to ceiling height. His father, still straight and tall, plays a dual role and leads the bride-to-be down the aisle, then takes a place in the front pew next to his wife.

His own hand has warmed the ring he slips on Mina's finger, and he is nearly overcome with her loveliness, with the silken feel of her skin as he touches her fingers, with his sheer good fortune at meeting her in law school. His mother cries when Mina gifts her with the traditional roses, her tears like crystal droplets against her age-softened skin . . .

. . . then cries again when he places her day-old grandson in her arms while a tired Mina beams from the hospital bed amid a spray of flowers and congratulatory balloons. . . .

His father's laughter is deep and rich as the family gathers around the Christmas tree at his parents' home, and with a stab of nostalgia he sees that little about the house has changed since he was a boy. Now, so many years later, his own son and two daughters play in the same family room and the sun on Christmas morning still blinds him when he sits in the recliner as it did when he was a child himself. Linda, his youngest, gives a delighted squeal as she tears into a package from her grandmother, while Ethan and Christine examine their presents more thoughtfully. . . .

Outside now, the Chicago wind wraps them in a frigid embrace as he huddles with his wife and parents and watches Christine and Ethan skate along the thick slab of ice that the lagoon in Lincoln Park has become. His mom and dad are older and becoming more fragile each year, yet they stand patiently and without complaint. Linda tugs at his hand fretfully but she is too young and he will not let her join her brother and sister; unsure, Christine wobbles on new skates along the shoreline as Ethan sweeps and whirls farther out, already a budding hockey player. The breeze slaps and stings and shrouds his vision with a faceful of blowing snow; with a start, he realizes that, somehow, his son is now eight years old. . . .

Kysleen stalled him there, then began a slow fade of the fantasy, unwilling to carry it to the end of anyone's life and destroy the sense of love, of *security*, that she had so carefully created. In the real world, David's life had veered drastically from the dreams of his boyhood; his aunt and uncle did not have the income to supplement a college or law degree, and the idea of becoming a lawyer had already been discarded in favor of more practical goals. The dreams David's mother and father had planted and would have seen to fruition were gone forever, with the memories of their lost lives and love serving only as bitter, pain-filled reminders.

But there was the matter of her payment.

Kysleen pocketed David's twenty dollars, then shot back into David's past, her mind wrapping sharp, hungry tentacles around the two things she had always wanted most to replace in her own life, pulling his memories of love and security free of the web of his thoughts and tucking them safely away in her own mind to be examined later. That done, she waited as his eyelids fluttered, then opened.

He frowned. "What's going on?"

She pulled David's money from her pocket and placed it on the table, fingers brushing reassuringly against the Piece. "I'm sorry," she said. "It didn't work. Sometimes that happens."

He looked confused. "I . . . wanted a fantasy, right?"

She nodded. "Yes. You wanted to . . . know your parents."

The boy frowned again, then stood and shoved the money in his pocket impatiently. "That's stupid. I don't have any parents. I live with my aunt and uncle. I always have."

Kysleen made her voice reproachful. "Well, that explains why I couldn't do it. You should have told me that first. I wouldn't have bothered trying."

"Sorry." He stepped to the tent flap, shrugged—

—then he was gone. Without looking back.

She felt Oz in the shadows behind her, silent, waiting, and suffered an instant of regret that she would not be able to keep the Piece with her for a little longer, look at it, touch it, feel its strange and alluring chill course through her skin. She knew she must think of the result, the greater good that the assembled Device would achieve for her and her kind, releasing them from the sorrow they had experienced most of their lives.

Just as she had released David.

She sighed and slipped a hand into her pocket. At her

touch, golden light exploded from the Piece, filling the tent with flecks of undulating pseudo-firelight. She offered it without turning to look at Oz, felt him lift it from her palm as surely as if he'd taken a part of her soul. Then he, too, was gone.

But, like David, Kysleen would look only ahead. Now David had the promise of a new life, free of the regrets once nourished by memories more painful than beneficial; Oz had yet another Piece of his precious Device, something from which she and the others could only benefit.

And she, of course, had her payment.

The ever-present pain along her neck and spine faded as she sat back to treasure the memory of her new parents.

YVONNE NAVARRO

The show rolled on . . .

ALONG THE MIDWAY (X)

St. Joseph County, Indiana

Ginger yawned as she opened the door to her trailer. The crowd that had come out from South Bend tonight had been a little rowdy but wildly enthusiastic. Their response had pumped her up for a while, but now she was just plain tired. Tomorrow would be a lazy day. A motel day. She and George already had the place picked. A long hot soak would do her—

Someone grabbed her hand as she reached for the light switch. It pulled her inside. A scream began in her throat but a hand clamped roughly over her mouth and cut it off. Her trailer door slammed closed as she was pulled to the floor. Then the lights came on.

There were two of them. One behind her, gagging her, pinning her arms, the other in front, staring, grinning. Both big, burly, and very drunk. The one in front popped the snaps on Ginger's cloak as he spread it and jammed two fingers between the front strap of her bikini top. He ripped it with a sharp downward yank. He grinned as her breasts fell free.

"Oh, baby." His grin broadened. "If you like that freak, you're gonna love us!"

Terror blasted through her. Terror so deep, so powerful, it blurred her vision and wrung her insides. She began to kick and writhe, trying to pull free just long enough to scream.

"I think you'd better quiet her down some, Hank," said the one behind.

"Yeah." Hank cocked his fist.

Suddenly her trailer door opened. Ginger couldn't see who it was but when she saw fleshy tentacles wrap around Hank's throat and right wrist, she knew it could only be George. Then she saw his face, white with fury as he looked down at her over Hank's shoulder. She saw the tentacle around the man's throat tighten, saw his face begin to purple as George dragged his struggling body from the trailer.

Suddenly she was free. The second attacker released his grip and leaped over her in a scrambling dash for the door.

"Hank! Hang on, man! I'm coming!"

Ginger rolled to her feet, rushed to the door and began screaming into the night at the top of her lungs: *"Hey, rube! Hey, rube!"*

As she continued to scream she saw the second man attack George from the rear, pummeling his ribs and kidneys, knocking George to his knees and forcing him to release his death grip on Hank. Hank staggered, then kicked George in the face. As George went down they stood over him and began kicking him. But not for long.

Bulky, growling shapes hurtled out of the darkness, leaping through the air, knocking the two attackers to the ground with flying tackles.

The freak roustabouts, the ones they called the Beagle Boys, had arrived. They pounded Hank and the other one into the dirt, then stood over them, growling. Others quickly arrived, nearly everyone from the circus and the freak show who had been within earshot. Oz worked his way to the front. He looked at the two attackers, looked at George's bloodied face as he lurched to his feet, glanced at Ginger—his gaze made her pull her cloak more tightly around her—then nodded.

"All right," he said in that strange basso voice. "Circus people go on about your business. They attacked one of ours. We'll handle this."

"They were after me," Ginger said.

"Yes," Oz said, and his eyes were not kind as he stared at her, "but it is one of *our* brothers who is bloodied. Go. All of you."

As the circus people straggled away, Dan Nolan brushed by her.

"That's what you get for hanging out with freaks."

She swung on him, her voice a low hiss. "George is *not* a freak!"

Dan's eyes widened with surprise, then narrowed as he jutted his chin toward George. "Well, excuuuuse me. What *is* he then?"

As Ginger watched him swagger away, she wondered at her own words. Of course George was a freak. But she hated to hear anyone call him that. He was a person. A good guy. The best. No one was going to call him a freak within earshot without hearing from her.

She turned back to her attackers. They were cowering in the dirt, utterly terrified. It looked like the one called Hank had wet himself. But even a seasoned war veteran might be yammering with fright if surrounded by this group. All the freaks seemed to be there—big, little, one like a snake. She was familiar with a number of them by now, but there was one here she'd never seen before, and she knew she wouldn't have forgotten him if she had. She heard someone call him Lance and he was the most repulsive creature she had ever seen.

"I hope you have learned a lesson from this," Oz told the two towners. "Never think you can attack one of us. Attack one, you attack us all. And then we *all* strike back. Get up and go. Petergello will escort you to the edge of the lot."

Ginger noticed a number of the freaks smiling and nudging each other as Petergello led the two men off. Ginger wanted to protest. From the rage she'd sensed in the freaks she'd been sure they were going to beat the two men to a pulp. But this was it? A warning and then a walk? It wasn't fair.

"The least he should have done was report them to the cops."

They were in the kitchenette of her trailer. Ginger held

one ice pack to the squishy lump on the back of George's head while he held a second to his swollen, purpling nose. The easy treatment those two creeps had received still rankled her.

George shook his head. "A walk with Petergello," he said softly. "I've heard about that. I'm seen as a deserter of sorts, and a first-of-May, to boot, but I've heard whispers about Petergello. When Oz sends someone on a walk with Petergello, they don't come back."

"You mean . . .?"

"I'm not sure exactly what they mean, but no one who gets sent on a walk with P-man is ever heard from again."

A chill rippled across her skin. She wondered what he did . . . then brushed the thought away. Nothing was too hideous for those two.

Her thoughts turned to George. From where she stood behind him as he sat in one of her kitchenette chairs, she could see his bruised scalp. His bloodied shirt was soaking in the sink. She rubbed his bare shoulder with her free hand.

"How's your nose?"

"Broken, I think. Got to be."

"Thank you," she said. "If you hadn't come along . . ."

"T'warn't nothin'. I just happened to be passing by and got a feeling something might be wrong by the way you seemed to *dive* into your trailer."

"But what were you doing out there? Your trailer's on the other side of the lot."

A long pause. Finally George cleared his throat and looked up at her. She might have laughed at his swollen nose if she hadn't known how he'd acquired it.

"I was following you."

"Following me?"

"Yeah. I follow you back to your trailer every night. Just to be sure you get home all right."

Her guardian angel. She was touched. She smoothed his curly hair and looked down at him. He really was handsome, even with a broken nose.

"You're a sweetheart."

She leaned over and kissed him. He returned the kiss. Contact with his lips was electric, awakening something within her. She pulled back for an instant but George stretched up and caught her lips again. She didn't resist. A golden warmth suffused her as she settled onto his lap and slipped her arms around his neck. It all seemed so good and right as her tongue found his.

The touch of his chest hairs against her right nipple shocked her. Then she realized that her cloak had fallen open and they were skin to skin. Suddenly she knew she wanted this good, decent, brave man, wanted him very much. Without breaking the kiss she slipped off the cloak and the torn bikini top, then pressed herself against him.

George groaned with the contact and the ends of his arms encircled her breasts in a soft, teasing caress. Ginger shuddered, not with revulsion but pleasure. It felt so good. And the vague kinkiness of it served only to heighten her excitement.

She found George's belt and began to unbuckle it.

Afterward, as they snuggled together on her narrow bed, George was strangely silent. Ginger lifted her head and looked at his troubled face.

"What's wrong?"

He shrugged. "Nothing. Everything. I don't know. This was wonderful, but what comes next? I'm afraid."

"Of what?"

"Of you. Of how you might wake up tomorrow and be disgusted with yourself. And then you'll start to blame me and hate me."

"You got beat up trying to save my life. How could I hate you?"

"Because I'm not exactly a normal person."

"No kidding. And I'm not the brightest or the best educated. I didn't even finish high school. But I'm not a kid and I've been traveling with this circus for a couple of years now. I'm long past the point where I let people take advantage of me. What just happened was my idea. You didn't trick me or seduce me or anything like that. I know who you are and what you are. And I like where I am right now."

She saw tears fill his eyes but they didn't spill over. He swallowed a couple of times before he spoke.

"I want to keep this a secret," he said. "I mean, I'd

like to shout it to the world, but you've been hassled enough for being with me in the ring. If they knew about this . . ."

"Yeah," Ginger said, disliking herself for being so relieved. "Maybe that'd be best for now."

The way he was holding his arms struck her as strange. His left was tucked between his flank and the mattress, the right was slipped under the left.

"Are you hiding your arms?"

He shrugged, like a guilty little boy. Ginger knew they were about the same age, but she felt so much older than George, so much worldlier.

"I know you don't like them."

She was stung by memories of how she'd treated him, how she must have made him feel. *You poor guy.*

"Didn't," she said, pulling his left arm free and raising it to her lips. *"Didn't."* She kissed the tip, then dragged it down between her breasts, across her belly, and slipped it between her legs. "Now there's nothing about you I don't like."

She kissed him and they began again.

Battle Creek, Michigan

Now that it was his turn, Haman was afraid.

Calm, he told himself.

He sat cross-legged in the grass, holding himself perfectly still, committing the morning to memory. Even here in the shade of Gore Edmund's coach it was hot, the air heavy and humid on his skin. Clouds of mosquitoes whined around his head, landing and taking off again in baffled rejection. He tried not to be annoyed at them. It was fine not to be bitten, but in a few hours, when he and his friends put themselves on display, the mosquitoes would suck their fill of towner blood. He would rather they sucked his, too, than to feel he and his kind were being used as bait by insects for more "normal" fare.

Dismissing the gloomy thought, Haman concentrated again on memorizing the scene around him. To his right, directly in his line of sight, the big top struggled up, acres of tan canvas swaying under the hot sun. In the shadows under the rising top he could see Lucy and Peanut straining against their poles. Sniffing, he drew in their pungent, gamey fragrance. Their brown backs bulged around the biting straps of their harnesses, jerking the jangling chains to silence. Yard by grudging yard, the butts of the giant poles creaked forward, plowing up twin bow waves of dirt as the poles straightened, pushing up another section of canvas. Haman noticed a couple of roustabouts shambling along between the "bulls," apparently less afraid of the elephants than of the Beagle Boys, who followed twenty yards behind. The quints stalked forward together in a row, their muscle-bound arms hanging out stiffly like gunslingers ready to draw. Grinning, they watched the bulls with rapt, hooded eyes, ready to close in if either of the beasts started to lag. Lucy rolled a fearful eye back at the Beagle Boys. Somehow, the elephant's fear panged Haman more than the roustabouts'. Are we really so loathsome? he wondered.

No. It is just that we are strange—outliers. When things change, the loathing will turn to awe, the fear to worship. Everyone will wish they were like us.

Turning his eyes toward the top, he blotted it from his vision, bringing the side of Gore's Ultracoach back into view. Beyond the end of the coach stretched the vast, dirt parade ground of Fort Custer. At the far border of the field, a pale building shimmered in the heat—the VA hospital, probably. He closed his eyes, content that he would remember it all now. Physically, Battle Creek was not that different from a hundred other fairgrounds he had blown through, a hundred other mornings he had waited for the tents to go up. But what he would do here made it worth remembering forever.

What he would *try* to do.

An invisible fist clenched in Haman's stomach. Sweat popped out on his forehead and streamed down the jutting length of his nose, painting a blurred silver line through the left third of his vision. The hell with it—he couldn't stay still any longer. Finding a handhold on the side of Gore's coach, he pulled himself to his feet.

"Who's there?" Gore called from inside, though the coach could not have sunk more than a hairsbreadth on its massive springs.

"It's only me, Haman. Go back to sleep, big guy."

Haman paced the length of the huge coach and back, thinking: The place where the Piece was hidden was on the other side of town. After the last show, he would go there and the hunt would begin. Hopefully he would find the Piece quickly. But Oz had said that the coordinates might not be exact. The place was big and old, full of other things.

What if I fail? Haman thought.

Taking a deep breath, he held it till it pushed at his lungs, then eased it out again. The others did their parts, he reminded himself. Even Kysleen. I can do mine. I won't fail. Please.

"Oh—there you are."

The familiar voice of Dub's frontface came from his left. He would have to turn his face to the wall of the coach to actually see him. No sense looking foolish, even in front of "family," so he faced Dub instead. "What's up?"

"Petergello wants us over at the main gate."

A mosquito whined into Haman's ear. He slapped it dead. "What's he want? We're not on until this afternoon."

Dub's frontface cleared his throat. "He didn't say."

"But you know."

Backface laughed. "How do you do that?"

Haman shrugged.

"I guess we all have our little talents, don't we," the frontface said. "Petergello wants us to muster out for some big shots. We're in the Cereal City now, you know. Kellogg's runs this town. Their corporate headquarters downtown bought a big block of tickets so naturally they think their people are entitled to a little preview."

Haman sighed. "Okay. Let's go." What the hell. The towners might take his mind off tonight.

At the front gate, Casket Thompson had already set up the props. Haman settled in front of the mock-up of a Martian spaceship, his face pointed toward Benjamin in his cage on the next stage so that he could see the Kellogg's people filing past his right shoulder. The size of the group surprised him. Judging by the obvious couples, half the crowd were husbands and wives of employees. There were even a few kids.

Swallowing, Haman nerved himself for the feel of their stares crawling across his skin. Now stay cool, he reminded himself, remembering Albuquerque: the big jerk, crossing the ropes, taunting him, ordering him to look. They never got it into their dim skulls that he *was* looking.

The old, familiar frustration gnawed at Haman. His eyes—they'd always caused the most trouble. He could have made it fine despite the pea-soup skin and Pinocchio nose, but his eyes pissed people off. Part of it was the pupils, slit like a snake's. That scared people, and anger lived very close to fear in the human psyche. But even worse than the reptilian pupils was the *way* he saw. "Retinal displacement," the doctors called it. His retinas had formed on the left within his eyeballs, so that when he appeared to be looking straight ahead, he was *seeing* to his right. It was no use explaining to people that he was not ignoring them—that, though he appeared to be staring left, he was really looking at them. They could never seem to grasp it. And that pissed *him* off.

But Oz didn't need him losing his cool, especially today. And anyway, hitting towners was like shooting fish in a barrel. Unaware that he was already looking at them, the silly jerks invariably were unprepared for his reaction. If he'd struck a little faster, that oaf back in Albuquerque wouldn't have had time to blink. He'd be blind now and Haman would be in jail and the mission would be on the rocks.

"Lookit the man in front of the spaceship," squealed a young voice. "His skin's all green, he's trying to look like a Martian. Hey, mister, where'd you get the green paint? It looks like pea soup. Hey, mister, look at me, c'mon. Look how long his nose is, Dad. And lookit those shoulders. How'd they do that, make them so big like that when the rest of him's so skinny?"

"Uh, they've got stuff—plastic skin, you know. How should I know? You're the one goes to all the monster movies. God, he's ugly, isn't he?"

Keep it up, Pops, Haman thought, feeling his knuckles flex. Just lean over the ropes—*no, stop it*. They act like this at the zoo, too, Haman thought. Making fools of themselves trying to get the gorillas to look at them. Maybe in the new order, the lordly gorillas could be freed. Bored no more, they would file past cages of humans. Imagining it, Haman smiled again.

"C'mon, look at me, mister."

Haman turned his eyes toward the kid.

"Smile, Mr. Martian!"

Haman pointed a grin at the kid and gave him a little wave.

The kid moved on and Haman kept his pupils pointed at the passing crowd so they would think he was paying attention to them. Unable to see them, he lost interest in them. Tonight rushed back in: Don't worry, Oz had said, you'll be able to sense the Piece when you're near. In fact, it will sense *you*. And only you will be able to pick it up.

What did that mean?

What if Oz was wrong and he could not "sense" it?

The anxiety hit him again, twisting in his gut. Oz was the closest thing to a father he had. Failing Oz was unthinkable—but the final cost would be even worse. They needed every Piece. If they lacked even one, then the perfect future would not come. These debased morons now passing by and gawking at him would be able to go on calling themselves normal. Only if they were brought to their knees and forced to see it would they realize that *they* were the true geeks. And if I fail tonight, Haman thought sourly, the geek shall go right on inheriting the earth.

". . . don't care for this at all."

A woman's voice, low, artificially sweet.

"Come on, Cathy, give it a chance," a male voice urged.

"They're frauds, Clarence. Con artists in makeup, laughing at us for being so gullible."

"Shhh," the man whispered. "Maybe, maybe not."

His interest pricked, Haman turned his face away from the voices, so he could spot the man and woman. They were standing at the rope in front of his setup. She was slim and dark haired, her pretty face marred by tension. The man beside her—Clarence—was paunchy around the middle, with thinning brown hair and worried eyes. He was sweating, holding his suit coat over one shoulder, his face gleaming.

"Anyway, the circus isn't only this," he said. "Wait until you see the acts tonight. Guys juggling with their *feet*, Cathy. And the high-wire act, the clowns—"

"Forget tonight. I'm not coming back here."

Clarence looked at her with distress. "But you may

never get to see something like this again. Circuses are dying. It's terrible—a grand old tradition, fading away in a world of cable TV and tractor pulls. Did you know the first circus in America dates back to 1793? George Washington attended it."

"I don't care if the pope and Pocahontas attended it." Seeing his hurt expression, Cathy gave his arm a brief, convulsive squeeze. "I'm sorry, Clarence. But that's the trouble with you. Always mooning over the past. The present doesn't even exist for you. And as for the future, well, we've seen how well you prepare for that. We're in hock up to our ears for Sandy, and God knows whether Tish will even get to go to college."

Cathy's voice was tight with resentment now. Haman listened, torn between revulsion and fascination. There was something else here—something he hadn't quite caught yet. Each was hiding something.

"Let's keep our voices down, okay?" Clarence said, glancing over, looking relieved when he saw that Haman's head was turned away. The relief interested Haman, too. Not many towners would care what a "freak" thought of them.

"You know I'm right," Cathy said.

"I'm sorry," Clarence said. "I've done my best—"

"Really? Well, your best must not be much when Ralph Bailey, who is ten years younger than you, gets the promotion. What do you get? A free pass to the circus—oh, hi, Liz, Ralph. How nice to see you!"

Cathy's voice was suddenly perky. Amused, Haman watched the ten-years-younger Ralph walk past with a well-dressed blonde on his arm. Clarence gazed, unknowing, right into Haman's eyes, his face a mask of suppressed misery.

"Take me home, Clarence," Cathy said.

"Couldn't you wait for me a few minutes in the car? I won't be long. I'd just like to go over there and watch the elephants finish putting up the big top."

Haman saw Cathy steal a glance at her watch as Clarence pointed. "I like to be there when Tish gets home from school, you know that."

"But that's not for three hours."

Of course, Haman thought, getting it.

"She had the sniffles today," Cathy said. "She may decide to cut her last class."

"The sniffles? I didn't notice—"

"You rarely do."

Clarence looked stung.

Don't you see? Haman thought. Come on, man, it's plain as the nose on your face.

"You can come back here after you drop me off," Cathy persisted—"if you have nothing better to do at work."

"Okay. Let's go."

Haman watched them pull away from the crowd of Kellogg's workers and walk toward the dusty field that had been turned into a parking lot for the day. Cathy's steps were long, eager; Clarence's dragging.

She's having an affair, Haman thought, you poor fool. She's going home now so she can bounce around in your bed with some broad-shouldered younger guy with hair—

Haman realized with surprise that he was feeling pity for this Clarence boob. He shook it off. The man is a towner, Haman thought.

And I've got worries of my own.

Clarence sat in a cool, dim corner of the Dew Drop Inn, nursing his third martini and wondering how to tell Cathy that he had been fired. One week left on his two weeks notice and he still couldn't summon the nerve. She'd go ballistic. It would be all over between them, twenty years of marriage down the drain, because he'd mistakenly turned in one of his doodles instead of the new ad copy.

Clarence traced a finger through the condensation on the side of his martini glass. It was a good glass, with the proper funnel shape. A good glass in a good place—one of the few old "lounges" left as wave after wave of progress swept Battle Creek. Not a window in the joint, thank God. The Dew Drop Inn was cozy, dark and secure, with that timeless nighttime look that let you believe, no matter what time you came in, that work was over for the day.

Spearing the olive at the bottom of his glass, Clarence popped it into his mouth, savoring the mingled tastes of oil and juniper. He gazed fondly out the slot of his booth at the corner of the long bar. Two guys with bowling bags and blue shirts that said Farley's Funeral Home sat, elbowed down with their beers. The smoke of their Camels curled up into the rich haze at the ceiling. Amazing. Here these guys worked for a funeral home, saw all the young ones rolled in from smoking. And still they lit up. Why? Clarence tried to puzzle it out, but the martinis had shorted out his more discerning synapses and he gave it up.

Simpler question: Should he go in to work tomorrow?

If he didn't, who would mind? The two weeks notice was a courtesy. They'd pay him off whether he came in or not. Kellogg's was good that way, he had to admit it. And, in fact, he deserved to be fired. He'd only meant to sketch in the essentials of the old cereal box he remembered from his boyhood. But then it had become a game of seeing how many details he could coax from his memory. His pens had taken on a life of their own and the doodle had ended up looking better than most of his finished copy.

Clarence groaned softly. If the foreman in packing hadn't caught the mistake, thousands of kids would be writing angry letters asking why a nonexistent Flash Gordon decoder ring wasn't inside their boxes. Most of them wouldn't even know who Flash Gordon was, but they'd want the rings anyway. That had been the great thing about those old cereal boxes of the past. No kid under fifteen could resist them. Clarence raised his glass: Hail the lost grand age of the trinket—Kellogg's and Post vying for the hearts of children not with Saturday morning cartoon spinoffs but with small magnifying glasses and space cadet whistles buried inside their cereal boxes. Tools of the imagination, treasures you could hold in your hand.

Clarence realized a moony grin had crept across his face. He wiped it off. There was nothing funny about this. Kellogg's had had to trash ten thousand Frosted Flakes boxes in the big dump behind the factory.

And he had trashed his marriage.

It would be the final proof of what had become Cathy's number one hypothesis: that he was living in the past.

Clarence put ten bucks on the table of his booth, pushed up slowly, and walked out of the Dew Drop Inn. Drop in, walk out, he reflected—there's something backward about that. Outside, he leaned against the brick and stood in the warm night air. The neon sign above his head sputtered and buzzed, his clothes ticking blue, then green under its flashing martini and beer glasses. The cobbled street stretched away from him, soft mists curling from the earth between its seams. Someday, in the interests of uniformity, the city fathers would blacktop this street, as they had all the others over the years. Of course, the city fathers would never have seen it like this, never savored the way the pearly light from the corner street lamp flowed across it, casting long, soft shadows from each fractional ridge of brick.

A train horn hooted in the night, the lost, lonely cry of a dinosaur. Clarence listened, soothed by the distant clank of iron on iron, remembering when he'd left Battle Creek for two years to go to college. That first month, waking up at two A.M. every night, listening in vain for the mournful hoot of the Soo Line. Lord love the freights, hauling the grain into Battle Creek, carrying away the cereal. The soul of the town, its protector. How many smart-ass bank robbers from places like Detroit and Chicago had been caught over the years because they didn't understand about Battle Creek trains? Racing away from the police sirens, laughing in their souped-up cars, only to fetch up, no matter which way they turned, against a railway crossing, blocked by the clanking crawl of a freight.

Of course, that was in the old days, before they started putting bridges over most of the tracks.

The train rumbled away. In its wake of silence, Clarence heard the soft burble of the Battle Creek River two blocks down, cutting between the abandoned warehouses which leaned over it like a sinking, lost borough of Venice. The river had been here before Battle Creek and would be here after it was gone—there was an odd comfort in that.

Suddenly Clarence realized why the two bowlers from Farley's smoked. It was *because* they worked for a funeral home, not in spite of it. They had seen enough. They knew they were dying. They had decided to do it their way.

"Hah!" Clarence said, struck by a revelation.

Okay, he thought, I'm dying. I can do it by default or by my fault. That's it, no other options. Defaulting is going home now and telling Cathy that I got sacked and listening to her yell and watching her pack, then going out tomorrow to find another job. At Post maybe, like Dad.

Cathy will probably pack *my* things, not hers.

Which would be entirely fair, too.

Clarence realized with surprise that he could admit that to himself with absolutely no sense of guilt. I'm not a bad man, he thought, not an evil man, not even an incapable man. For crying out loud, my doodle was so good it mesmerized them. They made up ten thousand boxes promising Flash Gordon rings before they came to their senses. That's how good I am. I bewitched them!

Clarence laughed out loud.

I wanted to give Cathy a good life, and I tried to do that, but it wasn't in me.

So what *is* in me? What do I *want*?

He sobered. It was obvious. He wanted a Flash Gordon decoder ring. That's why he had been doodling the old back of the cereal box in the first place. He'd never stopped wanting that ring. If only Dad had worked at Kellogg's instead of Post. Listening in his mind, Clarence heard the stern voice: *No Kellogg's cereals in my house.* God, Clarence thought, I came so close. Mom sneaked a box in, bless her, but by then the offer had expired. Thirty-five years ago.

Too late forever.

An idea started to nibble at the edge of Clarence's mind. He listened to the river, letting his mind float along with it. Too late, unless . . .

Where had Kellogg's taken the ten thousand misprinted cereal boxes? The same place they took everything they no longer needed or wanted—the place that had been here since the birth of Kellogg's itself. Clarence felt his heart begin to pound. Dickie and the airplanes! he thought. He would have remembered this sooner if he had not been asleep, dying by default, too narcotized to realize, even, what he wanted.

It was 1955—or '56, maybe—anyway, the summer

he'd played Little League: Dickie Guth had shown up at the ball field one day with a fistful of those little plastic airplanes Kellogg's had been offering until a few weeks before. All the kids had gathered around, asking him how he'd managed to eat so much cereal. He hadn't. He'd gone to the Kellogg's dump and found the planes lying in a vast pile. There were tons of other things, too—toy soldiers, cricket clickers, plastic rockets. You weren't supposed to go in. There was a tall fence and a fierce watchman who had yelled at Dickie and chased him—or at least that's what Dickie had boasted.

We talked about it for weeks afterward, Clarence remembered. We all wanted to go, but none of us had the guts. Except Dickie. He went back every few months like a kid commando and brought stuff out.

Is the stuff maybe still in there? Clarence wondered. After all, where would it go? The Flash Gordon ring had been plastic, and plastic, as everyone was so fond of saying these days, took forever to decay. Maybe he could . . .

Nah, it was crazy.

Hurrying to his Nash Rambler, Clarence drove east through town. To his left he could see the glow of the new mall rising like a halo above the skyline. At one end, the glow was brighter—Kellogg's massive new headquarters building, rising from the ashes of a city block of forgotten shops with the confident and pristine grandeur of a Mormon temple. Progress. Clarence grunted sourly, then caught himself. Cathy's absolutely right, he decided. I live in the past. So it's time I did it right.

The gate to the Kellogg's dump was closed. Fortunately, they'd replaced the old padlock version with a shiny new gate that rode on tracks. Clarence stuck his plastic ID tag in the box and the gate slid open. He grinned: *Progress outsmarts itself again!*

Driving through the gate, Clarence felt an incredible peace descending on him. He steered the Rambler carefully in the wash of his headlights along flattened bulldozer paths. The side wash of the beams showed him huge sliding mountains of spent cardboard. Glossy rivers of waxed cereal box liners glittered ahead of him. He drove deeper and deeper into the eerie, listing landscape. At intervals, hulking, steel machines, junked from the factory assembly lines, stood guard like armored sentinels. Clarence rolled down his window. A tide of warm, humid air rolled in, heavy with the malty smell of cereal. He inhaled deeply, savoring the familiar smell. An east wind from the factory. Maybe the gods of cereal were smiling on him tonight.

The northeast corner, Dickie had said, right by the big smokestack.

Filled with excitement, Clarence squinted through the windshield. Yes, there was the smokestack ahead, old and crumbling now, sitting atop a squat, brick building that had probably, in the days before pollution worries, served as an incinerator.

Clarence stopped the Rambler and got out, walking along beside his headlight beams, searching the ground. The packed dirt was stippled with the corners of buried boxes. He could smell the damp cardboard, mingled with dirt. Dropping to his hands and knees, he scraped at the dirt with his fingers.

All of a sudden, a sick feeling rippled through the pit of his stomach. Something flashed in his mind—a quick, searing image of a great city in flames, people screaming, running in panic.

Clarence pushed back on his heels, startled. As his fingers left the dirt, the images in his head winked out. What was *that?* he wondered. Had he seen something? No. It had just been a touch of dizziness.

Clarence sat, staring at the dirt, his excitement fading. This *was* crazy. How much dirt had been piled here by the bulldozers in the thirty-five years since Dickie's story? Three feet? Twenty feet?

What if the rings weren't buried here? What if he dug ten feet and found nothing but moldering cardboard?

Maybe the trinkets weren't even buried here anymore but had been burned up in that incinerator. Maybe Dickie had been lying in the first place. Furthermore, Clarence realized, it's night and I don't even have a shovel.

Face it, I'm not going to get the decoder ring.

Rocking on his heels, he put a hand over his eyes, trapping a sudden press of tears behind his lids. For a little bit, there, it had seemed so *right*. If he couldn't trust a feeling so strong, a conviction powerful enough to bring him out here to a dump in the middle of the night, then how was he ever going to know what was right? And if he didn't know what was right for himself, how could he have any hope of taking control of his own life?

With his eyes closed, Clarence became aware of an odd feeling, a tightening of nerves along his neck. *I'm being watched.* A chill ran up his spine. Trying to act natural, he stood and edged out of the headlight beams, giving his eyes a chance to adjust to the dark again. His throat dry, he scanned the roof of the old incinerator. In the dimming glow of his headlights, he could see the whole roof. No one was there.

Clarence scanned the nearby mountains of trash.

Oh, God, there he was!

Clarence felt his heart race. He stared, wide-eyed. The black image of a man stood on top of the tallest mountain of trash, silhouetted against the purplish radiance of Battle Creek to the west. The figure stood very still, one knee cocked, a foot on the crest of the mound.

But he's not looking at me, Clarence realized, puzzled. He's looking off the other way.

Suddenly the figure moved, disappearing from the crest, bounding down toward Clarence. In the dim wash of the headlights, Clarence could see him zigzagging through the trash with the agility of a mountain goat. Clarence's feet felt frozen to the ground. He's coming to get me, he thought. *Run!*

Clarence ran for the Rambler, fumbling at the door handle. As he started to plunge inside, a hand grabbed his arm and whirled him around, slamming him against the side of the car. Terrified, he stared into the horrid, snake-like eyes of—

"You're the Man from Mars," Clarence breathed. He stared at the green face, the bulging shoulders. This isn't real, he thought. I'm back home, having a nightmare.

The Man from Mars turned his head to the side, looking away from Clarence's right shoulder. "My name is Haman," he said. "What are you doing out here, Clarence?"

"How do you kn-know my name?" Clarence could barely find wind enough to speak. His knees felt spongy.

"You—you eavesdropped on Cathy and me," he realized. "When we were at the circus this morning."

"What are you doing out here?" Haman repeated, his voice edged with menace.

"I might ask you the same question," Clarence said, surprising himself.

Haman's face, still cocked to the right, hardened. "And I might beat your face bloody."

"I . . . I don't think so," Clarence ventured.

"Don't you?" Haman looked interested now. "How good a thinker *are* you, Clarence?"

"Not so good, maybe. What are you looking at?"

"You."

Clarence considered this. "Really?"

"Really."

Clarence felt a thrill of superstitious fear as he realized that, somehow, the reptilian pupils of Haman's eyes actually *were* looking not away from him, but *at* him. And that he was seeing more than Clarence would like him to see.

"I'll ask you again," Haman said. "Why are you here?"

Clarence told him about the Flash Gordon decoder ring.

When he had finished, Haman said nothing, his eyes staring off to the side, his green face unreadable. He has a very long nose, Clarence realized. He looks like Pinocchio after his fifth lie. "Uh, I told you why I was here. Why are you here?"

"That is none of your concern," Haman said.

"You're looking for something, too, aren't you?" Clarence said, nettled.

"Get out of here. Your wife needs you at home."

"No she doesn't." Clarence's throat was suddenly thick. "She's having an affair."

Haman's eyebrows shot up. "You know that?"

Clarence stared at him. "Yes, I know that. How the hell do *you* know it."

Haman shrugged.

It was the first normal thing Clarence had seen him do. It made him seem warmer, more human. "You see a lot, don't you?"

"Go home, Clarence."

"No."

Haman turned and walked away from him, away from the headlight beams, his head down and cocked to the side. Clarence watched, fascinated. The guy, this freakish man, *was* looking for something. But what could it possibly be? He had never even been in this town before, had he? Surely a guy who looked like this would stir up talk, and he would have heard that talk. I've lived here for forty-four years, Clarence thought, except when I went away to college, and I've never heard of any green man before.

Suddenly, Haman stopped walking. Clarence saw that a pulsing red glow had started up at the circus man's feet.

"Huh?" Clarence said. He ran over to Haman's side.

"Get back," Haman said.

Clarence stared at the ground, mesmerized. There was something down there, under the surface. It had a very odd shape, like a dumbbell that had been twisted and sheared off halfway through one bulbous end. It was bigger than a dumbbell though—about half again as big. Whatever it was, the earth seemed transparent around it. "This wasn't here before," Clarence said. "I'd have noticed the light."

"It was here," Haman said. "It's been here for a long time. I ask you once again to leave."

"What is it?" Clarence asked, fascinated.

Haman knelt and began to scoop at the dirt.

"You're digging in the wrong place," Clarence said. "It's over here to your right."

Ignoring him, Haman continued to dig. The earth seemed to melt like sand under his hands, giving way easily. But why was he digging over there? Clarence wondered. The red thing, whatever it was, was right here.

Suddenly, Haman stopped digging and straightened, a look of intense excitement transforming his grotesque, green face. "I've got it!" he said.

Clarence watched him bend into his empty hole and grasp nothing. As Haman stood again, the pulsing red thing rose through the earth beside him, surfacing, hovering in the air a yard to Haman's right. The green man's fingers were curled as if clutching it. "I can see!" Haman shouted. "I can see everything!"

Clarence inched over to the twisted red shape hovering in the air. Easing a finger out, he tried to touch it. His finger passed through emptiness.

He looked at Haman, baffled. "I want to touch it."

"No you don't, man."

"You've got it, don't you? Even though it looks like it's over here." On impulse, Clarence reached for Haman's hand.

"Don't"

A dizzying shock struck Clarence, tearing down from his throat to his stomach. He saw the burning city again. The towering skyline, black against a raging red sky, made him think of New York, or maybe Chicago. He watched, horrified, as a crowd of people ran toward him. Their faces were frozen in terror, their screams beating at his eardrums. Behind the panicked crowd a dozen dark figures marched forward, spread out in a row, herding the people ahead of them like cattle to the slaughter. The dark figures did not quite look human. At the center of their advancing row a larger shape loomed, its surface crawling and twisting like a horde of insects under black light.

Something struck his hand a stinging blow and the vision vanished. He was standing in the dark dump, staring at Haman, feeling like he'd lost a few seconds, somehow. But no, he was right here. Crickets chirped softly in the night. Relief flooded him—he could not imagine why. His hand stung and he realized Haman had slapped it away. *I tried to touch that thing floating beside him,* Clarence remembered. *But I guess he wants to keep it to himself. Fine. It's not what I came for anyway.*

Haman's green face was transfixed by rapture. "I can see into the ground!" he exulted. "Bones, a skeleton, right where you're standing. Very deep. A tomahawk, too—some arrows."

"An Ojibwa Indian," Clarence whispered, a shiver of awe passing through him. "They were here before us. We destroyed them in a big fight. I mean the settlers. That's why it's called Battle Creek."

Haman stared past him. "What?"

"Nothing. What else do you see?"

"Boxes. Parts of machines. Stones. It's like standing on the surface of a clear lake." Haman's hands were still curled, his elbows locked, as if he were holding the thing that hovered in the air beside him. Clarence understood that he actually *was* holding it—maybe he was the only man in the world who *could* hold it.

Clarence was stunned by a sudden rush of hope. "Do you . . . do you see . . . ?"

Haman shook his head. "No. No decoder rings."

"Maybe they're over there, near that chimney."

"Poor man," Haman said. "You can't live in the past."

"Oh yeah?" Clarence gestured around the dark dump, the mountains of trash, etched black against the maroon horizon of the city. "What do you think this is?"

"This is the past that no one wanted," Haman replied.

"I want it," Clarence said stubbornly.

"I have to go," Haman said.

"Please. Just come with me and look." Clarence set off without waiting for an answer, leading the way back to the edge of the old incinerator. He turned, breathless, hoping, and there was Haman, behind him, his head bowed and cocked to the side. Beside him, the red, sheared dumbbell hovered in the air.

"I see some little toy cars."

Clarence pinched his eyes shut, thinking. "Cars? Yes! They came after the rings! Try to look below them."

Haman bent closer to the ground. "Okay. The rings are there, hundreds of them. Do you want me to dig them out?"

"Yes—wait . . . No." Clarence grinned. His legs strained with the urge to caper and dance. The decoder rings were there. He was going to get them all—

No, he decided, just one. More than one would be worth less than one. I'm going to be the only kid on my block to have one! Clarence realized Haman was still waiting for an answer. "No, don't dig. I want to do it."

"They're quite deep."

"I have time. I've been fired." Clarence laughed.

Haman stood, profile on to him, studying him.

Clarence sobered, looking at the pulsing shape beside the other man. "What in God's name *is* that?"

"A piece of the new future," Haman said. "When it arrives, you will know."

Clarence nodded. He did not really understand and

wasn't sure he cared. If he wanted to, he could decipher it all later—when he had the decoder ring.

Dropping to his knees, he began to dig, feverish with need. The dirt was soft and fragrant between his fingers. I should thank Haman, he realized suddenly. He looked up, but the circus freak—and his strange, pulsing burden— were gone. South of town, in the coal black darkness of midnight, a freight train wailed its long requiem at the skewed wooden crosses as it passed.

Clarence went back to digging.

STEVEN SPRUILL

The show rolled on . . .

Drood Hollow, West Virginia

Lance Whiting sat alone in his tent on a small stool, separated from the gawkers by wire mesh and a million miles. The show supplied the wire, Lance the distance. He had to, or the strain of staring nightly into the face of so much loathing would have driven him crazy. Oz suggested he simply create another place to be, and he had. Tonight he was on a California beach, watching the evening sun set the sky afire as it dropped over the western horizon in an opera of color. Lance neither saw nor heard anything within the tent. Sunset blocked out the ashen faces and surf washed away the wretched sounds they made. He was protected, wrapped inside the beauty he knew existed within the shell of their horror.

Because, as he reminded himself at least twenty times a night, it was *their* horror, *their* ugliness, *their* guilt and fear they saw when they looked at him. Sometimes he would come back from the haven in his mind to look at the faces and wonder why they paid to see their own ugliness made manifest. Was it self-hate? Disbelief? Did they think the show was kidding when it told them they were about to see the worst thing they could imagine? Did he have the same attraction as a horoscope which dared to tell the truth; *today you will be shown the deformed creature made from discarded parts of every evil impulse*

236

you've ever had. You will see yourself as the Devil sees you. Stay indoors.

He marveled at the way they kept coming but, whatever the reason, they all wanted to see the Man of a Thousand Fears. They lined up outside his little tent to sign a liability waiver and then came in to face him. What they saw was always different, always horrible; gargoyle twisted stone-slime with bleeding eyes, or visions of erupting disease. Each individual saw the toxic waste of his own brain. Sometimes they threw up. Sometimes they fainted. Others were suddenly petrified, electrocuted eyes locked on to the hulking shape behind their own personal mirrors. In the beginning he'd pitied them, wanted to reach out and comfort them, tell them not to worry, that everyone carried an inherited sickness called fear which gave off a toxin named anger and a spore called lust, and they were destined to pass the sickness along to their children and it was no one's fault, least of all his. He had wanted to reach out and embrace them in sympathy, to give them absolution for their private agony as only one who bore the weight of their fear was able. Once or twice he even tried, but when they saw him open his arms it was as though they were peering through the gates of Hell itself. They'd run screaming, clawing their way through the tent's opening or under its sides. Once, after one of his fits of empathy, the show was hit with an injunction and forced to leave town. The wire had been erected then, to restrain his love as much as the loathing of the towners.

Not long after the wire went up Lance resolved to kill himself. He was in his camper with the barrel of a .357 magnum in his mouth when Oz came in and, as casually as if he were bumming a drag off a cigarette, took the gun away and sat down. Oz's giant torso slumped against the wall of the camper, spidery arms outstretched along the back of a bench seat, giant head rolled back, blank face looking at the ceiling as he spoke.

"Little brother," he said. "How old are you now, sixteen, seventeen?"

"You know how old I am," Lance answered. "You're always telling me about how you rescued me when I was born."

Oz didn't look at him but the deep voice was direct, as if it came out of the massive chest, or heart. "That's right, wise guy," he said. "You're sixteen. And why do you think I did that? They were going to kill you, you know. Or at least let you die. Put you in some corner like a sack of garbage and let you rot."

"Even my mother . . ."

"What do you want from her? She died when you were born."

"Because I was . . ."

"Because she thought she could pass for straight," said Oz. "She couldn't stand the shock of seeing you any more than the rest of them. It wasn't her fault she couldn't see beyond her own fears to what you are inside."

Lance started to cry, forcing the words out between clenched teeth. "What am I then?" he asked helplessly. "Maybe what I see is a lie and they see the truth."

From somewhere deep inside Oz came a laughlike rumble. "The truth," he said derisively, and held up the gun. "The immortal search for the truth has killed more people than bullets. You know the difference between us and them? We know that nothing this side of the Veil is truth."

Then Lance forgot his debt and turned on Oz for the first time in his life. "That's all damned nice and philosophical for you, but I'm the one who has to live it. I'm the one who has to sit in the tent and watch those people get sick when they see me. Don't you understand? I have to know they're wrong. If I don't know they're wrong I can't stand it. If they're right I want to die. Fuck them, fuck this life, and fuck you. I'd rather die."

Once, when a couple of the Beagle Boys were drunk and hassling towners on the midway, he'd seen Oz wrap one skinny arm around each of their heads and squeeze them to his huge torso until they looked like hanged men, dangling feet kicking, faces blue. Then he'd literally thrown them into a camper and locked the door for two days. So Lance half expected Oz to reach out and wring his neck as easily as a pigeon's, but instead he found himself being lifted gently and turned toward a full-length mirror on the bathroom door. Oz stepped out of the mirror's border and his voice seemed to come from somewhere as distant as time but as near as the inside of Lance's own mind.

"What do you see?" the almost soundless voice asked.

"You know what I see," answered Lance, subdued but not mollified.

"It's the same as always then?" asked the voice.

"Yes."

"Tall blond kid? Sun-bleached hair? Skin tanned the color of California beach sand? Jawline sharp enough to cut glass? Muscles perfect as a braille explanation of human anatomy?"

"Yes, yes, yes," Lance said irritably.

"Well then, it's not you they see, Lance. I've told you that. It's something chemical or electrical, some field around you. You're nothing more than a mirror to the worst parts of their minds. When they look at you they see the physical manifestation of all those things they don't want to admit about themselves. They project all their sins onto you. I know it's not fair, boy, and the day is coming soon when things will be reversed."

Lance bowed his head and walked away from the mirror. "Will that be any better, Oz?" he asked.

"Hang on, kid," advised Oz. "Just hang on and the world will turn your way. Anytime you feel down just look at yourself. Hell, most people would kill to look like that. Let it work for you."

"How? Everyone else gags at me."

"Not the freaks, kid. Carmella's always giving you the eye."

For the first time in a while, Lance laughed. "I wonder how often she's heard that one."

It was true. The female freaks seemed to see him as beautiful. He couldn't walk across the backyard without Carmella coming up to him, an extra button undone on her blouse, and making with the invitations. But even she didn't see him the way he saw himself. To her he was dark and Latin, some kind of Di Nicino creature. And that extra eye. It never seemed to close. He'd imagine it staring at him in bed like the eye of God and any passion he felt would dissipate. "I can't, Oz."

"Quinta then."

"She scares me, Oz. I hate to admit it but they all make me sick."

"Because you're so beautiful?" There was an acid sting in his tone.

"I can't help it."

"You're in a hell of a fix there, boy. But remember what I said. The day is coming, and when it does you'll lose your virginity, one way or another."

Oz was getting up to leave, taking the gun with him but it didn't matter. The impulse toward suicide was over. Lance would try to hang on like Oz said, wait for butterflies with the faith of a caterpillar. But still he couldn't resist a last question. "Oz," he asked. "What about you? What do I look like to you?"

"All you need to know you can learn from the mirror."

"Enough philosophy, Oz. Answer my question."

Oz's head rolled back almost involuntarily to stare up and over his own right shoulder, at what, Lance didn't have a clue. Now the voice was deep and round again, seeming to come straight out of Oz's exposed Adam's apple. "Little brother," it said. "You're forgetting one thing. My dreams are far darker than the straights'." With that he was out the door before Lance had a chance to ask again. But someday, someday he'd force the question. Without knowing why, he was sure Oz was the one person with a definitive answer.

Back in the tent: The sun's final quarter was dipping like a coral sail into the polished calm of evening water. The Pacific horizon curved away to either side in an eyeshadow arc, pulling him with it into a fruit-colored stretch of endless tomorrow. Something was calling to him from a brighter future, a dawn many mornings away when an eternal sky would reign royal blue over the butterfly's release from his mirrored cocoon. Something was calling him, something soft, feminine, a voice, a close voice.

"Hello. Hello, can you hear me in there? You look like you're asleep or something."

Lance's eyes popped open as if the voice had released a spring in his head. He was staring into the face of a girl, or rather was absorbing her stare. His first impulse was to close his eyes and go back to the beach. She was probably just another of the albino mutants who populated this graveyard of dead gas pumps calling itself Drood Hollow, West Virginia.

Sometimes he liked to look back at the horrified faces just to see their surface intelligence erased by the brute stupidity fear always brings, but in this town intelligence had already been erased by genetics.

As far as anyone in the show had been able to discover, there were only four family names in Drood Hollow, not surprising since most of the citizenry showed marked evidence of inbreeding. They seemed to come in two basic types; death white albinos with brick red hair and rabbit pink eyes, or lumpy hulks with weaselly eyes and noses like new potatoes. The intelligence level, however, appeared to be at least equal to that of a tribe of mountain gorillas.

Drood Hollow itself consisted of two ancient gas stations with globe-topped pumps still imprinted with the names Esso and Cities Service. The town's social center was a phone booth about a hundred yards up the road from the Esso station and directly across from a dank little store which sold mostly beer, cigarettes, and pickled pink sausages which decomposed slowly in a radish-colored brine like alien turds in a forgotten lab basement. The rest of the community was scattered up and down the dry creek beds in a spokelike arrangement of leaning gray houses with rotting-leaf lawns upon which sat the rusted hulks of former cars and farm machinery. All the decom-posing metal had furrowed the ground into poison trails which led like a virus track to forests of dead gray trees, bowed and broken into thickets of surrender by mountain winds looking for easy prey.

The show had hit town in the middle of the night and made its way through a driving rain to what a chicken-necked towner had referred to as "the playground." It turned out to be a five-acre tundra of scrub and mud reached by an ascending spiderweb of sloppy troughs which the locals referred to as "lanes." From atop the playground could be seen the whole incipient landfill which was Drood Hollow. At night the fog drifted up the lanes onto the flats and covered everyone's ankles, making the place look like some rural backwater of the river Styx, with bloodless pales floating in desperation from tent to tent looking for a way in or out.

If anyone needed proof that Oz had displaced Peabody as the boss of the show their presence in Drood Hollow was it. Some of the circus people objected lamely but they knew it was no use. The freaks were more curious than disturbed. Under Oz's tutelage they were, for the first time in their lives, gaining ascendance over a normal-looking group of people. They weren't about to buck the trend no matter where it took them. Oh, a few had asked him what they were doing there, but Oz just looked up and back in his loose-necked way and said he felt the place calling to him.

Since Lance's usual haunts were inside his mind or his camper it made no difference to him where they were. The locals would file through his tent, scream, gag, roar, or whatever, then go on their way. He'd only see the first few, just to establish their probable level of violence, then he'd drift away. Unless something called him back, like that voice, that girl. That girl who was now leaning closer to the wire, saying something again.

"Come on now, I know you can hear me. I caught you looking a few minutes ago, so come on and look up at me now, you cute thing you."

What was it she'd called him? *You cute thing.* Impossible. But then she did it again.

"Come on and look at me, cutey. I ain't going to bite you."

Lance looked up and saw two eyes on the verge of blue, eyes the color of rain on a clear day. They were large and round and staring at him with the exaggerated kindness you show to a new puppy. Lance was dumbstruck and awed, like a newborn baby emerging to an unimagined world. He looked closer to make sure it wasn't one of the girl freaks playing some kind of practical joke. What he saw was a round open face, not beautiful but abundantly female, pale but not albino, with a kind of sun spray of tiny freckles covering the bridge of her nose.

"There," she said. "I knew you was just playing possum, kinda to get away from everyone staring at you.

Must pluck your nerves a bit but then I guess you must be used to it by now, huh?"

She looked to be somewhere between sixteen and twenty, youthful skin still showing milk-fat over cheekbones that would someday emerge into photogenic prominence. Her hair was a faded russet on its way to wintry brown, November hair parted down the middle of her head and combed into well-behaved lifelessness, pinioned with barrettes apparently made from clothes pins. Lance thought she had the kind of Great Plains beauty you might see in a locket found on the body of a dead cowboy; a comparative beauty owing much to the barrenness of its surroundings and the fertility in the eye of its beholder. But what was he but a cowboy trekking parched and lonely through a wilderness in which only the cactus loved him. She also had big tits. No doubt about it, tits as big as Carmella's but attached to a normal body. He felt a stirring in his groin.

"Well," she said, rocking back with her hands on her hips. "Say something to me. Jeez, you'd think the cat had got your tongue. You can talk can't you?"

"Yes," Lance managed to croak.

"Well then, my name's Galena. It's someplace my ma saw on a map on the back of a spaghetti box. She's dead now but it don't make me too sad 'cause I never knew her much. Do you think that's mean of me?"

Lance didn't know what to say. His thinking hadn't progressed beyond the fact that a reasonably attractive girl with big tits was talking to him as if he were human.

"Well, do you?"

It dawned on him that she had the particularly rural trait of expecting answers to her questions.

"Uh, no," he said. "How would you know what to miss about her? Since you never knew her, I mean."

"That's right. Goddarned you're not only cute, you're smart too. Goddarned."

Lance was afraid to broach the question. He thought there might be some kind of hypnosis going on and that to ask would dissipate any kindly electrons attached to him. But he had to know. "You keep saying I'm cute. Could I ask you, ah, what you mean by that?"

She adopted a coy sort of implied wink as she turned to a three-quarter profile and gave a mock-frustrated snort which puffed her tits like edible balloons. "Well, what does a girl usually mean by cute?" she asked, pointing a coquettish finger. "It means I think you're, well, just pretty enough to put on the table for Sunday dinner. There, you made me say it, you bad thing."

Her moon-colored skin turned a deep red and Lance knew she must mean it. She thought he was "pretty." What did that mean? He wished Oz were there to tell him. He could ask her but she already seemed embarrassed and a little skittish. *The day is coming when it will all be reversed.* That's what Oz had said. Could it be true? Might this be the day? He had a flashlike vision of him and the girl together as old people, discussing the merits of their grandchildren while sitting hand-in-hand in front of a warm fire. He pulled himself back by visualizing the way he looked in the mirror and asking himself if she was really worthy of him. The answer was, who cares? *Have you had any better offers, any offers at all?* Oz had never steered him wrong and Oz said things were changing.

"I wasn't fishing for a compliment," he said. "It's just that I, uh . . . I'm not used to them."

She turned back toward him with a maternal anger that made him feel warm all over. "Well, gee damn willikers. I know what it says outside. You think I'm stupid or something? It says you're the man of a thousand fears and all that. And I seen them other people coming out of here looking like they was just down with the flu but I know one thing my Daddy Caleb told me. He says that the thing people are scared of the most is the thing they love." She blushed again and turned away. "Not that I'm saying I love you for goodness sake," came the words over her shoulder. "I don't even really know you, but like Caleb says, when something happens, let it. And all I'm saying is I think you're just cute enough to invite home for supper."

She made him feel like laughing and that was what he did, and not out of cynicism. "That's quite an expression," he said.

"Well, lordy," she replied in a responsive hoot. "It ain't no expression at all, it's a honest invitation."

Lance hoped she couldn't see him shaking. "You mean you actually, ah, want me to come out of the tent, to your house, for dinner?" he asked, unable to fully grasp the meaning of such a thing. What mayhem if the rest of her family ran screaming from the house, or worse, in their fright killed him.

"Well, of course," she said. "Is there some law agin it that I don't know about?"

"Will there be anyone else there?"

She winked and leaned close to the mesh. "Well, well, well," she said conspiratorially. "Kind of a fast worker ain'tcha? Of course Caleb will be there but he won't mind none, and of course I got my own room." She winked again and blew him a kiss.

"No, what I meant was, do they know, I mean they'll have to, ah, look at me."

Galena looked like she was going to cry. "Ahh, ain't that just the saddest thing," she clucked. "Just the saddest thing I ever heard. Don't you worry your pretty head about that. We're the kind of folks who don't worry as much as some do about what other people think. We see things our own way."

Lance almost began to cry himself, but out of joy rather than sadness. It was beginning to happen just like Oz said it would. Finally, people were beginning to see what had been trying to shine through forever, normal people, or maybe better than normal, simple people without enough evil in them to furnish evil visions. Maybe it would turn completely. Maybe the very fabric of whatever separate universe held him apart from the love of his planet was turning. Someday he might be the man of a thousand hopes, a source of beauty to the afflicted.

"They know it's me who's coming?" he asked just to be sure. "And who I am?"

"Now what did I just tell you," she answered. "You want me to ask you pretty please, with sugar on it?"

"No, that's okay." He smiled. "I'll come. Sure I will."

She did a little pirouette of joy, her skirt swirling out to show a pair of solid but soft-looking thighs. "Oh, great," she squealed, clapping her hands. "I'll be over by the candy apple cart. When you get done just come a-looking for me and I'll be there. I promise you won't be sorry."

She winked again and ducked out the exit flap, leaving him too stunned to even notice the parade of horrified goons who came after her. He was still visualizing the texture of her satin skin when the early show closed at six-thirty in the evening.

Lance was halfway through the backyard when the fear hit him like a falling weight. He was on his way to a shower and some borrowed aftershave preparatory to meeting Galena when he was crushed to the ground. He actually sat down, or rather was pushed by doubt. What if it was a mistake, a momentary ion storm, or sunspots, or a hallucinogenic drug the girl had been taking? What if he primped and shaved and showered and hoped and then saw her scream when he rounded the corner of the candy apple cart? What would then be left of life? Hope gone, confidence in change annihilated by the fascism of present circumstance. There would be no choice then but to die or worse, intentionally become what his audience beheld. The risk was too great, the potential reward too beatific. He was paralyzed, pinioned to hope, impaled by doubt, nailed to a crossroads. Who could deliver him but Oz?

Lance rose slowly, as though bearing a physical weight, and staggered to Oz's trailer. He brushed aside the chaff of empty food trays littering the steps and knocked, a terrible panic-light shining in his eyes, the music of spherical doom buzzing in his ears.

"Come in," said Oz.

"What do I look like?" croaked Lance. "Please, Oz, what do I look like?"

As Lance dropped onto the couch, Oz looked down from what seemed like an even greater height than usual and laughed, a bass drum echoing through the enclosed space. "You look like a person pained enough to be in love," he said.

Oz stood above him through the whole story, and when it was done he wasn't laughing.

"I'm building something, Lance," Oz said. "You know that, but you don't know how important it is. But this is strange. Very strange."

"I don't understand," Lance said in a whisper.

"You've just described innocence," replied Oz's voice.

"Go to her that way. Let it work for you. Let it work for all of us. Go on and meet yourself in what you fear. Feel the dimensions of reality. Learn the geometry of opposites, and the reason they pay to see you."

The dinner consisted of fried chicken, mashed potatoes, gravy, green beans, and apple pie for dessert, washed down by hard cider followed by moonshine and coffee. Caleb was a tall, rifle-thin, bullet-headed hillbilly with waxed hair smelling of honey in the comb. He looked about sixty years old, but only because of the crook in his nose and the break in his voice. It was a voice that, like a nighttime stair-creak, carried no distance but bore no comfort.

After dinner Galena excused them both and led him to her room over the barn. It was sheltered and insulated, reached by a short flight of stairs from the dirt floor below. Once up the stairs and through a hinged door in the ceiling, Lance found himself in a paneled two-room suite. The white walls were made of birch and covered with macrame tapestries hanging in the light of pink lamps with the glamour of ivy. The floors were solid oak and, he could tell by the muffled intimacy of their voices, virtually soundproof. The main room was covered by a woven rug and overseen by a crownlike wood stove glowing in the perfumed darkness with the same red as his new-fired lust.

No one had cried at supper. No one gagged or ran or stabbed him to the heart with the violence of their fear. They ate. They ate and looked, and talked, and even joked, about the others in the show, not him. He must be normal. The night and the coals and the perfumed air must be normal, because she opened the bones of her thighs so he could speak with his body of the oceans in his mind.

There in that soundproof oak distance from the otherness of others, he lay atop her and felt for the first time in his eighteen years on the planet of plenty what the poor only dream of in stuporous sleep. But he was awake, truly awake for the first time in his life, as she lifted her skirt, and slid down the panties of country cotton over thighs of city silk he'd seen only in dreams of far countries of flesh.

Then, in gratitude, he pressed his face to the slit that was the entrance to salty safe harbor.

Then he was inside her, letting her guide him home from lifelong exile to a land where the self he saw in the mirror stretched like a far horizon to the end of his life. He was warm, and infinite, liquid as the smile in a kiss, boundless as spreading wings in a shadowless sun, flying high in triumph over the rubbly plain of his previous life. Because now, in the timeless presence of her sliding thighs and crying sighs, years were distance, minutes were nothing but mythology, and seconds ran like water into the gravity of an exploding present.

He was sure it was the first time he had lived, a new birth into the heaven of opposites, strength becoming kindness, friendship burning itself to bones of want in the unsuspected flame of generosity. Arms became emotion, legs kicking and sliding into blocks of rib-poetry. All things were joined. All joinings were life. All life was contained in her distance-blue eyes, now looking at him closer than self, nearer than voice, as she whispered the song of wished-for memories.

"Oh yes," she crooned. "You're so big and so nice and so hard. Come to my lap. You're my biggest pet, yes, gawd, my best gift, 'cause you give it to me so good, so nice, like all ugly things, oh yes. Like all ugly things you wanta give so good, so bad, so good owww, don't worry, you only hurt me a little and there, that's nice again. Just do it. Just do like you feel. Oh yes, that's right my baby. My ugly. My furry, fuzzy, hard-hoof, horny-tailed pet. It's all right. Do it. I can feel the way you want to be nice 'cause you're so big and don't want to bite me 'cause of your teeth, but baby go on, you can bite me a little with those fangs, go on, it's all right 'cause they're not poison. I know your fangs aren't poison. . . ."

In a delirium of joy, Lance thought he was hearing the thoughts of his own past, coming to get him like imagined hands at the top of dark stairs. But they were being thrust into the bottom of his throat by the slippery enthusiasm of Galena's hot tongue.

Her words were like a cold iron bar that pried his stomach from hers and caused him to roll away, lapping air like a dog in a car on a hot day, searching for a friend but finding only a master.

"What's the matter, baby?" she cooed. "Did I stick you in the ribs with my knee? I'm sorry. But I get a little carried away, girlish of me, idn't it?" Then she laughed, a throaty yuk which almost made him roll back and reclaim the territory invaded by doubt, almost, but not quite.

"What did you say?" he asked, breathless and sweating.

Galena smiled at him and he noticed that her teeth were as white, clear, and evenly spaced as the midline on the road to hell. "Oh, baby," she moaned. "Don't ask a girl to repeat that kind of thing." Then she rolled toward him and hooked her thigh over his. "That's just a little tip 'cause I know it's your first time."

"How?" he asked, knowing the answer but afraid of it anyway.

She looked away, toward the far wall, or any place his eyes couldn't reach. "What do you mean, how?" she murmured into the distance.

"I mean how do you know it's my first time? How do you know I've never done this before?"

"You were doing just fine, really."

"I know that dammit," he screamed. "I'm not so stupid that I don't know when things feel right. So how did you know? Tell me. Tell me!" Lance grabbed her throat from behind, but couldn't bring himself to squeeze. She let out a defeated sigh, as ominous as a north wind on a Southern night.

"Why are you doing this?" she pleaded. He felt tears dropping onto the hand he saw was around her throat.

In a fury that surprised him, he turned her onto her stomach and straddled her back. "Describe me," he ordered. "Describe me!"

His weight forced her face into the bed, muffling her response. "You know," she said. "I don't want to. You know."

"Describe me," he screamed again. "Describe me or I swear I'll . . ." He squeezed her throat, already knowing the answer but afraid of it, afraid he would kill her, afraid he wouldn't. He tried to squeeze but couldn't. She felt his hesitation and reacted to it by turning in his hands and coming up against him.

"All right," she said with a kind of sad vengeance. "All right. But you know already. You're a big, clove-hooved thing with eyes like two fires way back in a couple tunnels in a couple hillsides. You have a little short tail and warts, and kind of a sheep's head, and you're just about the ugliest thing I ever seen."

If his back hadn't been against the wall he would have collapsed with despair. He knew. That was the terrible part. He knew she was going to say something like that. In all his hours of being stared at with horror he'd never once deigned to become an accomplice in the customers' psychic crimes, and now this. *A new life*. He choked and turned his face away from her.

"I'm sorry," he said into the wall. "I'm not like you think. I mean I'm only like you think."

She rolled away from him and off the bed; standing in the low-rose glow of the fading fire, she was lit from behind with red from the stove. She made no attempt to cover herself but spread her arms wide, pleading in a kind of muted desperation. "Oh, God," she wailed. "What must you think of me. What must you think of me?"

The question hit him in the stomach with greater force than the shock of her vision. *What must he think of her?* What should he think about a girl who would go to bed with a creature that looked more like an animal than a man? A hybrid animal from the lower depths of collective horror. How could she do it? How could she take to her body a thing? *A thing like him*. What must he think? The answer was that he didn't think anything, he felt, and what he felt was a bowel-clenching rush of pure revulsion. *How could she? How could she unless . . . unless she'd done it before, unless she was so inbred and mutated that ugliness and bestiality aroused her? Unless she'd slept with animals before.*

"Oh, my God," he stammered. "Where's my shoes. I have to go. I have to get out of here."

She took a step toward him, holding out her arms as if to comfort him. "It's all right," she said through the tears now covering her face.

"It's not all right," he shouted. "What must I think of

you? What must I think? I think you're some kind of mutant who's used to sleeping with animals. That's what I think. Let me out of here. Where are my damned shoes?"

"Oh, God," she cried. "Oh, God, no." Then she screamed, a spear through the eardrums in the closed room. "Daddy," she wailed. "Daddy, come quick, Daddy, please."

Lance used the time to put on the rest of his clothes, believing that her father wouldn't be able to hear any sound coming from inside her room. But in what seemed only seconds the door slammed against the wall and a male form barreled through it in a fury. Lance jumped away from the door but found himself face-to-face with Caleb.

"You mutants," screamed Lance. "You goddamn mutants. I'm getting out of here." He was halfway through the unhinged door when Caleb grabbed him by the shirt and hauled him back.

"Just a minute there, son," Caleb drawled, pulling him easily toward his face and speaking directly into his eyes. "Let's wait until we hear what the girl's got to say."

"You can't do this," Lance yelled, and tried to tear away but, despite his reedlike physique, the older man handled him as easily as if he were made of straw. He was actually lifted off his feet by the front of his shirt and shaken like a doll.

"Please now," Caleb said apologetically. "Be reasonable for just a minute. Ain't nobody going to make you do nothing but listen. All right?" Lance felt himself being shaken lightly, for emphasis. "All right?" asked Caleb again.

"I don't have much choice do I?" Lance hissed through his teeth. "But that's all I'm going to do, listen. I don't care if you kill me. That's all I'm going to do."

He saw a look of revulsion pass over Caleb's pickax face and then change to an expression of awe. "God, but you're scary looking when you get mad," the hillbilly said. "If I was anybody else I wouldn't know whether to run or try and kill you."

"Daddy," said Galena from the corner where she was covering herself with a bed sheet. "Daddy, show him, please. He's saying awful things about me." She was barely understandable through the sobs which were choking her.

"What?" Caleb asked, looking at Lance, beginning to lift him off the floor again. "What was he saying, honey?"

"It's all right, Daddy. He didn't know."

"What'd he say?" Caleb demanded.

"He didn't know."

"I asked what he said," roared Caleb, his sallow face turning red.

Galena stopped sobbing and spoke in a low, sorrowful voice, as if she were more ashamed for Lance than for herself. "He said I must be used to it, that I must be used to bedding with animals."

For a second Lance thought Caleb was going to snap his neck. The farm-tool hands tightened and anger heaved the furrowed face upward like a bulge of ground. Then Galena spoke again. "Remember, Daddy. Remember."

Caleb's hands relaxed and his face cracked into a rueful smile. He shook his head and lowered Lance into a chair by the stove. "What a world," he said, shaking his head continually. "You're really a mixed-up somebody, ah, what's your name?"

"Lance," Galena answered for him.

"Lance," Caleb said reflectively. "Kind of a movie-star kind of name. How'd you come by it?"

"I don't see what that's got to do with—"

"Oh, just indulge an old man and tell me."

"I picked it myself, in California."

"When was that?"

"A couple years ago."

"And what was it before that?"

"Joshua."

Caleb sighed. "Joshua, now there's a solid name, a good old country name. With a name like that you could be from around here. Why'd you change it?"

"Look," said Lance irritably. "Just let me go. This was a big mistake."

"I don't think so," Caleb replied. "Just answer that one question for me and I'll repay you better than you might think." He was now leaning easily against the wall, chewing a toothpick he'd produced from his shirt pocket.

His mood had changed to a sly irony, as if he were drawing out a joke. Lance had the feeling he was trying to be friendly so he answered.

"It just seemed to make me feel better."

"About yourself?"

"Yeah, I guess so."

Caleb came toward him, smiling now, and hunkered down to face him. "Boy," he said. "You must have had a rough go of it. I'm sorry I almost lost my temper, but that's my little girl you was talking about. And you had her all wrong, kind of. Look at this."

He opened his blue work shirt and removed a leather thong from around his neck. Hanging from it was what appeared to be an irregular piece of amethyst about an inch long and two inches across. It was purple like amethyst but suggested every other color he could think of and, as he looked at it, time seemed to change into silence. Motion in the room slowed until the purple piece seemed to be the only thing alive in a hall of statues. It seemed to pulse like a heart with energy collected from their now-still thoughts. Caleb reached out, placed the thing in Lance's hand, and covered the hand with his own so that the Piece was touching both of them. Now Lance could feel its pulse as Caleb spoke.

"Galena, come over here," her father said, and she seemed to glide across the room like a wish coming true. When she got there Caleb ordered her to put her hand on top of theirs and she did, forming a circle of quiet which vaulted to the ceiling like the sides of a small cathedral. "Now look at her, son," Caleb urged. "Look at her and tell me if you think she's ever slept with an animal."

Lance looked, and saw Galena shining, ivory against the birch walls, like an angel in the snow. The tears now drying on her face reflected the color of her eyes, tiny jewels faceted with fragments of sadness, cut from the diamond of her understanding.

"No," he said. "No, of course not."

"And how can you see that now, when you couldn't before?"

"I don't know," answered Lance. "She's just too beautiful. If she'd done that it would show, and it doesn't."

"You can see her the same way she saw you. She saw you, boy. Somewhere behind what you look like, she saw something a-shining. Same way I can."

"You can see me?" Lance asked in an explosion of quiet joy.

There was sadness in Caleb's voice when he answered. "No, boy, not really. What we see is pretty much like what everybody else sees, except that there's a kind of shining that comes out from behind, a kind of light that seems more real than what we think we're a-seeing."

"We feel you more than see you," purred Galena. "And what we feel ain't bad, it's a kind of beauty feeling, like you feel when someone's coming home. They ain't made it yet but you know they're on the way."

"But, boy, listen," added Caleb sternly. "What everyone else sees is still a sin. The only reason we're able to get past it is this stone we're holding. You gotta remember that and not get your hopes up too high."

"But how?"

"I don't know how. Once, a long time ago, I was out hunting and I seen a skinny man on a hill, or rather I heard him wailing like something with jaws was on his back. Then I saw him flang something out and into the brush in the valley before he ran back outta sight. I walked to where I saw the thing fall and found this here stone. Galena's ma died when she was young and I've always tried to make up for that as best I could. So when I saw the thing was right pretty, I took it home to her and, I swear, she's just had the best heart of anybody I ever knew."

"Oh, Daddy, now stop." Galena blushed, a red that added to the warmth of the stove.

"We take turns wearing the stone, and it's give us another kind of sight somehow. Lots of things in this world is covered, boy, and I expect you're one of them. Others can't see like we can, understand?"

Lance shook his head in the affirmative, too disappointed to speak.

"That's just the way it is," Caleb said gently, and rose, leaving the purple stone in Lance's hand. Galena covered it with hers and they were alone.

They said nothing for a while, just sat staring into their closed hands, feeling the pulse replace their separate heartbeats with one. Then she stood and pulled his hand. "Come back," she whispered. "Come on back to bed with me now."

He followed her to the edge of the bed where he stood facing her. "But your father, won't he . . ."

She put a finger over his lips. "You mean how can he be peaceful with the fact that his little girl is up here . . . doing what we want? The answer is kindness, sweety, just simple country kindness. The kind that knows the time is more important than the place."

"I'm not sure I can."

"You mean still knowing what you look like to me?"

"Yes, I guess so."

She doubled his hand into a fist over the stone, then moved it to a position over his heart. "You can," she said. "You need it, and I'm the only one who can give it to you. But first you got to believe what you look like to me. And you got to accept it like I do. If I can, you can. Lord-a-mercy, honey, for the first time in your life let feeling be more important than seeing."

And then they were together again on the bed, fang to flesh with small bites of laughter, hoof to toe, spurring hairy arm to lift plaster-white back with soft sable brush toward light behind loin. And the room glowed red with the heat of the two-backed meld of two hearts to one piece, and one piece to the compass of limitless horizon at the edge of a semen-seed nova. And when it was over there were tears, sweat, prayers of gratitude uttered in spaces between breaths, and another time, and another, and then whispering sleep, and morning.

"Take it," she said, pressing the stone into his hand.

"I can't."

"You have to, you'll need it, to remind yourself what you really are."

"You don't understand." He laughed. "I can always see who I am."

"Feeling," she said in exasperation. "Don't you remember, honey? Feeling. You got to feel who you are, not see." She ran her hands through her hair, turning from angel white to ghostly pale. "Lord," she said. "What's this been about if it ain't that?"

In truth, he did want the thing. It made him feel a substance to the perfect image he was used to seeing in the mirror. "But what about your father? I couldn't."

She held his face in the palms of her hands. "Listen," she said. "This is as plain as I know how to say it. He gave it to me 'cause he's a kind man. I'm giving it to you because I'm a kind woman. It's already done what it's going to do for us. Besides, I don't usually go to them kind of shows. I think it was a-looking for you. You got to take it. Nobody's going to be satisfied unless you do."

So, with plain kindness, she persuaded him to do what he wanted and take it. And the thing was warm in his hands. It made it possible for him to leave her warmth, and it occurred to him as he descended the stairs that maybe she gave it to him partly for that reason. But when he got to the bottom he saw he was wrong.

Parked in a stall was an old but well-maintained tractor. The thing must have been Caleb's pride and joy because its green fenders were freshly painted and polished, polished to such a shine that he could see himself in them. And what he saw took the legs from under him. *You got to accept it like I do. You got to believe what you look like to me.* He had, and now he saw in the tractor's mirrored fenders a hooved, hairy, horn-headed man-creature with tunneled red eyes and long teeth. "Oh, God, where am I?" he choked. "Where did I go?" And then he saw the light, glowing around the edges of the creature in the mirror like a corona around an eclipsed sun, and he felt himself within; whole, unassailable, but angry enough to run all the way back to Oz.

Oz reached out to help him inside the camper. "What are you so mad about?" he asked, guiding Lance to a seat on the couch.

"Look at me," shouted Lance, jumping in front of the mirror to see the same apparition as the one in the fender of Caleb's tractor.

"You look just the same to me," Oz said.

"But not to me, goddamnit. Now I look to myself just like everyone else sees me."

"Everyone?" asked Oz.

"No, I mean yes . . . no."

"Who, then?"

Lance turned his head away from the mirror. Clutching the piece in his pocket he stared at Oz. "I think you know," he said.

"What?" said an innocent, almost youthful voice from Oz.

"Yeah, sure. You knew. You sent me to get this, didn't you?" Lance took the glass from his pocket and threw it on the couch. "You've been looking at my pocket ever since I got here. You knew it was there. You sent me for it."

"Only because it was always yours," Oz answered in a hoarse whisper.

"How?" Lance demanded. "How did you know?"

"Because I know the territory," answered Oz. "I knew how my father got rid of it, and when I heard the girl had invited you home I knew she must have it. How else could she have found you attractive?"

"Sure, how else?" Lance said bitterly as he turned again to the mirror. "And now what?"

"Now you're in here, Joshua," said a voice like a warm blanket. Oz gently picked up the Piece. "You're in here with the rest of us now."

"Why, Oz? Why did you do this to me? Why couldn't you let me have my illusion?"

Once again Oz directed him to the couch and spoke in the voice of a far-off mother. "Remember when you were ready to kill yourself for contact? Well, you found it. Be glad. You've found home. You've known real contact. You've found Joshua." Oz stood above him, torso swelling, a giant, sucking power like a vacuum. "But you paid the price we all have to pay. You always thought you were separate from us as well as from the straights. The Piece is your birthright but, like all birthrights, it has to be paid for with birth. Tonight was your birth. Before tonight you were just an idea to yourself. Be glad for what she gave you, and glad for what you gave her."

Lance looked up at Oz in total stupefaction. "What, Oz? What is it I gave her? What is it possible for me to . . ."

"Hope," Oz said simply. "Not that they deserve it. Remember when I told you to go find out why they pay to see you? They pay for hope, kid. They hope for what your girl had, the ability to see beauty in ugliness. And why? Because they know, deep inside somewhere they know that the ugliness they see is in themselves and they hope to find some beauty in it. Don't you see? There's no answer to whether it's better to be horrified or a horror because we're all both. Everyone's horrified at the horrors they can be. Everyone's afraid they're a freak. But only a few people will know that until I finish what I'm building."

Oz held the amulet under Lance's eyes. "For this, you're a hero. And like all heroes, you've exchanged tame water for savage seas, but the depth, Lance, the depth. Are you willing to let me handle the depth?"

"I have no choice, now."

"Choice is only experienced once in this lifetime," Oz answered.

Lance felt suddenly sick and hungry for night air. He got up and moved toward Oz. Stopping within arm's length, remembering Galena, he asked Oz the last of his first-show questions.

"Oz, once more, and answer, or fight me for the Piece. What do you see when you look at me?"

Oz stood tall, taller than nature made him or artifice added. When he spoke it was from everywhere, and beyond always.

"All right," he echoed like a quiet cannon. "I see Joshua; someone who looks exactly like me.'"

LEE MOLER

The show rolled on . . .

ALONG THE MIDWAY (XI)

Frederick County, Maryland

George was passing Oz's trailer when he noticed the
light, a pale, violet glow leaking around the edges of the
door, diffusing through the curtains pulled across the
windows.

It was late. He'd sneaked off to Ginger's trailer after
the show, and now that the crowds from Emmitsburg and
Gettysburg were gone and most of the show folk were
either asleep or dead drunk, George was quietly making
his way into the freak section of the backyard. He was
beat. He'd have loved to spend the night wrapped in
Ginger's arms but that would risk being spotted leaving
her door in the morning. And then the tongues would start
to wag. A lot of folks guessed there might be something
going on between them, but so far they'd been discreet
enough so that nobody could be really sure.

George was allowing himself to get used to the idea
that he was happy, happier than at any other time in his
life. A scary thing, happiness. Suddenly it was there. He
hadn't done anything to summon it, and he didn't feel he
deserved it, and he didn't know how to keep it. So what
was to prevent it from slipping away as quickly and easily
and mysteriously as it had come?

It seemed to be slipping away now as he watched those
violet flashes from Oz's trailer. Something about them

stripped away the warm afterglow of his hours with Ginger, made him forget his fatigue, and drew him closer.

He didn't dare knock. Instead he crept around the trailer looking for a window that wasn't completely blocked, that had an opening big enough to peek through. He found it in the rear corner. A shaft of violet light was beaming heavenward through a gap between the sash and the shade. But the gap was a good eight feet off the ground. No way George could get a look inside through that.

So he watched the light. Something about that particular shade of violet simultaneously attracted and repelled him. And strange the way the color shifted and grayed, as if odd-shaped forms were passing through it, even though the night sky was clear and empty. George had a feeling of teetering on the edge of some horrific epiphany, that a revelation was near but just beyond his reach.

Abruptly it faded, leaving George blinking and shivering in the darkness. And then he noticed that his tentacles were raised in the air. With no effort on his part, without his consent or knowledge, they had reached toward the light.

Thoroughly shaken, he hurried on to his own trailer. The Device and the Pieces his fellow freaks had been collecting along the tour route had something to do with that light. He was certain of it.

He decided he'd better learn a little more about this Device. And soon.

Bird-in-Hand, Pennsylvania

Jacob Zook was just beginning to drive the cows home when he heard the music. It seemed to drift from somewhere in the trees across the pasture, and Jacob froze and listened, fearing to make a sound, as if a single breath would blow away the music forever.

Jacob seldom heard music, and to hear it now, now on a cool summer evening, alone with the placid cows who looked but never laughed or smiled, was wonderful. It filled his ten-year-old soul with the kind of glory he had not yet found in God, but which he had been told over and over again was there. He had never said this to anyone, but he thought that maybe God laughed at him too, snickering behind his big, pink, five-fingered hands of power and majesty.

But he didn't think about God or anyone else laughing now. He only thought about the music, soft and airy, as though the breeze itself was singing. As he walked closer to the trees, he could hear the melody, but he didn't know what kind of instrument made it. He knew no music beyond the memorized chants of the *Ausbund*. Oh, the few times his parents took him among the English in the little town of Bird-in-Hand, he heard from passing radios the savage roars of what he thought must be songs, but the only true instrument he knew was the wheezy mouth organ he had kept hidden in the hayloft for the past two years, and all he could do on that was breathe in and out, in and out.

Still, it was satisfying. Sometimes he went fast, sometimes slow, stretching his mouth wide to play as many tones as possible, and holding the notes as long as he could until they finally died away on his breath, but reverberated in his memory long afterward. Often he took the mouth organ with him when he gathered in the cows at night, but this evening his father and brothers were working in the hayloft, and he had no chance to rescue the instrument from its hiding place between two boards.

So now he walked with empty pockets toward the trees, powerless in the grip of the music, unable to turn back and drive in the cows. Then he was among the trees, and as he walked through them he saw that the field on the other side of the woods was different, filled with things he had never seen there before. And he looked through the trees as through the bars of a cage, and the fragmented images coalesced as he drew closer, until he saw that there were *real* cages there in Mr. Murphy's field, cages and tents and trucks and wagons, poles and lights and trailers.

A *fair*.

No. It couldn't be, not yet. The local fair wasn't until early fall, and this was still summer. His brothers had gone to the fair, though he had never been to one. Abraham and Levi sneaked to it last year, and had told Jacob afterward about the rides and the food and the girls, and Jacob wanted to go, but he knew his brothers would never take him, and he would never go alone. Whatever this was, he decided, it wasn't a fair. It was too early, and there were no rides.

He walked closer until he stood right at the edge of the woods that separated the English Murphy's property from the Zook farm. He heard other noises now, men shouting as they set up tents, unloaded platforms from trucks, hauled on pulleys that lifted colorfully painted signs into place. Jacob looked at the first sign aloft. *Ozymandias Oddities,* it read, and he had no idea what either word meant.

But his gaze lingered on the sign only a moment, for his attention was captured by the man who sat thirty yards away in a canvas folding chair outside a small trailer. His back was to Jacob, but the boy could see that he was the source of the music. The man was bent over something, something that he worked with his left arm while he held it with his right. Jacob saw a graceful curve of polished wood under that right arm, but nothing more. What was it, he wondered, that made that wonderful sound of several voices singing together at once, like the mouth organ, yet softer and sweeter, and singing on their own, not bound by a single breath?

He went closer, slowly, tiptoeing so that the man would not hear him, and began to circle around, walking through knee-high weeds, when he stepped on an unseen corn husk that crackled beneath his black-shod feet.

The man's head swiveled, smoothly, so that Jacob, caught, saw the curve of his cheek as smooth and brown as the thing he held, then his profile, sharp, angular, and noble, and finally his eyes, blue and soft as the morning sky.

A colored man.

Then the man smiled, showing even, white teeth, and nodded. "Well, hey there," he said gently, and Jacob thought the voice sounded a little like the music the man had made. "Hey there, white boy," he said, then gave a little laugh that sounded like still more music. It wasn't a cruel laugh. "And I *do* mean *white* boy. Come join the party."

Jacob didn't smile back, didn't move. He couldn't.

"Oh, come on," the colored man said. "Don't be shy. We're all a little different here." Then the man beckoned with his right hand, and Jacob's stomach went cold.

It was as though a giant spider wriggled, belly-up, at the end of the colored man's arm. There seemed as many fingers as belonged on a *pair* of hands, and they waved like wheat stalks in the wind, showing Jacob the way.

The man looked at his hand, then at Jacob, and his smile widened. "Somethin' to see, aren't they? They're what makes me Musical Mitts. Now come on over here and let's see you better."

The man's words were kind, and Jacob walked slowly toward him, his head cocked, his legs tense, ready to run.

"You surely are pale," the man said. "Albino?"

Jacob nodded, unable to take his pink eyes from the man, who then looked Jacob up and down, taking in his dark blue shirt, black pants and suspenders, and broad-brimmed straw hat.

"And Amish too, from the cut of your duds." The man pronounced it with a long *A*.

"*Ah*-mish," Jacob corrected him, but so softly that the man couldn't have heard him, so he cleared his throat and repeated it.

"Okay, *Ah*-mish," the man said correctly. "Well, welcome to Ozymandias Oddities and Peabody's Traveling Circus, little Amishman. My name's Herbert Brooks, but everybody calls me Mitts. Pleased to meetcha." He turned around the whole way so that Jacob could see that his left hand, the one that clutched the strange and wonderful instrument, was just as bizarre as his right, which he now extended to Jacob.

Jacob licked his lips, swallowed, and held out his own right hand, which Mitts shook. It was like being held by a bundle of pussy willow branches, soft, but stiff and strong underneath.

"Hmm," Mitts said, releasing Jacob's hand, but keeping his eyes on it. "I see you've got an additional appendage of your own there."

"A . . . what?"

"Extra digit. The same kind of gift that sets me so far above my fellow practitioners of the musical arts. You play?"

"Uh, no."

"Sing?"

"Just the *Ausbund*." Jacob looked at the thing on the colored man's lap. "What is that?"

"The *Ausbund*, and you don't know what a guitar is. Looks like we speak different languages, friend. Sit down, visit a bit." He gestured with his riot of fingers toward a wooden box, and Jacob sat. "Now. What's this *Ausbund*?"

"It's a . . . a hymn book. They sing from it at services."

"Ah. Then you can read music?"

"No. It's just words. We, um . . ." He looked for the right term.

"Memorize the music?" the man named Mitts said, and Jacob nodded. "Pass it on down the line. Just like in Africa. Just like the blues." Jacob tried to smile to show that he understood what the man was talking about, even though he didn't. "You never seen a guitar before, huh?"

Jacob shook his head. "No. We don't have things like that."

"You mean musical instruments? How do you sing hymns without a piano or organ or something?"

"We just . . . sing."

"*A capella,*" the man said, then looked down at his guitar. "Yeah, I guess this would be quite a novelty then."

"I heard you. Over in the pasture," and he nodded his head toward the trees.

"Pasture over there, huh? This your farm?"

"Oh no," Jacob said. "My papa wouldn't ever . . ." He let it trail off.

"Wouldn't ever rent his land to folks like us, huh?" There was no resentment in the man's voice.

"It's not . . . people like you," Jacob said, realizing that he had never had to explain this to anyone before, then realizing with an even greater shock that he had never spoken to an English at such length. "It's just anything English."

Mitts Brooks gave a wry smile. "We ain't English."

"No, not . . . not from England. Anything that isn't Amish. Well, almost anything," he added, thinking of his father's solar-powered calculator he used to figure out the farm's finances.

"Uh-huh." Mitts chuckled. "That's the first time I've ever been accused of being English. So you heard the music and snuck over here to . . . what? You wanta join up?"

Jacob's eyes widened. "Oh no!" he said.

"That's good. An albino with an extra itty-bitty finger wouldn't stand out a whole lot around here." He nodded toward Jacob's right hand. "That work good? I mean your auxiliary there."

Jacob realized his hand was clenched into a fist, but

now he opened it, showing the man the extra, smaller finger that protruded from between his ring and middle fingers' interdigital pads. He had heard the doctor call them that one time, and had remembered the name. "It works," he said softly. "Just got one joint though."

"Mmmm." Mitts reached out a hand, and Jacob felt the branchy fingers touch his own again. He kept himself from shivering for the first seconds, and after that found that the touch was cool and soft, as some of the man's fingers gently flexed and bent his own. "That's not bad." Still holding Jacob's hand, he looked into his eyes. He was not smiling now. "But people laugh, huh? Or act strange?"

Jacob nodded. He didn't want to say anything for fear that his voice would break.

"Price we pay for being different. You don't know it, son, but maybe you've been given a gift here. People just don't realize it."

"The English," Jacob finally said, "they joke me. They say it's because the Amish, we . . ."

"Incest." Jacob had never heard the word. "Brothers and sisters, or people related, having babies, is that it?"

Jacob nodded. "But it's not true," he said. "Amish would never do that."

"I know. But there aren't all that many of you. Bound to be related somehow, huh? Still, more genetics than I know about." Another word Jacob didn't recognize. "Just make the best of it you can. I did."

"You're . . . a musician," Jacob said.

"I am indeed." He struck a flowing arpeggio on the guitar. "Musical Mitts Brooks is the appellation I go by. Play guitar, fiddle, piano, saxophone, clarinet, hell, all the reeds."

"How about . . . mouth organ?"

"Mouth organ?" He crooked his fingers into a thicket and mimed blowing, and the boy nodded. "A little. But not very good at it. Can't cup it tight enough. Not with these utensils." And he waggled his fingers. "But they're good for everything else I said. Take a look." He laid the guitar on his lap and held out his hands palm up. Jacob leaned forward and examined them.

There were nearly twenty fingers altogether, and the

biggest one looked to be almost a foot long. Jacob counted
five separate joints on that one. Growing out the side of
that finger and several of the other long ones were secondary digits which Mitts moved one at a time as if proud to
display his separate control of each. The fingernails were
polished and long, too long, Jacob thought, for anything
like farm work.

"They obey me just like little soldiers," he said. "I just
think it and they do it. Listen."

He placed his hands on the guitar and began to play.
The tune was soft and delicate, but very fast, and Jacob
watched, his mouth open slightly, unable to take his eyes
off the many fingers dancing over the frets and strings,
hearing the notes and the other sounds beneath, the
little buzz when the fingers ran up and down the bass
strings, the rhythmic raps that the outside finger of
the right hand made on the guitar's body, the high har-
monics that resulted when Brooks laid a strong finger
across all the frets, and made the guitar sound like a ghost
of itself.

Then, too quickly, the tune was over, and the fingers
came together like the legs of a dying spider, and the man
grinned.

"You don't know this," he said, "but nobody plays
like that. Nobody in the world ever has, and nobody else
ever will. Oh, lots of people have the talent, the musi-
cianship, but nobody else," he said, unfolding his hands,
"has these." Then he wrapped his magic fingers around
the guitar, sat back, and smiled.

"Hey, *boy.*" The words were flat and cold, and when
Jacob turned and saw the face of the man who had spoken
them, he saw that it was as flat and cold as the words. The
man was big, well over six feet, but stocky, and his red,
wide hands were as stubby fingered as Mitts's were long.
He looked as if he could have picked up two hay bales at a
time and tossed them through the loft door.

" 'Lo, Lowdge," Mitts Brooks said quietly.

"Oz says he wants to see everybody. Five minutes.
Main tent."

"I'll be there."

"You better be there, Mitsubishi," the big man said.
"And get that kid outta here. Now." Then he turned and

walked away, looking back over his massive shoulder.

"Who's he?" Jacob asked.

"That's Lowdge. He's a roustabout."

"What's that?"

"A worker. No talent. No soul."

"What'd he call you? Mitsu . . . su-bee-shee?" Jacob
said.

"Kind of car. Japanese. It's a little joke of Lowdge's.
Says I should've been a Jap nigger. Calls me Mitts-ubishi.
Get it? Like a Japanese name."

Jacob nodded. "Is it . . . supposed to be funny?"

Brooks shook his head, and Jacob saw him look sad
for the first time. "He doesn't mean for me to think it's
funny. He means for me to think it's as nasty as it is."

"Like 'Bunny,'" Jacob said.

"Huh?"

"The boys call me that. Bunny. Like a white bunny
with pink eyes. But my real name is Jacob."

"Mmmm. People can be pretty mean. They don't like
things different from them. They did, I'd be playing in
concert halls, making records, be on TV instead of playing in a"—he gestured around him—"a freak show. See,
people don't think that anything that looks this awful can
make anything beautiful."

"But it is. The music, I mean. It's beautiful."

"You know it and I know it, but there are more of them
than there are of us. Even here, in the show, people like
Lowdge still . . ." He left it unfinished, then turned to
Jacob with the smile back on his face. "So what we gotta
do is be as good as we can, you know? Find something we
can do better than anyone else, and do it." He cocked his
head. "Maybe you could learn to play an instrument. If
your folks'd let you."

"They wouldn't," Jacob said, and then he leaned forward and told Mitts Brooks what he had never told anyone before. "But I got one anyway," he whispered.

"You do?"

"Yah."

"Yah?"

"I mean yes. A mouth organ."

"A harmonica?"

"Is that what you call it?"

"What most people call it. *Mouth organ*'s kind of old-fashioned."

"Harmonica," Jacob said, and the word felt as sweet as a fresh pear in his mouth. "I got a . . . harmonica."

"Now where'd you get that?"

"My mama used to work for a hotel in Lancaster when I was little, cleaning the sheets. And sometimes she took me with her. And there was a man worked in the laundry there, a colored man like you."

"*African-American* is the current patois, but no offense taken," Mitts said. "And he gave it to you?"

"Yah. He said it was lucky. That he won it a long time ago."

"Won it."

"Yah. And he told me not to let my mama see it, that it was a secret, but to hide it and take good care of it and only play it when nobody else was around."

"So they wouldn't take it away."

"Yah."

"You play good?"

Jacob shook his head. "I don't know how. I just make it go . . ." And Jacob gave a demonstration with his voice, breathing in and out in a treble "Hee-haw" that made Mitts laugh.

"Sounds like you could use a lesson. Tell you what. You come to the show tonight—"

"Oh no, I couldn't do that . . . if anybody'd see me . . ."

"I get you. All right then. Come around through the trees again. The back way here. Come knock on the door of that trailer. I'll put you where you can watch the show and see me play *all* my instruments, but nobody else'll see you. How's that sound?"

Jacob thought about his father's stern face, but then he thought of the beauty of the guitar's song, and the names of the other instruments—piano, fiddle, something-phone, and what was it, clarinet? What were they, and what kind of music did *they* make?

"All right," he said. "All right. If I can . . ." He paused. He had been about to say *sneak out*, but it made him sound like someone bad, a boy who fooled his parents. So he said no more.

"Good for you." Mitts had his hand in his lap, but when he pointed a long finger upward, the tip still touched his lips. "We'll keep it a secret. Now. I got to go to a meeting." He leaned down and put his guitar in its case, then closed it and stood up. "See you tonight. And it was real good meeting you, Jacob." This time Jacob held out his hand, and Mitts shook it, then started walking in the direction of the largest tent. Jacob watched his long, lean figure move effortlessly away, the fingers only inches from the ground.

He had just turned and started for home when he heard Mitts's voice. "Hey, Jacob!" Jacob turned and looked at the man. "Bring that harmonica of yours along tonight," Mitts said. "We'll jam! And maybe I can even show you a lick or two." Then he waved, and vanished behind a trailer.

Jacob turned and started to walk briskly away, hoping that the cows were all together so that it wouldn't take him too long to drive them back to the barnyard. His heart was beating quickly at the thought of sneaking away from his home to go to a fair, so that when the other voice called after him, he jumped in fear.

"Kid!"

He looked around and saw the big man Mitts had called Lowdge twenty yards away. His face was set and angry. "Come here," he said roughly, beckoning with hands that looked fat and useless after having seen those of Mitts.

Jacob stopped walking, but didn't go toward the big man.

"You hear me? I said come *here*. Wanta tell you somethin'."

No. This wasn't right. This man didn't want to tell him a thing. He wanted to *do* something to him, Jacob knew it. *Just awful things* were what he wanted to do. That was how his mama had put it, when she told him to stay away from people who wanted to get him alone where nobody could see. Stay away, because they wanted to do . . .

Just awful things.

"Goddamnit, *c'mere!*"

Jacob turned and ran into the woods, ran as fast as he could, not looking back, afraid the big man named Lowdge was right behind him, the mean man who called Mitts bad names and talked hard to him, the red-faced man with the fat hands that could do . . .

Just awful things.

Then he was in the pasture, and there were the cows, and the sun going down, and no sounds but the wind and his breathing, quick and heavy. There was no one behind him, no beast visible through the cage of the trees.

Jacob bent over and breathed easier, until the stitches in his side went away and he could straighten up without pain. Then he began to gather the cows, shouting and waving his arms until they headed in the right direction. After that, all he had to do was follow them. They knew what it was time for, and where they were going.

As he walked behind them, he thought about the night. He wanted to go back, back to the fair or carnival or whatever was in Mr. Murphy's field. Despite disobedience, despite his fears of strangers and the stranger named Lowdge, he wanted to go and hear the music, all the music, hear Mitts play and have him teach him about the harmonica.

He and the cows got to the barn later than usual, but his father said nothing about it over dinner. After the family ate, it was still light, and Jacob went outside with his younger brothers and sisters and played around the farm equipment, free for an all too brief time of the chores that life on an Amish farm made necessary.

Jacob was crawling under a horse-drawn harrow when he caught his foot on something half buried in the earth. At first he thought it might be one of the harrow's teeth that had fallen from the blade, but when he pulled it from the dirt he saw that it was far too small, little more than two inches long and an inch wide, though it widened, nearly imperceptibly, at one end. It may, he thought, have come from another piece of machinery, and he brushed the moist soil from it and shoved it into his pants pocket. He would show it to his father later. His mind was on other things now.

When his brothers and sisters were concentrating on a crayfish they found in the stream, he scurried away in the dusk into the hay barn, climbed the ladder to the loft, and, in the half-light, found the two boards between which rested his treasure. It was safer to get it now than later, when it was fully dark, and his father might be curious about strange sounds in the barn.

He began to slip it into his right pocket, but remembered the strange piece of metal there, and the dirt that still clung to it. So he put the harmonica in his left pocket, climbed down the ladder, and rejoined the other children.

That night, instead of putting his dirty clothes in the clothes basket, he folded them up and put them under the bed he shared with Timothy, his eight-year-old brother. After evening prayers and a sponge bath, they crawled into bed together and closed their eyes. Timothy was soon asleep, and Jacob lay there waiting until his mama opened the bedroom door and looked in for a few seconds, then closed the door again. He waited several minutes more, then crept out of bed carefully, dressed, and went through the open window onto the porch roof, from which he climbed down a trellis.

The moon was full and high, so he had no trouble crossing the pasture. The patch of woods was darker, but he tripped only once on a root he could not see. Eventually the glow from the show helped to guide him, and in a few more minutes he was standing at the edge of the woods, bathed in red and orange lights, and he heard the sound of many voices, and the raucous tones of calliope music. Between the trailers and trucks and tents he glimpsed the people of Bird-in-Hand and the surrounding towns, probably many from Lancaster, come to see . . . whatever there was to see. And yes, to hear the music.

Jacob walked to where he had talked to Mitts Brooks earlier that day, looking around frequently in search of Lowdge skulking in the shadows, but seeing no one. He knocked at the trailer door, and Mitts opened it within seconds, his face breaking into a grin when he saw who stood there.

"Well well well. You came in the nick of time. Just about to start my second—" He broke off suddenly, his face tensing, like Jacob's cat Snowball did when he smelled or saw something in the air that people couldn't. His spidery fingers clutched the door frame so hard that

Jacob was afraid they might snap like twigs. But then they relaxed, and Mitts smiled again, and finished softly, ". . . my second show." He stepped down from the trailer and shut the door behind him. "Come on. I'll get you situated."

Now Jacob could see that Mitts was wearing some kind of black suit with shiny strips down the pants legs and the same shiny stuff on the lapels. He had on a black bow tie, and there were two bright black buttons in the front of his white shirt, although Jacob couldn't see what they were holding together. The man led the way through a labyrinth of trucks and trailers until they reached a large tent. Mitts drew back a panel of canvas and said, "Enter my caravanserai, good sir."

"Huh?"

"Go on in."

Jacob did, and found himself at the side of a small stage. Voices came from around the edge of a big curtain. Mitts opened a folding chair, and gestured for Jacob to sit down. "Now," he said. "You just stay here and you can see me play, but nobody in the audience can see you, how's that?"

Jacob sat, then looked at the array of devices out on the stage. "What *are* all those things?" he asked.

"Well, the big one's a piano, of course. That gold curvy one's a saxophone, the straight black one's a clarinet, the little wooden one with the strings is a violin, and you know my guitar. Now you stay put, huh? It's show time."

He grinned, put his hands behind his back, and walked out onto the stage. A few people clapped, some shouted things Jacob couldn't make out, but the buzz of conversation died, and everyone grew quiet when Mitts began to talk.

Jacob didn't understand much of what he said. He said some things that made some of the people laugh, and one of them shouted something at Mitts, but then Mitts said something else that made almost everybody laugh, and the person who shouted didn't shout again. Finally, he brought his hands from behind his back, and held them up, their backs to the audience. There was a gasp, and Jacob heard people suck in their breath when Mitts wiggled his fingers. Nobody shouted now.

Then Mitts stepped over to the piano and began to make music. Although Jacob had heard a piano before, it had not been like this. It sounded as though three people were playing on the same keyboard, hands on all parts of it, high, low, and in-between, giant clumps of music that nearly deafened the boy, and then something softer, like a rippling stream of notes, and he watched in amazement as Mitts's hands filled the keyboard, going up and down, back and forth like a pack of trained animals, getting faster and faster until they were nothing but a blur of brown, and Jacob blinked, but the hands would not come into focus, and he thought he must be dreaming, that no one could move their fingers that fast.

But finally they stopped, with a crashing chord that seemed to last forever, and the man's shoulders slumped as if he were exhausted, and the people clapped and yelled (but good things this time), and Mitts got up and bowed so low that his fingers tapped a fast rhythm on the floor of the platform.

Then he grabbed the thing he had called a clarinet and a thin keening sound got louder and louder, and notes chattered like angry bees and everyone got quiet again. The notes dipped and swooped and climbed as Jacob's eyes got wider and wider, and when that was over and the people clapped Mitts picked up the saxophone thing, and the sound was deeper, like a man's voice instead of a girl's, and that thing sang and wailed and wept and finally started to laugh, laugh so hard that Jacob laughed too, tears rolling down his face, and he never could remember laughing like that. He laughed until he forgot what and who he was, and that felt so good, *so* good.

Then came the fiddle, and Mitts wrapped some of the fingers of his right hand around the long wooden stick, but used some of his other, longer fingers on that same hand to press the strings down the way the left-hand fingers did. Jacob figured that most people couldn't do it that way, because the audience ooohed and aaahed and clapped as soon as he started, but soon the applause died away and Jacob could hear the music again. It was fast and there were many notes, but there was something else, a feeling that had not been there in either the piano or the instruments you blew into. And as the man played slower, and the eyes in his dark face closed, Jacob heard music he had never thought to hear and felt things he had never known he could feel.

He closed his own eyes then, and felt sad and lonely and brave and beautiful. He felt as though he would die in this instant, as though he would live forever. He felt joy and pain at once.

Happy, he wept. Devastated, he rejoiced.

And at last the notes slowed, ended, faded from hearing. It seemed an eternity before anyone began to applaud, and when they did, the sound deafened Jacob, filled his head so that he could hardly breathe. It stopped only when Mitts picked up his guitar, sat on a stool, and began to play.

If the sound of the violin was that of an angel, here was the voice of God. Ever since Jacob could remember, his ten short years of life had been filled with words, with the promises of knowing God, of walking with him, seeing him, speaking to him and having him answer, a God that would make you strong and ease your pain. But he had never heard God speak to him, had never sensed that still, small voice, never until this night. The Sunday-long church services, the words of the deacons, the admonitions of his elders, all the humility and unworldliness around which his life revolved, had not once touched his soul the way this music did. These simple notes and harmonies, the skill and the intensity with which they were expressed, these alone permitted him to see God's face, to tear aside the veil that discipline and his church had placed between him and the Almighty.

Then the music was over, and through the rush of angel wings that still sounded in his ears (or was it, he wondered, the breath of God?) he heard applause, stately and awed, and saw through a film of tears Mitts Brooks, carrying his guitar, coming toward him, waving his hand, his long, thin, brown, blessed fingers, to the people, but coming to see him, Jacob.

Jacob blinked until he could see clearly again, and saw that Mitts was wiping a tear from his own eye. "Outdid myself tonight," he said. "Sometimes it gets to me, too. Did you like it?"

"It was wonderful," Jacob said.

"Thank you. Much appreciated. Well. Let's go for a walk. I'll take this." He held up his guitar. "You got your harp?" Jacob looked at him quizzically. "Your harmonica?"

"Oh. Oh yah," and he patted his right pocket, felt the metal, remembered, and patted his left.

"Good for you. Come on. Let's see if we can't turn you into Sonny Boy Zook, huh? You, uh, didn't see Lowdge anywhere?"

"No."

"Tell you what, he doesn't like to see you around, so let's get out of here. Maybe find a clearing over in those trees of yours. Moon's bright, and that way we won't hear that darn calliope. Whaddya say, Sonny Boy?"

"All right."

Together they walked across the open patch of ground behind the carnival until they reached the trees. "There are some rocks in here," Jacob said.

"Rocks?"

"To sit down on." Enough moonlight fell through the branches that Jacob was easily able to find the rocks. He sat on one, and Mitts sat on another several feet away. He looked funny sitting there in his fancy clothes, holding his guitar in the moonlight, Jacob thought. There were few trees near the rocks, and he could see Mitts Brooks's face as clearly as if it were day. He was smiling, and started to strum his guitar.

"So let's see this harmonica," Mitts said.

Jacob dug in his pocket. "Aw," he said, taking out the small chunk of metal he had been carrying, "that's not it."

"What is it?" Mitts asked, and Jacob thought his voice sounded queer, nervous like.

"Just a piece of metal I found. Half buried at the farm."

"Toss it here." The tone of the words left no room for refusal, and Jacob lofted the thing to Mitts, whose hand entrapped it like a net gathering in fish. "Interesting," he said as he turned it in his fingers. "What do you think it is?"

"I don't know. Maybe something off our harrow. Or some other machine maybe. I thought I'd give it to my papa."

Mitts shook his head. "No," he said. "Don't bother your papa with this. It's nothing. Just a piece of junk. Who knows how long it was buried before you found it. It's nothing at all." And he dropped it on the ground at his feet, then looked back up and smiled. "Now," he said, "let's hear you play that harp, huh?"

Jacob smiled back and nodded, then took out the mouth organ and held it up to his mouth. He took a breath, then blew in and out, moving the instrument back and forth along his thin lips. He did that several times, then stopped. "That sounds just awful," he said.

Mitts chuckled. "Even I sounded awful when I started. Tell you what, though. I don't think the harp's really your instrument. I'm going to propose something to you."

Jacob had no idea what the man was talking about, but he listened.

"I think, Jacob, from the way you looked tonight when you heard me play, that this is the instrument for you." And he held up his guitar. Jacob couldn't speak. "I want you to have it."

Jacob shook his head. "Ach, no, I couldn't. I couldn't take that. That's yours."

"It's meant for you, son."

"No. No, I couldn't."

"All right then. How about we make a trade? You give me . . ." Mitts seemed to concentrate, then his face brightened. "Give me your harmonica, how about that? An instrument for an instrument, isn't that fair?"

"Well . . ."

"Here. Chuck it here."

Jacob hesitated a moment, then tossed the mouth organ to Mitts. It vanished in his hand, which then went to his mouth. Jacob heard, very softly, in and out breaths, the notes wistful in the night air.

"That's nice," Mitts said, and slipped the instrument inside his jacket pocket. "Now here. Come take it." Jacob sat on the rock, not believing what was happening. "Come on," Mitts said. "It's yours."

Jacob stood and crossed the few feet separating them like a pilgrim come into the presence of a saint's shrine. Here was the instrument that had shown him God's face, and it was his, all his. He reached out, and Mitts put it into his hands. He looked down at it in awe.

"Now," the man said, "all you got to do is learn to *play* it. Here, sit down next to me."

Jacob sat on Mitts's left and cradled the instrument in his lap as he had seen Mitts do. He wrapped one hand around the neck, and strummed the strings with the other. There was a sound, but it was not music, and Mitts laughed.

"Here," he said. "Let me show you." He put his left arm around the boy and positioned his hand on the neck, bent Jacob's fingers with his own. He took Jacob's right hand, the one with the extra finger, and held it across the flat of the guitar, just over the strings. "There," he said.

"There."

He held the position, his hands on Jacob's, his arm on Jacob's shoulder, his side against Jacob's side, and Jacob felt him tremble, felt the long fingers of Mitts's right hand slip away, leaving warm sweat on Jacob's white skin.

"It's a wonderful instrument," Mitts said. "Maybe a harmonica isn't enough in trade. Maybe . . . there should be something else—"

The world shook. There was a sound like a rock hitting a barrel, and Jacob felt the man's weight on him, pushing him down so that he was falling off the rock. He twisted so that he would not land on the guitar, and fell on his side, Mitts's face against his, and when Jacob looked at the face he saw that the eyes were rolling upward to show the whites, and the jaw was dropping open, and blood and spit was trickling out of the mouth.

Then he saw the man named Lowdge standing over them, holding a thick branch like a baseball bat.

Jacob took his hands off the guitar and pushed himself to his feet, ready to run, but Lowdge grasped his arm and held him there. He opened his mouth to shout, but Lowdge dropped the club and clapped his other hand over Jacob's mouth.

"Shut up, kid! They'll all be over here, you yell."

Awful things, Jacob thought. Just awful things. And he got ready to die.

"I tried to tell you today," Lowdge said, his fat hand

still over Jacob's mouth. "Tried to tell you about him, but you ran away. Now you gonna be quiet?"

Jacob nodded, his eyes wide, and Lowdge took his hand away, but kept holding his arm. He reached down next to Mitts, picked up something with a shiny handle, then pushed a little button. A five-inch blade snapped open.

"That was for you," Lowdge said, his voice shaking, and threw the knife into the darkness of the trees. "Got a skull hard as a bull. Let's go before he wakes up. Which way's home?"

Jacob pointed with his chin into the trees.

"You a farm boy? Got a barn?" Lowdge asked, and Jacob nodded. "I've had enough of this, enough of him, enough of my buddies havin' accidents. And after this I ain't worth two bits. Sleep in your barn tonight? I'll be gone before first light."

"I . . . yah. All right."

"Bastard." Lowdge looked down and spat on Mitts's fancy coat. "Saw him with you today. Then saw you walk out of the backyard with him tonight. And I knew. I knew what that nigger was up to."

"Don't . . . call him that."

"Jesus, kid. Don't you ever learn? You know what he was gonna do to you?"

". . . Awful things."

"You bet your life."

"But . . . the music . . ." The word drifted away.

"Listen, just because somebody makes music like an angel don't mean he is one. And just because I say nigger don't mean I'm a devil. Now come on. I'd kill the bastard, but . . ." Lowdge blew a puff of air from his nose. "Ah hell, I ain't got it in me. Not even him. Now lead the way."

Jacob started walking toward his home. He hadn't gone ten steps before he was crying.

"Forget him, kid. Forget his damn music, too. All it does is hide what he is. You'll see past them things someday, you live long enough."

When they came out of the woods, Lowdge stopped and looked back through the trees at the lights. "Bastard killed my best buddy. Couldn't never prove it. Found him in the donniker, his whole throat tore up inside and not a mark on his neck. Internal bleeding, they said. Yeah. Mitts standin' there, had blood under his nails. Musta stuck his fingers right down . . ." Lowdge broke off, his voice thick. Finally he said, "No more. I'm away from it now. Work my way home again. Home."

"He still has my harmonica," Jacob said softly.

"He might be awake by now. Forget it. He got more than just a harmonica. Forget it. I get home, I'll send you one."

They started walking across the pasture toward the dark house and the ghostly barns. When Jacob looked at Lowdge again, he saw a tear gleaming on the man's face. He reached out and took his thick, stubby-fingered hand.

Lowdge kept walking, but looked at Jacob and smiled. It was not an easy smile, not the way Mitts had smiled, but it was a smile, and they walked on.

Back by the rocks, Mitts sat up rubbing his head, cursing under his breath. Who the hell was it, he wondered, and where had the boy gone? Home, probably. Gone for good now.

He reached down and examined his guitar. It would be all right. One of the tuning pegs was bent, and the back was scraped, but he could straighten the peg and it would still sound fine, better than fine, beautiful.

Mitts put a hand on the ground to push himself to his feet, and the tip of a secondary finger brushed something smooth and cold. He picked up the piece of metal, turned it over in his hands, and then snapped his wrist and fingers, whirling it away into the deeper darkness until he heard it strike a tree and ricochet into the brush. Junk. Just junk.

He picked himself up, rubbing his head with his most delicate fingers, and walked back toward the lights, his guitar under one arm. He entered his trailer, put his guitar in its case, and looked in the mirror. He would have to change before his final show.

He took off his tuxedo jacket, reached into the pocket, and came out with Jacob Zook's harmonica, the one somebody won a long time ago, maybe won at a carnival. His flesh tingled when he touched it, and he smiled that easy smile, the smile that so many children had known was true. And it was. He loved his music, and he loved the children.

His long wiry fingers grasped the two pieces of housing where they were open at the back, and pulled. They snapped apart easily, and the other Piece, the hidden Piece that he had known the boy was carrying when he opened his door that night, fell to the carpet.

Mitts knelt and picked it up, examined it, touching, tasting, smelling. Yes, he thought. This is it. He would give it to Oz after the last show. But now he had to change, change his dirty, rumpled clothes, and play again.

He opened a drawer and moved some folded socks aside to reveal a wooden box ten inches long and six inches wide. He opened the lid and tossed the Piece inside so that it rattled among the dozens of white and yellow bones that lay within, none of them longer than the distance between a child's finger joints.

Then he changed his clothes, stepped outside into the warm night, sat on the steps of his trailer, and played his guitar, played with so much compassion and feeling and love that the towners who heard it stopped in the middle of the midway and listened, and tears came to the women's eyes, and the men had to clear their throats before they spoke again.

And on the Zook farm, young Jacob slept next to his brother in their bed, and heard it through the open window, but only in his dreams. Lowdge, sleeping in the barn, waiting for the night to end, heard nothing.

CHET WILLIAMSON

The show rolled on . . .

ALONG THE MIDWAY (XII)

Monroe County, New York

Oz had been surprised to find George standing in the doorway of his trailer. He'd invited him in and they'd talked about how the tour was going, how well his aerial act with Ginger was being received. He looked for signs of distress at mention of the girl but saw none. Perhaps things were going *too* well there. And then George got to what Oz sensed was the real reason for his visit.

"You know the Device you told us about before starting the tour, the instrument you said would change the way the world looks at us? How's that coming along?"

"Very well," Oz said cautiously. "Your brothers and sisters have been very successful in claiming its components. We're progressing steadily toward our day."

"May I . . . may I see it?"

Oz studied George. The troupe had circled three-quarters of the country and he hadn't shown the slightest interest in anything but the normal he was playing footsie with on the trapeze. Now he wanted to see the Device. What was up?

"Of course," Oz said. "This way."

Why not show it to him? Maybe he'd reveal what was on his mind.

Oz unlocked the back room and ushered George in ahead of him. Not much room left over with the two of them in there, and no way George could miss the Device. Oz watched the younger man's face as he studied the instrument.

"That's one strange-looking contraption," George said softly. "It looks almost . . . familiar. Kind of hard to believe it'll change the world."

"It will, brother," Oz said. "It will."

"But how?"

"Just as I explained: It will change the way the world sees us. When our day comes we will no longer be considered freaks. We will be accepted. We will get our due."

Our revenge.

"But how's this weird little thing going to accomplish that?"

"You must trust me that it will. Of course, if we don't retrieve *all* the components, the Device will be useless. In fact, it will not be a device at all, but little more than a curious construct of peculiar components. And then we won't have our day, and we'll remain freaks and rejects."

George glanced up at him and Oz saw defiance in his eyes, read *Speak for yourself* there.

And Oz envied him that confidence that somehow, some way, he was going to make it in this world as it was, make it accept *him* as he was. Oz had never known that feeling, not for an instant. How could he? But he wanted that feeling of belonging, craved it.

And he would belong. The Device would see to it.

"Is there—?"

He suddenly noticed that George had turned away from the Device and was peering at the bookshelf. A special bookshelf. Most of the tomes that lined it were old, some ancient, many of them stolen from the restricted sections of various libraries across the country. George reached up and touched a short leatherbound volume.

My father's journal!

"Please don't touch those, George. Some of them are very fragile. Have you seen enough?"

"I suppose so," George said. "But I don't understand."

"You will," Oz said, clapping George's shoulder in

what he hoped was a friendly gesture. "Trust me, you will."

He was going to have to keep an eye on George.

Petergello arrived shortly after George left.

"How's Lover Boy doing?"

"Acting strange. I hope this little matchmaking plot of ours doesn't backfire. How did Louella do at the museum?"

"Fine. She snatched the Piece easily—and helped herself to a few other things as well."

Oz sighed. Another Piece—this one obtained without fuss.

"That's Louella. Where is it?"

"She wants to play with it awhile. I gave her a couple of days if she swore not to lose it. That all right with you?"

Oz didn't like it but he nodded.

"I suppose so. Louella must have her fun."

Rochester, New York

It was certainly hot enough for the circus.

Everything he could see was covered with flies. They rose up in great black swarms above the fields behind the house, and moved slowly across the hazy blue sky; whole, ragged, living clouds full of them, looking for a place to eat and breed.

Glenn looked out from the relative safety of the screened-in porch. It was too hot out there under the sun, the kind of heat you only got at the end of the summer. Even here in the shade, the sweltering, wet air pressed down on him as if he were trapped within a mound of woolen blankets. And there was never a breeze to give any relief, as if the ever-blazing sun had dried up the wind.

On days such as this, the last dead days of August, he would start to sweat even before he started to move. And the moment the salty moisture was on his skin, the flies descended. No yard work would get done today, no matter what Anna said. He glanced again at the paper in his hands: Old Time Circus in Chili Fairground.

Glenn checked out the address. He knew just where the place was, down the way from that park with the antique merry-go-round. They had tried putting up yet another shopping mall out there, but, with the economy in the shape it was, things had fallen apart in a hurry. The town fathers decided to make the best of bad times, renting out the lot to flea markets, craft shows, and anybody else who could give the town some money. And now they had a circus.

The lot was also up close to Lake Ontario. Even on a day like this, there'd be some sort of breeze. You had to do something when August got like this, or you'd go crazy. Something, he thought, like taking in a two-bit circus in Chili. He chuckled, both at the thought and the name of the town. He always loved the way they pronounced it, not like you pronounced the country south-of-the-border or the dish with beans, but with the *"i"* sound long and drawn-out. *Chii-lii*. No pretensions in upstate New York. He watched a beetle, a big, brown ugly thing as long as his thumb, waddle across the porch floor toward the door that led inside. He was going to the circus. It made him feel like a kid again.

"Glenn?" A voice from the house cut through his concentration. "What are you doing, Glenn?"

There were no pretensions, that is, unless you happened to mention his wife. Glenn moved his foot forward and crushed the beetle beneath the heel of his shoe.

"I'm reading the paper!" he called into the house.

"You can do that any time, honey," was Anna's curt reply. "That lawn has to be mowed before it gets completely out of hand."

Glenn knew there was no use arguing that it was too hot to work; if the lawn wasn't perfect, it would reflect badly on Anna. She needed everything just so. But they had been married long enough for Glenn to have figured out other means of escape. "You wouldn't want me to do that, honey. It's too hot. If the grass gets too short, it'll dry out and die."

There was an uncommon silence from the house. For a change, Anna couldn't contradict his point of view. A dead lawn was even more improper than a ragged one.

Glenn almost started to whistle. Not only was he going to the circus, but for once he'd gotten the better of the lawn work. He hadn't felt this good in ten years.

Still, if he wanted this feeling to last, he'd have to get a couple of his cameras and go, before Anna got any other ideas.

He walked briskly into the house, smiling to himself all the time. The circus. This was the sort of thing the two of them used to do before they were married. For a minute, he thought of asking his wife to go along with him.

But only for a minute.

The Nikon had a good, solid heft to it. He always felt better when he had a camera in his hands.

There was a wind off the lake. It ruffled his clothing and blew away the biting flies, and brought the smells of popcorn and cotton candy. And this place was even better than he could have imagined. It wasn't just a circus; there was a full-blown sideshow, too.

Glenn raised his viewfinder to his eye, and snapped the row of gaudy canvas banners, advertising the world's fattest man, "A Ton of Quivering Flesh," Carmella the fortune-teller, the slithering snake man, the incredible Man from Mars. He'd stumbled on a real old-fashioned ten-in-one, a real carney show. He'd seen a couple of these at state fairs when he was a kid, had even done some reading about them, but he'd never dreamed he would be able to see one of them through his camera. He had always thought that this sort of thing was history.

A tall man in a striped suit stood on a platform in front of the main tent, waving a cane at the entranceway. An insistent voice drifted on the breeze: "Inside this tent are the secrets of the world—hidden from the eyes of man for hundreds of years. Ladies and gentlemen, you won't see this on TV!"

Glenn decided to ignore the big show. They wouldn't let him take photos inside that tent, anyway. Instead, the freaks always sold cheaply printed cards with their likenesses on them. They used to cost a quarter, back in the fifties. He wondered what happened to the ones he had bought way back then. His mother had thrown them out, probably; or maybe his wife had.

A little way up the midway, he saw a huge trailer with a canvas protection to keep away unpaying eyes. A sign said The World's Fattest Man Is Here! He must really be something to see, Glenn thought, if they gave him his own separate admission. The pit shows were only reserved for the very best freaks.

Still, he didn't want to look at what was up front and intended for the public. He wanted to get inside this place, back where the rubes never traveled, and take a picture of its darkest secrets. His camera was loaded with fast film to get the best out of the natural light, because he hated using a flash. A second camera body fitted with a tele-photo lens was stashed in his bag, in case one of the freaks dared to show himself in daylight. He wanted to be ready for anything.

But to really get what he wanted, Glenn had to move away from the midway. He walked around the tent, paus-ing to let a forklift truck loaded with hay pass. Later on, he might follow one of those trucks and get some pictures of the elephants. Right now, though, he was stalking stran-ger game.

There, beyond the main attraction, was a smaller tent, a dark tan color where the main tent was all bright reds and blues. Unlike the fat man's trailer, there was no sign for the public to show it might be a pit show. It must be some of the freaks' living quarters. What a place to add to his photo collection.

Glenn almost jumped when he heard a percussive noise, almost like a drumbeat. The tent before him had a loose piece of canvas folded away from the entryway and tied, very loosely, to a nearby pole. The canvas made that heavy noise whenever it caught the wind, a sound some-where between a person beating a rug and the firm slap of a hand against a backside, as if the tent were made out of some more substantial material than simple burlap.

He walked past the noisy canvas to the entranceway and couldn't hear any other noise from inside. The freaks were probably on the job. But he'd never find anything if he didn't take a look around. He took a step across the threshold.

He lost his balance when his foot sank into the soft flooring. They must have put up this tent over thick grass, or maybe even moss. He took one more tentative step, then another. He felt like he was walking across a feather bed. His feet made no sound.

The outside sunshine didn't reach very far inside; only

a small circle of gray at the entranceway managed to penetrate the total dark. He made out some dim shapes before him, but the light was so bad they could be anything from barrels to bodies.

Glenn wished he carried a lighter. He waved his right hand before him, trying to find a pole with a switch or some sort of hanging cord; some way to bring light into this place.

Perhaps, he thought, he could get his bearings if he flashed his strobe a couple of times. He unzipped his camera bag.

"Don't allow no photos in here," came a voice from the far side of the tent, husky, but the voice of a woman. "People got to stay alive, after all."

He thought about the main tent, the ten-in-one, and how the Armless and Legless Wonder would pass out twenty-five-cent photos of himself using only his teeth. But he wasn't interested in profit here. He was making historical documents by taking photos behind the scenes, and maybe he could talk this woman into changing her mind.

Glenn realized there *was* light in the tent. At first, he had thought his eyes were only getting used to the darkness, but the tent around him continued to gain color and definition, as if someone were slowly turning up a dimmer switch. He blinked and the shapes around him became recognizable.

These weren't living quarters after all. The part of the tent he was in was almost empty, with nothing but a stack of boxes and a couple of worn folding chairs. A curtain, fashioned from the same dull tan as the outside of the tent, hung across the midsection to either side of the center pole. Maybe, Glenn thought, this half of the tent was used for some kind of storage, and there were living quarters beyond the curtain.

He couldn't see any sign of the woman who had spoken. Perhaps she was behind the curtain as well.

"Behind you now," the voice declared. "Have to move pretty fast to keep up with Louella."

He turned around slowly, a smile on his face. You got a lot more photo opportunities with the proper attitude.

He forgot the smile when he saw Louella.

She was a fat lady, but more than fat. She was immense. And she didn't appear to be wearing any clothing.

Glenn was not a small man. His wife was always nagging him to "lose twenty pounds." But he could have fit three times across within the mass of flesh that regarded him from the other side of the tent. Her body was a series of great horizontal folds, like someone had taken logs of flesh and piled them one atop another in some exaggerated parody of a torso. Somewhere in the middle of all that were her breasts, which Glenn could now see were held in place by a strip of tan fabric almost lost by the overwhelming corpulence that surrounded it. She was wearing some sort of bikini, then, made of the same burlap as the tent. The fat woman's coloring was so close to that of the burlap wall behind her that it made her appear even more immense. It was difficult to tell exactly where Louella ended and the tent began.

The tiny head atop the massive poundage smiled. "Now ain't I a sight for sore eyes."

"Oh." Glenn realized he was staring. "I'm sorry."

"Ain't you now?" Louella's smile widened. Her teeth were small, well-placed, and perfectly white. Glenn wondered if they were her original set. "But I'm used to bein' looked at. Comes with the territory." Her tongue darted between her teeth for an instant. For some reason, it made Glenn think of some tiny, pink prisoner, trying to escape.

She walked toward him then. Glenn had thought that a woman of her size would have difficulty moving at all. Instead, she seemed to stride almost without effort, pushing the muscles within her great legs in such a way that she almost flowed from one spot to another, as if her mass were so great she simply pushed gravity out of her way.

He could see her flesh undulate slowly as she walked nearer, the fat rippling like gentle waves lapping at a beach. Up this close, she smelled of sweat and something else. It reminded Glenn of bittersweet chocolate. The mixture was oddly appealing. He watched a bead of perspiration run down her ample flesh to the sudden angle of her elbow. He had to resist the urge to reach out his hand and touch her quivering arm.

She was taller than he was, too, Glenn realized, rising

almost a full head above him. This close, her huge form nearly blocked out everything else in his vision.

Her tiny smile broadened as she looked down past Glenn's chest.

"Kind of fancy camera," she remarked.

Somehow, she had the camera in her hands.

"Don't break it!" Glenn gasped in surprise. He hadn't even seen her hands move.

"Hey, I never break nothin'." She laughed, a great, booming noise that seemed to burst upward from her immense belly. "Somethin' comes to Louella Snard, well, she only makes it better."

She swung the camera away from him with her right hand, her pudgy fingers so large that they almost completely covered the camera body. Glenn saw that she held something in her left hand as well, although he hadn't seen where this second object had come from. It was a long, twisted thing, but with hard, angular edges, as if an artist had wanted to reproduce a tree root in metal. Then there was the bottom of it, a rounded object of a different color altogether; in fact the color of the thing seemed to change as Glenn watched, so that the knob looked smaller one instant, larger the next. The only thing certain about this piece was that it didn't belong at all with the metal above. Glenn had a wild thought about Louella hiding objects within the folds of her flesh.

She swiveled her hips. "Like the way Louella struts her stuff? Could have been a coochie dancer, if I set my mind to it."

What was she doing to his camera? That rig in her hand had cost him close to a grand. He was beginning to regret his little adventure into a place where he obviously didn't belong.

At least she was still talking to him. Maybe he could coax his Nikon back out of her hands.

"Look," he said, careful to have his own smile back in place. "Maybe I shouldn't have come in here. I was just wandering around the circus, looking to take some good pictures. It's my hobby. But if you don't like cameras around, I'll be glad to take it and—"

"Hobby?" Louella replied with what sounded like a

girlish giggle. "We can make this much more than a hobby, honey."

With that, she brought her two hands together.

"No!" Glenn called out, having visions of smashed lenses and shredded film.

But there was no crack or crash. There was no sound at all.

"Hold your water," Louella commanded. "I may be big, but I ain't clumsy. Here's your precious camera." Her hands opened. "Catch."

Something flashed from her hand. He caught it more by reflex than by thought.

It wasn't the camera. As his fingers closed around it, he realized it was that other, twisted thing. It seemed smaller than when the fat lady had held it.

He dropped the object with a yell.

"Like a hot potato, huh?" She chuckled. "Meant to toss you this."

But the thing hadn't been hot. It had been cold as a metal pole in the subzero Rochester winter.

She handed him the camera. His fingers were still numb, but he managed to hold on to it anyway.

"Next time you come," she drawled, "bring your pictures with you."

Glenn stared at her. He would be happy just to get out of here with his camera in one piece. Why would he ever return?

"My gentlemen callers always come a second time," she replied before he could even ask.

Something soft brushed his cheek as he turned to go. Glenn realized it was her hand. It was surprisingly cool.

He stumbled out into the light and looked down at the camera. It appeared to be perfectly fine, not a scratch or dent on the lens or body. Louella had probably been playing some sort of trick on him, a sleight of hand, three-card monte carney joke, trying to get a rise out of him.

Well, she certainly had. But he wasn't going to let this one strange meeting spoil what he came here for in the first place. And—not that he was really worried—he wanted to try out the camera and rid himself of any worry that it somehow might have gotten damaged.

Besides, it was time to get to work. It was only late afternoon, and this time of year, he still had a couple hours of good sunlight. It was a shame, though, that he hadn't gotten a good picture of the fat lady.

All thoughts of Louella left him when he saw the father, son, and cotton candy. The cotton candy had taken over. It appeared to have landed everywhere on the boy but the child's mouth. The father, in his quest to help, had managed to get a great wad of pink spun candy stuck to his wrist and sleeve. And they were both laughing.

Glenn focused and pressed the shutter.

Click.

It was a great shot. And he got it just in time. He noticed as he lowered his camera that the smiles had vanished from their faces. The father looked irritated, the child sad. But Glenn had managed to capture that golden moment just before on film.

Glenn shooed away the first few gnats of evening. He spotted a little girl staring in wonder at a clown. He swung his camera up and . . .

Click.

The little girl started to cry as he turned away. It was a shame, Glenn thought, about the fat lady. It would have been a great shot. Maybe Glenn would visit Louella a second time after all. And, next time, he'd show her just whose camera it was.

When he came home, he thought he would be exhausted. He had taken half a dozen rolls of film at the circus, one wonderful shot after another. In an odd sort of way, rather than break the camera, the fat lady had blessed it. For the rest of the afternoon, Glenn had been in the right place at the right moment. And the shutter always clicked in that instant before the right moment passed.

He had rushed around the circus for three hours, in such a good mood that not even the flies could bother him. But the energy had left him as he drove toward the inner loop and home. By the time he had reached his driveway, his arms felt like lead pipes at his sides. But there were things he had to do. At the very least, he had to develop the film.

His wife was reading the evening paper at the kitchen table.

"What's this world coming to?" she demanded, waving the newspaper in his face. "Not that you'd notice, you and your camera."

The headline on her paper read: Break-In at the Museum.

Glenn sighed. The world wasn't keeping up with Anna's standards again. He glanced at the article. This actually did interest him. Someone had stolen two objects from the photographic museum, the George Eastman House. One seemed to be some kind of totem, the sort of thing that some people believed protected them from having their spirits captured by the camera—unless it caused those spirits to be captured. The translation of old documents was apparently unclear. The newspaper piece was rather vague about the exact nature of this thing's power, and mentioned something about a curse. The other missing piece was a kind of photographic curiosity; no matter how many pictures you took of the object, it never appeared the same way twice on film. The article was continued on page two.

"Glenn? Is there something wrong?" Anna asked as he took the paper from her hands.

There was a picture of the objects on page two. If you put the two of them together, Glenn thought they formed the strange device the fat lady had used to pretend to smash the camera. Glenn stared at the smudged black-and-white image, not very well reproduced on the rough newsprint. It was hard to be sure. Why, after all, would something as obscure as a stolen relic show up in a freak show?

He gave the paper back to Anna. "No, nothing's wrong." He smiled and held up his camera. "In fact, everything's great."

She actually laughed at that. How long had it been since he had heard her laugh? "Oh," she said, and this time her voice was filled with humor. "You and your pictures!"

He felt a sudden mischief, as if he had spent too much time today among the twelve-year-olds. His grin broadened as he lifted his viewfinder back to his eye. "I'll take your picture, little girl!"

"Oh, Glenn!" She pushed her chair back and jumped away. "Not now! I look a mess!"

But Glenn would not be denied. "Smile pretty for the photographer, little girl."

"Glenn, it's much too hot—" She shrieked as he swung the camera toward her, but it was a shriek of delight. "Glenn!" She laughed. "I'm serious now."

Glenn lowered the camera. "Does the little girl want a surprise before we take her picture?"

"A surprise?" Anna paused in her flight, intrigued. "What kind of surprise?"

He leaned forward and kissed her. She made a little noise in the back of her throat, half surprise, half pleasure. Glenn hadn't heard that noise in a long time.

They kissed a second time, longer and deeper. His arms moved around her shoulders, her hands pressed his waist. Why didn't they do this more often?

His hands hesitated as they moved down her ribs.

As soon as the moment came, it was gone again. Somehow, it was all wrong. His hands felt awkward in their caresses. Her body was too bony, her breasts far too small. He pulled his hands away. All desire left him.

"That's better," she said, resuming her prim and proper tone. "Glenn, we are full-grown adults." She still had a smile. "I was thinking. It's getting late. Maybe we should go to bed."

"In a few minutes." He looked down at his camera. "I've got to put the film away."

"I'll be waiting for you." How long had it been since Anna had smiled for this long?

Why not? Glenn thought. He still had a couple shots left on that last roll. "Time for that picture."

He pressed the shutter before she could renew her protests.

Click.

He escaped before Anna could say anything else, down to the basement and his darkroom.

He turned on the fluorescent lamps for a minute to gather the paraphernalia to develop the film. He swatted at a buzzing near his ear, then glanced at a dark blur that moved toward the ceiling.

There were even flies down here. There were flies everywhere.

Except, he thought, inside Louella's tent.

Nonsense. His attention, after all, had been directed elsewhere. Louella had been strange enough without him imagining things.

He switched to the darkroom lighting, and mixed the chemicals quickly, then plucked the other rolls of film from the outer pocket of his camera bag. With practiced hands, he freed the film rolls from their canisters within the lightproof bag and transferred them one by one to their developing canisters. He shook each container in turn, then rescued the film, hanging each roll to dry below that single red light.

He hadn't realized how anxious he still was until he freed the first roll from its canister. Even in the dim darkroom light, he could see the lights and darks of the negative image etched on the celluloid. The camera was working fine. Why had he ever thought otherwise? These were going to be great pictures!

Now that he had seen that his precious pictures were safe, he had used up the last of his energy. He turned out the lights and climbed the stairs.

Would Anna be waiting for him? He was so tired, and the desire had not returned.

It was with relief that he saw a lump at the far side of their king-size bed. There didn't have to be any explanations or accusations if Anna had fallen asleep first.

Glenn fell into bed, as far away from his wife as possible.

Louella was waiting for him.

It was dark, the circus closed for the night. But Louella's tent was glowing, the skin of the shell giving off the kind of light Glenn had seen in pictures of iridescent fish that lived far beneath the sea. As Glenn approached, he could see that the light pulsed with a regular rhythm, like that of a heartbeat. *Thub-thub. Thub-thub.* But that was his own heart, wasn't it?

Maybe, he thought, it was that noisy tent flap. The

entrance was suddenly before him, and the flap beat the
heart's rhythm. Maybe he shouldn't go back into that tent
this late at night. But, before he could think of what else
to do, he was inside.

"Back again this late?" Louella's voice called out.
"You catch a lady at a disadvantage." She was behind him
again. "I don't know if I'm that kind of girl."

"Well," he found himself explaining, "your light was
still on—"

"Hey, I do some of my best work at night." She
laughed as he turned to face her. She no longer wore her
bikini. Without the cloth restraints, she looked twice as
big as before. He glanced at her smile, and saw her teeth
were gone as well, the perfect tiny white molars replaced
by a few haphazard black stumps.

"So you like the real me?" she asked coquettishly.

He could swear her teeth were moving, shifting back
and forth across her gums. He had the sudden feeling that
they weren't teeth at all, but shiny black beetles that lived
in her mouth.

He realized he had to be dreaming.

"Don't you wish," Louella drawled as she approached. "Honey, you're gonna love the real me."

His nostrils were filled with the smell of bittersweet
chocolate. She was almost touching him. He stared above
the great mounds of fat, high in her face, at her two tiny
eyes.

And then the two black spots grew wings and flew
away.

He was surrounded by flesh before he could scream.

He couldn't breathe.

Glenn opened his eyes and struggled free of the bed-
clothes. Somehow, he had gotten tangled up in the blanket
during the night. He was all alone in bed and covered with
sweat.

He realized he also had an erection.

Well, that happened in the morning sometimes, even
with a middle-aged guy like himself. He was sure it had
nothing to do with the dream.

Still, he was relieved that Anna was no longer in bed
with him. He was surprised she hadn't tried to get him up.

There was a proper time to get up, according to her, even on Sunday. Maybe, he thought, this was an extra benefit of last night's playfulness.

He rose quickly. Maybe he'd be doubly lucky, and Anna would be out somewhere. He'd like nothing better than to go right down to the darkroom and print the best of his pictures before the heat of the day.

The morning paper sat on the kitchen table. There was no sign of his wife. Usually by now she would have outlined a full day of chores and criticized at least three of his bad habits. Glenn had a quick thought about gift horses and proceeded immediately to the darkroom.

He kept his curiosity about the pictures in check as he cut the film and laid it out to make contact sheets. He developed each sheet in turn, hanging them with clothespins to dry. Normally, the next thing he'd do is examine each shot with a magnifying glass to see which would be the best to print. But he didn't have the patience today. He had seen the father-and-son shot at the beginning of the third contact sheet. The first picture he'd taken would be the first he'd develop.

The result was wonderful. It was a great picture. They looked even happier on film than they had in person. Now he was really excited, and he decided to develop the little girl with the clown next.

He frowned as he focused the photo in preparation to make the print. The little girl was in the exact middle of the shot, her eyes wide open in wonder. But the clown was nowhere to be seen.

How could he have missed the clown? His viewfinder looked right through the lens. It was the sort of mistake an amateur would make. Had he been too nervous after the fat lady, too excited at the very thought of the circus?

He wondered what else could have gone wrong.

He pulled down a still damp contact sheet and examined it with his magnifying glass.

It was terrible.

He had taken pictures of dozens of circus performers, and, toward the end of the day, had even managed to capture a couple of freaks out on the platform before the big tent. But there wasn't a single circus performer on his rolls of film. And the platform before the tent was empty.

What had gone wrong? It couldn't have been his error—not this many times. Were the circus performers not really there? Was something wrong with the film?

Was something wrong with the camera?

Glenn closed his eyes at a sudden headache pain. He had been staring too intently at the tiny images.

He opened his eyes again and saw the photo of Anna.

She was radiant. When she smiled that way, she looked ten years younger. For the first time in so long, he remembered what he had felt when he had married her.

He thought he heard footsteps upstairs.

"Anna?" he called.

It seemed suddenly very important to find his wife. He grabbed the contact sheets and ran upstairs.

She wasn't there.

"Anna?" he called again. There was no answer. He thought he heard footsteps in the other room. He was about to follow the sound when he saw the open paper on the table.

FURTHER EVIDENCE IN MUSEUM BREAK-IN
Valuable Camera Found at Crime Scene

He frowned. The camera's description was very familiar. It was crazy, but today, everything seemed crazy.

He thought he heard someone moving in the basement.

"Anna?" he called as he hurried down the stairs. He thought he saw movement in the far corner of the room, a shifting of shadows, but the light was so bad down here, it could just as well be his imagination.

Anna didn't answer. Why didn't she answer?

He stepped into the darkroom. She wasn't here either.

He checked his camera bag. His second camera, the one that matched the description in the paper, wasn't there.

He remembered when he had unzipped his bag in Louella's tent. When he had left the tent, the bag was zipped again. When had he done that? Wouldn't he have noticed the difference in weight if the camera was gone? How could they have replaced the stolen artifact with the camera, if Louella already had the artifact? Had they broken into the museum twice, the second time, no doubt, right in front of any number of police and security guards?

It was doubly crazy. Only one thing really made sense. Louella had played him for a sucker. And she wanted to make sure she would see him again.

He grabbed his remaining camera and ran back up the stairs. He took the contact sheets, too. He'd find out what was going on. No one took advantage of him for long.

The gate was closed and locked. On Sunday, the circus didn't open until noon. There was hardly anybody around. It was fairly easy, even for someone as big as Glenn, to slip on through a spot where the temporary fence hadn't quite been joined properly.

He came up to Louella's tent from the back. He paused, listening for any sound. A fat lady should make a lot of noise, if this made any sense at all.

It didn't. There was no noise except the wind and the buzzing of flies.

His hand brushed the tent as he walked cautiously toward the entrance. The burlap was warm to the touch, probably warmed by the morning sun. Except that this tent didn't really feel like burlap. It felt a little bit like leather. It felt even more like living, human flesh.

It was his imagination again. This whole thing was too much for him. He hesitated at the entrance. A great hand grabbed his arm and pulled him inside.

"You're not gonna yell or nothin'," Louella's voice demanded. "Don't tell me you don't like this."

Glenn hadn't yelled. He must have been too startled. "My camera—" he began.

Louella spun him around so he could see her. "Took you long enough to get here. What I have to do to get a man's attention." She wore her bikini, and she had her teeth, thank God.

Glenn was about to demand an explanation when he realized they weren't alone. It was dark behind Louella, but something was moving there. It was like the shadow he had seen in his basement, but there were a lot of shadows, maybe a hundred of them.

Were they other freaks? Why didn't they come out into the light?

Glenn realized he wasn't angry anymore. He was confused, and maybe he was afraid.

"Who are you really?" he asked. "What do you do here?"

"I take care of things around here. Make sure there's no leftovers." Louella laughed. "And, let me tell you, honey, I can work up an appetite."

The tent grew lighter behind him, and Glenn could better see the crowd of shadows. If that was what they were. Even if he squinted, they were fuzzy, ill-defined, like an out-of-focus shot or a photo that was only half-developed. But Glenn thought he saw a father and son, a girl who had stared in wonder at a clown, and a hundred other subjects of his camera the day before.

Is this what he had done? Were all the subjects here?

"Anna?" he called.

He thought he heard a whispered reply, but maybe it was only the wind.

Louella laughed, maybe at him, maybe at the shadows. "Once their spirit's left them, they don't know what to do."

She pulled the contact sheets from his hand. "Nice of you to do my collectin' for me. One thing about all these pounds. Make me stand out in public." She stroked his shoulder with her free hand. "Much rather be in private. Know you would, too."

Glenn felt a sudden rush of anger. He wouldn't give into her this easily. He reached out to grab the contact sheets back, but the photos had turned to ash.

The shadows were growing less distinct as the tent brightened, shrinking until they seemed to be little more than a hundred dark dust motes, buzzing about like flies. Flies? Maybe, Glenn thought, there had been nothing but flies and shadows after all.

The last specks of darkness disappeared behind the fat lady. Behind her, Glenn thought, or inside her. Louella burped.

"But you and me got business," she said, both her hands on his shoulders. "I like a live one, now and again."

What was she talking about? Glenn heard a buzzing in his ears. Those flies again. It gave him a headache, and made it hard to think. This close, all he could smell was sweat and bitter chocolate.

The camera bumped against his neck. He had forgotten it was there. Louella's hands rubbed across his naked back. What had happened to his shirt?

He couldn't breathe. The buzzing was everywhere. Where were the flies? It felt as if they filled the inside of his head.

"It's time, honey."

His world was filled with the buzzing of flies and the smell of bitter chocolate. He stood there, naked, covered with sweat. His skin tingled as if a thousand tiny insects crawled inside his veins. His entire body felt alive.

He had to finish this. But where was Louella?

Her voice came from the far side of the curtain.

"I'm waitin' here. I ain't got all day!"

He opened the inner flap of the tent.

CRAIG SHAW GARDNER

The show rolled on . . .

Quarry, Massachusetts

Please don't take him!

They take him anyway, and with him, her dignity, leaving her crying and begging on her knees. Webbed hands clasped in rigid-fingered prayer, she throws herself at their feet. Tears rolling down her beak, she pleads with all her heart and soul.

Don't take my baby!

They don't listen. They don't care.

In her recurring dream, the last thing Mother Goose sees before hyperventilating is her son's beautiful face as her father bends over to kiss his grandson good-bye. He slips something inside the baby's blanket as he hands him over to the social worker and that bitch Mrs. Butterman, then he turns and says, "What goes around, comes around, Em."

As they leave with her baby, she's never sure who screams first, her or her dream baby, but scream they do and the screaming usually wakes Mother Goose.

But not tonight.

Tonight, when her father turns, it's not her father at all. Tonight it's Ozymandias Prather. "What goes around, comes around, Em," he says, but the words don't fit the movement of his lips. Unlike her father, Ozymandias slips something into her *left hand instead of into the baby's blanket.*

Mother Goose woke sitting up in bed, looking out the tiny window as though she'd been that way for a while. It was a dream, she told herself. Her clenched left hand opened to reveal a crumpled piece of paper. Her webbed fingers trembling, Mother Goose unfolded and read it by the faint light coming in the tiny trailer window: *62 Warren Road, Quarry, Massachusetts.*

It was Ozymandias Prather's handwriting. She hadn't been dreaming after all.

She got out of bed with care. Though she was only forty-one, arthritis and rheumatism, coupled with occasional flare-ups of phlebitis, tortured her body, making her feel more like eighty. She slipped her feet into the pair of fuzzy pink slippers with the sides cut out to accommodate her wide, webbed feet, and shuffled through the kitchenette. In just a few steps she was at the other end of the small trailer where she found her son Joey's stowaway bed empty. She raised the greasy red checkered curtain on the window over the dry sink and looked out at the large green army surplus bus in which her "children" had sleeping compartments.

One of them must have come and gotten Joey to go get breakfast at the kitchen truck. Mother Goose thought about joining them, but her dream—she realized she'd had it every night for the past week—and Ozymandias's visit, coupled with the thought of the task ahead, left her appetite lost in a sour stew of anxious apprehension that boiled in the bottom of her gut. She needed a drink, even if it was too early for one. She reached under the dry sink and let out a cry.

The bear had got her bottle!

Scrambling to her knees, she looked under the sink for her gin. It was gone. Mother Goose got to her feet and went to the door. She opened it and looked out. Standing a short distance away, staring at her trailer as if waiting for her to show her face, was one of the Beagle Boys. He smiled and nodded and Mother Goose got the message: Ozymandias wanted her sober until after she had brought the Piece to him. She realized she had been foolish to think she could hide her drinking from Oz.

She closed the door quickly. Within a couple of steps she was sitting at her dressing and makeup table. To take her mind off things, she picked up her abalone-handled brush and began nervously brushing her long red hair.

Emily Gibbs had never minded her looks. Being raised in the carney sideshow life she felt accepted for what she was from the beginning, which gave her an inner confidence and strength that helped her deal with what would happen later. It wasn't until she began doing shows with her father and not only saw the way the rubes looked at her, but also felt their disgust and abhorrence that she understood what being different really meant.

From the bridge of her nose up, Emily was normal, even pretty. Her long hair was a rich red with the slightest touch of gray in front. She had large, bright blue, intelligent eyes that were spaced just far enough apart to bestow a gentle, innocent look to her deformed visage, and which were capable of instantly winning the trust of any child. Her nose was long and would have been noble if it didn't meld with her extended upper jaw, leaving only two, tiny, teardrop nostrils in the same general position they would be in on a goose's upper beak. Combined with her webbed fingers and toes, the Mother Goose schtick was inevitable.

Emily finished brushing her hair and decided not to put on any makeup. She glanced over her shoulder at the piece of paper on the shelf above her bed. Not for the first, nor the last time, she rued the day she had ever heard of Ozymandias Prather.

Her parents, Walter and Rita Gibbs, had been good friends with Oz's father, Jacob Prather, in the old days when they'd toured with Taber & Sons mud show until Rita gave birth to Emily. Unable to deal with the sight of her deformed daughter, she fled, leaving all her belongings behind, never to be heard from again. Later, when Jacob went crazy and dismantled the Device, Walter took a small Piece shaped like a pastry French horn and which could be sharp as a razor, but was usually dull as stone, as a good luck talisman.

Walter raised Emily on his own, and when she met and married Bob Butterman he had the Piece put on a gold chain as a wedding present for her. Walter told her the

Piece had power and would someday bring her great luck, but her life was proof that that had been bullshit. She didn't know what had happened to the Piece over the years. She'd lost it right around the time James and Joey were born.

When Ozymandias finally tracked her down and invited her to join his carnival, Emily hadn't been surprised when he told her of his search for the Pieces of the Device, the coming of the Otherness, and explained that he knew where her Piece was and that he wanted her to get it. After securing his promise that her children wouldn't be involved and would receive safe passage when the Otherness was let loose, Emily had reluctantly agreed for one reason only. On his deathbed, eaten up with lung cancer and barely able to talk, her father had told Emily that someday the son of Jacob Prather would come looking for her. He made her promise that when that day came she would follow him and do what he asked of her.

Now that day was here.

After the evening show, as the last of the rubes filed out to their cars, Emily gathered her children together in the bus for a meeting. Her "children," as she fondly referred to them, were a collection of deformed and normal dwarves and midgets whose abnormalities worked well with her nursery rhyme schtick. Their sideshow tent was called *Mother Goose's House of Rhymes*.

Each of her children represented a particular nursery rhyme by way of their individual deformities. Don Barlow, a hermaphrodite, played Jack and Jill. His lover, Homer Graise, had a deformity of the skull that made his head overly large and shaped like a pumpkin. He played Peter Peter Pumpkin-eater. George Lemay, who was all torso— born without arms or legs—was Humpty Dumpty. John Beane, whose thumbs were the size of tennis balls, was Little Jack Horner. A married couple, Billy and Betty Leiderman, who were fairly normal-looking dwarves, played Jack Be Nimble and Little Miss Muffet. Jack Sprat and his wife were played by Henry Wallski, who was so skinny he looked like a concentration camp victim, and his sister, Gerta, who was a midget version of Gore Edmund, the world's fattest man. A pair of Siamese twins,

Dennis and David Roma, were Tweedle-dee and Tweedle-dum. Ginny Dowd, who, along with Betty Leiderman, was Emily's closest friend, was thirty-five with a one-hundred-year-old face that was a sagging mass of wrinkles. She played Cross Patch.

Always sitting at Emily's feet, as close to her as he could get, was mute Joey, whom everyone else called Simon. He was the only one of her "children" who was really her offspring, and the only one who hadn't been taken away from her on that awful day she dreamt about every night. At five feet, Joey was an inch shorter than Emily. He'd been born severely retarded and had a face that showed it. He was Simple Simon in the sideshow.

Emily looked them over as they talked among themselves. She truly loved each of them as if they were her real children, even though most were close to her own age. She knew they didn't belong with Oz and his strange collection of sinister freaks, but because of her promise to her father, here they were.

Emily stumbled through excuses as to why she couldn't engage in the nightly drinking and playing of canasta, and tried to tell them each how much they meant to her. Though Ozymandias had assured her everything would be all right once she had contributed her Piece, Emily had a terrible sense of foreboding. She realized this meeting was really a fumbling attempt to say good-bye.

Later, driving in search of Warren Road, Quarry, Massachusetts, looked familiar to Emily. She'd been in hundreds of cities just like it all over the country—cities so small that if it weren't for the industries each was built around, they'd be nothing but large towns.

Quarry appeared to be barely that now. Textile mills and paper factories along the river that ran through town all appeared abandoned. The granite quarry jutting up over the center of town, and from which the city took its name, was a dark, barren-looking crag overgrown with shadowy trees and brush.

The house at 62 Warren Road was set back from the street a good fifty yards. It was large and wide, of uneven dimensions and styles ranging from excesses of Victorianism, to useless Colonial gables everywhere on the roof, to modern glass and steel skyscraper effects with a large glass wall on the left side of the mansion. The outline of the top of the house against the night sky gave it a castlelike appearance. At the right front corner facing the street, a square tower with a conical roof rose another story above the house. It had a single tiny window.

The front yard was literally a dump, piled six feet high in some areas with trash bags that overflowed with last summer's brown lawn clippings. Even with the eyesore of the front lawn, the striking presence of the house was undiminished.

She parked the van in front of the house, where it was darkest and there were no streetlights.

"Where the hell are we?"

Emily jumped at the voice, looking with astonishment at Joey as if he had spoken.

"What are you up to, Em?" Ginny Dowd said, poking her wrinkled visage over the backseat she'd been hiding behind. "I knew your story about looking up a distant relative was baloney!"

Next to Ginny, Betty Leiderman's pixieish face appeared. "Yeah!" she said firmly in support of Ginny.

"What are you doing here?" Emily asked them. Joey smiled happily and clapped his hands.

"We asked you first, Em," Ginny countered.

Emily looked at her two friends and despaired. This was not what she had wanted to happen. "You have to get out of here!" she shouted at them. "Go back to the carney."

"Fat chance!" Ginny said.

"Yeah!" Betty said again.

"You've been acting strange this whole tour," Ginny said. "You're in some kind of trouble with creepy old Oz, aren't you? What is it? We're your friends and we're not leaving, so you might as well tell us what's going on," Ginny said with a tone of finality that defied argument.

Pressed for time, and secretly glad for the company, Emily gave in. She explained she was only doing a favor for Ozymandias. Keeping the facts to a minimum, she told them she was looking for a piece of jewelry, a family heirloom, that Oz's father had given to her father, and which had been lost over the years but now Oz believed was in this deserted house.

Though Ginny and Betty exchanged doubtful glances, they didn't push her for more information. "So let's go get it!" Ginny said.

"Yeah!" said Betty.

As quietly as possible, the four of them departed the van and slid under the old cyclone fence that ran haphazardly around the place. Emily checked the front door and found it was locked. She started around the porch, motioning for the others to follow. As they did, a shudder, like a minor earth tremor, rolled through the house bringing Emily, Ginny, and Betty to a panicked halt on the porch.

They whirled to see Emily's idiot son standing frozen before the wide open front door, an eerie, faint, half-light creeping out to him. His mouth worked strenuously, whipping up a froth that dripped from the corner of his lips and ran to his chin. There were tears in his eyes.

Emily rushed to him and took him in her arms. "Joey? Are you okay?" He looked at her, blinked dual lines of tears down his cheeks, and smiled. He looked at the open front door and back at his mother and nodded his head excitedly. "Yes, honey," Emily said softly. "You did a good thing."

Another shudder moved through the house when Joey stepped across the threshold. It was softer, more subtle than the first one. It rippled through the structure, setting the old wood and stone to humming faintly and buzzing the bottom of their feet.

"Since when does New England feel like California?" Ginny wisecracked.

Is this really worth it? Mother Goose wondered. She didn't like the house and its thick darkness. It was dank, musty, almost heavy and stifling when combined with the moisture-laden humidity of the August night air. Emily wanted to be back in her trailer, the shades drawn against prying eyes, her small, battery-operated fan propped on the shelf above her bed, her bottle of Beefeaters cradled in her lap. But her promise to her father made her follow Joey into the house.

With a flashlight in her hand, she and Joey were climbing the wide front hall stairs to the second floor. The higher they got, the more oppressive the atmosphere became. Emily had to stop to get a decent breath. She leaned over the railing to watch Ginny and Betty—who were searching downstairs by the light of a candle—disappear into a dark hallway. She had tried to describe the Piece to them as best she could without mentioning its strange, shape-shifting properties.

Emily's light fell on Joey and she was suddenly reminded of his father. Emily was eighteen when she met Big Bob Butterman. At six-foot-four and built like a stone wall, Bob was true to his nickname, but his intelligence was a dwarf compared to his physique. His eyes crossed terribly and a set of protruding horse's teeth gave Bob's mental status away at a glance, but his massive, powerful body brought him respect.

Emily and her dad were with Boone's Big Top and Sideshow Extraordinaire the summer they played Bob's hometown of Greendale, New Hampshire—not too far north of Quarry—for three days. The town was centrally located to a lot of small towns around it which made it a worthwhile spot to stop for more than a one-night stand. At the urging of her father, Emily had started doing the Mother Goose schtick as the middle part of his act to give his arthritic legs a break.

Big Bob Butterman fell in love with Emily Gibbs the moment he laid eyes on her. As a child he had loved a book of Mother Goose rhymes his mother used to read to him at bedtime. Since his adult state of mind had remained more or less that of a child's, Bob had immediately seen Emily as the living embodiment of something he'd previously thought was make-believe. Bob hung around after each show, matinee and evening, waiting for Emily. He brought her flowers and candy and his time-worn nursery book for her to autograph.

Initially, Emily tried to explain to the gentle giant that she really wasn't Mother Goose, but the realization that it would break his heart kept her from pushing it. For the first time in her life, Emily came to understand the difference between loneliness and having someone who loves you to spend the rest of your life with. When the carney pulled out of Greendale, heading south for Long

Island, Bob Butterman went with it, signing on as a grunt, putting up and taking down canvas and lumber.

Emily and Bob were married in Maryland by a dwarf justice of the peace her father knew. By the time they reached winter quarters in Florida, she was pregnant. Nine months later, the sight of her twin boys, perfect and normal looking in every way right out of her womb, had brought Emily tears of joy, relief, and gratitude to God for answering her prayers that the children not be cursed with her deformities. Emily was in paradise with James and Joey and could ask for nothing more from life—except maybe a little more time in paradise.

Six weeks after the twins were born, Bob's mother, Barbara Butterman, an overbearing, domineering, *cruel* woman, tracked her son down and convinced the authorities in Florida that between her son's lack of brains and Emily's deformities, not to mention the life they would subject the children to in the carney, they were unfit parents. Based on her son's mental incompetence, Bob's mother had their marriage annulled, forced Emily to give up the Butterman name, and arranged to take the children and her son back to New Hampshire with her.

By then, it was obvious the twins weren't identical, as had been thought at birth. Joey's head never lost its conical shape from passing through Emily's small birth canal, and his eyes were more severely crossed, his teeth more buck, than even his father's. James, on the other hand, was a beautifully perfect baby. To Emily, he looked like the Ivory Snow baby, so cherubic and cute. Emily couldn't believe James was hers.

When Barbara Butterman was told by doctors of Joey's retardation and that it would be best for all concerned if the boy was institutionalized, she decided that Emily *was* fit to care for an idiot. A woman of some wealth and influence (her father had been a U.S. Senator), she wielded her power to split up the twins, taking James, and leaving Emily with Joey and a future full of bitterness and nightmares.

Emily felt that her life ended then for all intents and purposes. Then what are you doing here? she asked herself. Oz was offering hope, a new beginning, a new world. What use did she have for such things when everything that had ever mattered to her had been lost in the old world? If Oz was successful with the Device and this old world passed away, shouldn't she pass on with it? She was quite sure there would be nothing for her in the world Oz was planning to unleash.

"I should be home with my bottle," she grunted, and turned quick to see if Joey had heard her. To her surprise, she was alone. She took the last few steps to the second floor and played her light around the landing. Where had Joey gone? It wasn't like him to leave her side like this, especially in a strange place.

"Joey?" she called in a whisper and laughed inwardly. She could barely hear her own voice, how could she expect Joey to. "Joey!" she called louder. There was no sign of him.

Maybe he saw something shiny—Joey loved shiny things—and wandered away and was lost. If that were true, he must be terrified, the poor thing. She bustled down the right side hallway, flashing her light and calling his name.

Joey.
Mama Goose?
Noise.
Loud.
Hurt.
Roar in ear. Pound in head.
Mama Goose?
Dark.
Don't like.
Joey!
Mama Goose?
A light, silvery green and shining like sun on the ocean.

Been waiting for you, Joey. So long. Come here, Joey. Come here. Come. Come to me, Joey. Waiting so long. Here. Come now. Come, Joey, come come come come come come now!
Joey hear.
Joey come.

Shadows and fear.

Follow the light and come to me, Joey. I need you. We need you. Need you bad.

A door. The silvery green light glows around its edges. Door open. Stairs going up up up.

Another door. A room behind it. Filled with the silver and green light. Feels like Christmas.

A baby's crib. The wall behind it. The light comes from there. Green glows it. The wall moves. Out. In. Heartbeat.

Out. Out. Waiting so long for you, Joey. Let me out, Joey. Let us out. Out out out, now!

Joey do.

Hands against heartbeat wall. Tear the teddy bear paper away. Tear the plaster off. Green and silver light glows brighter. Tiny silver eyes peering through the darkness under the plaster.

Who there?

Come see.

Betty Leiderman followed Ginny Dowd into the corridor to the immediate right of the stairs. It was dark and got darker the farther they went. Betty kept looking back at the moonlight in the front hall but all too soon it was gone, swallowed in shadow. Ginny had the candle and Betty followed its glow, but before long the darkness became so overwhelming that she felt her vision blotting out and she couldn't see the candlelight at all for long frightening seconds; like a rabbit suffering from snow blindness.

"Hold my hand, Ginny." She stretched and found Ginny's hand and clasped it tightly. It was cold and clammy but Betty wasn't surprised. Ginny could talk tough, but she didn't fool Betty. She was scared, and if she was *half* as scared as Betty was, then she was *terrified*. If ever a house looked haunted it was this one!

Ginny led her into deeper darkness. It seemed to Betty that they had walked an awfully long way without getting anywhere.

"Ginny?" she asked softly. She heard a door close far down the hall behind her. She looked over her shoulder and saw a tiny flame appear, as if floating in the air, and begin moving toward her. Ginny pulled her hard in the opposite direction.

"Ginny, what's that light? What's wrong?" Betty asked, her voice going up a register with anxiety.

"Betty? Where are you?" Ginny called. Her voice was coming from *the end of the hall behind her where the light was!*

The hand holding hers felt like a tightening vise and tugged her farther into the darkness, away from Ginny. Betty tried to scream and pull away at the same time.

"Ginny!"

Another hand closed on her arm. She screamed again. Over her shoulder, as she struggled, she saw that her friend's light was farther away and retreating with every step she was dragged. The darkness was so thick it was almost liquid around her. Ginny's light was becoming a mere pinpoint behind her.

"Gi-n-n-n-n-y!" she screamed frantically. Her voice sounded bubbly and weak, swallowed up by the hungry darkness. Before she could scream again, something shiny and sharp flashed out of the darkness, slicing into her neck, cutting off her air.

In the last few bloody seconds of her life, Betty Leiderman saw a pair of shining eyes over her. She recognized the face even as she was dying, but it was the eyes that held her. The eyes grew larger and she experienced a sense of slow-motion falling.

A bubbly sigh escaped her lips as the eyes pulled her in, leaving her body behind.

Leading the way, Ginny held her candle high to illuminate the hallway. "This place is creepy," she said to Betty. "I bet everyone in town thinks it's haunted," she added in a whisper and giggled at herself.

The hallway was narrow and high-ceilinged. The walls were covered with a faded gold pattern that was indiscernible in the shadowy light of the candle. The floor was carpeted with a braided rug of no color in the weak illumination. It gave off a pungent, damp, musty odor capable of clogging the sinuses as badly as spring pollen.

"Stinks in here," Ginny muttered.

"Ginny?" Betty asked behind her, taking her hand.

"What?" Ginny asked, half-turning, looking at her friend's shadowy silhouette behind her.

"Never mind."

Ginny shrugged and went on, holding Betty's hand all the while though she found it annoying to have to do so. "Seems we should have seen a door by now," Ginny said.

Betty squeezed her hand uncomfortably. "Ginny?" she said a moment later.

"What is wrong with you, girl?" Ginny asked. Out of the corner of her eye, she saw a door ahead on the left side. She turned away from Betty, disengaging her hand as she did, and hurried forward.

"Ginny?" Betty called from behind her.

"Come on!" Ginny didn't stop until she got to the door. She grabbed the doorknob and angrily pushed the door open. Candle in front of her, she entered a large, empty room. Its walls were covered with mildewed and peeling wallpaper and the floor was warped hardwood. A few steps into the room, Ginny heard Betty follow her, then the door shut.

"Why'd you close the door?" Ginny asked, turning and thrusting the light in her friend's direction.

"Never mind," Betty said, directly behind her.

Ginny whirled. Betty wasn't there. Ginny spun around, nearly extinguishing the candle as she searched for Betty.

She wasn't in the room.

"What the hell?" Ginny whispered. She felt suddenly cold. She went back to the door to the hallway, opened it, and stepped through. *It wasn't the hallway she'd just come through. It was another room!* She struggled to retain her equilibrium and sense of reality. She was *certain* she had gone through the correct door. She turned back to it. It was closed though she hadn't heard it. She opened it.

Her throat went dry as she walked into the room she and Betty had just been in—it was a completely different room.

She turned. The door had closed silently behind her again. It *looked* like the same door she'd just come through—oh, what the hell was she thinking? Of course it was the same door. It *had* to be.

Slowly she turned the knob and opened the door,

holding her candle high to illuminate another room she was certain she hadn't been in yet. She looked over her shoulder. The room she was in *wasn't the same one it had been only moments ago.*

Waves of dizziness and nausea swept over her. She felt suddenly weak.

"Betty!" she called. Her voice sounded small and distant. There was no answering sound. Trembling and unsteady on her legs, Ginny stepped through and heard the door click shut behind her. This is not happening, she numbly told herself, trying to remain calm and rational but failing. She turned around and faced the door. She took a step toward it and stumbled over something. She lowered the candle and looked at the open-throated, blood-bepooled body of Betty Leiderman lying at her feet.

A near soundless shriek spilled from Ginny's open mouth like air escaping suddenly from a balloon.

"Ginny?" The slit in Betty's throat moved like lips, speaking her name.

Ginny's reflex was to scream as her mind snapped, but there wasn't enough air.

"Ginny?" Betty's throat said again.

Ginny felt as though something were interfering with her vision and cutting off her oxygen. She put a hand to her face and felt plastic. There *was* something. She looked and saw a face looming over her. She struggled to see it, finally recognizing Emily's son, Joey. With a jolt of panic, she realized he was holding a plastic bag tightly over her head.

"Ginny?" he said. His newfound ability to speak barely registered in her air-starved brain as did the fact that Betty's voice came from his mouth.

"Simon . . ." Ginny barely gasped, the air in the bag almost gone. "Wha—?"

"Never mind," Simon said reassuringly as his expanding silver eyes swallowed her.

Her body convulsed several times as she left it.

"Joey?" Emily called into the darkness of a small room. She'd searched all the second-floor rooms, this one being the last, and had not found any sign of Joey. She passed the flashlight beam around the room, illuminating a couple of broken ladderback chairs, but no Joey. As the light passed the window, Emily caught a flicker of something glowing that was more than just the light reflecting in the broken windowpane.

Next to the window frame, nestled into a slim crevice in the wall, she found a thin, leatherbound book with *Diary* printed on the spine in gold lettering that glowed with a light of its own in the dark. Her webbed fingers made it difficult, but Emily managed to get the book out and blow the dust from it.

My Diary it said on the cover in the same phosphorescent gold lettering as on the spine. The first few pages were unreadable, the ink smeared from water damage. Emily was going to tuck the book into her pocket, to peruse later at her leisure, but noticed legible writing on the fourth page.

> *The baby comes today! Oh, how I've waited. The woman at the adoption agency told us the poor thing's family all perished in a fire. Now, Roger and I shall be its new family.*

Emily flipped the pages until another entry caught her eye.

> *Little Roger is perfect. What a joy he is. The only things he came to us with were a book of nursery rhymes and a shiny, funny shaped thing, both of which he cried for terribly. He played with the shiny thing for hours when we gave it to him and fell asleep hugging the book. Roger is making a mobile to put over the baby's crib and is going to hang the doodad from it.*

She glanced at the date at the top of the page: April 21, 1968. Less than a year after the twins had been born and her beautiful baby James taken away from her. Emily felt an overwhelming urge to put the book back and just leave the house, but she couldn't go without Joey.

She pushed her forebodings away and started to tuck

the diary into her pocket when the pages of the book seemed to move of themselves, flipping open at another entry about midway through the book.

> *The baby won't stop crying. I'm afraid Roger will hurt him if left alone too long with him. The doctor says it is just colic and he will outgrow it, but I notice that even he is on edge around little Roger and seems to avoid touching him as much as possible.*

Emily tried to close the book again but the pages flipped as before to another entry farther on.

> *I think I am going mad. The baby talks to me in my dreams, makes me see things, horrible things. The worst of the dreams is where Mother Goose from his book chases me, accusing me of stealing something of hers. . . .*

Emily's breath left her in a shocked expulsion. "No. It can't be!" she half whispered. Thoughts of finding Joey disappeared as she frantically turned pages, scanning the increasingly cramped and near illegible writing that depicted a family in severe disintegration. She stopped on an entry scrawled in wobbly frantic letters.

> *Roger is dead and I fear the baby killed him. I found him in the tower room, lying at the foot of the crib, the mobile he made for little Roger clutched in his hand. At the hospital, they said it was a heart attack, but I know the truth—it was the baby. Now he wants to kill me. Every night I dream of Mother Goose chasing me and every night she gets a little faster, a little closer. I fear what will happen when she catches me. I must do something before that happens. I must do it. I must . . . kill little Roger.*

"Oh, dear God, no!" Emily gasped. *Did she hurt my baby?* It couldn't be James, could it? What if Bill and his mother were the ones killed in the fire the diary mentioned? If James survived, he would have been put up for adoption.

Emily's thoughts turned to the tower room. Closing the book, Emily tucked it into her dress, successfully this time, and headed for the tower.

Upon achieving the second-floor landing again, Emily noticed a light coming from the open doorway that led up a narrow flight of stairs that must lead to the tower. She went to it and began to climb. The light, an eerie, silver greenish glow, grew stronger the higher she went.

There was another door at the top of the stairs. The weird light spilled around its edges. Emily climbed to it, sweat dripping from her with the exertion. With some effort, she pushed the door open and was engulfed in brilliance. The first thing she saw was that the light was emanating from behind what looked like an old, broken-down crib. The second thing she saw was that someone was standing near the crib.

"Joey!" she said with relief. The third thing she noticed, as she crossed the room, was two bodies on the floor of the onetime nursery.

"We've been waiting for you, Mother Goose," Joey said.

His sudden ability to speak nearly stopped Emily's heart with shock. But his voice sounded strange, quad-raphonic, as if more than one person were speaking the words at the same time.

"Joey, what is this?" Emily stammered. Despite the shock of hearing her formerly mute son speak, her eyes were drawn back to the figures on the floor. She recognized the corpses of her two best friends.

"Oh, God!"

"It's all right, Mother," Joey said softly, moving to her side. "You were right. They didn't belong with Ozymandias and the rest of us. None of them do. Now they will. They're safe now here with us." His multiple voices echoed faintly in the room.

Was that Ginny's voice she heard, and Betty's, mixed together and coming out of her son's mouth? Emily thought she was going to pass out or get sick, or both. Joey took her arm to steady her, and a sense of calm came over her as if transfused from him by his touch.

"I am here, Mother. Me. *James*," Joey said, motioning to the wall behind the crib where the light lived. There was a large hole in the wall revealing a dumbwaiter and laundry chute that had been sealed up and covered over with plasterboard. Lying in the dumbwaiter was the dried, shriveled body of a baby.

Joey went to the hole, reached in, and picked up the dead baby. The light in the room was coming from a familiar silver object on an equally familiar gold chain attached to a mobile draped over the tiny corpse's body.

Emily saw that the thing emitting the light was the Piece her father had given her and she thought she'd lost. Her dream had been right after all: Her father *had* slipped something into James's blanket as they took her son away.

"Yes," Joey said in his many voices as if reading her mind. He carried the remains of his twin brother to his mother. "The Piece was with me all along. It nurtured my pain and anger and sang to me of revenge. Aided by it, the power I inherited from you grew, and I learned to use it to enter and control the minds of others before I was six months old.

"I used it to destroy those who had taken me from you. The woman whose diary I showed you—the woman who adopted me after the Buttermans all died in a fire I made Barbara Butterman set—managed to resist me long enough to drug me and wall me up in there. She blew her head off with a shotgun afterward to escape me.

"All these years, Mother, I've been waiting, feeding on human suffering, growing stronger; becoming like those who wait in the Otherness for the Device to bring them over. I've been waiting for you to bring Joey to meld with me. Now I'm free of this place."

Joey handed the dead baby to Emily. She took it lovingly, tears running down her beak, and didn't even blink when its head swiveled to look up at her through eyes that glowed with the same light as the Piece; the same light that blazed in Joey's eyes as he stepped closer and put his hands around her throat.

"Now we go together into the Otherness," James, Joey, Ginny, and Betty whispered. Emily could clearly hear each of their voices speaking the same words through her son's mouth and she finally, completely, understood what Ozymandias Prather had meant when he'd guaranteed her children's safe passage into the Otherness.

It is the dark, empty time just before dawn when no one is up; no one to see. The sound of the van's engine seems to be muffled by the hollow hour. As the vehicle moves through the civic center parking lot, it disturbs none but the leader of the carney freaks, and he only sits in darkness and watches.

The large old bus squeaks lightly as it rocks back and forth with the motion of Simple Simon's arm raking the nasty edge of the Piece across the throats of Mother Goose's sleeping children. The windows of the bus glow with silver-green light with every passing life.

Within twenty minutes it is over and the bloodied empty bodies of the nursery rhymes are piled in the back of the van. With the mummified corpse of his brother on the seat next to him, Simple Simon returns to the house where Mother Goose, Cross Patch, and Little Miss Muffet's vacant bodies lie. He carries the rest of Mother Goose's children inside and arranges them around her before setting a match to her clothes.

Simple Simon steps back, staring at the flame, and concentrates. He wills the fire to grow white-hot and spread, and it obeys. The other bodies and the rest of the room are aflame in seconds. Picking up his twin's corpse, Simple Simon casts a last look at the room, and waves bye-bye.

The fire burns all night, despite the efforts of several area fire departments, and leaves an ash so fine it yields nothing even when put through a sieve.

The sun crowns the horizon, making the gold dome of the abandoned planetarium glow. The dawn light burns on the tops of the dark shapes of the vehicles lined up in the civic center's vast parking lot. The show is shut down, packed up, and ready to roll.

The growing light catches a tall figure standing opposite a short one at the rear of the lot and casts their shadows in long grotesque forms.

"We won't be needing the van and trailer anymore," the shorter of the two says. *His words are spoken with*

many voices, like an unrehearsed chorus. A light, silver and green with the depth of a thousand precious gems, flashes between them, illuminating their faces.

"There's a used car dealership down the road. Clean them up and take them there in a few hours when it opens, and sell them. Catch up with us on the road in the bus." *Ozymandias Prather holds the Piece Simple Simon brought him. He pats the dead baby in Simple Simon's arms on the head. Its eyes shine like twin mirrors with the light of the Piece.*

"We will," *Mother Goose and her children agree through Simple Simon's mouth, whether they want to or not..*

R. PATRICK GATES

The show rolled on . . .

ALONG THE MIDWAY (XIII)

New Haven County, Connecticut

"I don't like this, George," Ginger said as they crept through the darkness.

"Neither do I," George said. "But hang in there. This won't take long."

She didn't understand what had come over George lately. He'd been talking about some sort of device Oz was constructing and how it was supposed to change the world or some such nonsense and how he had to know more about it. He was positively obsessed with it. So when they'd pulled into Ivoryton today, George had made sure he positioned his trailer with a full view of Oz's. He and Ginger had sat inside for hours tonight in complete darkness waiting for the big man to leave. Finally Petergello came by and the two of them drove off in the old Mercedes.

"What if we get caught?" she said. She didn't want to have to take one of those walks with Petergello.

"We won't if you just stand guard. Will you do that for me?"

"You know I will. But I'm scared."

"So am I. That's why this will be the quickest in-and-out you've ever seen."

They stopped by the front of Oz's trailer. George had a beat-up credit card wrapped in his left tentacle. He slipped it between the door and the jamb and worked it up and down. A few seconds later Ginger heard the latch pop.

"Where'd you learn to do that?"

"After I lost my scholarship I spent some time on the streets of Gainesville. I got *very* hungry. You learn to do what you've got to do." He gestured to the shadows by the corner of the trailer. "Okay. You wait over there. I'll be right back. You know what to do."

She nodded. She knew: bang twice on the wall of the trailer if she spotted Oz coming. George would climb out a rear window.

With her nerves stretched as tight as the high wire, she retreated to the shadows and waited. The night was quiet. All she heard were the crickets and the constant jingle from the elephants as they pulled on their chains, trying to get free.

Oz had left a light on so George moved in a crouch to keep from casting a shadow on the window shades. He moved straight to the back room.

A lot of strange stuff going down lately. Emily had up and left with all her "children." He could buy her blowing the show, but not leaving her son behind. And Joey . . . he no longer seemed like Simple Simon. And Benjamin—where had Benjamin gone? A few hours ago George had seen Petergello load him cage and all into the back of a van and head out toward the woods. When he'd returned the van was empty.

He entered the tiny room where the Device sat on its stand. It was bigger now, and again he was struck by how familiar it looked. Something from his past . . .

No time for that now. He picked a slim volume from the bookshelf by the X-ray machine, the book Oz had stopped him from examining a few days ago, and brought it back to the lighted front room. He squatted under the lamp and opened the cover. A journal, handwritten. On the first page:

> *To my son, Ozymandias.*
> *In the hope that he will*
> *someday understand.*
> *And forgive.*
> *Jacob Prather*

George flipped through the pages, pausing here and there when he saw "the contraption" mentioned. Apparently it was something Jacob had discovered in one of the deep shafts during his younger days as a coal miner. He found that people were fascinated by it so he joined the old Taber & Sons circus and exhibited it as a sideshow attraction. Jacob billed it as "The Mystery Machine" but did not seem to be aware that it served any function.

The occasion of the birth of Jacob's first and only child stopped George cold.

My son, my Ozymandias, is hideously deformed. He is a monster. Martha and I have wept every night since his birth. How did this happen? What can we do for him?

George swallowed. Monster? Oz was a weird-looking duck, but compared to the freaks in his show he was pretty damn near normal. He read on as Jacob described his years of searching for the cause of his son's birth defects. Modern medicine offered no answers, so Jacob began looking elsewhere. But along the way he realized that his son's deformity was not an isolated phenomenon. Many people connected with Taber & Sons mud show had given birth to freakish children over the years.

That was a clue. At first Jacob was sure that the answer lay along the tour route, that the teratogenic influence would be found at one of the show's stops—maybe in the water supply. But then wouldn't the locals there have produced an extraordinary cluster of freaks? There was no record of any such cluster.

Jacob came to the conclusion then that the key to the deformities lay *within* the show. His research led him to arcane sources, and in one of those sources he came across a drawing of his own "Mystery Machine."

The handwriting in the journal began to change here, becoming increasingly agitated and difficult to read. George struggled through it.

The story took a bizarre turn. Jacob's search through unorthodox sources revealed that the Device, as his curio was called, was a link to "the Otherness." Jacob did not quite understand what the Otherness was, but he learned that it existed on the far side of "the Veil" and that the Device was a gateway to the Otherness. (Apparently whoever had translated the old texts had a penchant for capitalizing key words.) When the Device was intact, it maintained a pinhole breach in the Veil, allowing a tiny stream of the Otherness to leak through. According to the texts, that tiny stream had no effect on our world at large.

But Jacob was devastated by the realization that the Device had a terrible effect on unborn children. Every freakish child born by members of the Taber & Sons show—and to people along the tour route—had been exposed in utero to the Device, including his own son. It was all a matter of timing and degree. Brief exposure late in pregnancy resulted in negligible damage, while long exposure during the first few weeks or months yielded hideous deformities, some virtually incompatible with life. Which explained his wife Martha's long series of miscarriages. But during most of her final pregnancy she had skipped the tour and stayed with her mother. As a result their son was viable but deformed.

My son is a monster and it is all my fault! I can't tell Martha, but perhaps someday I can explain it to Ozymandias. But not before I destroy the Device.

Jacob went on to describe his unsuccessful efforts to destroy the Device. Finally he dismantled its components and spread them around the country. Ever compulsive about details, he described every hiding place.

Then he said good-bye to his son.

The rest of the pages were blank. George wondered briefly where Jacob was now, but that question was overwhelmed by the childhood memories . . . the Taber & Sons circus . . . standing with his mother before the Device, coming back to it again and again, sharing her fascination with it.

He held up his tentacles and stared at them.

She must have stood before it when she was carrying

him, early in her pregnancy. The exposure had left him with these things in place of hands.

Then it must be true. Jacob Prather wasn't crazy.

He closed his eyes as his throat constricted. If only Mom had been fascinated with the elephants, or the clowns, his life would have been so different.

He shook it off. He'd have never met Ginger. She made up for everything.

But why was Oz reassembling the Device? How was this link to the Otherness—whatever that was—going to change the world's perception of the children it had deformed?

George headed for the back room again. The answer was waiting there.

"Come *on*, George," Ginger whispered to the night. Despite the August heat she was shivering. What was he *doing* in there?

And then she noticed that the jingling of the elephants' chains had stopped. Suddenly a sound behind her. A growl. She whirled and wanted to scream but the sound choked in her throat. She stumbled back a few steps.

There were five of them there behind the trailer, hulking shadows in the starlight. The ones they called the Beagle Boys. One of them growled again and made shooing motions. They moved closer, edging her away from the trailer. The message was clear. *Get out of here. This is Freakville.*

How was she going to warn George? These . . . things were between her and the trailer now. She couldn't reach the wall to bang on it.

"I'm looking for George," she said. "You know George—Octoman? He was supposed to meet me around here." She cupped her hands around her mouth and began calling. "George! *George!*"

The growls were many now, and more menacing as the Beagle Boys began to encircle her. Ginger couldn't help it. They terrified her. She ran.

Back in George's trailer, she lifted a corner of a curtain and watched Oz's trailer, waiting for a chance to return. Finally the Beagles wandered off. She opened the door, ready to dash over there to warn George, but she slammed it shut again when she saw a tall ungainly figure hurrying toward the trailer.

Oz was returning.

A number of the older books were in foreign languages—Latin, Greek, German, and one that seemed to be in some sort of Arabic script—none of any use to George. Finally he found one in English. *Mysteries of the Veil* was stamped on its spine. He brought it back to the front room but groaned when he opened it. It was in English, all right, but strange, old-fashioned English that was practically a foreign language.

Suddenly he heard a key in the door lock. In a panic he scrambled along the floor to the far corner of the room and rolled behind the end of the couch. He didn't look up as he heard someone enter and hurry toward the back room.

From the back room he heard snatches of words and phrases in Oz's deep voice—"Yes! . . . I *thought* that's where you'd fit! . . . Yes! . . . Too bad you can't be here to see this, Benjamin . . . Now we'll see what your Piece can do!" Was he talking to himself?

As George was wondering if he should risk sneaking out, Oz suddenly returned to the front room and went to the kitchen. George caught a glimpse of Oz's hands; they looked . . . bloody. He rinsed them, fooled in the refrigerator for a moment, then returned to the rear of the trailer.

George began to sweat. Whether he stayed or made a break for it, he was going to get caught, no two ways about it. He was wondering what the price would be. A walk with Petergello?

A silent explosion of light from the back room erased all questions. The same kind of light he'd seen shooting from Oz's window the other night. Violet light, *violent* light that flowed twisting and churning from the back room, alive with shadows and erratic motion. As the light swirled around George, a roaring grew in his brain, a call, a beckoning. Vast open vistas reaching toward strange horizons filled with mad, groping forms of twisted life flashed in his vision. He feared it even as he hungered for it.

Abandoning all caution, he struggled to rise and forced his feet to move him across the room. The door was a vague outline ahead of him. He prayed the roaring would mask his exit.

Echoing above the sound was Oz's voice, distant, deeper than ever.

"One more Piece. One more Piece and it's done!"

With the thick old book clutched tight against his chest, George slipped through the door and stumbled into the blessed darkness outside.

Oyster Bay, New York

"I had the dream again," said Carmella Cerami. She looked across the breakfast table at George Swenson.

"About the guy in the hat?"

She nodded, pushed a strand of long dark hair from her cheek. "It's more than a dream, George. I *know* it is."

He sipped from his coffee mug, his gaze alternating between her dark eyes and the red-and-white checks of the tablecloth. "One of your 'visions,' huh?"

"For what they're worth," she said, half-grinning. "Sometimes they mean something, and sometimes, you know, nothing. . . . But *this* one—this one's so real! He's so handsome and well-dressed, but I can't see his face because of the hat being kind of slanted down. And he comes to see me, but not when I'm in the sideshow, and he doesn't see me as a freak. But . . ."

"But what?" asked George.

"But there's something different about him, something almost . . . dangerous."

"Does he try to hurt you?"

Carmella smiled wistfully. "Oh no, nothing like that. He's kind of mysterious—like those men in the old black-and-white movies, like Garfield or Bogart."

"I don't get to see many movies . . ." George rippled a tentacle and fidgeted with his coffee mug. He seemed to have something on his mind.

"The old movies are the best," said Carmella, feeling her mood begin to brighten. It was always like that—the more she distanced herself from her dreams and her sometimes prescient visions, the happier she would feel.

She drew a breath slowly; autumn was in the air. A woodsy sachet which always comforted her. It was her favorite time of year—the end of the hot, dusty weather of summer and the change of season's colors. Time to switch from iced lemonade to hot cider and a cinnamon stick; time to end the roadshow for another year. They were on the home run now. No more gawking faces, no more—

"Hey, Carmella, you okay?"

She looked up at her friend as though he were a stranger. What had he been saying?

"I'm sorry," she said softly. "I was just thinking . . . and drifting away . . . 'woolgathering,' my mother used to call it."

George nodded, tried to smile, doing an awkward job of it. She knew he wasn't trying to court her; he had a girl—a straight. Just like Carmella wanted. She'd always had a wish-fantasy that someday she would leave the show and end up with a normal man—a straight of her own. Despite her reputation as a flirt with a great body, she liked to think of herself as a dreamer. Blowing the show was a fantasy she'd sheltered and protected like a baby bird with a broken wing.

More importantly, it was one of the things she'd promised her mother when she died two seasons back—

Like a cruel hand, the black memory slapped her. Blinking her eyes against the vision, she fought against reseeing the grim tableau: the dark interior of their trailer near the last days of her mother's life. Dying oh-so-slowly, she had curled herself into the depths of her bed where the light could not reveal her sagging flesh. As the cancer continued to feed, speech became almost impossible, but Carmella's mother had forced the words to come. It had been a time of last things—last words and last chances—and both mother and daughter knew the importance of such things. Her mother had been rehashing a familiar wish—that Carmella find a man who would be good to her, who would stay with her. ". . . and not run off like your father did."

The words had become like a well-known litany, but this time her mother added something new.

"Carmella, listen to me . . ."

"Not now, Momma. Rest."

Her mother had smiled weakly. "Plenty of time for that. Listen."

Carmella nodded.

"I want you to blow the show."

The words had shocked her so. "What? Momma, why?"

"Mellow, this is no life for a young woman. You deserve better, you deserve a *life*."

"The show's the only life I've ever known. . . . It's okay."

Her mother winced. "That's my fault," she said. "I should've given you a better chance . . ."

"Momma, don't talk like that. You've been good to me."

Her mother looked directly into her eyes, her gaze dark, piercing. "Just promise me, Carmella."

"All right, I promise."

"There's one other thing—" A cough savaged her sagging chest before she could continue. "You won't be able to leave until you . . . you do something for Oz."

"Mr. Prather? Do what? Momma, what're you talking about?"

—And that's how Carmella had learned about the Device. Her mother had tried to hide and protect her from the knowledge. She hadn't wanted Mr. Prather harassing Carmella about finding something so alien and unknown. But death would shift the mantle of responsibility to her daughter's shoulders.

She'd never forgotten her mother's final warning: Find the Piece, Carmella; Oz won't let you leave until you do. Don't be trapped like I was. *Trapped*. Carmella had never let the word fade from her mind.

"Oz has you hunting for the last Piece, doesn't he?" George said abruptly.

"Uh . . . yes, he does." She looked at George's face—his expression seemed odd, unreadable.

"Maybe it'd be better for everybody, Carmella, if you didn't find it."

"What? How can you say that, George? What do you—"

"Shit," said George, getting up quickly from the table. "I'd better get to work. See ya."

Carmella had been staring absently toward the woods at the opposite end of the field when she suddenly focused on George's exit. Beyond him, she saw the reason for it. One of the bullnecked Beagle Boys lurched through his rounds among the trailers, making sure everybody was heading out to their stalls in the sideshow tent.

And immediately behind him, walking in long purposeful strides, came Ozymandias Prather. He seemed to be looking at her in his oddly indirect way as he drew closer.

"Hello, Carmella," he said in his deep, resonant voice.

"Good morning, Mr. Prather." She stood up, started gathering her breakfast things to leave. "I was just getting ready to—"

"I know you were. Just one moment, my dear."

There was something commanding about Ozymandias Prather. Whether it was the way he looked at you, or the inflection in his voice, or perhaps something altogether indefinable, one thing was certain—people paid attention to him. Carmella stopped in midstep. "What is it?" she asked, already knowing what he would be saying.

"Oyster Bay is our last chance this season," he said. "Almost everyone has come through for me—and now it's your turn."

"Mr. Prather, I don't even know what I'm looking for. Even *you* can't tell me what it looks like."

"You'll know when you've come near it," he said. "You'll *feel* it and you'll simply *know*."

"I hope so," she said. "I hope you're not upset with me."

Prather smiled and it was a clumsy gesture. "Of course not. It's only that I grow impatient. To be so close and yet so far is most frustrating. I'm sure you can understand that. Although I can't explain it yet, you must be-

lieve me when I promise a better life for *all* of us when the
Device is complete."

Carmella nodded. Prather's words had become a familiar refrain and she almost could recite them by heart.

He turned and moved away from her, long legs scissor-
ing him along the path between the trailers. One of the
Beagles pulled in beside him like an ugly tugboat eager to
service a cruiser, and the pair headed back toward the
midway.

Cleaning up quickly, she retreated to her trailer where
she applied overly dramatic makeup—false eyelashes,
pencil-arched brows, Chinese-red lipstick and rouge—
and slipped into her costume. When she emerged she had
transformed herself into "Madame Cerami, Seeress of the
Mediterranean Isles." Her garishly painted billboards
portrayed her to the public seated behind a crystal ball,
holding it so that the sixth finger on each hand was clearly
and obviously visible. The same for her jeweled, satin
headdress, which had been designed to accent the third
eye in the center of her forehead.

Growing up among the freaks, Carmella had never
been overly sensitive or neurotic about her mutations.
Indeed, her mother had always seemed far more disturbed
about her differences than Carmella ever had. And yet,
when she traveled among the straight people she wore her
hair in ways which concealed her extra eye, or wore hats
which performed the same function. All those "normal"
people—most of them would get very bothered by her
extra eye even though, if they took the time to really look
at it, they would realize it was as beautiful an eye as a
woman could have. The shape a perfect Sicilian almond,
long lashed, an iris of gold-flecked chestnut, clear, and
radiant.

But it was a false perfection; the eye was blind. Had it
been blue-frosted by a hideous cataract, it could see no
less.

No, Carmella's special eye, the source of her special
sight, actually lay within the dark folds of her mind, in the
place where dreams and fears and hope break free. Her
visions were full of mist and mystery, brooding views:
dark and personal things often fraught with symbols of
sex and romance. So full of shadow and smoke—these

visions were—that she'd long ago learned not to trust them, even if she *could* understand them clearly.

The boards called her a "Seeress," and she had to smile at that. The stories she made up for the rubes who paid for a quick look at the future were inspired by the horoscopes in the morning papers. Cheap prophecies for crippled spirits. Carmella believed it was a fair exchange and nobody ever came back to complain anyway.

As she entered her tent through the back entrance, she could feel the pent-up expectations of the crowd about to be loosed upon the freaks; could smell anxiety coming off their pack like the sour-musk scent of bad sex.

Her stall was set up as a space-within-a-space so that she was visible to everyone who passed by, close enough so that no one could not notice the fingers and the eye. The crowd could press against the sheer canopy and peer into her inner sanctum where she sat under dramatic purple-gelled light, fondling a cheap glass ball. For an extra few dollars, one of the carnies dressed in mufti would let one of them into her tacky salon for a quick reading from the crystal globe. And as always, she could hear the sting of their voices.

As diverse as the freaks might be, there was one experience they all shared: listening to the straights talk about them as if they weren't there. As if they were dumb circus beasts; as if they were insensate lumps who couldn't be touched by human speech; as if they had no feelings and could not be hurt.

"Jeez, check out this one!"

"Oh-my-God . . . what a shame . . . !"

"Is it real? Did you see it blink!"

"How can she stand that?"

"And she would've been such a pretty girl . . ."

"Nice set-a jugs on her, though."

Carmella had heard them for so long, it was no longer surprising how unoriginal their responses had become, how numbingly similar. And yet, their words had never lost their power to deal out the pain.

She looked into their faces as they filed past. They seemed better dressed, better groomed than most. Oyster Bay was near a few colleges and some high-tax real estate. It had been a traditional spot on the tour for a long, long time, before the area had become a place of wealth and influence, but the people still came each year to get funky with Peabody's Traveling Circus. Maybe they needed a break from their VCRs and their BMWs and their CPAs; maybe they wanted a taste of the way life used to be.

Most filed past, with Labor Day indolence, pleased enough to gawk and stare and mouth an insult, but some paid their dues and dared to enter her sanctum. Carmella gave them her inscrutable smile as she coaxed visions from her crystal with six-digit strokes:

There is money in your future.
Watch out for friendly strangers.
Your love life will take a fortuitous turn.
Next month is a good month for starting new projects.
A lifelong dream will soon come true.
Your family is concealing shocking news.

The usual platitudes of hollow hopes and fears flowed from her full lips like the promises of a virgin. Everyone loved it whether they believed it or not. The night slouched past her and finally a bullhorned voice dispatched the hangers-on, the deadbeats, and the latecomers. After she closed up her stall, she pulled off the headdress, ran fingers through her long auburn hair. It felt good to be free of it.

Leaving through the back entrance, she could smell the blended scents of the midway: cotton candy, fried food oil, and crowd-sweat. Even though the tension of the night's performance was easing out of her, she still felt anxious, as though she sensed something frustratingly unclear. Just knowing the tour was drawing to a close was making her what momma used to call "antsy."

By the time she reached her trailer, she decided she would go into Glen Cove, a neighboring town with a strip of friendly late-night restaurants and bars. She needed a change of scenery. After shedding her costume, and a quick and rare shower courtesy of the Nassau County Recreation and Parks Department, Carmella prepared herself for a late evening among the straights.

When the cab picked her up, she looked like any other

casually fashionable young woman. Wearing a baggy silk blouse, a sleekly cut skirt, and a pair of white cotton-lace gloves, she could have easily passed as a C. W. Post college student wearing the latest trendy styles. Thick bangs covered her forehead, and the gloves concealed her extra fingers. The costume was perfect and no one would ever suspect she wasn't One of Them. She smiled wanly as she considered her life as a series of changes from one costume to another. Maybe it was time to change all that.

"Where to, madam-lady?" The cabbie checked her out in his rearview mirror as he punched in his meter. He sat on a seat cover of woven wooden beads and spoke with a Middle Eastern accent. He didn't seem to notice anything strange about her. Good. She assumed her "disguise" was flawless.

"Glen Cove. The Gold Coast."

He nodded. "Gold Coast. No problem. You have been visiting the bazaar?"

Carmella smiled. "You mean Peabody's—the road show?"

"Yes, yes. The 'road show.' I am thinking the wrong word. It is not *bazaar,* no?"

She smiled again. "Well, I don't know about that. Most people think it's pretty bizarre . . ."

The cabbie nodded and grinned, obviously not catching her play on words. He turned his attention to the road, abandoning Carmella to her thoughts.

The darkness and the sense of impending adventure made her think of her mother's wish for her to blow the show. She squinted against headlights of oncoming traffic and wondered what it would be like to own her own car, to learn how to drive it. Traveling with the mud show all her life had left her oddly unprepared for life in the straight world. Even a simple thing like climbing into the family wagon and driving off to the food market was totally alien to her.

She wondered what other complexities awaited her, and how fearful, how difficult, it might prove to be. But despite such thoughts, she still clung to vague dreams of romance and money and plastic surgery. Her tickets to the land of straight living.

The cab burrowed into the darkness between the

North Shore towns as she settled back into the vinyl-covered seat. A familiar tingling across her forehead signaled the onset of another vision and she recoiled from it with an equally familiar tightening in her stomach. Her third eye began to tear, and she closed all her eyes tightly. The movie screen in her head, the place where the twenty-four-hour skull-cinema ran, was misting up, getting foggy. She could see the now-familiar man in the slouch hat standing in a pool of street-lamp light like a guy in an old movie. She tried to make out his features, but his face remained in shadows. He reached out to her; the gesture could have been menacing, but maybe not.

Blinking her eyes, Carmella realized she'd been clenching her teeth. Her jaw muscles ached, and she concentrated on the pain as the vision faded. She was left with the notion that tonight was the night she would finally meet him.

The thought charged her with comfort and fear . . . and a surge of sexual excitement.

It had been a good summer for John LoMedico. From a bookie's point of view, sports had never been better—what with neither the American nor the National League showing any really great teams, none of his bettors had a chance of doing much damage; and of course, *nobody* picked horse races! That, plus all the *finocchios* playing daily numbers, and a little loan-sharking here and there, and you were talking some serious profit taking. Pretty good, when you figured that the NFL hadn't really cranked it up yet. That's when you really raked in the dimes.

At forty-six, "Johnny Doc" LoMedico had never done an honest, hard day's labor in his life." And it showed. His hands were smooth and soft and accented by several tastefully extravagant rings. His hair was still dark and full, and not a wrinkle in his stress-free, dago-handsome face. Not a day older than thirty-five, he looked. Not a day. And all because he never bought that whole ramadoola about working hard and being honest.

His uncle Paulie'd told him, back when he was just a kid hanging out at the family candy store in Flatbush, that working stiffs were the biggest suckers in the world, that nobody should even get outta bed in the morning for what most dummies brought home in a *month*. Johnny remembered all the neighborhood dads; how the poor bastards used to drag themselves home from shit-paying shit-jobs every day.

He was fourteen years old when he swore he'd never let that happen to *him*.

That's when he started running numbers out of the candy store for Uncle Paulie. That's when he was making more in a *night* as a high school punk than a lot of his friends' fathers took home all week. Eventually, when he got a little older, he started keeping a sports book, getting his own stable of customers together, kicking back some *trib* to the Manzaras, and generally just lovin' life. He made excellent money and he never got greedy. That was the secret—never get greedy and everybody left you alone. Nobody fucked with you. The years rolled by and Johnny Doc never tried to horn in on somebody else's action, never tired to chisel or jam anybody, and he got a rep among the wiseguys as a very straight player. This helped in a couple of very important ways—everybody trusted him, plus the Manzaras protected him fiercely because he contributed so much to the Family's honorable image.

John smiled as he drove his Infiniti down Jericho Turnpike. He'd just picked up a big payoff from an Oyster Bay dentist who'd liked the Buccaneers plus the points. There wasn't a better feeling in the world than riding around with a chunk of tax-free, folded green in your pocket. Nothing like it—not even great sex, and he'd had enough of both to know, thank you.

Entering the town of Glen Cove, he headed for Manny's Place and parked in the side lot. The evening was grinding down, but there were still plenty of cars huddled in the spaces. He could hear music leaking into the night as he adjusted his hat and straightened his tie. His reflection in the car's dark glass pleased him—Johnny Doc looked good.

Despite the lingering humidity outside, the bar's interior was comfortable. Some couples were draped over each other on a postage stamp dance floor; others traded *bon mots* as they solidified earlier pickups and connections. The witching hour approached when the lucky ones would start draining off into the night for a few hours of sweat and passion. It was getting late, but it wasn't *too* late. As the door closed behind him, all the heads at the bar turned to measure his entrance. Some of the women allowed themselves glances which lingered and John clocked each and every one of the interested parties.

Plenty of time for that later. Business always came first.

Scanning the tables and booths, he found Jimmy back in the corner with two older guys who figured to be horseplayers.

"Mr. John!" said Jimmy. He looked to be about thirty-seven or so, dressed like he was always getting ready to play golf, and had a habit of smiling even when there was nothing funny going down. He stood up and shook John's hand vigorously, then introduced him to his companions. "This is Augie—my father-in-law, and this is Marv, he's a buddy."

Handshakes all around. Normally, when there were new faces unexpectedly in attendance—like Augie and Marv—John was a very suspicious man. But after all the years in the business, you got to know who's a cop and who's a *cetriole,* and John could lay heavy odds that Augie and Marv couldn't find their own behinds with a coupla funnels. If they were cops, he *deserved* to get busted.

So John took the end seat of the corner booth, and calmly waited. Jimmy handed him an envelope discreetly. No need to check it. Jimmy sold commercial real estate and his paper-count was always jake. Music and cigarette smoke swirled and eddied around them like fog in a cheap mystery movie as Jimmy continued to smile. "Can I get you a drink, John?"

"No, thanks," he said. "I think I'm going to do a little trolling at the bar . . . see who bites, huh, Augie?"

Jimmy and the old man chuckled. "They *all* bite," said Marv. "Watch it, son."

"Yeah," said John. "Everybody's got a set of choppers when it comes to love, don't they?"

They all had a good laugh at this and John used the natural pause to make good his exit lines. The last thing he wanted to do was sit around with a bunch of losers and talk sports. Truth to tell, Johnny Doc was sick of the whole sports thing. He couldn't give a shit who had the best quarterback, or the worst bullpen, or the loudest home fans. He didn't understand how *anybody* could care about the outcome of something so trivial as a *game* unless they had some money on it. A client of his who taught philosophy at Hofstra told John he'd become jaded, that he'd lost the appreciation of sport as a pure expression of desire and performance. Yeah, sure. That too.

Turning away from Jimmy's table, John adjusted the rake of his hat and focused in on the row of females sitting at the bar. That was one of the good things about Manny's—it had become a great place to meet people who just wanted to meet people. No Great Expectations, and no searches for your soul mate, and no questions asked.

He wedged in next to two housewives zeroing in on the gray horizon of fortysomething and got Frankie's attention. "George Dickel—rock it, with a chase of Coke on the side," he called out.

"George's what!" asked the frizzy-haired blonde closest to him. She punctuated her wit with a witless chuckle. "I'd be afraid to ask for a drink with a name like that."

"It's sour mash," said John, mildly interested as he scanned the topography of her face. The lines beneath the makeup spoke of kids off to college and a husband lost within the circles of corporate hell.

"Sour mash? Why would anybody want to drink something that sounds like it should be mopped up off the floor?"

"Because it tastes good?" Frankie dropped the two glasses in front of him and he sipped at the Tennessee ambrosia.

"Can I try it?" asked the blonde. At least she seemed adventurous.

He looked at her tutie-fruitie cocktail, grimaced, and did a little Bogie on her. "This ain't gonna taste like that neon light you're drinking, shweetheart . . ."

She giggled and sipped cautiously from his glass. Coughed. Rolled her eyes.

"Whew! Why would *anybody* want to do that to themself?"

"It makes me horny as a hoot-owl," said John. He took back the glass, turning it to avoid a rim-smear of dark lipstick, and knocked back half of it. A tiny sip of Coke and he was in business.

"I never did it with a hoot-owl," said Frizzy Blonde.

John laughed politely and glanced across the bar where a dark-haired woman of maybe thirty was nursing a daiquiri. He'd seen her when he'd first walked in, and she'd been watching him then, as she was now. He smiled and touched the low-slanted rim of his hat. She nodded and proffered a small smile in response. She wasn't just attractive or pretty; she was centerfold material. Her hair was an explosion of auburn, framing a face that spoke of classic Mediterranean statuary. Eyes as dark as the windows in a stretch limo and as full of the secrets behind its glass. Lips that had been designed to do nothing but the best finished off a face that could only be Italian. A woman like her was used to things like the utter impracticality of linen napkins, the joys of Paganini, the cool rush of satin sheets, the necessity of *paté de foie*, the comfort of silk kimonos and leather upholstery.

And even if she wasn't, she should be.

He finished his Dickel, signaled Frankie for another. Still plenty of time to make some kind of significant contact. He watched her send the guy next to her crashing and burning a couple of times, but he was too stupid or too wasted to realize he might as well be a leper to her.

"So what's your name? And how come you still got your hat on? Do you keep it on in bed, too?"

He looked back to Frizzy Blonde and made a point of not smiling. "You ask a lot of questions."

"I like a lot of answers," she said with a giggle which wouldn't've sounded right even on a teenager.

John looked at her and smiled, touched her shoulder softly. "Listen, could you excuse me for a minute? I think I see my sister over there."

"Your sister?" said the blonde, looking disappointed.

"Yeah, and I've got a message from Mom I gotta make sure she gets."

Before the woman could say anything, he was up and moving around the horseshoe of the bar. Gliding to a stop next to the wild mane of auburn, he cleared his throat softly. "For a second there I thought you might be my sister, but now that I get up close, I can see I made a mistake."

"Maybe you didn't," she said.

"Really?" Inside he was grinning widely. Yeah, the old radar was still in working order—just like all the other equipment.

"I know this is going to sound funny," she said. "But I had a . . . a funny feeling, almost like a dream, that I was going to meet you."

He smiled. "You mean I'm the Man of Your Dreams?"

"Not exactly," she said. "I'm not sure what you are."

"What's that supposed to mean?"

She brushed her long fingers down the wave of hair on her forehead. It was an automatic gesture, born of long habit. She started to speak, paused, seemed to think better of it. Finally: "I don't know why I told you that . . . I'm sorry."

"Hey, no problem. You want to sit at one of the booths?"

She smiled, obviously grateful to be let off the hook so easily. "That would be fine."

An hour later, they had managed to divulge enough information about each other to make things interesting. But John wasn't taking any bets on how the night might end.

He wasn't surprised when she admitted she was Italian, and that she'd always dreamed of being a dancer or an artist or maybe even an actress. But when she hit him with the carnival road show, he kind of did a double take. She wasn't the type you'd expect to be part of a bunch of social rejects like that. Something funny about it, but he wasn't in a mood to play detective.

Doctor, maybe, if he could find the right nurse. And maybe he had.

She didn't ask him to further define his work when he told her he was a "short-term investment broker," and that was just as well. Despite her work in the "mud show," as she called it, she sounded like the type who wouldn't be impressed with a bookmaker. Funny, but the longer they talked the more he was getting the impression she was overly fascinated with him.

But why? He hadn't said anything all that dazzling, and had in fact let her do a lot of the talking. So what was going on here?

Carmella felt like she was falling down the rabbit hole—like Alice in the book. The longer she talked to John, the more convinced she'd become that he was the one she'd already dreamed about. He'd taken off the stylishly raked hat, fully revealing the rugged good looks the dreams had always kept obscure. She found herself attracted to his down-to-earth mannerisms and his lack of a need to try to impress her. From the moment he spoke to her, there was something *different* about him, something that was reaching her on some intense psychic level. It was like the low-frequency signal from the reptile part of our brains, that thumping, blood-beating rhythm that spoke of sex and danger. Excitement and dread flowed into her, commingling like oil and water, to produce a hybrid emotion that she could not identify.

There was something about him. Something that kept her on edge. Expectant—but of what she was not sure.

She talked a lot to mask her anxiety. She needed time to sort out her feelings and yet she knew there was no time. She had a sense of the storm just beginning to gather power, of the impending maelstrom, the white-hot star ready to nova.

She was suddenly reminded of a memory from childhood. It was cold and snowy and Christmastime; she and Momma were visiting with people up north, relatives, maybe. It was an old house, and Carmella had found the steps leading to the basement where a great coal furnace squatted and glowed in blue-edged darkness. She could remember standing in front of its heavy, slatted door from which a terrible heat radiated with red teeth. Like a torpid beast, the furnace slouched and whispered its coal-fire voice at her. In her child's mind, there was something horrible behind that slatted door, something that danced in unimaginable heat and anger, something that beckoned to young Carmella.

Come here, child. Touch my hot metal. Open me. Look into my burning heart, if you dare.

The memory seared her and for an instant John's words went away and she was a little girl again, standing in the pit of the cellar, before the glowing, grinning beast. The door of red teeth like a giant jack-o'-lantern was speaking again. Carmella had reached up and sprung the latch on the grate and fell back screaming as the dragon-breath roared.

Sitting before John was like that. She wanted to reach out, to throw open the door and let whatever would come screaming out consume her. More than lust. More than dread. Whatever it was, she knew she could not leave him until she understood why the fates had brought him to her.

And so she did not hesitate when he suggested they take a ride by the coast. The moon was rising above the Sound, he said, and the dark water was speckled with the mooring lights of pleasure craft—it was pretty, romantic even, if that's what she was looking for. He spoke straight-forwardly, didn't play around with his words, and she liked that. She wanted him and he wanted her—they just had to work out the final logistics.

His black Infiniti crouched by the coastline like a predator waiting to pounce. She sat in the soft leather of its passenger seat looking out at the moon-freckled water, feeling the effects of the liquor spin through her head. Neither of them spoke for several minutes, but the silence had not become awkward. Rather, it drew them closer, bonding them in some yet to be understood way.

Finally, he touched her shoulder. Gently. With *rispetto*. Respect. "Hey, it's getting late. You want to come to my place, or do I take you home?"

Turning, she paused to let her heart stop racing. "Yes," she said without letting herself think about it. "Your place. Hurry."

He nodded, and keyed the ignition. As the car glided away from the shoulder of the coastal road, she kept herself from thinking about what was happening. The risks didn't matter this time. There was something urgent, something important, in their meeting. She hated to use such a cliché, but she knew it was something *fated*. She had no choice now but to play it out.

The house was more ordinary than she expected. It resided in an older neighborhood of Oyster Bay—the kind of place that usually included the wife, the kids, and the station wagon. The usual suburban tableau. John LoMedico didn't seem to fit in that picture, but she didn't care.

Once he guided her inside, they moved through the maze of rooms and hallways in semidarkness, both of them aware of an animal urgency, of that familiar, unquenchable and searing *need*. It was like a third presence, pushing them together, pulling them through the shadowed house.

Half-closed vertical blinds painted the king-size bed in thick stripes of shadow and pale light from a moon as high and full as her breasts. He kissed her gently with a hint of more passion to come, teasing, promising. She slipped off his jacket, unbuttoned his shirt; he fumbled with the catches and zippers of her ensemble. There was something wonderfully erotic in being slowly undressed by a lover, and she tried to control the pace, to savor each moment.

As their clothes began to fall away, some with effort and others with a clumsy tug, they began to lose themselves in the dark pool of each other's desire. A mutual abandonment, a magic chemical bonding that spoke of a closeness neither could have anticipated. Exhilarating and fearful at once, Carmella had never felt anything like it. No man had ever made her feel like this. . . .

"Do you feel it?" she whispered as he kissed her swollen nipples. "What's happening to us?"

"I don't know . . . I've been trying to ignore it. . . ." There was a sincerity in his voice. He wasn't humoring her, he sounded wary, cautious. "You feel it too, huh . . . ?"

She nodded, arched her back in response. Whatever it was, she had fallen prey to the aura of danger which had enveloped him. Intoxicating, alluring, teetering on the edge of control. He was kissing her, tonguing and licking her, and nothing mattered beyond that single moment. Moving up to kiss her cheek and blow warmly in her ear, he stopped suddenly.

"Oh, Jesus . . ." he whispered hoarsely.

"What's the matter?" she asked, sitting up as he backed away from her. Even in the slatted light, she could see the revulsion, the abject fear in his eyes, and she knew what had happened. Automatically, her hand moved to her forehead, to protect, to conceal.

"Jesus Running Christ!" John LoMedico didn't so much as move away from her as he *leaped* backward into the shadows of the room. He slammed into a closet door and sagged down to the carpet where he buried his face against drawn-up knees. His breath came in ragged sobs.

"I'm sorry . . ." she offered, trying to maintain control of her voice. This had never happened before. She didn't know what to say, how to handle it. She had no idea he would react so . . . negatively. Was she *that* repulsive? "I . . . I don't know . . . maybe I should have told you . . ."

He looked up, his eyes catching just enough moonlight so she knew he was staring at her. "Oh God . . . you don't understand, honey . . . you don't understand . . . Oh Christ! Is this crazy or *what?"*

"From the show . . ." She started to talk without thinking, rambling. "We're all like this . . . well, not exactly like *this,* but—"

He gestured for her to stop, forced himself to stare at her. "You don't get it . . . you don't get it, Carmella." John LoMedico crawled over to the bed, touched her knee as he struggled to stifle his sobs and his jagged breathing.

"Tell me," she whispered, feeling comfort in his touch.

"Hey, don't think it's you, honey. You're beautiful," he said, letting the words leak out of him like water from a cracked vase. "You've always been beautiful . . . you were a beautiful baby . . ."

He stopped, letting his words echo in her mind. And just that quickly she *knew* what he meant.

"Oh no . . ." She managed the two words before a stringent pulse of pure pain/joy spiked through her.

John LoMedico forced himself to stand, gathering his clothes about him, turning his back and awkwardly stepping into his pants. The task seemed to calm him, give him strength. The words rambled out of him. "I met your mother almost thirty years ago—Jesus, at a fucking carnival!—I should've thought something was funny right away when you called it 'mud show.' And you kinda looked familiar to me . . . Your mother, she was older than me. I was just a kid . . ."

"You don't have to—"

"No, lemme get this out. Christ, I've been carrying this around for a long time, honey."

"I never knew anything about you . . ."

"That's because your mother didn't either, I guess. When the carnival came back the next summer—right here on the Island—she surprised me with the baby . . . *our* baby. It was you . . . and you were . . . you were different, and I guess I went kinda wacko. Hey, I was sixteen years old—what did I know about being a man?"

"So you split?"

He hung his head, shook it slowly, then nodded. "Oh yeah," he whispered. "I told her I never wanted to see her again . . . and I didn't . . ."

He moved to the wall, leaned against it as though he wanted to melt into it, and he started to cry. Softly, in a dignified way, but she could feel the pain coming off in hot sheets like the furnace of her childhood. "I'm . . . sorry . . . Carmella . . ."

"Please, don't be," she said, pulling her clothes together, dressing quickly. She felt like there was so much they could say to each other, but she knew it wasn't necessary. Her half-toned dreams made sense now, in their usual muddy way, and with such understanding, she felt a sense of peace, of release.

"I'd better go," she said softly.

"Yeah . . ." He continued trying to fade into the wall. "Give me a minute or two and I'll drive you. Wherever you want to go."

She sighed, shook her head. "You can't take me *there,* but you've got me started in the right direction."

"Huh?"

"Never mind. Too hard to explain."

"You mean you don't want a ride?" He looked at her for an instant, then toward the window.

"I think I need to be alone. I need to sort things out."

Her father moved to the bedside table and picked up the phone. "Let me at least get you a cab."

She considered the option of walking the deserted streets, but not for long. "All right . . . thanks. I'll wait out by the door."

As he called for directory assistance, Carmella slipped down the shadowed hallway, into the living room. Even the absence of light could not diminish the gaudy accessories and furnishings. Lots of draperies, fake Roman columns and statuary. As her gaze traversed the fireplace mantel, the silhouettes of framed photos and knickknacks failed to catch her attention . . . until she noticed a patch of moonlight caught on something round and smooth.

A crystal ball. Smaller than a real one, like hers. But there was beauty in its petite symmetry. Its glass held pale power of the moon. Fascinated, she moved to touch it but stopped halfway. Rather than merely looking at the object, she seemed to be listening to it. A subsonic hum. Soft, gentle. Like a ballad in a minor key.

The Piece.

No, it couldn't be. And yet the feeling and the knowledge engulfed her. The words of Oz haunted her: *When you've come near it . . . you'll simply know.*

Her pulse jacked behind her ear, the tips of her fingers tingled. Reaching out, she picked up the crystal sphere, and felt its coldness.

No. Something was wrong.

It was dead. Its promise a lie. Carmella felt dizzy. Anxiety catching up with her. The emotional floodgates had been loosed and she was going to get caught in the backwash. It was too much. Too much at once.

"The cab will be here in a minute or two," said her father. His voice had been not more than a whisper, but she started, almost dropping the crystal.

"Hey, something the matter?" He walked closer, but not too close.

"I . . . I don't know. I thought I recognized this glass."

He almost smiled. "You *should*—your mother gave it to me. That first summer."

Wait! Oz was right. Too many coincidences. It had to be the Piece. And yet . . .

"Maybe you should take it," he said. "Maybe if you gave it back to . . . to your mother . . . maybe it would make things a little better."

She could not tell him her mother was dead. For a lot of reasons.

"I don't know," she said, slowly replacing the sphere on the mantel and the silvery ring stand which held it. As her hand drew closer to the polished mahogany ledge, her fingertips grew warmer.

The stand . . .

"Did she give you this part, too?" she asked, already knowing the answer.

"Sure," he said. "Take it, go ahead. Give it to your mom; I want you to."

Carmella picked up the stand—three graduated rings given form by external braces that looked like the flying buttresses of a Gothic cathedral. The metal was almost pearlescent, like platinum. There was a *density,* a sense of great mass about the metal object; it spoke to her. Tonight she had found both her past and her future.

The Piece.

"My mother would be very grateful . . . if you would give it to me."

"Take it. It was never mine. Your mother said it would bring me luck, and I gotta tell you—I think it always did."

"Thank you," she said, carefully placing the worthless glass and its magical stand in her purse.

The man named John, her father, almost smiled this time. He was about to speak when an auto horn beeped briefly, respectful of the hour and the neighborhood.

"Go on," he said, kissing her forehead, almost brushing the lid of her third eye. "My daughter . . ."

Carmella looked at him and he looked sadder than any man should ever be. "Thank you," she said. "I'll come back someday, and maybe then I can call you 'father.'"

"Yeah, okay . . . I can settle for that."

The cabbie beeped again, and she opened the screen door, looked back and smiled. "Good-bye," she said.

Oz was waiting for her in her trailer.

"How could you know?" she asked, clutching her handbag to her breasts.

The tall, gangly man shrugged. It was a disconcerting gesture, almost mechanical. "Sometimes we just know things, don't we, Carmella?"

"Sometimes . . ."

"I'll be needing it, my dear," he said as he stared at her purse.

Opening the clasp, she reached in past the crystal globe, to touch the light-heavy metal. It reacted to the warmth of her hand as though alive and she could almost swear it had begun to glow. She handed it to Oz, who held it up to the dangling light above her tiny kitchen table.

"Yes," he said. His hand trembled. "I knew this one, this final one, must be circular. I would have never imagined the struts like this, but yes, very ingenious, actually . . ."

Carmella watched him become absorbed in the warm glow of the Piece, which seemed to have acquired a soft incandescence under his touch. She suddenly felt his presence in her trailer intrusive, and something not at all desired. She cleared her throat and he looked at her as one might regard a slight irritation.

"So you're done with me?"

"Yes, you've done well. All of you have done very well. We head south in the morning."

"I won't be coming back," she said.

He nodded. "Yes, I remember your mother always wanting you to be free of us."

"I promised her."

Oz smiled. It was an awkward gesture. "Yes, well, I suppose you did . . . but you must know you're not going anywhere."

"What? What did you say?" Her stomach began to twist as she glared at him.

"No one blows the show unless I say. And especially not now. The Device will be ready soon."

"I don't care about your Device!" The words exploded from her like lava. She had never raised her voice to him before, and a bleak point of fear touched her mind.

But Oz just smiled. "Oh, but it cares very much about *you*, my dear."

"I can't believe this . . ." Tears came, despite her wanting to retain control. "Oh, Momma . . ."

He pocketed the series of concentric platinum rings, turned toward the door, then wheeled back upon her. "Carmella, someday you will thank me for this. Someday very soon."

He closed the door and it sealed shut with the sound of a final breath. She fell against it, biting her lower lip against the pain of frustration. What good was it to find the truth if it could never set you free?

Carmella felt herself sagging to the floor, where she drew up her knees to huddle within the prison of the night. At dawn, the wheels would turn; a new hope clanking south to be born.

THOMAS F. MONTELEONE

The show rolled on . . .

THE PINE BARRENS

Cape May County, New Jersey

"I don't know what my uncle is thinking these days," Ginger said as she stood outside George's trailer and stared at the darkened main top looming under the overcast night sky. They were due in Towson, Maryland, tomorrow. Why wasn't anyone striking the canvas? "Why have we been playing all these one-horse dates in Jersey anyway?"

"Your uncle Joe hasn't done much more than smoke his pipe since June," George said. "He won't listen to Shuman or Nolan or anyone. It's Oz. He's in charge and he's just been killing time until tonight."

"How do you know?"

"It's all in the book."

That book. That damn book. George had become obsessed with it, spending every free waking moment buried in it. Their sex life had dropped to zilch.

"Okay, what's so special about tonight besides being the last day of summer and the day before your birthday?"

He didn't smile. "It's the equinox."

"So?"

"So a lot of weird stuff happens during the equinox. The weirdest thing the world has ever seen could happen during this one."

George was bothered by the strangest things lately. He'd made such a big deal about Oz trading in his car and a couple of the trucks for a number of off-road vehicles.

"I'm going to take a look around, see what's going on," George said.

She didn't want to pout but her lower lip seemed to push out on its own. "I thought you were going to stay with me tonight. You'll be twenty-three at midnight and—"

"I'll only be a few minutes."

He gave her a quick kiss and walked off. Feeling thoroughly frustrated, Ginger watched him disappear into the darkness, then went inside. Hard to believe how attached she'd become to George. Just a little over three months ago, after Carlo got hurt, she'd been sickened by the thought of touching him; now she couldn't imagine living without him. She had to snap him out of this.

Because she had a surprise for him.

And the best way she could think of to surprise him was to get naked. Quickly she stripped off her clothes, wishing she were in her own trailer where she could put on something sexy and wait for him. But she was in George's so buck naked would have to do. She was just stepping out of her panties when she heard the door open behind her. She whirled.

"Surpri—!"

The word died in her throat. It was Oz. He towered over her, looking like a scientist staring down at a bug. Ginger turned to run but he caught her arm and roughly pulled her around. She tried to cover herself with her free arm.

"Where is he?" The voice boomed through the room. "Where's my book?"

"Not here!" Her voice sounded so tiny after Oz's. "Let me go!"

"You'll tell me or so help me—!"

Oz reached for his waist. For a blood-freezing second Ginger thought he was going to unbuckle his belt and visions of being raped by Oz sliced through her mind. But his hand stopped above his belt, at his lowest shirt button. As he undid it he pulled her closer and shoved her hand— her *arm*—into the gap. There was no skin there, just a warm, moist empty space that—

Something hard clamped on to her arm just above the elbow. She screamed and tried to pull free but she was trapped. How? *How?* She screamed louder and struggled harder as something soft and coarse and very wet squirmed against her forearm, layering it with thick fluid. She retched and looked up at Oz.

Oz said nothing. His eyes were steely, his smile a hard, thin line as he pulled his shirt open, sending the buttons flying in all directions. Fearfully, Ginger lowered her gaze to see what had trapped her arm. She screamed again as the room swam around her.

A mouth. Oh God, a *mouth!* There, in Oz's belly, along his waistline, a huge lipless mouth, at least a dozen inches across and full of thick, heavy, yellow teeth the size of cigarette packs, clamped down on her arm. The huge tongue within licked her hand again, then spit her out.

Ginger tumbled back and sprawled on the thin carpet. She was only dimly aware of her nakedness. Part of her could think of nothing but wiping the smelly saliva off her arm, while the rest of her would not allow her eyes to turn away from the hideous deformities of Oz's upper torso.

For the huge mouth was only part of the horror. Above it, just below the breastbone, was a vestigial lump that vaguely resembled a nose. And above that were two egg-size eyes, white as eggs, too, so they could only be blind, but they moved and fixed their blank stare on her.

"No further need for pretense," said the belly mouth with Oz's basso voice while the normal mouth in the head hung slack and immobile.

Ginger realized that Oz must have spoken through the belly mouth all along with the head mouth merely lip-synching the words. He stepped closer, towering over her. She tried to crawl away but there was nowhere to go.

"I'm not going to hurt you," he said. "That would be gratuitous—especially at this juncture. I simply want the book. I noticed it was missing tonight and could think of only one person who might have taken it. Give it to me. *Now!*"

The booming volume of the last word shattered her nerve. Sobbing, unable to speak, she pointed a trembling finger to the bottom door of the bureau to her right. Oz went to it and retrieved the old book. Then he pulled a piece of paper from his pocket and tossed it at her.

"Give that to George. Tell him to meet the rest of us at the bald spot if he wants to witness the remaking of the world."

And then he turned and was gone.

George wrapped his arms around Ginger. Her clothes were back on but she shivered and shuddered as she told him what had happened.

"But he didn't hurt you?" he said. "He didn't . . ." George could barely bring himself to think about it, let alone say it.

"No. Beyond putting my arm in his muh-mouth, he didn't touch me. He said it would be 'gratuitous.' What did he mean by that?"

George understood—perfectly. But how to explain it to Ginger?

"He has a machine, a Device, as he calls it, that he's been reconstructing from components retrieved along the route of this tour. He got the last Piece back on Long Island. Now he's just been killing time until the equinox when he can put the Device to work."

"But what's it do?"

"He's been telling us since winter quarters that it's an instrument of change, that it will bring us justice, understanding, acceptance, and compensation, that it will alter the world's perception of us, change our place in the world so that we'll no longer be considered freaks."

"Maybe it's working already," Ginger said, looking up at him and trying a smile. "I don't consider you a freak."

George tightened his hold on her, but even Ginger's warmth and nearness could not reach the cold fear that had been growing within him since he'd begun reading that book.

"But Oz hasn't been telling us the whole story—or at least not me. You see, according to Oz's father and the book I took from him, there's another world, another reality that borders on our own. *Borders* isn't even the right word—*coexists* is better. We somehow occupy the same space but we can't perceive each other. We're separated from that other place—'the Otherness'—by what the book calls 'the Veil,' some sort of barrier that keeps our two realities from intermingling. The Device can breach that barrier, can create a pin hole between the two realities and let some of the Otherness through."

"Is that bad?"

"I'd say so. Look, almost all of us in the Oddity Emporium are a special kind of freak. Our deformities are the result of exposure as fetuses to the Otherness that leaked through the Device. The Otherness is a much older, more dominant, more powerful reality than ours. It changes any of our reality it touches."

"Well, then how is that pin hole going to help people understand you?"

"It won't. But Oz isn't planning a pin hole. He has a special substance"—*now* George understood all the first-class treatment and special privileges accorded Malaleik throughout the tour—"that when used to fuel the Device at the proper time and place will cause a permanent rip in the Veil."

Ginger drew back and stared at him. "What will that mean?"

"The Otherness will flood into our world, infiltrate our reality, changing it, overwhelming it until both sides of the Veil are the same."

"Why would he want that?"

"Because then *you'll* be the freaks and *we'll* be the norms."

"But that's awful. I mean, that's horrible! He'd destroy everything? Why?"

George looked away. "You'd have to spend your life on our side of the fence before you could completely understand."

Ginger got up and paced the tiny room in a tight circle.

"What are we *talking* about? The whole thing's *crazy!* Why are we buying into it? Oz is obviously nuts, or he's been dropping acid, or both!"

"Maybe," George said. "But it's in the book, too. There's too many correlations to be just coincidence. I can't risk him being right. I've got to find this bald spot."

"Why?" Ginger said, standing back and staring at him. "If he's going to make you a normal, why should you want to stop him?"

"Because of you," George said, rising and facing her. "I'm used to being a freak. I've had a lifetime of practice; you haven't. So I want things to stay as they are. Because with you by my side there's nothing this world can throw at me that I can't handle."

Ginger ran forward and leaped into his arms. She sobbed against his neck for a while, then stepped back.

"I'm going with you."

Try as he might, there was no way of talking her out of it.

"Are we lost?" Ginger said as she guided the borrowed aging Honda along the sandy rut that passed for a road in this wilderness. Twice already they'd become mired in sand. The Honda's front-wheel drive and George's shoulder against the trunk had got them free, but the next time they might not be so lucky.

"I don't think so." George sat in the passenger seat, a map on his lap, one tentacle pinning Oz's instructions to the map, the other curled around a flashlight. "How many miles since that last turn?"

Ginger checked the trip odometer. "Three."

"Keep going till we hit five and a half."

They'd followed the directions up the Garden State Parkway to Exit 44, then they'd followed a state highway, then a county road, then an unlabeled blacktop. With each turn the road had become narrower, the pavement rougher, the surroundings more deserted and desolate until they were now on this sandy path in the middle of a huge nowhere known as the Jersey Pine Barrens.

The night seemed to have congealed around them. So dark. Not even stars above. Ginger would never have thought it possible to feel trapped outside in the open like this, but that was what she was feeling now. The overcast sky seemed to press down on them; the scraggly, angular pines lining the road leaned over them like the bars of a cage.

"Turn here!" George said suddenly.

Ginger skidded to a stop, backed up, then swung left onto an even narrower road. She braked to a halt.

"Let's face it, George. We're lost."

George opened his mouth to speak, but leaned forward instead, staring up through the windshield.

"Look."

Lights were moving through the sky, globules of pale fire floating overhead in a line parallel to the road they were on. Ginger's mouth got dry and a crawly sensation wormed through her belly.

"This is scary, George. Let's go home."

"You might not have a home to return to if we turn back now. Follow them. They seem to know where they're going. Maybe they're headed for the bald spot, too."

Reluctantly, Ginger put the Honda into gear again and headed down the road.

"What's this bald spot anyway?"

"It's what the book calls a 'nexus point.' It's real complicated and I couldn't understand half of it, but from what I gather there are places on earth where the Veil that separates us from the Otherness comes loose for a little while during the equinox. This bald spot is one of those nexus points."

"Why do they call it that?"

"Because after being exposed to the Otherness twice a year for who knows how long, nothing grows there. Not even a weed."

Ginger drove on, her sweaty palms slick against the wheel. She drove until there was nowhere left to go, until the road ended in a little cul-de-sac. Theirs wasn't the only car there—half a dozen vehicles were already scattered around the clearing. Her headlights flashed across words like Jeep and Isuzu as she swerved to avoid them.

"I guess we're not lost after all," George said. "Those belong to Oz."

Ginger got out and looked around. "Where do we—?"

No need to ask. Behind the trees was a rise. The globs of light were streaming that way. Many streams, gliding in from all directions, all converging somewhere beyond that rise. As she watched, pale violet light flashed, silhouetting the gnarled, twisted pines.

She glanced at George. In the backwash from the headlights she could see his face. His eyes were wide, his expression strange. None of the unease creeping through

her was there. Something else. A yearning. He looked
almost . . . eager.

"Let's go," he said.

He didn't wait for her to agree or disagree. He simply
began walking, shining the flashlight along the narrow
sandy path that led through the trees. Ginger hurried after
him. They passed through a collection of shanties, recently deserted. Whoever lived here had run off.

Good idea, she thought. If I had half a brain, I'd be out
of here, too.

The violet flashes grew brighter and more frequent as
they trudged up the slope. George didn't say a word the
entire trek. It was like he had a one-track mind, like
someone had a rope around his neck and was pulling him
toward the light.

George stopped dead when he reached the top of the
slope. Ginger crept up behind him and peeked around his
left side. There was a clearing atop the rise—a grassy field
rimmed with pines that were especially stunted and
twisted. She froze when she saw what was happening in
the clearing.

Madness. That was the only way to describe it. Madness and chaos. Globs of light swirled and swooped over,
around, and through the air above the clearing, dipping in
and out of a dome of violet light that flashed and sparked
at its center. The dome of light covered what had to be the
bald spot—a roughly circular area devoid of the slightest
hint of vegetation.

And in the center of the bald spot, at the pulsating
heart of the violet light, were clustered Oz and the people
from his freak show. The landscape around and behind
them didn't match the landscape here. There were no
pines, only a wide flat plain and some sort of mountain
range in the distance. The perspective was somehow
wrong. It made her dizzy. They weren't here. They were
someplace else. They were in the Otherness.

But Ginger's eyes were drawn to the freaks, all naked,
all their awful deformities exposed to the night, all standing in a loose circle around some strange assemblage of
odd-shaped parts seated in a shallow tray. That could only
be the Device George had told her about. As she watched,
Oz tilted a black box and poured a smokey fluid over it.

For a long moment, nothing happened. Then she saw Oz point to the Device and she noticed how some of its components had begun to move and writhe and twist. And then the dome itself began to writhe and twist. Tendrils of violet light wormed out of its surface and began stretching into the air, along the ground, spreading beyond the border of the bald spot, coiling around the stunted vegetation nearby, engulfing it, changing it.

The dome of Otherness expanded, rising higher, spreading wider, following its pathfinding pseudopods.

"It's coming this way, George!"

George made no reply, only stood there, staring.

"George!"

He shook himself and looked at her. His expression was slack but his eyes were alive, dancing with reflections of violet light.

"It's working," he said softly. "The Device is working. It's widening the gap, tearing the Veil. The Otherness is coming."

Why wasn't he afraid? Why didn't his face show any of the terror that was ripping through her? What was happening to him?

Ginger glanced again at the bald spot and cried out with alarm at how far the Otherness had spread. It had taken over most of the clearing now. It had moved to within a dozen feet of them. The trees and vegetation touched by the Otherness were changing, twisting, and spreading into new, alien shapes, blossoming with heavy, salivating flowers and spiny, pulsing fruit.

As Ginger watched, a rabbit bolted from its burrow and ran in panicked circles in the violet light. Suddenly something long and thin and white with slavering jaws whipped out of the empty burrow and fastened its teeth on the rabbit's back. The poor creature screamed briefly as it was shaken violently until its neck snapped. Then the white thing dragged the limp and silent meal back to its former home.

Without a word, George began walking forward.

"What are you doing?" Ginger said.

"I've got to go."

She grabbed his arm. "George, you can't go in there!"

"I've got to," he said, shaking her off. "It wants me. And I . . . I want it."

He strode forward, away from her, into the violet light. Ginger started to follow him, to try to drag him back, but as she reached into the light she *felt* the Otherness, sensed its alienness, its implacable enmity. Her arm snatched her hand back of its own accord, so violently that she stumbled backward and fell. She couldn't go into that light, not in a million years.

And as she saw the leading edge of the Otherness creep toward her she scrambled to her feet and retreated, screaming George's name, but he gave no sign that he heard her.

It wasn't night here. And it wasn't like any sort of day George had ever seen.

He stared around in fearful fascination as he scuffed through the blue sand toward Oz and the rest where they stood in the Otherness-equivalent of the bald spot. The Otherness. It was so much bigger than the reality he knew, the horizon had no curve, seemed so much farther away. The violet light had no source; it seemed to radiate from the clear sky; dim, boulder-rough moons raced across that sky while the clouds stayed low, roaming the endless plain at ground level. Far off to his right a range of sharp-edged ebony mountains stretched into the stratosphere. His own movements seemed slower, the air thicker. This reality felt so much *older;* the incalculable age of this place weighed upon him like a shroud.

And yet as much as he feared it, as much as it repulsed him, a part of him was responding to it. Something deep inside knew this place, called it . . . home.

Ahead, Oz turned and waved him toward the circle. The smile of welcome on his face was magnified in the huge mouth in his belly. George had wondered at the nature of the "hideous deformity" that Jacob Prather had mentioned. Now he knew.

"George," the mouth boomed—sound, too, was different here. "You've come to join us. Welcome home."

Carmella, startlingly beautiful in her nakedness, stepped forward and grabbed his arm, pulled him into the circle. Violet light flashed from her eyes, from all the eyes gathered on the bald spot. They were all there: Petergello, the Beagle Boys, Mitts and Gator and Kysleen and Dub, Tripper and Lance and all the rest. Tane faced him across the circle, his wings spread.

"George!" he said, his voice breaking. "I can see here. I can *see!*"

And in the center of the circle sat the Device, wreathed in smoke from the fluid pooled at its base. A couple of Virgie's monstrous little offspring were squatting before it, alive and well, watching it like regular kids might watch a TV.

Oz had an onyx box in his hand. He stepped forward and poured more of the smoking fluid over the Device.

"We're creating a new world from the old one, George," he said. "A new world where *we'll* be the norms and *they'll* be the freaks. The tear is small now, but already the Otherness is moving into our old world. Slowly now, but as we extend the tear, its rate of flow will increase. And soon the tear will be irreparable. Then it will be *Genesis*, George. A new Genesis. And this time *we* get to play God."

George turned and looked back the way he had come. He saw footprints—his and the others'—leading this way through the blue sand that stretched on forever, but a few dozen feet away they stopped, as if someone had swept the sand clean of all markings. He saw Otherness-mutated trees and brush, but where were the millions of acres of the pine barrens? Where was Ginger?

Ginger! The memory of her was like a splash of icy water in the face. She was out there somewhere, terrified—for herself, but mostly for him. He knew that. For *him*.

And what was he feeling for her? He could stand here and let Oz and these people have their way. These people who were deformed like him, who were outcasts like him, who'd taken him in and made him part of their family when everyone else had discarded him. They wanted this.

And damn it, he wanted it, too. Or at least a part of him did. And another part of him wanted to be back with Ginger, wanted to protect her from the horror that the Otherness would make of her daily existence.

And yet . . . he felt he *belonged* here. He held up his

tentacles and stared at them, coiling and uncoiling them before his face. Not to have to hide them, to *flaunt* them instead. What would that be like?

No. It wasn't enough. The belonging he felt here couldn't replace how he felt with Ginger. Nothing the Otherness could offer would ever top that.

George turned again toward the Device. Oz had just finished emptying the contents of still another onyx box over it. Without allowing himself to think, without giving himself a chance to change his mind, George made two quick steps into the center of the circle and booted the Device, putting all the force he could muster behind the kick.

Pain shot up his leg as pieces of the Device were knocked loose and sent flying, tumbling through the air in a dozen directions. Shouts of shock and rage rose on all sides as bolts of light—white, pure light—flashed from the damaged Device and arced into the sky. A wind began to blow, swirling the sand into stinging blue vortices.

"The tear!" Oz shouted. "It's closing! Everything's being undone. Find those Pieces and bring them to me!"

Not enough, George realized. Not enough merely to knock the Pieces loose. Oz could simply reassemble them. George had to bury them, scatter them where they couldn't find them, or better yet, put one beyond their reach. Just one. The Device couldn't perform the task for which it was designed if it was incomplete.

George spotted a Piece at his feet. He wrapped one of his tentacles around it and ran. Back. Back along the way he'd come. He squinted against the swirling sand, trying to stay on course, but the gusts were filling in and smoothing over his tracks. Ahead of him the air shimmered and flashed with darkness, while behind him George heard baying howls of the Beagle Boys as they took up the chase. He kicked up his speed. If they got hold of him, who knew what they might do?

The steady advance of the violet light of the Otherness had backed Ginger over the edge of the rise, and now she was retreating down the slope.

She sobbed with every backward step. George had left her, deserted her for the other freaks. She'd seen the way he'd let Carmella take his hand and lead him into that circle. And now the Otherness was coming, changing everything, taking over—

Then she noticed a change in the violet light. Its questing tendrils withdrew as its leading edge flickered and began to pull back. Hesitantly, she followed its retreat.

When she regained the top of the rise she could see the clearing again, still within the shrinking dome of violet light. But the light from within had a grainy, ground-glass appearance. She thought she saw a shadow moving within—a number of shadows.

Suddenly a figure burst from the violet light and came bounding across the clearing toward her, running as if the hounds of hell were on his tail.

"George!" she cried.

His features were dim in the violet glow, but his expression was frightened, desperate. Without a word he pushed her back into the shadowy brush at the edge of the clearing and thrust something into her hand.

"Hide here. Don't move. Don't make a sound no matter what happens. I'll be okay. I'll be back for you."

Then he kissed her and ran down the slope. No sooner had he been swallowed by the darkness than five hulking, growling forms burst from the steadily shrinking light and pursued him. Moments later they returned, dragging him along in their midst. Ginger locked a scream in her throat and fought the urge to rush to his aid. He'd told her to stay hidden. And besides, what could she do? She'd be swatted like a fly. So she huddled in the brush and watched the Beagle Boys hustle George back into the Otherness.

. . . I'll be okay . . . I'll be back for you . . .

Only those words kept her from screaming out her terror that she'd never see him again.

Vaguely through the swirling violet light she could see the circle of freaks in the bald spot. They seemed to be searching the ground for something. When George was brought back to them they searched him, then began beating him. Finally they pushed him aside and resumed sifting the sand around them.

Ginger held up the thing in her hand. It felt cold and

fuzzy, almost furry. Was this what they were searching for?

When she looked up again she was startled at how small the violet dome had become, how quickly its light was fading. Panic tightened its fist within her chest. What was happening? And what would happen to anyone caught inside if and when it faded completely? She dropped the Piece and ran forward.

"George!"

She saw him. He'd staggered to his feet and was staring around him. He looked lost. She shouted his name but he gave no indication that he heard. She screamed his name. The dome was shrinking so *fast!*

Maybe he heard her, maybe it was some sort of instinct—whatever the reason, he began to stumble in her direction. The others didn't seem to notice. They were still searching through the sand around the Device. But George seemed to be moving in slow motion, tilted forward, head down, as if fighting a gale. His tentacles were stretched out straight and stiff before him, reaching blindly.

Still calling his name, Ginger inched up to the receding edge of the light and forced herself to thrust her hand within. The enmity, the alienness, coursed through her again but she forced her hand in farther. It was cold in there and she felt the blast of the wind, the sting of the sand. She pushed her arm still deeper into the light, up to the shoulder, stretched and managed to touch the tip of George's right tentacle. It responded immediately to her touch, stretching, writhing through her palm and wrapping around her wrist in the catch grip they'd done so many thousands of times in midair. George looked up and smiled, though she knew he couldn't see her. He said something she couldn't hear but she read his lips.

Pull!

Ginger planted her feet and leaned back, trying to haul him through, but the drag was too strong, she was losing ground, especially now that the dome was shrinking faster—*collapsing.* Her feet were sliding through the sandy soil of the barrens. Instead of pulling George out, she was being pulled in. She dropped to her knees and with her free hand grabbed a gnarled dead root looping out of the soil. It stopped her slide, and for a moment she thought she was going to win. But the pull was too great. Her hand slipped free and once more she was heading into the violet light. George must have realized this. He began wriggling his tentacle free of her grasp.

"No!" she cried. "Don't let go! I'll get you out!"

He shook his head and his lips formed a firm *no*. He touched his free tentacle to his lips then pressed it against the back of her hand.

"Please, George! Don't let me go!" She tried desperately to keep a grip on him but his flesh was so loose and flexible that he managed to slip free. "George, *no!*"

But he was going, sliding backward toward the bald spot and the others within it. He waved. He looked like he was crying.

And then George was gone. Everything was gone. A loud bang, like a giant balloon exploding, and suddenly the light, the Otherness, Oz, the freaks, George—everything. Gone.

Gone!

"Oh no! Oh, please, God—*No!*"

Sobbing, crying, refusing to believe this was real, Ginger ran forward into the bald spot and staggered around in blind circles, screaming out George's name until her throat was raw and her voice was torn and useless. But there was no answer. Even the night insects were quiet. Only the cold eye of the moon bore witness to what had happened here.

She dropped to her knees. George . . . he was gone . . . lost inside the Otherness . . . maybe even dead now . . .

And what time was it? Had to be after midnight. George's birthday. His present . . . she hadn't been able to tell him about it . . . he'd been taken from her before she'd had a chance to tell him about the baby.

F. PAUL WILSON

The Authors

Douglas Borton (Mr. Tane and Bowser) is a Los Angeles–based writer who worked as a screenwriter for several years before publishing his first novel, *Manstopper*, in 1988. Since then he has written four more novels of horror and dark fantasy: *Dreamhouse, Deathsong, Kane,* and *Shadow Dance*.

Richard Lee Byers (Virgie Bone) is a refugee from an emergency psychiatric treatment facility (a former clinician and administrator, not a patient) who is now a full-time writer. He is the author of three novels—*Deathward, Fright Line,* and his latest, *The Vampire's Apprentice*. His short fiction has appeared in *New Blood, 2AM, Amazing Experiences, Quick Chills,* and the Tampa *Tribune*.

Scott A. Cupp (Señorita Gato) has written fiction for *The New Frontiers, Razored Saddles,* and *Obsessions*. He was a nominee for the John W. Campbell Award for best new writer at the 1991 World Science Fiction Convention. He lives in Texas with his wife Sandi and their three cats—Ace, Wolfgang, and Leon Trotsky.

Morgan Fields (Theron "Tripper" Rawley) is the author of three horror novels: *Play Time, Deadly Harvest,* and *Shaman Woods*. Writing as J. M. Morgan, her ecological thriller *Desert Eden* was published in 1991. *Beyond Eden, Future Eden,* and *Between the Devil and the Deep* are scheduled for publication in 1992. Morgan is also the author of one historical novel, *Emerald Destiny,* written under the pseudonym Meredith Morgan. More of Morgan Fields' short fiction will be published in *Stalkers III*.

Craig Shaw Gardner (Louella Snard) has had over two dozen short stories published in original anthologies, including *Final Shadows*, *The Complete Werewolf*, *Life on the Border*, and *The Seaharp Hotel*. He is also the author of sixteen novels, the most recent of which include *The Other Sinbad*, *A Bad Day for Ali Baba*, and *Revenge of the Fluffy Bunnies*.

R. Patrick Gates (Emily "Mother Goose" Butterman and Jamie) is the author of the critically acclaimed novels *Tunnelvision*, *Fear*, and *Grimm Memorials*. *Funny Bones*, a collection of his humorously macabre short stories, is in the works. He wishes to thank John S. Sampson III, D.M.D., for his help with his story here.

Nancy Kilpatrick (Malaleik) has published horror in *Karl Wagner's Year's Best Horror XX*, *Northern Frights*, *Book of Shadows*, *Eldritch Tales*, *Prisoners of the Night*, *The Standing Stone*, *The Vampire's Crypt*, and elsewhere. She has a penchant for vampires and is currently working on a bloodsucker novel.

Rex Miller (Petergello and Gore Edmund) once had a major market broadcasting career ranging from comedy production to national TV voice-overs. *Slob*, *Frenzy*, *Stone Shadow*, *Slice*, *Ice Man*, and *Profane Men*, all published since 1987, have brought him mainstream readership. His forthcoming novel *Chaingang* is a Pocket Star Books lead title for November 1992.

Lee Moler (Lance Whiting) has been published previously in the first *Borderlands* anthology.

Thomas F. Monteleone (Carmella Cerami) is the author of eighteen novels and eighty short stories; his irreverent column of personal commentary runs regularly in *Cemetery Dance* magazine. Recently he has crossed the trenches and joined the ranks of the specialty publishers with his own imprint, Borderlands Press. He is editor of the highly regarded *Borderlands* anthologies. His most recent novel is *The Blood of the Lamb*.

Yvonne Navarro (Kysleen) lives in Roselle, Illinois. To keep herself and an old dog in food she works in a law office during the day. Her horror fiction has appeared in *Women of Darkness II, Pulphouse,* and *The Blood Review,* among others. She dreams of cactus, desert lizards, and relocating to Arizona.

Gregory Nicoll (Doubleface, Rattles, and Slither) is a Southern writer whose novelette "Dead Air" appeared in *The Year's Best Horror Stories XVII.* He also writes articles on horror movies for *Fangoria* and was involved in the production of the feature film *Blood Salvage.*

Kathryn Ptacek (Quinta Romero) is the author of eighteen novels and the editor of three anthologies, among them the award-winning *Women of the West* and the critically acclaimed *Women of Darkness.* She also edits *The Gila Queen's Guide to Markets,* a nationally distributed magazine for writers.

Dan Simmons (Benjamin Willis Ashley-Montague) has won the Hugo Award (*Hyperion*), the World Fantasy Award (*Song of Kali*), and the Bram Stoker Award (*Carrion Comfort*).

Steven Spruill (Haman) grew up in Battle Creek with the smell of corn flakes and the rumble of trains. He is the versatile author of eight novels ranging from science fiction to horror. His medical thriller *Painkiller* was a selection of the Literary Guild, Doubleday Book Club, and Mystery Guild. His most recent novel is *Before I Wake* from St. Martin's Press.

Brad Strickland (Claude "Gator" Bledsoe) has been writing fantastic fiction since 1981. Two of his tales have appeared in *The Year's Best Horror,* and two of his six novels have been horror: *ShadowShow* and *Children of the Knife.* He would like to thank Dr. Bill Cribbs for teaching him how to get in and out of the Okefenokee relatively intact.

Chet Williamson (Herbert "Mitts" Brooks) is a former vice president of Horror Writers of America. Among his novels are *Reign, Dreamthorp*, and *Ash Wednesday*. Over sixty of his short stories have appeared in such magazines as *The New Yorker, Playboy, Esquire, F&SF*, and other magazines and anthologies. He lives in Pennsylvania's Amish country with his wife Laurie and son Colin.

F. Paul Wilson (Oz, George "Octoman" Swenson, the Beagle Boys) is the author of thirteen novels and a short-story collection. *Freak Show* is the first anthology he has edited. It is also the last.